The Time of the Cat

Gaea Ascendant 1

Eric S. Martell

Second Initiative Press

The Time of the Cat

Copyright © 2014 by Eric S. Martell

Second Initiative Press

Printed in the USA
ISBN: 978-0-9989805-3-9

Cover Design by Krzysztof (Kris) Krygier

Vox audita perit littera scripta manet.

This is a work of fiction. All the characters and events portrayed in this book are fictional, and any resemblance to real people or incidents is purely coincidental.

Dedication

This book is dedicated to my wife, Sally, whose suggestions and patient listening greatly improved my telling of the story.

I'd also like to say, "Thank You!" to the talented authors of all of the hundreds of science fiction stories I've read over the years. They provided me with inspiration and enough background ideas that this story practically wrote itself.

My grateful thanks to Krzysztof (Kris) Krygier for the original cover art. Working with him was easy and he created a wonderful, graphic interpretation of the story elements.

Contents

1

The Drunk

From Umberto Eco's novel, Foucault's Pendulum: "People walk by and they don't know the truth... That the house is a fake. It's a facade, an enclosure with no room, no interior. It is really a chimney, a ventilation flue that serves to release the vapors of the regional Metro. And once you know this you feel you are standing at the mouth of the underworld..."

It was just another spring day in the city, until the drunk limped by. He was a bearded urban-outdoors-man type stumbling down the sidewalk. He was pretty typical. Inebriated, unwashed body and a filthy mouth that opened a little too often. It was nearly summer and the weather was warming up. I didn't think it was hot yet, but he was suffering from the heat. I got a quick whiff of his horrible body odor on the breeze as he staggered by. It was a safe bet that he had no interest in water either for drinking or washing.

The drunk's teeth were yellowed and broken, and he slurred parts of a melancholy song as he limped along with alcohol showing in his gait.

"She doesn't give you time for hmm-hmm your arm hmm," he crooned in a scratchy baritone.

I couldn't quite think of the name of the song and it didn't help that he was slightly out of tune. Nor, did the fact that he couldn't remember most of the words.

He continued with an unpleasant quaver in his voice, "And you follow 'til hmm-hmm disappears. By the blue-tiled walls hmm-hmm there's a hidden door she leads you to."

The passersby veered to the edge of the street to give him as wide a berth as possible. He staggered and stopped to lean on a bicycle rack diagonally in front of where I was standing.

I was across the street from the door of a non-nondescript, three-story building which happened to be the tallest building on this part of Steinway. There was a closed pet shop next door and the other side boasted a mosque and a couple of sickly trees.

The mosque was obvious to any casual observer. It was decorated garishly with gold columns on either side of the front entrance and windows with filigreed cutouts. The view of the building was one reason I was standing by a shoe store entrance. I'd also picked this location because it was shaded by another dejected oak. The poor tree was making the best of its ill fortune to be planted by the street. I felt sorry for it, but was glad of the shade.

The drunk started on the next line of the song, "These days, she says, I feel a hmm-hmm ..." It was irritating. By this point, I had my own feeling. It was that I was going to throw something at him, if he didn't stop.

His voice trailed off. Then he abruptly leaned over and voided the contents of his stomach, managing to splash some on the feet of a swiftly walking pedestrian. There was a considerable amount of cursing, but the drunk seemed oblivious. The violated woman, stomped her feet, shook her fist at him and then continued toward a corner restaurant. Uncaring, the drunk staggered across the street, moving away from me and toward the mosque.

I looked both ways down the sidewalk, keeping tabs on the pedestrians in case someone was on to me. Mentally, though, I was still trying to place the drunk's tune when suddenly there was a screech of brakes on the street as someone swerved to miss him and cut-off another car. The screech was followed by horns and some more shouted curses. Typical big-city behavior; lots of noise and swearing but no actual physical contact.

I glanced at the narrowly avoided collision and when I turned back, the drunk wasn't on the far sidewalk. He wasn't up the street or down the street either. He hadn't gone into the closed pet shop; the hand-written sign on the front notified any interested parties that it was "Close for Vacates."

The sign's message had me mystified. I couldn't decide if the owners had closed permanently and were vacating the property or had simply gone off on vacation.

He certainly wasn't the type who would go into a mosque. He was obviously drunk and would have been denied entrance or worse. I thought, he must have gone into the three-story building. The only problem was that it was entirely too nice looking a building for him to have any business inside or to find anyone there who would be willing to give him any sort of sanctuary or anything but a push towards the exit.

I wasn't busy at the moment. In fact, I was waiting for the man I'd been following to come out of the mosque. I do that sometimes. My consulting business is very discrete and quite expensive and often involves locating some pretty unsavory characters, sometimes in unsavory locations. Anyway, I wasn't busy, so I watched for the drunk to come out while I waited for my target.

You must understand that I'm not normally interested in drunks. I am, however, interested in people doing unusual or unexpected things, because my experience has taught me that this can be important. Anyway, I remained on watch, but I walked over and relaxed in the front seat of my car. It was parked nearby, under the unhappy tree in the darkest patch of shade that I could find. The wind was cool, but the sun was hot, so the shade was definitely appreciated.

The street was heavy with the usual traffic; a mix of private vehicles and some cabs along with delivery trucks and the occasional bus. The atmosphere was thick with exhaust fumes: both from the automobiles and the numerous restaurants in the area. The exhaust fans from the restaurants exhaled a thick, cloying smell of burnt grease, intermixed with some more appetizing odors of various types of food. The sidewalk was covered with black spots where chewing gum had been discarded, indicating with a high degree of accuracy the type of thinking (or lack, thereof) that was predominant among the local residents.

Sixty-two minutes later, my target came out of the mosque. He walked out of the door, paused and glanced both directions, then headed toward a black Mercedes 600 S Class that he'd thoughtfully parked right in front of a fire hydrant. I'd been sort of hoping for the fire department or parking patrol to come by, but they hadn't shown up in the time that I'd been there. My hope on that score was simply a form of amusement based on my imagination of the expression on the guy's face when he saw his car had been booted.

He walked down the street, stopped and looked both ways again. If he was trying to act nonchalantly, he was failing miserably. Without another pause, he walked swiftly around to the street side, unlocked the car door, and got in. He pulled out into traffic without even a sideways glance, causing a considerable amount of honking and cursing. I'm used to the commotion, but it still keeps me on edge. I'd previously placed a GPS tracker on the frame of the vehicle, so I didn't worry about following.

Instead, I went into a doughnut shop and got a cup of iced mocha and then stood around under the tree outside for another ten minutes while I sipped my drink. Still no drunk. Crossing the street gave me a closer view of the door where I guessed that he had entered. It was a brass door with two windows that gave me a view into the lobby. There was nothing inside but a small lobby with a pot holding a dusty, artificial palm and a plain-looking, metal elevator door at the rear.

I was about to quit looking through the glass door, but there was something that looked like a second elevator on one of the side walls. It hadn't been there a moment ago. It just somehow appeared. The appearance made me doubt myself, but I'm good at observing details, so it was only a flicker of doubt. That door had popped into existence right by the corner of the room. Its edge touched the edge of the original elevator's frame on the back wall.

As I watched, the new door flicked open far more quickly than any normal elevator. A slightly deformed hand on a skinny wrist reached out and pressed the adjacent call button for the elevator at the back. I couldn't see who or what the hand was attached to. The rear wall elevator opened and a man-shaped figure with unusual taste in haberdashery shot out of the side elevator disappeared into the back one. The doors both closed; the back elevator light flickered for a moment. It didn't go up or down, just turned red and then faded out slowly.

I wondered what I had just seen. An ordinary person, passing by, probably wouldn't have noticed anything. The entire action occurred in only a second or two.

Most people don't really look anyhow. I was reminded of this fact when I suddenly realized that the sidewall elevator door had disappeared again and I'd missed its disappearance. That was weird enough to keep me looking through the glass, just in case something else happened.

The being...creature, whatever it was, that had changed elevators was, or appeared to be, only superficially human. I'd gotten the impression of smooth skin with rippling muscles, but the angularity of the shape was definitely not within the normal human spectrum. And, the clothing! The clothes would probably be a hit in any number of edgy clubs in the Village, but most people wouldn't be wearing something that odd looking even if they were that odd looking.

Don't get me wrong; I've seen some pretty strange people not only in New York. However, what I'd seen definitely had not looked human.

2

DOORS?

I work in many cities and under many names as a rather highly paid and respected, if I do say it myself, counter-terrorism expert. I'm not above active intervention, if the situation requires it, but I prefer to simply observe and report developing situations to whomever hired me or to the local authorities at the appropriate time.

My background is, well, not something that I speak about, but in addition to being a moderately attractive, brown-haired guy of above average height and being muscular without looking steroidal, I'm expert at both armed and unarmed combat and a highly trained investigator.

I'd been assigned by a multinational corporation to watch a particular group of Middle-Easterners who seemed to be loosely associated with another group that had taken their jihad a little too enthusiastically and had, in the process, previously blown up one of the corporation's local headquarters in the Middle-East.

The current group was trying to act professional, but it was apparent that they'd been poorly trained. The real key of the matter was that I was slowly moving in on their source of funds. They seemed to be well paid. Mercedes, and the like, and better than the average religious fanatic's clothing. They also seemed to be tied in with a lot of illegal drugs that had recently been coming into the country.

My working hypothesis was that a competitor of the corporation had an "in" with some Imam who had recruited the cell I was watching under the guise of a religious fatwa. The cell members seemed to sincerely believe they were working under the command of Allah and were apparently dedicated to bringing down the infidel as represented by my client.

The financial issue was complex. Funding moved through the Cayman Islands and possibly Mexico, but it seemed to come from multiple accounts in Switzerland. I hadn't yet worked out the location where the Swiss accounts funds were sourced.

This wasn't my first soiree in the seedy underworld of international terrorism. I thought I'd seen it all – black market explosive devices in Ghana, perverted so-called "holy men" laundering money for priceless treasures, warlords bartering human flesh and trampling on the rights of their fellow man, and New Haven, Connecticut – but the simple act of my curious observation of a homeless man that day involved me in weirdness that I could never have imagined.

What had started as an act of simple curiosity had now become far more interesting. I figured I owed it to myself to investigate a little farther. Tracking amateur terrorists through New York sometimes gets a little boring. I was ready for some additional intellectual complexity, so I opened the door and entered the lobby.

The second elevator door on the sidewall was still missing. New York is a strange city and Astoria even stranger, but it wasn't usual to have elevators appear and disappear. I spent some time feeling the wainscoting, but nothing out of the ordinary appeared. As far as my inspection went, it was a perfectly ordinary wall; it was true that it was painted an ugly shade of institutional green, but there was definitely no sign of a second elevator door.

Half expecting to see the original elevator missing, I turned to the back wall, but it was still there. It was enough to make me pause a moment, the thought of pushing the elevator button, but I went ahead and pushed it. The door opened immediately.

At first glance, the inside of the elevator looked normal. It was decorated with pale blue walls that roughly matched the lobby decor. As I entered, I looked at the control panel, which, I thought should have three floors on it. I was holding the door with one hand, but when I saw the panel, I dropped my hand in astonishment. There were two buttons there, arranged side-by-side rather than in an up and down pattern. It was going to be hard to get upstairs with that button arrangement. Neither of the buttons had any recognizable numbers. There were some odd symbols, but nothing I could read. There was also a much smaller blue button, located immediately over the other two. It might or might not be necessary to activate the elevator, but the other two looked slightly worn as if they were the most important ones.

Suddenly, the nerves attached to the small hairs on the back of my neck tingled, my version of a premonition of danger. It has saved me more than once. This time, I had sensed a change in the system, because the door snapped shut before I could move.

The light flickered. Reflexively, I pulled my carry piece – a Sig Sauer P220. It's a little large for a concealed weapon, but I'm pretty big-boned and I really like the knockdown power of a forty-five.

The thought came to me that I wasn't really in an elevator, but some form of matter transmitter. I've watched sci-fi movies and figured I had an idea about how that was supposed to work. What I was experiencing was a lot less dramatic than the things that Hollywood seemed to favor, but it had an effect that I sensed physically. It seemed to be like speeding down a roller coaster. The physical sensations of movement were so bewildering and so disorienting that I might as well have been unconscious for all the details I could give – then or later – about what happens during such a journey.

For a brief moment the walls shimmered around me and gravity seemed to let go abruptly inside my body, so that I felt like my attention had wandered for a moment. The walls suddenly steadied and were not pale blue any longer. Now they were a hard, dull steel with rivets showing where plates overlapped, and here and there a streak of rust. The inside of the elevator seemed somewhat smaller than before and the lighting was much dimmer and redder. Suddenly the door snapped open and I was somewhere else. The potted palm had disappeared.

Rather than seeing a flustered Scottish engineer or a humanoid with pointy ears desperately trying to beam me in, my first view was of a lovely face. She was probably the most beautiful woman I'd ever seen. Her hair was about shoulder length and blond and she had an unusually well proportioned face with high cheekbones and, yet, she didn't look at all like some magazine model. She had a wholesome, girl-next-door appeal. Her face was perfectly proportioned and her body was incredible.

Her hands were handcuffed behind her back and she was being escorted by what I initially thought was a really ugly man. I supposed that he'd summoned the elevator. For a moment, Mr. Ugly looked surprised at seeing me, but then went for the weapon that was strapped to his belt. Not fast enough. I shot him high and off center with the idea of asking some questions. The woman's mouth fell open in shock, but she didn't make any sound.

Ugly went down and then came back up with his gun in his other hand pointing directly at me. A standard double tap followed by a round to the head dropped him again. He didn't get up this time.

"Oh, oh, I knew that I wasn't going to make it out of this alive! Are you going to kill me too?" Her eyes were wide with fear and so dark blue that they were almost purple.

I smiled at her, still in awe of her looks, gathered my courage and said, "Probably not. I'm Declan, and you might be..?"

I realized after I'd said it that I sounded like an idiot, considering the circumstances, but she was so beautiful that it seemed to shut down my brain.

She answered with a brief hesitation, "Elizabeth, but you can call me 'Betty' or what I really prefer, 'Liz', but I'm babbling and we really need to get out of here. Fast!"

While she was talking, I took a quick look up and down the hall. Lucky for us, it was empty in both directions. There was a door at one end of the hall with an odd red light beside it. Shortly beyond the door, the hall made a right turn. The other end of the hall was only a few feet away and revealed nothing but a surprisingly ordinary Colonial-styled chest of drawers with a vase holding a silk plant on top.

She continued talking at a high rate of adrenaline-induced speed and eventually told me she had been captured in what I thought sounded like somewhere in Greece, along with some other stuff about aliens and invasions that I didn't quite get. It was apparent to me that her accent wasn't Greek, but rather more mid-western American. I put the problem of her place of origin in the back of my mind until later, while I admired her looks.

While she spoke, I figured I had a few seconds at most to learn what I could about "Mr. Ugly" before someone else showed up. The first thing I did was to insert a fresh clip into my Sig.

The second thing was to check Ugly's body for any wallet, keys, and other items of interest. He had a wallet, which I opened. There was nothing in it except for several crisp and new hundred dollar bills along with a discount coupon for tire service. I took the money and left the coupon. I wasn't in the market for new tires at the moment, but the hundreds might come in handy. He wasn't going to need them in his current state.

He also had a door key with no key chain. I took it, but there was no way of knowing what, if anything, it unlocked. Then I took some pictures with my phone before I picked up his pistol – and here my jaw dropped. It was like nothing I'd ever seen before.

It looked similar to a cheap automatic pistol, but the caliber was tiny, it was smaller than a BB gun, perhaps about a millimeter. I moved the plastic bolt carrier mechanism back and was rewarded with a view of a needle-like projectile that might have been made of glass. It had a small amount of yellowish fluid inside the tip. The source of the projectile seemed to be a more or less conventionally styled magazine. I pushed the release button and the magazine dropped out in my hand. None of the needles in it had any fluid in their tips. There was another tubular knob on the bottom of the grip that I thought could be its source.

I stuck the weapon into my belt holster for later investigation and was pleased to see that it fit reasonably well. As I finished stowing it away, I was reminded that I'd been ignoring my rescuee. She abruptly stopped talking and stomped firmly on my foot and then turned, holding out her cuffed hands. I guess I hadn't been paying close enough attention to her, so it was my fault, in a way.

Fortunately, I carry lock-picking equipment in neat little package that also holds a standard handcuff key. She really unloaded with that stomp and I wondered if I'd be able to walk normally as I worked on the cuffs. When they came off, I tossed them onto Mr. Ugly, figuring I had no more use for them than he did, and then looked around the narrow hallway. There was nowhere to conceal the body, except in the elevator; so, I dragged it in there and let the door go shut.

We moved down the short hall; she walked rapidly as I limped along, trying to keep up. When I stopped to look at the door with the red light, she said, "You don't want to go in there! There's likely to be a lot more of them in that area."

Shrugging, I turned to the right. We went around the corner and found a door that led outside. It had a conventional "Exit" sign overhead. After going through the door and out, I stopped for a moment in astonishment while she kept walking down the street. We were somewhere on the Upper West Side. Central Park was directly in front of us.

I was still assimilating this change when I realized that she was getting away from me. Despite the pain in my foot, I took off after her and caught up about halfway down the block. We headed south as fast as possible. In my experience, it doesn't do to hang around a recently deceased body, especially when you are responsible for the state of the corpse.

We hadn't gone more than another block when she started up the steps of a small, rather dilapidated brownstone. I said, "Whoa! Where are you headed?"

"There's another transporter in here and we can use it to get away from this area," she answered.

I asked, "You know about these things?"

"I've been through several, yes. The one here isn't used often and it can place us in Durban, South Africa and then we can move from there to, I think, Florida. They don't all connect," she said, anticipating my next question as she pulled on the solid front door with both hands.

It seemed to be unlocked, to my surprise, but then I realized that she'd pulled the door handle down while lifting the thumb-tab upwards.

"The locks are coded for an unusual opening action," she explained, noticing my interest.

We went through the door and found ourselves in another matter transporter thing. There were two buttons on a metal panel in what seemed to be the standard side-by-side pattern. Looking over her shoulder at me with an unreadable expression, Elizabeth pressed one.

3

LIZ

I led Declan out onto the street and headed south towards the Museum of Natural History. I wasn't sure, but thought that was the direction we needed to go. As we walked, I briefly reviewed my past six months with special emphasis on the last ten days.

It was about six months ago that my boss stuck his head out of his office and called, "Elizabeth, come in here."

His wire-framed spectacles were down at the end of his nose and he had his head tilted forward in order to look over them at me. Between that look and his wrinkled, cheap suit, he looked like my idealized version of a clueless accountant. I knew him too well, though, and his use of my full name indicated that he wasn't interested in any delay. I jumped to my feet and followed close on his heels as he turned back and shuffled around his desk, dropping into his saggy chair.

I paused momentarily and then, when he was settled, I picked out one of the two chairs facing the desk and sat down, ready for either a new assignment or what he called a helpful critique of my previous mission. His idea of constructive criticism was usually unjustified and was always more in the line of an acrimonious attack on both the target's intelligence and their maturity, so I took a deep breath and prepared myself.

He sighed and pushed a slim, brown folder over to me. It was marked "Top Secret" though why it should have that level of security was questionable. It was a simple briefing on some high-quality counterfeit bills that were beginning to come into circulation in several of the major cities including New York.

"Elizabeth, I'd prefer to send someone else to check this out, but you're the only one of my personnel who isn't currently assigned. The other people are all committed to more important tasks, so I'm afraid that you're my only option."

In addition to holding the opinion that women weren't really able to investigate anything but recipes, he also automatically held my looks against me. I'd heard him tell one of the other men, when he thought I was too far away to hear, that I was too good-looking to be serious about law-enforcement work. It didn't help that I was also the rookie in the group. I had over a year's worth of experience in another division, but had just transferred to this one and I'd taken a lot of kidding over my 'new' status.

I closed the folder and answered, "I'll get right on it, boss."

As I stood up and turned to go out, he added, unnecessarily, "I hope I don't regret trusting you with this."

I turned back and gave him my sweetest smile and said, "Don't worry, it can't be harder than baking a cake." Then I pushed open the door, inwardly snickering at the look on his face.

Using the information in the folder (which was scanty at best), my various connections and the Internet, I was able to trace the flow of the counterfeits from Mexico back to New York. I had a lead that indicated the origin of the bills was in DC. The bills themselves used the same paper that the US Mint used and the various experts I'd consulted thought that the plates used to print the fakes were such high quality that they might have been stolen from the Mint. The only way to tell they were fake was that the serial numbers overlapped some already existing, older bills. None of the legitimate bills were in newly minted condition.

Based on that information, I went to DC and got lucky. I was able to locate some rental trucks that were being used to transport the bills to Mexico and other locations as well. I'm making this sound easy, but it wasn't. It took a lot of grinding-hard street-work and months of labor to get this far. I wasn't able to locate exactly where the bills were being printed, but it seemed like they were coming from somewhere in DC.

By this time, I was getting desperate. I figured that my boss was going to pull me off the case due to lack of real progress. However, I finally got a break. I accidentally located one of the rental trucks parked at an all-night diner. I waited until the driver came out and followed the truck to see where he was headed.

I reasoned that if I couldn't figure out where they came from it would be the next best thing to see where they were going. I trailed the guy all the way from DC to New York, but then lost him in the traffic.

The next day, I checked in with the boss. He was not too pleased with my lack of progress, but after begging for him not to take me off the case, he said that he'd give me a couple of more days.

Not wanting to waste any time, I checked out of the office and hit the streets. I had one really good source that I wanted to check first. A pawnshop owner who always had his ear to the ground. I'd used him carefully and sparingly, because I didn't want him to get a reputation of passing info on to the cops. I suppose that it was a little bit unfair that he was my uncle's brother-in-law, but the family connection meant that he was always happy to see me, even if he didn't have anything useful to say.

I walked into his store and pretended to be interested in some jewelry while he dealt with an enormous woman dressed in a gaudy caftan. She was shouting at him with a Jamaican accent about getting her TV out of pawn. When he'd finished with her and she was on her way with the flat-screen tucked against her ample bosom, he turned to me.

"Hi, Liz. What's up with you? Not some more information, is it?" he smiled.

"Yeah, Uncle Frank. It's easy, though. Have you heard anything about some new paper that's coming in from somewhere?"

It was obvious that he knew exactly what I was talking about. He frowned, "I got burned for a couple of hundred and I didn't even know it until I went to the bank." He prided himself on his ability to catch counterfeits and he was pretty pissed about taking a couple of bills without realizing it.

"I've got one right here," he said as he opened his cash register and pulled out a new-looking one hundred dollar bill and handed it to me.

"How do you know?" I asked, examining the bill and then holding it up to the light to peer through.

"The bill is high quality, but the serial numbers are in a sequence that overlap some real bills that were printed last year, so you have to remember the numbers," he answered.

That squared with my information and I was happy to hear from him that the counterfeits weren't so secret after all.

"I'm supposed to find out where it's coming from," I sighed.

He shrugged, "It's anyone's guess, but if I were you, I'd go talk to Mustapha Varkey. He mostly has an in with anything of that nature."

"OK. Where can I find him?"

"He's probably over around the convenience store on Sixth Avenue run by that Paki, what's his name? Oh, yeah. Mamoud Al Waziri."

I said, "Thanks, Uncle Frank!"

As I turned to leave, he added with a cautionary tone, "Watch yourself over there. Those guys are pretty hard-core and they don't like liberated women very much."

"I will and thanks again!" I waved at him and left.

My next stop was along Sixth Avenue. It turned out to be easier than I thought. I didn't see Varkey, but as I drove up, Al Waziri was standing by a vacant parking space in front of the aforesaid convenience store. I pulled in and got his attention by rolling down the passenger window. I think he thought I was soliciting, because he bent down and looked in with a lecherous grin.

His grin faded as I held the bill out to him, "What? You want to pay me? Normally, I'm the one who pays, but if that's what you want, I'm ready!"

I shook my head, "Don't go off half-cocked! I'm not that sort of girl."

"What sort are you?" The grin was back.

"I'm looking for more of this stuff," I waved the bill at him.

His attitude changed immediately, "Law enforcement?"

"No." I smiled at him and answered, "I'm just a working girl, but my fiance asked me to find out how to get some of this,"

"And who is your fiance?" he asked, starting to back away.

"Roberto d'Angelico," I answered, naming one of the most well-known and reputedly dangerous mob members in town.

"I know nothing," he answered moving towards the middle of the sidewalk.

"Do you want Roberto to come and ask you? He's within about five minutes of here right now and I can call him to come over. He'll be sure to bring some help with him and I'm not sure they're in a very good mood, since they think this paper is infringing on their territory."

He stepped back towards the car with a fearful look in his eyes, "No. It's not needed to have them come by. My family owns the store and they are very poor. They don't need trouble." He was ignoring the fact that he was usually the source of the trouble in the neighborhood. He continued, "I know nothing, but I happened to hear that some new paper would be coming into a warehouse on the west river about three AM."

He gave me the address nervously, looking over his shoulder at times. He knew a lot for someone who knew nothing. I was determined to be there when the stuff came in. I left after threatening to tell Roberto whom to blame, if the information wasn't accurate. As I pulled out, he trotted heavily inside.

I realized that he'd undoubtedly make a phone call to alert someone and perhaps the shipment would be delayed or, considering Roberto's reputation, the delivery would turn into a set-up. The Middle-Easterners were intent on moving in and there was already bad blood between the two groups. In either event, I decided to get there plenty early in order to check out the situation.

4

Rescued

About one am, I arrived and carefully looked the warehouse over. It didn't seem like there was anything going on that would indicate a trap, so I settled down to wait. I didn't have to wait long, because about fifteen minutes later, a delivery truck pulled up. It was the same type as the delivery trucks that I'd been following. When it pulled up, the warehouse doors opened. It looked like they'd decided to speed up the exchange to avoid the mob.

I waited until the truck left and everything was quiet. I thought that I'd check the place out surreptitiously to make sure the counterfeits were in there. It was dark and no one was around, so I got out of my car and sneaked around to the back. There was a door there that opened easily with my lock-pick. In I went and that's when everything went weird.

Once inside, I realized that the place was empty. That didn't square with the load that I thought had come out of the truck. It had been squatted down on its axles when it arrived and looked empty when it left. Puzzled, I looked around. There was an elevator on one wall. It was a one-story warehouse and that didn't compute at all. Nevertheless, I tried the elevator, since the only place the fakes could have gone was through it.

It seems like I've lost track of exactly how long it was, but I think that elevator ride was about ten days ago.

There were only a couple of buttons, so I pressed one, thinking that I had a fifty-fifty chance of finding the money. When I came out of the thing, I was flabbergasted. I was in some kind of glass dome and it looked like I was on another planet. Through the glass, stars were brightly shining and not flickering. The lack of flickering indicated to me that there was no atmosphere outside the dome.

As I watched, standing there with my mouth open, Jupiter rose over the horizon. It moved quickly and I was awestruck by the size of the thing looming over me. I could see the great red spot, so I was reasonably sure that I was looking at Jupiter. That meant that I was on one of its moons.

I knew from somewhere that Jupiter has about fifty moons, but try identifying one without references. There wasn't a convenient signpost nearby. I settled on the name 'Io' as a moon that I remembered.

Well, after my shock, I decided to explore a little bit. I hadn't gone five feet before two unusually strong individuals grabbed me from behind. I tried to fight, but nothing doing. They handled me easily and dragged me around a corner into a brighter light.

That was when I got a good look at the guys who had me and they didn't look so good. They almost looked as if they weren't human. I went limp with surprise as they removed my gun and phone. Then they hustled me across the lighted space and up to a group of similar individuals that were standing there. They looked me over and made some hissing noises, seemingly directing my captors as to what to do with me.

We went into an office and there was another elevator door.

"Where now?" I thought to myself as we entered.

They pushed the button and the elevator got kind of woozy and wavered and we exited into a large room that didn't look as if it were part of the same dome, since it had rock walls and was very cold. The other thing that gave it away was a huge window with a view that showed Jupiter from another direction. We'd either moved a long distance across the moon or to another moon entirely, because the great red spot was a quarter of the way from the left-hand side of the disk and it had been on the right-hand side when I first saw it.

I started to shake and then made an effort to get control of myself. It helped when I observed a large number of pallets holding what I presumed were the counterfeit bills I'd been following. They were stored in neat rows across the floor.

There was a group of humans working listlessly on arranging more of the pallets under the supervision of two of the ugly aliens. The men were dragging loads into line by hand and it looked like a difficult task from the effort they were putting into it.

One of the men quit working and leaned on one of the stacks of bills to recover. The closest supervisor had an awful, spider-like thing perched on his shoulder. The alien hissed something and the spider jumped off and ran over, climbed up the stack of bills and bit the recovering man on the arm.

He screamed as the bite instantly swelled up like a balloon. It burst and green fluid sprayed out over the screaming man's face. The fluid turned his skin black and it started to dissolve. He thrashed around for a few seconds and then quit with a few final spasms of his legs.

The supervisor turned to the other humans who had stopped in horror and hissed, "Work! Now!"

My two escorts didn't seem to care about the killing. They dragged me across the space and down a hall. They didn't talk at all and finally left me by myself in a dimly lighted cell with a bucket and a twenty-four pack of bottled water. I was thankful for the water, but it seemed to indicate that I might be there for quite a while.

Time passed and I tried to rest and conserve the water. It was quite a long period and I was alone for the entire time. Finally, after twenty of the bottles were empty and the bucket nearly full, the door opened.

This time, there was a single, ugly guy who had a strange pistol pointed at me. He handcuffed me and pushed me through the door, down a hall and around a corner. We stopped in front of a bank of elevators. He called one and we entered.

This time I observed something that I'd hadn't thought about before: The buttons were arranged in a horizontal pattern and there were only a couple of them. He pressed one and we came out of a door next to a boulangerie in Paris.

I could hear people speaking French in the near distance, but saw no one. We walked several yards and then he approached what I recognized as Berthier's door, an art project that was simply a fake door on a building side. As I recalled, it led nowhere, but I was wrong.

He looked around, somewhat nervously, and then opened the door and hustled me into a small enclosure behind it. It made me feel claustrophobic; it was so small. It was another of the transport boxes and he hit one of the buttons immediately and we went somewhere. I don't know where. I never saw anything that gave me a clue as to where I was at this location.

All I knew was that it was inside an office-like building with lots of closed doors facing long, vacant halls. It didn't seem like it was occupied. We went a long distance down a featureless hall, and then into a room to face an inquisition panel of three odd-looking creatures. They looked mostly human, but there was a strangeness about them that let me know they were alien.

They asked me some questions about where I'd come from and what I was doing. Their voices were full of sibilants and it sounded like they were hissing at me. Their English was understandable, though. What I found out as they interrogated me was shocking.

They told me they were members of a superior race from another planet. They'd chosen to call themselves by a name we would recognize: "Pugs." They told me that they were superior to us physically because their bodies had a silicon matrix that made them much more difficult to kill than pure carbon-based life forms. They wanted me to understand that the human race had no chance at resisting their invasion of our planet. They were going to take over.

I faked my way through the questions, trying to be as consistent as I could and acting as if I were totally ignorant of everything. This seemed to throw them off. After a few minutes of this, they put their heads together and conferred in a hissing language. Then they spoke to my guard and he led me out of the room.

We went down a hall and stopped in front of another transporter. Once we went inside, he dithered a bit, finally selecting the left-hand button. We came out in a brownstone on the upper west side in New York.

He hustled me into a florist van that was parked right in front of the stairs and it pulled out into traffic. It wasn't long before we passed the Museum of Natural History and I realized that we were going south. The driver then turned across Central Park and we finally ended up in a parking garage off of Madison Avenue.

The ugly guy dragged me out of the van and into another transport unit that was in an odd location at the back of a service closet. This time we came out in a penthouse at the top of a high-rise that was in the North Beach area of Durban, South Africa. Fortunately, I'd been there before and recognized the view out over the ocean, so I was sure where I was.

We only stayed there long enough for me to critique the owner's taste in art. It wasn't good. There was a large, unattractive modern art painting across from the transporter exit.

Apparently, this was a transfer point. We immediately entered another elevator and came out of it through an exit in the side of a warehouse. I could see a large apartment complex with the name, "The Miami Stadium Apartments" on the front. I knew that these apartments were situated on the former site of the Bobby Maduro Miami Stadium. It had been used as a summer home of the Baltimore Orioles until the Florida Marlins were established in 1993. The Marlins opted to use Joe Robbie Stadium and the old Miami Stadium was eventually razzed to make way for the apartments. You might wonder at this knowledge, but my grandfather was a rabid baseball fan and I spent many Sunday afternoons watching games with him when I was a girl.

This destination, too, wasn't the end point, because we went on to the next warehouse, through a door that opened to reveal some more pallets of fake money and another transporter. He pushed me into this one and we transferred to the back room of a bookstore. At least there were stacks of books lying around in considerable disarray.

He paused when the door opened, seemed to think better of the idea and pressed the second button. The door shut and then opened to a cavern. It was empty and he made a hiss of, I thought, exasperation. Then he hit the return button and we were in the room with books again.

It was the back room of a bookstore that was near Times Square. He pushed me out and we walked through the shelves of books, brushing by the proprietor as we went out of the front door. Then he took me across the street and up a flight of stairs to a janitor's closet that held another transporter. This one took us to a room that frightened me out of my wits.

There were rows and rows of humanoid-looking aliens hanging in racks. My escort wasted no time in dragging me around the room and into another elevator-like door. He pushed the activation button and we came out in a short hall. There was nowhere to go but down the hall. We walked rapidly down to the end and he shoved the door open and we exited into another hall. The door we had come through had a red light beside it, but what it represented or warned against, I couldn't understand, unless it was the rows of hanging aliens.

My unattractive escort dragged me down the longer part of the hall away from the red light and stopped in front of yet another transporter. He pushed the call button and, after a moment, the door popped open to reveal a rather large man holding a pistol pointed in my general direction.

The barrel appeared to be about a foot in diameter and I thought my number was up, but he aimed and shot my escort once, then twice more when he didn't go down. The man paused and then shot him one final time right between the eyes.

In the shock of the moment, I started babbling. I thought that he'd saved me, but I was so overwrought that I couldn't seem to stop talking and none of what I was saying seemed to be making sense to him.

Even in my excitement, I realized that he was at least a couple of inches over six feet and very well built. He wasn't movie-star handsome, but, for some reason, I found him very attractive – maybe it was due to being relieved at seeing a human who was apparently working against my captors. Anyway, he bent over and checked out the ugly guy. While he did, I took the opportunity to check out his backside. It looked lean and hard and his shoulders were wide enough to make me feel like a little girl. I figuratively put a check mark on the "he meets all of my physical qualifications" line under his description in my mind.

Then he had to spoil the good impression I had started to form by getting engrossed in the alien pistol he picked up. It kind of irritated me. I was used to men paying me more attention than he showed, so I unfortunately stamped on his foot. This got his attention and he took the handcuffs off. He didn't show any resentment for my rude stamp and I was forced to give him additional credit for restraint.

One thing led to another and I shortly found myself trying to lead him through what I could recall of the maze of interlinking transporters. We finally reached the brownstone I remembered and I showed him how to activate the latch. As I was about to press the button for Durban, I looked at him and finally had the thought, "Just who is this guy, anyway, and can I trust him?"

5

KIDNAPPED

As Liz pressed the control button, the same sensation of movement without movement that I'd previously experienced almost turned my stomach inside out, but we arrived at the next destination before I could feel sick. The door snapped open and I stepped out with my pistol held in both hands near my chest. There was a large, ugly modern-art painting on the far wall that caught my attention as I cleared the room.

Assuring myself that there were no immediate threats, I glanced back at the painting. Yes, it was exactly as unattractive as I'd first thought. Hearing a small noise, I turned around in time to see the door snap shut behind me with Liz still inside.

I pressed the single call button and the door immediately opened, but she wasn't there. Stepping inside, there were the same three buttons on the control panel as before. I was strictly leaving the blue button alone. I didn't know what it did, perhaps called service or something else undesirable. As for the other two, I didn't know which was which, so I randomly pushed one of them. The button clicked and the system engaged. When it stopped, the door opened.

"Must have been the wrong button!" I thought. There was a huge room in front of me that appeared to have been carved out of a cave. There were machine tool marks showing in the stone of the walls. The main problem that I had to deal with immediately was that there were several large and alert creatures waiting for the transporter.

These guys were like the one that I'd first seen. Humanoid, but not human. It took them a second to realize that I was poking my nose into their business and only a second more for them to decide that it needed to be cut off. They unlimbered the most unlikely set of weapons and pointed them at me, but by that time I'd shot two of them with my right hand, slowing them down, and pressed the same elevator button again with my left simultaneously. The door snapped closed. I reasoned that the same button would take me back to my point of origin rather than to some other location. As it turned out, I was at least partially correct.

This was going from bad to unbelievably bad. Not only had I lost Liz, I now had a bunch of hostile somethings looking for me. The two I'd shot hadn't gone down and my last view of them indicated that my two shots had only irritated them extremely. The forty-five wasn't enough to stop them permanently. I rapidly substituted the splinter-shooting gun for my Sig. It seemed easy enough to operate and I thought that it might have slightly more effect on the bad guys.

In this case, my reasoning about the buttons was right, because when the door snapped open, I was in Durban again. The painting across the way was still there. That was really one ugly painting.

After a little thought, I stepped back into the transporter and pressed my second choice, the other button. I was ready to shoot when the door opened, but this time I ended up coming out of a door in a back alley of what later proved to be Greenwich Village.

I realized that even though I didn't fully understand how the elevator controls and network functioned, at least I was back in New York. I deduced that I was probably in the alley behind a Chinese restaurant based on two factors: the burned grease odor that thickened the air and the garbage bin full of cartons with indecipherable labels on them. The labels looked like they were written in Cantonese and not something that might have come from another world. The usual New York traffic noise rumbled down the alley making me feel more at home.

I looked around and since there was no one in sight I headed for the entrance to the alley. All of this solo traveling and shooting had only taken me about thirty seconds. As I came out onto the street, I was just in time to see Liz being hustled into a black Mercedes 600 S by two dark-skinned guys wearing expensive, but poorly fitting suits. It didn't look as if she was very happy about it, either. One of them was limping and I figured that he'd gotten the foot-stomping treatment.

I headed that way in a hurry, but they pulled out quickly and all I was left with was the license plate number. There were a lot of people on the street, but none of them had seemed to notice anything unusual happening with Liz and the two men, so I figured she'd done her stomping before they got out in full view. My toe twinged a little bit in sympathy. I hoped that she'd broken his.

Of course there were no nearby cabs. Funny how there is always a cab available in the movies, so that the hero can follow the lady being kidnapped. It didn't work out that way for me. Regretting that I didn't have the opportunity to say, "Driver! Follow that car!" I headed for the subway.

6

TRACKING

In a reasonably short time, I was in my "branch office" in midtown. This particular office was in a very unassuming building. I had rented a cheap, walk-up suite on the third floor under an assumed corporate name. An offshore corporation that was in yet another corporate name paid the monthly rent. The space I rented was a simple room with a desk and a filing cabinet. It was located in the middle of the sidewall of the adjacent building, so there wasn't a window. That lack didn't bother me because I really didn't want to look out and I didn't want anyone looking in at me while I was in there.

I had a number of such "offices" scattered around town in convenient locations. This had proven useful on a number of occasions. I couldn't be traced to any one particular location and that made it a little harder for the opposition.

I sat down at the desk and turned on the computer. It was an older model with a copy of Firefox installed on it. I fired up a secure browser and network connection, thinking that I should be as secure as possible. While the computer was grinding away, I opened the filing cabinet and took a quick inventory. It wasn't an ordinary filing cabinet. The entire front of it opened up and then both sides folded around to reveal a rather complete armory.

There was a secure latch that required my fingerprints in order to open. If someone had taken the time to force the armory open, they would have been rather surprised. There was a small block of C-4 that was hooked onto a switch that would engage if someone opened one of the doors by force. I had made sure that the explosion would not be large enough to hurt anyone in any adjacent rooms, but it would be quite large enough to give the burglar a severe headache. Probably severe enough to take his head right off.

I took out a spare left-side holster and fitted the splinter-shooter into it, then hung it on my left side. My Sig went back into its accustomed place. I had been missing its weight because the splinter gun was much lighter. Feeling the heavy pistol in its holster made me feel better. This arrangement gave me an easy option. Left side for aliens, right side for humans.

The computer beeped, showing that it had made connection with the Internet, so I turned around and sat down. It was the work of a few more minutes on some web sites that I really had no business looking into, to track the license plate to a man who nominally owned a restaurant serving bad falafel. It took somewhat longer to check some more secure, private law enforcement databases. I had prior access to these from another job so I didn't have to spend any time breaking in through their security.

I tried to maintain a good relationship with all of my previous employers. I've found that it helps if I do a good job. It seems like there are too many people out there that feel that they can get by if they just show up. At any rate, part of my contract negotiation tactics involved working out deals that would allow me to continue to use valuable resources from my previous employers. Many of them would allow that. The worst of the bunch were government-related agencies that had a vastly inflated sense of the importance of their data. I usually turned down offers from those types of groups.

I determined that the restaurant was a Hezbollah related enterprise that probably was partially funded by the proceeds from cigarette smuggling, although it also looked as if they may have gotten some US government funding for "health" related services in Benghazi.

With that information, I used some other passwords that I really shouldn't have known and tapped into a real-time satellite data feed, also not public, just in time to catch a black Mercedes coupe pulling into the parking garage which was adjacent to the restaurant. I couldn't tell if it was the particular 600 S that I'd been tracking, but the timing seemed about right.

I felt pretty good about this, since I figured that I could continue to bill my corporate employer for the job on which I'd started off the day. The group that ran the restaurant conveniently included my suspect from the mosque in Astoria. Sometimes things seem to have a way of working out nicely. In this case, I was becoming suspicious that there was some factor that tied things together that I was overlooking. I resolved to keep that question in the back of my mind in the hopes that the answer would present itself.

Feeling a little overloaded, I ran out to the restroom and relieved myself. Action heroes never seem to do this in the movies, but it's an unfortunate fact of real life that humans create waste products. I checked the hall carefully before I exited the door, made sure that the office was completely locked and carefully eased myself into the restroom. It was a one-person accommodation so there was no chance that anyone else was in there.

Finishing my business, I checked the hall again and went through the process of unlocking my office once more. As I came back into the office, my imagination got the better of me and I thoughtfully re-armed myself with an H&K UMP in forty-five caliber. I concealed the small machine pistol in a specially designed, over sized bag with a convenient, quick-action lock and was shortly en-route to the restaurant, using a rather battered, white delivery van that I kept in the parking garage adjacent to the office building.

As I drove, I considered my situation. I'd gone from an ordinary stakeout to chasing around with a blonde and a bunch of homicidal aliens with unknown motivations. Things were complicated and I don't like complicated. I'd prefer facing a bad guy while holding my gun in my hand. Nevertheless, it was obvious that this was a very unusual situation, even for New York. I realized that it amounted to an invasion of Earth and I wasn't sure I was prepared to be the savior of humanity. I wasn't even wearing an all-black suit like the stars in a re-run that I'd recently watched on the tube. I didn't have an alien sidekick disguised as a small dog, either.

All mental kidding aside, I figured that I at least owed it to Liz to try and rescue her. From there, I'd play along and see what was up and what, if anything, I could do about it.

The traffic was about normal; somewhere between suicidal and criminally insane, but I was used to it and it didn't take too long to get where I was headed. After several minutes of New York-style driving that would be considered crazed anywhere else, I pulled into the alley that led to the rear entrance of the restaurant.

I parked in the alley and checked out the situation. There were no other cars visible in the immediate vicinity and no open doors either. I could see people walking by on the street end to the west, but there was no one walking along the street to the east. It turned out that the other end of the alley opened onto a street that dead-ended a few feet past the intersection.

I walked down and peeked around the corner and saw that the dead-end street was clear. The other end of it exited into traffic about half a block further on. My van was pointed that way and I could drive out rapidly in the event of some sort of heavy pressure.

Just as I had that thought, the heavy pressure started. Some bearded guy stuck his head out of the rear door of the restaurant and tried to shoot me.

It was a big mistake. He dropped instantly with the report of my H&K and I slid through the building door with the machine pistol held at the ready. It turned out that the door opened into the kitchen. There were two startled cooks in the room. They dropped their cooking and cowered in a corner.

As I walked past them on the other side of the kitchen, my sixth sense suddenly kicked in,warning me. I ducked as one of the cooks threw a French bread knife at my back. It clattered on the wall, and I fired a round that hit the miscreant in the arm. He sat down and looked as if he was done trying things. His buddy was already heading out the door into the alley, so I let him go in the interest of saving ammunition.

The kitchen had swinging doors to the main restaurant; I peeked through the glass. There was no one out there. That was good as they would have been thoroughly alerted by the gunfire. I walked through the door and immediately saw another one of those odd elevator doors on the wall.

Crossing the room carefully, I pushed the call button and stepped in when the doors popped open. Once again, there were only two large buttons and the enigmatic blue one. Given a fifty percent chance of being correct, I hoped that I'd be lucky and guess the right one.

It never seems to work that way for me. If I drive onto a street that is a loop, I invariably end up heading the wrong way and drive all the way around before finding the address I'm looking for next to the loop entrance. That's about what happened this time, too.

I tried the left button and nearly dropped my teeth when the door opened. I was in a huge vacant, glass-enclosed area on an icy planet. As I watched, a huge planet, that could only be Jupiter, rose over the horizon. There was no other living creature in the place, so I pressed the left button again and thankfully ended up back in the restaurant shaking my head in amazement about the view I had just seen.

The second button got me more trouble than the first, so maybe it wasn't so lucky after all. Fortunately, I was prepared and was holding my weapon at the ready while I pressed the button.

I popped into a room that was full of people. Human people. Luckily, most of them weren't armed. The real problem was that the two who were, weren't humans. They were the oddly shaped aliens who were so hard to put down. They had their glass splinter guns out and ready and it got pretty dicey for a moment, but the H&K came through for me again. Both of the aliens were down and kicking after I burned through about half a mag.

I turned my attention to the humans in the room. Four of them had been near one side of the elevator door when I let go at the two aliens. Three of them had been struck by return fire, possibly by parts of the glass projectiles that splintered on the elevator frame.

The wounds didn't seem serious to me, but the victims were gasping for breath and beginning to spasm as if they'd been exposed to some nerve poison. Before I could complete my threat assessment of the rest of the room, they'd all expired.

"Those glass-splinter guns are a very nasty weapon," I thought. I resolved to stay as far away from the splinters as possible.

7

Rescued Again

After a little discussion with the eight survivors, it turned out that the rest of the people in the room were captives who had no idea what was going on. I sent them back through the elevator with instructions to get as far away from the restaurant as they could, as fast as possible.

I hoped they'd move quietly and not attract any additional attention to the building. Just about the last thing I wanted right now was some of NY's "Finest" blundering into a fire-fight and mistaking me for the aggressor. At the very least, it might take some elaborate explaining to ease them into the idea of "aliens-from-outer-space." If the evacuees would only run a few blocks before panicking, it would be great.

There was a single door out of the room directly across from the elevator door. I cleared it and then headed rapidly down a long hall. About halfway down the hall there was another door with a window. On inspection, it was locked and the small cell behind the door contained a chair on which Liz was sitting.

I wasted no time in opening the lock and letting her out. She fell into my arms and gave me a huge hug, followed by a hesitant and somewhat teary look as she said, "My God! I'd completely given up on ever seeing you again."

I reflexively tightened my arms around her and she looked up at me from a temptingly close distance with a question in her eyes. I'll be the first to admit it, although women frighten me because I don't know how to deal with them, I'm also amazingly romantic in my orientation. I cry at weddings and enjoy good love stories. I couldn't help myself, the scene was too perfect and demanded what came next. I bent my head and kissed her softly. She sighed and snuggled against me.

Then two things hit my mind at the same time. The first was that she'd left me in Durban and the second was the name of the song that the drunk had been singing. I got confused (my mental processes were still involved with the kiss, I guess) and blurted out, "The Year of the Cat! Al Stewart, 1976!"

She drew back with a start, displaying a puzzled look on her face, "What are you talking about? You big, crazed idiot! What's that have to do with us right now?"

"Oh," I sheepishly looked down. "I just remembered it was the song that a drunk was singing. He disappeared and I followed him and discovered the aliens' transportation system and – you!" I looked into her eyes again and that reminded me of my other thought.

"Why did you take off on me in Durban?" I demanded in an accusatory tone of voice.

"I didn't!" she denied. She looked in my eyes and then continued. "I was getting ready to follow you out of the door and it snapped shut in front of me. The next thing I knew, it popped open again and some Middle-Eastern looking guy jammed a gun in my face. I started to fight, but he grabbed my arm and then another one got hold of my other arm and they handcuffed me again!" This last part was spoken in a rising voice that betrayed her anger at being captured so easily.

"It was in a Chinese restaurant, so they might be involved also. You can get there by pressing the other button in the brownstone where we took the route through South Africa. I think it's somewhere in the Chinatown area. They dragged me outside and into a car – "

I interrupted, "I know, I came out of the alley just in time to see them drag you in and drive off."

She looked distressed, "I wish you'd been a little faster." She paused, thinking and then continued. "The first guy dragged me down the hall and into this cell. I was trying to get up the nerve to attack the next one that came in, when you found me. He removed the handcuffs and I thought I might have a chance. I'm not too bad at hand-to-hand."

Thinking about the hug, I responded, "No, I imagine that you're pretty good at close quarters." Then I had the good grace, but ill luck to blush. I didn't mean it to come out that way; it's only that I kind of lose my mind in the presence of pretty women.

She looked at me sternly and slowly shook her head back and forth. She was apparently trying to suppress a grin. To prevent any other embarrassing statements, I resolved to keep my mind on business. I said, "Let's get out of here before anyone else shows up."

We hurried back through the door, down the hall and into the first room. I was disappointed to see that the machine pistol had failed to finish the two aliens. They were staggering to their feet in a kind of woozy way, and were both looking daggers at us. Their guns were on the floor and had bounced several feet away from them. One grabbed the others' arm and pointed in a human-like manner. They started to sidle towards the weapons.

I thoughtfully let the H&K dangle from its sling and pulled the splinter gun. The trigger had an abominable action, but it went "thump-poof" and one of the aliens flopped. I shot the other and they both expired. I took a thankful breath and then stepped over to them to check. There was no doubt about it; they were completely inert. In fact their bodies had reacted violently to the poison and they were quite dead. It was not a pretty sight.

I looked at Liz. "They're hard to kill."

"They're not human, obviously," she said. "When I was captured, one of them told me that they've got a dermal layer that has a lot of silica in it and it makes them as tough as nails. That's why they use those poisoned-glass splinter-shooters. The poison kills them as fast as it kills a human. The other thing about them is they wear a sort of body armor-skin that is very smooth, almost slippery, so a glancing shot sometimes won't even penetrate; the bullet just slips off. I also think that their skeletal structure has silica in it, rather than calcium."

"Well, knowing is half the battle," I said as I picked up both of their weapons. I gave one to her. "Know how to use this?"

"You better believe I do!" she said, with a rather evil grin that didn't bode well for the next alien we encountered.

As I walked past one of the now uncaring aliens, I noticed something funny that made me stop and take a closer look. The skin on its face had slipped to one side deforming in a way that didn't seem right. I grabbed its cheek and realized that the skin on its head was loose. In fact, as I pulled, it stretched and then came off with a slurping sound. The result was even less pleasant to look at.

"Wow! That must be the real creature! The body-armor must cover the entire body including the face." I looked closer, "It's a suit alright, but it looks like it's needed to protect the creature from our atmosphere."

The skin of the creature's face was bubbling up from exposure to the air or possibly from reaction to the poison. As I watched, the skin formed bubbles and then sort of dissolved into a wet mess, running back through the skeletal-like structure of the thing's skull. Liz, who was looking over my shoulder, made a gagging noise and turned pale. She turned her back and stepped away. I shrugged and filed this latest information under the interesting-and-to-be-dealt-with-later category.

We turned back to what I was still calling the "elevator." The other dead alien had rolled partly inside. The door was opening and closing on the corpse. Stepping over, I bent and grabbed its ankle and pulled it out. It felt funny and I wiped my hands on my pants after I let go.

This time Liz didn't waste any time over the body. "Let's go," she said.

We went back into the transporter and pressed the button that took us to the restaurant. It'd been vacant when we left, but now it seemed to be hosting a regular convention of my erstwhile terrorist buddies. I shot them up pretty good with the H&K because they seemed disposed to argue about our presence. Their arguments included reaching for various concealed weapons, and neither Liz nor I were in the mood for such a discussion. At the first opportunity and with our ears ringing, we slipped out the back door into the alley, leaving them licking their wounds, or rather, some of them licking their wounds and the rest dead or dying.

Liz had used the splinter-shooter and had proven deadly with it. It didn't wound anyone. They died from even a minor hit, while my shots had killed some and wounded others. I guessed if I had to be shot, I'd opt not to be shot with one of the splinters. I might have a chance if it were only a lead slug.

We drove the van out of the area and cruised along the street heading uptown. I looked at Liz and she had the grace to blush a little. She apparently realized that I was rather impressed at her weapons handling. She'd gotten more than half of the hits in the restaurant.

I didn't say anything and the silence got to her. She finally cleared her throat and admitted that she was a US Treasury agent and had been following up on a lead that might have something to do with a recent influx of high-grade, hundred-dollar counterfeit-bills. "These are even better than the ones the North Koreans have been making," she added.

She'd tracked the source to a warehouse. She paused, thinking, and then continued. She'd accidentally gone through a transporter to Jupiter and there she'd been caught by some of the aliens who'd imprisoned her for several days. They'd eventually handed her over to the one I'd called Mr. Ugly to transport to somewhere unknown where she was asked a series of questions by a panel of the aliens. They turned her back over to Mr. Ugly to take somewhere after a brief conversation. She had thought that the somewhere she was headed for was a one-way destination, a short walk followed by a bullet to the head.

Their interrogation didn't extract much information from her, but they told her enough about themselves to let her know they intended to take over the Earth.

"The aliens call themselves 'Pugs'. I don't know if that's their racial name or only the name of their group, but it kind of fits because they're fighters and are hard to kill," she said. "Some of them can speak English, but they all seem to understand it. Generally, they use their own language. They sound kind of like snakes hissing."

I thought to myself, "That nixes the idea that I could have a small pug-dog as an alien ally, at least." I was relieved. I don't much care for pugs anyway.

She'd been pretty surprised and grateful when I'd rescued her the first time and, now that I'd pulled her out of the fire the second time, she was positively my biggest fan, at least for the moment. From past experience, I knew how quickly this sort of thing could change.

While she'd been in the holding cell where I'd found her, she'd watched through the window for a while and she'd seen the aliens herding a group of humans down the hall. A few minutes later, she'd seen a larger group of Pugs come through on the reverse trip.

She'd been in the windowed cell for only a short time until I'd gotten there. From the traffic she'd seen going back and forth, it was apparent that the Pugs were shipping a lot of people somewhere and building up a pretty significant, and undoubtedly, armed force at the same time. She'd also seen them carrying some suspicious packages that looked exactly like the package that she'd previously found that was full of counterfeit bills. Her thought that the Pugs were bringing in the counterfeits was probably right on target.

We wondered a moment, to no avail, why the aliens were pushing counterfeit currency. My best guess was that they hoped to retire in Florida, or something. Liz seemed to think that it was an attempt to destabilize the system by flooding the world with fake bills. Thinking about it, I agreed that her thought was probably more accurate than mine. Based on her speculation, my subconscious suddenly put two and two together and came out with five. I could probably teach common core math, if I ever decided to retire and take up a profession that was even more dangerous than my current one.

"I think that the Middle-Easterners I've been watching must somehow be in on the action. They are amazingly well funded, so perhaps they are getting some of the counterfeits. I wonder if they know that they are working for aliens? I'll bet that the Prophet, praise be upon him, would roll over in his grave at the thought of such a thing!" This last remark was spoken sarcastically and was probably uncalled for. Liz did me the favor of ignoring it and we moved on to other information.

She only knew a few of the transport stations. Luck was needed to tell the buildings from their neighbors.

The transporters were located in numerous, different and unlikely places. Since they seemed to be more or less dimensionless, they could be mounted on a flat, thin surface. Despite being flat, the transporter opened to a small, elevator-like room that linked to the destination when activated. To the occupant, the transition appeared to be instantaneous.

Most of the transporters had a permanent facade that looked like an elevator, but the facade of some of them could appear and disappear. These were usually placed in locations that were difficult to secure. Despite the disappearing facade, the underlying transporter link was always to the same physical location.

The Pugs exhibited an odd strategic sense in the locations they picked. They'd used closets in police stations and heavily trafficked offices. One of the portals was even behind Berthier's door in Paris.

I hadn't heard of it, so Liz explained that it was a fake door that had been installed against a solid wall by a couple of artists. The city keeps it clean of graffiti. The door even gets mail and advertising delivered to it. What the artists don't know is that the Pugs co-opted the door and rather than opening to a blank wall, there was now a transporter head behind it. Some of the other transporters she knew about were in false buildings that sometimes served as vents for the subway or undergrounds in other cities.

Right about then I was feeling pretty happy. She was sitting very close to me on the van's cheap bench seat. She'd turned partially towards me and it only took a little daring for me to put my right arm around her. Liz didn't seem to mind and she was such a nice armful. I found that I was distracted from my driving. Luckily the traffic was pretty light.

We drove in silence for a few minutes and then she proceeded to tell me more of what had happened to her, starting a few months ago.

"I've been working on tracing some high-quality counterfeit hundreds. Really good stuff. The trail led from the US to Mexico and from one group to the next. From all signs it was pointing straight to the Middle East. Just before I was captured, I'd gotten a couple of little facts that seem to show that the Middle East isn't the ultimate source of the paper. The technology is too good. The bills are exactly like the real thing. The only way to tell is that there are some serial numbers that are duplicates of real Federal Reserve Notes. It's like the counterfeiters didn't know or care exactly where the bill printing process was in the numeric sequence and, of course the bills were so good that they really don't have to worry much. The chances of being found out are tiny, except some bankers got lucky and found some duplicates and then alerted the Treasury."

Then Liz dropped a bomb, "I'm now of the opinion that the printing presses being used to create these bills are in Washington and in, or near the Mint."

"Wait a minute," I said. "Doesn't that mean that they aren't counterfeit, but the real thing?" Then, like the idiot I sometimes was, I had to add, "I don't know what difference it makes anyway. Counterfeit or real, these days the value is about the same."

She didn't seem to approve of my sentiment, looking away before she continued in her exposition.

"In a sense they are real, but they are unauthorized, as far as the government knows. I think they're being shipped through the transport system to the North Koreans and to some terrorist groups, drug cartels in South America and some other nasties for distribution where they will do the most good. Uh, I mean harm, " she said, correcting herself.

"Lately, I've been trying to find out exactly who is behind the extra printing and how it's getting done outside of the normal controls. I believe that the Pugs have something to do with the actual process, which is pretty clear, since they're providing the transport to the destination groups," she added, then continued, "But, I'm really frightened!"

"Yeah, being captured and then rescued a couple of times will do that to you."

"No," she said and I could see that she really was afraid. "I think that they are kidnapping people in large groups and I don't think that any of them are being left alive. I'm... I'm afraid that something horrible is happening to the ones who get captured."

One minute, she was tough and the next trembling like a child. I asked, "What do you think could be happening to them?"

All I could get out of her was: "I think the Pugs are meat eaters." Then she looked away quickly and shuddered. I hugged her even tighter, despite the fact that the traffic had picked up and was now wall-to-wall.

Liz's answer led me to consider the latest statistics of which I was aware. I happened to know that literally hundreds of thousands of people go missing in the US alone on an annual basis. Trying to extend this to the entire world led me to a mind-boggling estimate. If even a few percent of these people were being taken by the Pugs and either removed from the planet or, and here I shuddered mentally, eaten, it would amount to a number that would qualify in the world's view as worthy of being called genocide.

That thought led me to wonder how many Pugs were on Earth at the present time. We'd seen some, but they apparently weren't here in large enough numbers to openly invade. I also realized that they had an environmental issue with our planet. They needed protection from some gas or compound in the air that we breathed. The lack of enough protective suits could be a limiting factor.

Earth was also brighter than they liked and that might be a limiting factor. They seemed to prefer dimmer lighting with a reddish hue. I had to assume that they were from a dimmer environment and perhaps their local star was redder than ours.

I was becoming more and more convinced that this was the real thing. An alien invasion of Earth. It didn't start with spacecraft plunking down into the ocean or with huge saucers hovering overhead. It started with a bunch of nasty creatures trying to sabotage our society. Something definitely needed to be done and I was becoming determined that I was the one to do it. Now, if only I could figure out what to do.

About this time we arrived at the parking garage near our destination. This was a hideout that had been provided by my present employers. They knew about it, so it wasn't too secure, but it was a pretty good place to hide out. I hadn't used it before and, based on the depth of the problems we had, I'd probably never use it again.

It was in a building served by a concierge. I had asked them to set it up for contingencies. The unique thing was that it wasn't on the list of addresses in the building. The doorman would have been amazed to know that it was there.

8

Δ Respite

I used my remote to open the parking garage gate and we parked in the basement in a service parking space where the van looked at home. We then went through a service door, down a hall, and found a door that didn't have a keyhole or handle. I looked closely at a crack in the concrete located conveniently at eye height. The retinal scanner concealed in the crack seemed to think that I was OK because the door opened.

We went in. Understand that this was actually the first time I'd used this hideout, so I wasn't too sure about the facilities. A brief check showed me that there were weapons (good), computers (exactly what we needed for more research), and a small, fully stocked kitchen (great, as we were both starved). There was also a room with two sets of bunk beds, in case someone needed a nap.

While we looked around, Liz continued to talk, "I got involved in this mess about six months ago. I was assigned to trace some bogus bills that were coming over the border at Tijuana. One thing led to another and I eventually followed the trail back to DC, as I mentioned."

"After considerable digging, I discovered that the bills were being printed at a secret facility that I think is near the Mint. The paper was apparently being transported from the Mint to the location of the other press. The dies themselves look to be the real thing. Perhaps they're spares that have been stolen or... borrowed." She looked at me with a speculative air.

"It seems that a number of Federal employees are moonlighting on this and I don't think the citizens of the country would approve. At least, I don't," she said and then sighed deeply.

"Anyway, I followed a shipment of the bills that was being moved in an unmarked delivery van from DC to New York. The deliverymen off-loaded the pallets at a warehouse near the Hudson. I had to get smart and go sneaking into the building and the first elevator I tried – "

I grinned and interjected, "Wasn't like any elevator you'd ever been in before."

She looked disgusted, "No, it wasn't. I ended up on some moon of, I think, Jupiter."

"I went there," I interjected. "It was amazing. The view of Jupiter coming up over the horizon was like nothing I'd ever imagined. Wait a minute, didn't you say you were captured in Greece?"

"If you can just forget what you thought I said," she said, sarcastically, "I'd like to continue with more important things." She paused to see if I was going to talk again.

I have that effect on women. I don't know what it is, but I often seem to bring out the worst in them.

She continued, "It wasn't in Greece, it was on Io, a moon of Jupiter. At least, that's what moon I think it was. Maybe you simply heard Io and assumed Greece. But, let me go on." She looked to ensure I wasn't going to interrupt and then said, "There was a mess of Pugs there and they grabbed me immediately. I don't know where they thought I was from, but they were puzzled enough to hold on to me and investigate, rather than killing me out-of-hand."

I interjected, "I was lucky, then. The place was empty when I poked my head out."

She continued, "From what I've gathered, they're meaning to take over the Earth, but they don't seem to have the force to invade directly." She sighed again and looked at the wall. "I think that their overall strategy might be to create a series of financial crises that disorganize us and create internal problems. If governments were fighting internal battles for power, it might be possible for the Pugs to force us to a tipping point where they would be able to take control without too much risk. Who knows, they may have done this before. They certainly seem to know what they're doing and they are sticking to what looks like a long-term plan. We'd better figure out a way to counter them fast, or we might end up as slaves or," she shuddered, "cattle."

Well, I'd once read a quote from some famous investor who remarked that, "Only when the tide goes out do you discover who's been swimming naked." That's exactly what happens in really bad monetary crises. It was beginning to look like the Pugs and possibly some unknown members of our government were trying to create a financial storm by dropping even more worthless currency on the population than normal. It seemed like they were trying to discover exactly how stupid humans could be.

You can figure out roughly how safe a bank is by looking at its liquidity. One way of doing that is to calculate how much cash it has on hand as a percentage of customer deposits. Banks don't actually pile up stacks of paper money these days; they simply have electronic records of deposits with the central banks. In general, the more cash the bank has on hand, the safer it is, because in a financial crisis, people always panic and want to withdraw cold, hard cash in physical form.

In a crisis, banks bleed cash and, if the government doesn't close them with a banking "holiday," the bleeding will look like a cut jugular vein. The reverse of this problem involves creating so much physical cash in circulation that it begins to loose value. In that case, Gresham's Law comes into play and people will horde other stores of value such as precious metals, drugs, food, and probably ammunition. Those types of valuables will become the desired medium of exchange.

Banks, on the other hand, really don't have any business hording ammunition, so they'll try to raise as much cash as they can to meet the increased demand. If they are poorly run and don't have the necessary reserves, they'll start liquidating assets such as loans, stock, and even shares of the bank itself. The only problem with that process is, in a full-blown crisis, one never gets the true value of the asset. Everything goes at a huge discount. This means that the banks with thin reserves will either go out of business or go to the government for a bail-out.

The Pugs didn't even have to be very good planners. We'd shown them the easiest way to disrupt our society with the crash and bail-out of 2009. The only thing that would make it worse would be to somehow destroy all electronic records of finances. I didn't know it then, but we later found out the Pugs were working on that. My general conclusion was that using financial disruption as a means to take over was only too possible.

Just at that point, my stomach rumbled. Liz laughed and walked into the kitchen, shooing me out when I followed. I heard some cooking noises and shortly after that some really interesting smells came wafting out. I was trying to ignore my hunger by working on some satellite recon with the aid of a reasonably fast computer and anonymous Internet connection.

I was afraid, and rightfully so, as it turned out, the Internet was compromised and any open inquiries might be monitored, not only by NSA, but by other entities as well. Our location was protected by the encryption system that was in place.

Shortly, Liz came in to get me. We returned to the kitchen and had a satisfying meal. I kidded her about her cooking ability and she feigned embarrassment, but I could tell that she was pleased that I liked the food. She simply hadn't scrounged up any old thing. She'd fixed a complete Italian meal with spaghetti and meatballs and a great Greek salad. Unfortunately, this really wasn't the time or place to open a bottle of Chianti, even though there actually was one sitting on one of the pantry shelves.

We looked at each other across the table, laughing a little as we sat down and tucked into the food. We were both tense from our various escapes, but as we started to eat we began to relax. I think food tastes better if I take the time to enjoy it. I found out long ago that eating slowly helps burn off the stress of action. We were really hungry, so we kept our heads down and stayed too involved in eating to carry on much conversation.

When we were done, we went back to the computer and, this time, Liz helped by giving me locations of the few transport stations that she knew of. She was reasonably certain of the locations. The one or two that she was dubious about, we flagged with question marks. In our travels today and her prior captivity, she'd gone through some parts of the system more than once and she had a good memory for that sort of thing.

The pattern that started to emerge was patchy, but its implications were chilling. The aliens seemed to be covering a large part of the globe. Most of the transporters Liz and I had seen were in New York. If other cities in the United States had as many, it implied that there were a lot of transporters in the network.

She had no idea if they had spread evenly across the country or if the west coast was also involved. We decided that we'd better presume that the Pugs were everywhere and work on that assumption.

We were speculating about the pattern and what to do next, when I unexpectedly kissed her again. This action was met with only token protest.

My heart rate skyrocketed as her arms went around my neck.

My reactions seemed funny to me, because I never really had encountered a woman with whom I'd had such an instant connection. Thinking about it, I guess I had unreasonable expectations. It always seemed that there was no girl next door who fit into my rather active and dangerous lifestyle. The women that I had met were for the most part either actively working for the opposition or were basically incompatible with my subconscious image of a mate. She wasn't. In fact she seemed to be all that I'd ever dreamed of. I only hoped that I was as attractive to her she was to me.

Quite some time later, after we calmed down, we managed to make a decision about going back into the transporter system. She was of the opinion that we had no choice.

Liz said, "Look, the aliens are obviously dangerous and they don't mean us well. It's up to us to see if there's anything we can do."

"I'm game," I responded. "Let's see what we can find out, but let's get equipped first."

Liz took a large briefcase that was already stocked with an UMP, a Glock 9MM pistol, four frag grenades and a new tool that I'd not used before. It was a state-of-the-art laser projector that could be adjusted momentarily from a modest flashlight-like mode to an intense weapon beam that would burn skin and instantly burn out the retina of any eye that happened to be in its way. In the high-power mode, the laser was almost invisible. There was barely enough visible light to aid in aiming over a medium distance.

I found another one of the lasers and put it in my bag, along with my UMP, and a couple of additional full magazines for the gun. I lightened her load by taking two of her four grenades. The went into the bag, then I, arranged a towel to cover all of the weaponry from prying eyes.

In our work at mapping the system, she had remembered that there were a couple of transporters nearby. They were not far from Times Square.

9

Δ CAT

It was only a short distance, so we left the van where it was and walked. The pedestrian traffic paid us no heed and we ended up at a small bookstore that specialized in arcane books. I took out my Sig, just in case.

We went in and found that the store was empty of people. There were numerous shelves of dusty books and an odor that was reminiscent of a long-undisturbed library. The clock over the register ticked loudly in the dead silence. Dim light filtered through the dusty front windows. A single faded bar of sunlight illuminated the dust motes dancing on the air we'd stirred up when we opened the front door.

The available light was quite dim, and as we approached the rear of the store it faded and grew dimmer and dimmer. It didn't help that the book shelves were arranged in such a way that the light from the front windows was mostly blocked. I pulled out the laser projector and used a diffused beam to help illuminate our path. This was helpful because there were stacks of books on the floor and some of them were lying in the middle of the aisles. It was dark and spooky and I really wasn't getting a good feeling as we walked towards the back.

We looked around. There was no clerk and no one else in there either. As we moved toward the back of the store, we heard a funny gurgling sound that came through a slightly opened door in the back wall. We approached cautiously and I peeked around the doorjamb. I really wasn't prepared for the horrendous sight that I encountered.

One of the Pugs was holding an elderly man in much the same position I'd once seen a praying mantis hold a grasshopper. The man's head was partially gnawed off and the gurgling was his blood running out onto the floor. The creature took another bite while I watched. The sight aroused me to an extreme intensity of anger and without thinking I instantly thumbed the laser projector to full power and flashed it into the Pug's eyes. It let out a scream and dropped the dead man. I held the pointer shining directly into its eyes for a little over a second. It seemed to be stunned by the light. Suddenly it shuddered, screamed again, then flopped on the floor, twitched for a few seconds and then stilled.

I cautiously stepped into the room and kicked its foot. No movement. It was stone dead. The Pugs had a true vulnerability to light. It apparently fried their brain in some fashion. After the difficulty I'd encountered with my forty-five, this was a welcome and somewhat encouraging discovery, particularly since we didn't know if we'd be able to keep the splinter-shooters in ammunition for very long.

Using the enemies' weapons against them was a viable tactic only so long as we could keep ahead of them enough to find more ammo. I knew I could get .45 cartridges, but they really didn't work well and I was worried about killing enough of the Pugs to keep a supply of glass splinters to carry us through a major battle.

I turned back to look at Liz who had an astonished look on her face. Her mouth was partly opened. She gasped and said, "I didn't know anyone could move that fast! That laser must be really powerful. It looks like it burned his brain completely out!"

"It's not terribly powerful," I replied quietly. "It will burn a human's retina out, though, so don't ever look directly at it, but the Pugs must be much more sensitive to it than humans."

Liz was already moving towards the transporter door set in the rear wall. As she reached it, the door flipped open and two more aliens popped out. I flashed the first of them with the laser and he dropped. This kill gave me a large amount of satisfaction, especially since I'd gotten a close look at the dead man's shoulders and realized that one of his arms had also been mostly gnawed off before he had died.

Dropping two of them with the laser took a little too much time. The second one was pointing a gun at me, but Liz shot him between the eyes with her Glock. She'd pulled it, following my instinctive choice of weapons, when I'd taken out my Sig. The shot knocked the Pug down.

It was making vague motions like it was trying to swim across the floor on its back, so I stepped up and held the laser beam on its right eye. It died within a couple of seconds, exactly like the first one. The laser worked, but it was a little bit too slow to work as a truly effective weapon.

The really scary thing was the creature's forehead had a thumb-print-sized dent over the right eye., but The slug had failed to penetrate, bounced off, and was lying nearby on the floor. Our weapons simply weren't designed for something that tough. I kicked at the thing's head as I walked by, then turned to Liz and said, "Nice shooting! Keep it up and I'll give you a master marksman rating."

She was still a little worked up over the situation and she snapped, "Already have that! Why not get into the transporter so we can go?"

I thoughtfully replied, "I've been mostly calling them elevators, but transporter is a much better name. Is that what the Pugs call it, it is Pugs, isn't it?"

She had calmed down and smiled, "Yes, it is Pugs and no, I don't know what they call the transporters. That's just what I decided they were."

It only took a few seconds to gather up our gear and move into the transporter unit. As we'd planned, she activated the button for the cavern where I'd been previously, but before starting, she pressed the blue one before I could stop her. By this time I had practically developed a phobia about that button. I had even imagined that it could be a self-destruct system. However, all it did was to activate a hidden video display on the seemingly smooth wall above the button panel. The display lit up and showed nothing but an empty room with a stack of boxes showing in the distance.

"The blue button activates a video function," she said with a smile in response to my gasp and aborted raising of my hand in a vain attempt to block her from pushing it. "That way you can see if you're going to encounter anyone at your destination."

"What happens if they look through and see us? Can they do that?" I asked.

"They probably can. To be safe, we should always try to stay to one side of the door, so we'll be mostly out of the field of vision. But, the thing is, not all of the units have the video function. Maybe they are older models that have fewer features. Maybe they're developing the technology and don't have too many of the new ones, or maybe Earth is so unimportant that they are using their old stuff to get rid of it."

While I was thinking about that, she hit the button for the cavern and we were there. This time there were no occupants. The sound of our footsteps echoed off of the distant walls. The place seemed totally deserted. The overhead lights were on, but dim. To our right, the lights faded out into shady rows that receded toward the distant wall.

The place seemed man-made and longer than it was wide. There were machine marks on the unfinished rock walls just as I'd previously noticed.

Overall, it was a depressing scene. Most of the floor was empty, but here and there were piles of litter and some stacks of boxes.

Liz stopped for a moment, opening her case to remove the sub-machine gun. She made sure it was loaded and arranged the sling over her shoulder. Never one to be outdone, I did the same. It was pretty spooky in the cavern.

We moved across the floor to the largest array of stacked boxes. One was standing by itself at the edge of the pile and its lid had been partially removed. We looked inside and the box was nearly full of Federal Reserve Notes in the one hundred dollar denomination.

She said, "Guessing from the size of this stack, there must be at about a trillion dollars stored here."

"Do you think they're real?" I asked, rather naively. My excuse was that I was kind of in shock. It's not every day you get to see that much cash.

"I'm positive they are all counterfeit. This must be the storage place of the bills I've been tracking." She started, paused and looked around.

"What is it?"

"I thought I heard something!"

There was a scrabbling sound and then a rush as a dozen large, insect-like creatures darted around the other end of the boxes and moved quickly towards us. The creatures were like nothing I'd ever seen.

They seemed insect-like at first, but I decided they were better viewed as a combination of spider and scorpion. Although they were only about a foot high, suspended on long, jointed legs, they looked formidable. They had a vertically oriented set of jaws that were complete with several large fangs. I was glad to see that they didn't have a scorpion-type stinger on their tail, but the fangs were quite evil looking and more than made up for the lack of stinger.

Liz shrieked and started blasting away with her UMP at the group. It blew pieces off of them, but they continued to advance as long as they had enough legs to move.

As she shot, I suddenly realized that the top level of the boxes was covered with a large number of the creatures moving stealthily towards our end of the stack. I flashed them with the laser. They backed up momentarily, but none dropped. Drat the luck! Just when I needed a super weapon, the laser had no effect. In fact, once they had gotten over the momentary effect of the flash, they accelerated towards us.

I had no idea what they would do if they actually reached us, but I didn't think that they intended to congratulate us for finding the money. Liz was still shooting at some of the survivors near the other end of the boxes. Whatever advantage we'd had by being quiet was now gone, so I dropped the laser, pulled out a grenade and lobbed it into the thickest part of the pack on the top of the stack. Bodies and parts flew all over, although none reached our location. To finish things off, I brought my UMP into action and fired short bursts into groups of the things along with Liz.

We burned through almost all of our available clips before we'd gotten them all.

Liz sighed a sigh of relief. I glanced at her and saw that she was shaking.

"I've seen one of these things bite a human. They carry a poison that causes the bitten part to instantly swell up to twice its size with a green fluid and then burst. The green fluid splatters out all over and wherever it touches, the skin turns black and then dissolves. The human doesn't have a chance. The bitten man screamed for about thirty seconds before his upper body was almost totally black. When his torso started to dissolve, he thrashed around for a bit and then died."

"That's horrible and nasty!" I said. "What are these things anyway?"

Before she could answer, we heard some scraping from the other side of the boxes. We looked at each other and then ran away from the door we'd initially come through, heading towards a door in the opposite wall. I didn't consciously plan to go that way; it was simply a lot closer.

About halfway there, I looked over my shoulder and saw another huge mass of the blasted things coming across the floor at high speed. Their legs may have looked flimsy, but they could really run. It was good that we had a head start.

I didn't waste any time shooting, I grabbed Liz's hand and we dashed through the door, bolting it after us. The creatures hit the other side with a series of thumps, but it held.

I turned around and looked to see where we were. There was a short, faintly lit corridor facing us. Without hesitating, we ran down it and emerged through an unlocked door into what looked like a dark subway tunnel.

Liz said, "I guess we must still be in New York, if this is the subway."

"Yeah. Don't touch the third rail," I cautioned. "They must be storing some of the money in one of the old, original tunnels. It might be easier to distribute it from there, considering the proximity of the financial centers and banks in the city."

We were able to see the lights of a station in the far distance, so we walked down the shadowy tunnel as fast as we could. Once I quit panting from exertion, it still took me a little time to regain my composure.

"What are they? Some kind of spiders?" I repeated the question that I'd asked before we were interrupted by the second wave of the attack.

"I think they're some kind of life form from the Pugs' planet. I saw one of the Pugs carrying one around on his shoulder. He had it kill the guy I told you about. Maybe they're a pet of some sort."

"I'll take a cat over these things, any day," I joked weakly. I've never really liked cats. Perhaps they're a little too devious or too independent. Anyway, I've never had the urge to have one around.

As if my words had somehow invoked the reality, there was a tentative "Meep" from behind a support beam and an inquisitive cat face peered out. Seeing us, he paraded around the beam and came right over to me and started rubbing on my leg.

He was a large, somewhat chewed-up orange Tom. One ear was kind of ripped, but otherwise he looked like a regular tough guy who won his fights as a matter of course. I reached down and let him smell my hand.

He approved of my fingers and I scratched his head and was rewarded by a loud rumbling purr.

Liz looked at me in astonishment, then snorted, "You can't make time for a cat now. We've got places to go."

The cat looked at her and then started leading us down the track as if he'd understood what she was saying. We looked at each other, shrugged and followed.

The cat trotted ahead and stopped by a bundle of rags that turned out to be a blackened and mostly dissolved corpse. This discovery didn't help our confidence, since we now realized that the alien pets had access to the tunnel. A few yards farther on, we found another corpse. This was definitely a bad sign.

The cat led us towards the glowing lights of the station that now seemed to be about a quarter of a mile down the track. Suddenly, it stopped and bristled with a hiss.

My pistol was out and I fired as soon as there was movement. There was a clacking noise and a scrabble as one of the spider-like creatures crawled towards us despite being blown almost in half. I fired again and this time the shot sounded abnormally loud. The alien exploded into pieces.

I shook my head to try to clear my hearing and then realized that Liz had shot at precisely the same moment as I, but since she was standing partially behind me, her muzzle blast had done a number on my right ear. It sounded like she was talking through a pipe.

"Let's keep moving, these things are feeding in this tunnel."

We followed the cat and were almost at the station when we heard a train coming from behind us. We dashed ahead and then found shelter in an alcove. The cat was nowhere to be seen for a moment, but then I saw him across the tracks huddled in a small hole in the concrete wall. He obviously knew what he was doing and had dodged trains before.

The train moved rapidly past us and began to slow for the station. As the last car rolled slowly up to us, a Pug jumped off of the end of the train and headed towards us.

I shot him twice with my UMP and then the clip was out. Liz shot and was out also. Too late, I remembered that I'd left the laser in the cavern. The Pug was still moving rapidly. As he came within twenty feet, he jumped towards me with an incredibly powerful leap.

He'd have been on me then, but I'd fumbled around under my shirt and retrieved the pistol I'd taken from Mr. Ugly. The gun thumped lightly and the creature died in the middle of his leap. He dropped to the ground at our feet and began to dissolve. A thin yellow fluid dripped out of his eyes. In a few seconds, his tissue started to dissolve into a black mass of slime that filled the body-armor that the alien had worn.

"Wow! Why do you think this one fell apart so much faster than the others we shot?"

Liz shook her head, "Maybe it was due to his sprinting at us."

The yellow fluid in the projectiles killed rapidly. We learned later that its action was much faster if the Pug was engaged in stressful activity. If one was resting, it simply died, but any strenuous exertion caused its body to react far more violently.

Knowing that the toxin would kill humans with almost equal facility, I carefully tucked the weapon back into my belt holster with a little cringe as I thought of what an accidental discharge might do to my leg. The dratted thing didn't have any safety, except to keep your finger off the firing button.

The cat edged past the alien's liquid remains, stopping momentarily to scratch some gravel at the mess. We both laughed. He obviously didn't have much use for Pugs either.

We moved on to the station, just as the train pulled out. There were only a few people there at the moment and they looked like normal New Yorkers and not Pugs, so we went up to the street without pausing. When we came out of the subway, it seemed like we were emerging from the depths of Hell. This feeling was exacerbated by the fact that we were disoriented. I'd seen the sign that said Lexington Exit down below, but it didn't compute until I came onto the street. I was looking back and forth, trying to get my bearings when the cat rubbed against my leg.

I looked down, thought about it for a moment, and then unzipped my bag. I held it down near the sidewalk and without any hesitation the cat jumped in. He looked at me and made another "meep" noise in an inquiring tone of voice. I gathered up the handles and picked up the bag as he ducked down inside.

"I've got to check in with my superior," Liz said.

10

No Help

Liz struck off at a quick pace down the street as if she knew where she was going.

I looked over my shoulder a couple of times, trying to make sure I knew where we were, and then ran to catch her arm.

"Hey, wait a minute! I've got a secure office a couple of blocks away from here," I said. "Let's go there and regroup."

She nodded and in a few minutes, we were back in my mid-town office. When I put the duffle down, the cat jumped out and began to explore the room.

Liz asked, "Do you have any way for me to communicate with my boss in this place?"

I waved toward the computer. "Use that, but be sure to encrypt your conversation. I feel pretty vulnerable as it is and we don't need them walking down our throats before you get half-way through."

"I'm already on it," she said. "It's protocol for my people to use a private system with full encryption."

She was, too. It was only a few seconds before the screen showed an office background and then a gray-haired, distinguished looking man leaned forward with surprise on his face. "Elizabeth! Is that really you? I thought that you were gone for sure! Where are you?"

"Right here in town, boss," she answered. "I've got a friend and we need help. I've located the source of the fake Federal Reserve Notes, but the situation is going to require some pretty heavy force to even begin to slow it down."

He looked over his shoulder and then back. "You need to report in, immediately. Come on in to the office now!"

"I don't think I've been followed, but I don't know for sure," she said, a frown on her face.

He frowned in return, then looked up, as if he were looking at something behind his computer screen.

"No, come on in," he insisted, momentarily glancing again at something out of the corner of his eyes. "We'll discuss a plan while I raise a response force. I'll have Peggy send out for some food, since it's almost time to eat. When can I expect you?"

"In about thirty minutes," she answered, hanging up.

She turned to me with a serious expression. "He didn't ask about you when I mentioned that I had a friend. That's not like him. He's usually extremely proactive and he likes to control all aspects of a situation."

She looked puzzled for a moment and then said, "Well, maybe he's just waiting until we get there, but he is acting a little strange."

"I don't like this very much," I said. "I'm already worried about the situation and going to meet people I don't know in a location that I'm not familiar with isn't really what I want to be doing right at the moment."

"Just trust me. The boss is the real stuff and he'll be able to help, you'll see," she smiled and stepped towards me.

My arms opened and she snuggled close with her head under my chin. "It's about time we caught a bit of a break in this situation," she said. "The Pugs won't know what hit them when we get into their transporter system with reinforcements. Especially now that we know their vulnerabilities."

"OK," I sighed. "Where do we have to go?"

"Back downtown, near Battery Park."

The cat made a "meep" noise and we turned to see that he was already standing at the door waiting for us. Liz laughed, "I think he must understand us!"

I responded, "He's more on top of things than some professionals I've worked with."

The traffic had eased somewhat and after only three insanely close calls, we were there and parked. Must have been my lucky day because a parking space opened as if I'd called ahead for it.

Our orange cat seemed bored. He was busy cleaning a hind foot and pulling at his claws with his teeth. I opened the rear windows a few inches and left him in the car. It was in the shade, so I figured he'd be OK for a few minutes. He didn't pay much attention to us as we walked off.

We left most of our weapons in the trunk, although I retrieved the second laser from my bag. Then we walked to a hardware store adjacent to a Chinese restaurant. There was a door between the two and we walked in and Liz started up some stairs that opened onto the foyer. I followed her up three flights and then into a hallway. As we headed up the stairs my danger sense began going off like crazy.

As we stepped into the hallway, we were in time to see a wall panel slide shut over what might have been a transporter door, leaving the wall looking as if it were seamless. We halted and looked at each other, with an uneasy surmise. I was pleased to see that her splinter gun was already out and in her hand. She was as fast a draw as I was. My gun was also out and we moved carefully down the hall towards the door at the end.

She placed her hand on a scanner plate beside the door. It clicked, and the door swung open. We'd moved where we could cover the opening and it was a good thing we were ready. There were about twenty Pugs waiting inside for us.

There was no sign of Liz's boss, but I briefly glimpsed what looked like some bodies lying against the wall behind the Pugs.

Our guns made soft thump-thump noises and we ducked back. The Pugs weren't too anxious to come around the corner, but shortly two of them tried it. They didn't live to regret their hurry.

We retreated down the hall, but then I had my sixth sense warning go off again. It had proved to be a useful indicator of danger in the past and it was right on track now. I swung around and started shooting just as the hidden transporter door snapped open and four more Pugs came out. They were all down, dead or dying. I heard Liz's gun continue to "thump-poof" several times more behind me.

We fought our way out of that building as quickly as we could. I lagged back on the stairs and got two more on the landings as they tried to come around the corners. It didn't seem as if their idea of tactics was too good. Perhaps they were so used to beating up on unarmed humans that they didn't really expect too much out of us. I'm proud to say that they were surprised, or at least the ones that we didn't shoot were probably surprised.

We were on the street and nearly in our car when some Pug fired off an RPG or something similar from the building's roof. The front of our car jumped about five feet in the air with the explosion. The windows in the car broke and our cat came flying out of the rear like his tail was on fire. It wasn't really, but the front seat was.

We bypassed the car and ducked around the corner before the shooter could reload and try for a second score. The cat was right with us, and hissing mad. He raced ahead and then stopped at an alley, looked down it and bristled his tail. He let out a full-throated battle cry, took a few running steps and leaped right up to the face of a Pug as it came running out of the alley, looking for us.

Mr. Cat proceeded to give the Pug a severe beating around the head and shoulders. It didn't slow the creature down. He quickly brushed the cat off, but now there was yellow fluid leaking out of numerous cuts and scratches in his body suit. That didn't bother him nearly as much as the laser did when I flashed it in his eyes. He dropped slowly to his knees and then expired, exactly like the others.

The cat looked startled and then sniffed carefully at the body. He hadn't heard the laser; it was soundless. I don't know if he'd seen it. He probably thought he'd killed the creature himself. It did seem like he had even more of a swagger as we moved down the street.

Around the next corner I was able to steal another car from a naive individual who thought it was safe to walk off and leave his door unlocked. The car did not have an electronic ignition, so I fiddled with the wires for a moment before getting it started. Then we headed back uptown.

As we drove, we discussed the ambush. I was of the opinion that Liz's boss was helping the Pugs, but she insisted that he must have been trying to get us there under duress. She was sure that he was too decent a guy to be on their side. After a few blocks, we'd exhausted the topic. She seemed to think that she'd convinced me, but I simply wanted to keep an open mind and resolve it whenever I had the opportunity.

11

The System is Corrupt

We went to a parking garage near my main downtown apartment. This was not the apartment that my current employers had set up, but one that I had owned for several years. I hadn't used it in six months.

We left the car on the top floor of the parking garage and then boosted a second car on the next floor down. We left it on the street a couple of blocks away from my apartment and then walked, carrying the cased weapons. The cat walked beside us with somewhat of a proprietary air. He'd definitely adopted us and, by default, our cause.

Several tourists stopped to look him over and made comments, but he paid no attention to them and simply paced onward between the two of us.

When we reached my building, he looked at me and said, "Meep?"

I looked at him and nodded. I don't know what he was asking, but he seemed to think the building was fine, so we all walked in and headed up to the suite.

I was relatively confident that we hadn't been followed, but, if we have drones and high- resolution satellite-borne cameras that we can use for military and civilian surveillance (and we do), then the Pugs might have something equally as troublesome or worse. The current generation of our sat-cams can resolve things down to somewhat less than a meter and advances are happening rapidly, given the government's apparent desire to keep track on everyone, everywhere, all-of-the-time.

Personally, I learned early in my career that too much data is worse than not enough. With too much, one tends to become paralyzed by trying to keep up with it all. If you use computer analysis to flag only suspicious events, it tends to make you complacent. I'd rather be alert and worrying about what the other guy is going to do that will impact me directly and in the immediately foreseeable future. I have a basic reluctance to rely on anything other than my own judgment.

As it turned out later, the Pugs had access to several human surveillance data streams. They'd been able to crack through NSA's security and simply tapped into the data flow in a number of ways. However, that was quite bad enough, since it allowed them to keep tabs on individuals that were of interest.

Their problem was they didn't know me. By now, they must have realized that someone had done some major damage to a number of their personnel. So far, none of them had survived an encounter with me,

I spent some time wondering if they had been foresighted enough to place a camera in the transporter booths. That would have given them my picture and advanced facial recognition software would easily generate my particulars. I decided that I couldn't do anything about this potential problem except to try and stay ahead of them. Speed was our helper. That and not returning to any location that might be associated with me.

I was relatively secure in my various "offices," since they were all carefully located in buildings without surveillance (except for the pervasive New York street camera system – also easily hacked). In addition, I had arranged the rent for each location through a series of shell-corporations and other entities that created a complex chain that was almost impossible to untangle and trace back. I'd encountered many such chains while tracing bad-guys in my work, and I knew how they worked. I also knew how to crack them and where they usually failed. I made sure that mine didn't have any such weaknesses. I set up the computer to tap into the Mayor's expensive, downtown surveillance-camera network and then linked that feed up to an A.I. program which would set off an alarm if anything looked odd. This was exactly what I feared the Pugs would think of, but as long as it was working for us, I couldn't complain.

Once that was done, I switched in some sensors of my own that were located in and around the office building. The monitor program wasn't perfect. In my experience it sometimes gave a false positive, but I wasn't going to stay up all night watching it and I trusted it to not miss any enemy activity, even if it did sometimes go off when it recognized police or parades of Shriners.

The cat had appropriated the most comfortable chair in the place, located in a convenient corner near a window and was napping. He seemed to be a remarkably calm and yet competent individual and I supposed that I'd have to decide to like him. It wasn't too hard, given how he'd jumped that Pug and nearly clawed its eyes out.

It was getting on towards suppertime and we decided we'd better eat while we had the chance.

Liz went into the tiny kitchen that I kept stocked with easily stored food. We didn't have any cat food, that not being covered in my standard operations manual, but she did manage to find some frozen chicken pieces that the cat approved of. She saved some of them back and made a meal that I approved also.

The cat finished eating and then looked wildly around and I realized that he was going to need a litter box. He dashed out of the kitchen and I followed him to the bathroom. The toilet was a commercial toilet with a seat, but no lid. By the time I'd gotten there, he was perched on the seat.

He looked at me with an expression of pained disgust as if to say, "Can't a guy get any privacy around here?"

I apologized and backed out, so I didn't see what happened next, but as I walked down the hall, I heard the flush activate. That was one smart cat! Someone had spent a long time training him or he was really good at learning.

The cat and I arrived back in the computer area at about the same time. He ran past me with his tail held straight up with a little crook in the very end, so it looked like a flag.

Liz was already there checking on the Internet connection with her command. It seemed to be down and there was nothing she could do to contact anyone. She was trying to get through to the New York office where we'd been ambushed when suddenly the video window opened and she got a picture of a wild-eyed man in a black suit.

"Liz? Is that you? Oh, God! They're all dead! The whole building is full of corpses!"

"Calm down, Alf!" she ordered. He took a breath and visibly got control of himself. My opinion of their training went up a notch as I watched. He was obviously in a tight place and his self-control was impressive.

"I just got back from Boca," he said. "They're all gone down there. No bodies, no nothing. The place is totally empty. What's going on? How did these people here die? They all look as if some kind of poison killed them. Are there terrorists active in New York? I've tried to reach the boss on his cell, but he won't answer. I don't know if it's safe in here." He looked apprehensive.

"Worse," she said sadly. "We've got a real problem and I'm afraid that the boss has been taken out or captured along with the rest of the HQ staff. I'm currently in a safe place and I suggest that you locate one also and hole up."

"Where are you?" he asked.

"You know I can't tell you that," she said, exasperated.

At that moment, Alf looked over his shoulder and jumped up with his pistol blazing towards the side of the room. He paused, looked, and shot again, but a patch of blood erupted on his throat and he staggered, gasped and then began to shake violently. He'd been hit with a splinter and the toxin acted quickly. He had only enough time to turn towards us and reach out for the computer. He wasn't able to complete the motion. He slumped onto the desk and then rolled off onto the floor.

I switched the room light off so the only light was from the computer screen. Liz placed her hand over the video camera lens and motioned me towards her.

A partial view of a Pug appeared. He was apparently looking down at the man. Then he turned swiftly towards the screen and his features enlarged as he leaned towards the camera.

"Who's there?" he said in slurred, but recognizable English. We were quiet. Her boss came into sight and the Pug straightened and began to speak to him.

They definitely weren't speaking English this time. The sound was somewhat like two snakes hissing combined with cricket chirps and odd clicks. Whatever was said, her boss leaned over the computer and started typing on the keys.

I reached over Liz and pressed the disconnect switch. This wasn't part of the computer itself. I'd installed it myself and it had the effect of disconnecting the network instantly.

"Well, that tears it!" she said with a depressed sound to her voice. Her eyes were wide and distressed. "I can't believe that my boss is one of them! I've known him too long and I just can't figure it out. We're not going to get any help from my people. For all I know, I don't have any people left."

Thinking rapidly, I asked, "Was there any time in the recent past that he seemed to be not himself? Perhaps he was out of the office for a few days or something."

She thought about it. "Let's see. I know! I heard that he called in sick for a week. That was last month. I met with him a little over a week ago and I didn't notice anything, but I wasn't really looking closely. Then I went back out in the field and was captured."

She finished with a tremor in her voice, "They must have co-opted him somehow. I wonder how they did it?"

"Best not to think about it now," I reassured her. "Let's go into the kitchen and have a drink and then get some rest."

I'd made sure that the kitchen was remarkably well stocked and even had a small selection of wines. We opened a bottle of Rioja, which proved to be excellent.

After some conversation about ourselves, which led to some flirting, which led to some slightly more intimate activity, we ended up in the bedroom. The cat had already staked out a top bunk and was lying in complete comfort, curled on his side.

The bunks weren't made for two, but we did our best to get comfortable.

Sometime around two in the morning, the monitor program let out a beep and got us out of bed. We hovered over the screen and watched a group of Pugs work their way down the street outside the building. They were checking on some kind of device one of them was carrying. If it was some kind of locator, it apparently couldn't find us, because they continued on down and out of sight.

The Pugs looked somewhat human at first glance, especially with their masks and, as long as they kept their sinuous motions slowed down to roughly human speed, city dwellers weren't likely to pay much attention to them, especially since they were dressed conservatively. I've noticed that most people in cities don't actually look at the people that they encounter on the street. It's normal for them to glance down or look away as they pass. It's a defense mechanism, of course. There are far too many people gathered too closely to deal with, so everyone simply tries to ignore everyone else.

The local residents were out clubbing, even though it was pretty late and they were much more likely to gather attention. Quite a few of them looked more alien than the actual aliens, in my opinion. In fact if the aliens had a problem about blending in, it was that they looked more conservatively dressed than most of the humans on the street.

About five, we tried to contact Liz's national headquarters in DC. For some reason, a lot of the Internet was down. I could reach some nodes, but any that led to DC were down. It was a really strange breakdown of the system. I reasoned that one of the main things that would happen in any sort of invasion was that the invading force would make every effort to disrupt our communications. We've reached the point at which the Internet is the primary mode of mass communication and disabling it would paralyze much of our society.

About six, we got ready, had some breakfast and then slipped out. The cat followed us closely. He wasn't going to let us leave him there. If there was going to be some action, he wanted in.

There had been several groups of Pugs on the street in the intervening hours and I figured that they'd somehow managed to get a fix on our general location. However, they hadn't found us and probably didn't know what I looked like. We were sure that they knew Liz, since she'd been a prisoner twice.

We decided that it might be a good idea if she wore her hair differently. To this point she'd worn it hanging loose, but she took a moment and put into French braids. We really couldn't do anything about her facial structure, but she changed her makeup slightly and highlighted her cheekbones so that she actually did look a little different.

She stepped into a drug store holding my bag with the cat inside and watched out the window as I went around a corner. It wasn't long before I came back in a new Mercedes M Class. The driver had actually left it running as he went into a doughnut shop to get some coffee. What an idiot! I was sure that he was on his phone to the cops at this moment, so I got out and openly changed the license plates with another car parked in front of the drugstore. No one seemed to notice.

Liz got in with the cat and the weapons packages. We hit the road and were heading off the island within a few minutes.

"You know, Liz, we've really got to name this cat pretty soon." I was scratching around his ears with my right hand, while I drove with my left. My scratching efforts resulted in a steady low purr of contentment.

"That's not necessary. I've already got it covered. He told me his name was 'Jefferson' last night."

I goggled at her for a moment and then turned my attention back to the street in front of us. "Now, exactly how did he manage to do that?"

"I tried several names and he made it clear he disapproved of them. 'Jefferson' was the one he answered to." Jefferson was watching her closely and he started to purr again when she said his name.

Obviously that was settled. I knew that cats were kind of picky and seem to have distinct preferences of their own. I also knew that they had about one billion more neurons in their brains than dogs. I had previously figured that they used those neurons in keeping a superior attitude. Now I was beginning to wonder if that was true for all cats. Jefferson appeared to be far more intelligent than the average cat, at least to a non-cat lover like me.

12

DC

We had been driving for about an hour and a half on our way towards DC at Liz's request. I didn't like it, but she was really adamant that she needed to check with her department there, assuming that it still existed. The problem was that she did not know of any transporter link from New York to Washington. I'm sure there must have been one since there is so much happening in both locations relating to governing this country.

Our peace was interrupted when a large panel van pulled up beside us in the outside lane. Jefferson had been acting uneasy for several minutes and he immediately jumped onto the back seat and bristled his tail and then let out his war cry; a low, deep-throated growl with evil overtones.

I glanced at the van. The driver was looking at us. He raised a pistol and pointed it at Liz. I jammed on the brakes and the van shot ahead momentarily. As it passed us, the back door opened and I could see two Pugs kneeling and aiming some kind of new weapon; not the splinter gun, but a malicious looking long, tripod-mounted weapon with a flared muzzle. There were two more Pugs standing behind those two, but I couldn't see how they were armed.

I wasn't having any of that; it was too early in the morning. I swerved wildly to the right just as the weapon fired. A bolt of light or energy of some kind flew by my side of the car. I know that I shouldn't have even been able to see it, but it moved visibly past and I swear it made a crackling noise as it went by my window. On the other hand, I didn't hear any explosion so I thought at first that it had simply continued on down the road. I was wrong on that account.

When I looked in the rear view mirror, there was a huge hole in the road and the car that had been tailgating us for the last forty miles was fetched up in the hole with its rear wheels spinning in the air. This didn't look pleasant. Shooting the Pugs with their own splinter guns was OK, but they'd upped the ante with these new weapons and I didn't want to be on the receiving end of any of those charges.

I finished opening my window fully and pulled up along side to the right of the van. Sure enough, the driver had probably watched his share of Hollywood movies. He tried to force us off the road. Why do they always try to do that?

Since the van outweighed us by at least a thousand pounds, he'd have been successful in pushing us off the road, except for the concrete and metal barrier that we were trapped against. The Mercedes' owner wasn't going to be happy. The left side of the M-Class was being crunched by the van, while the right side was generating a large stream of sparks and screeching noises as it ground against the guard barrier.

I took a shot at him through my open window when I had the chance. The glass splinter shattered on his closed passenger side window and I narrowly missed being splattered by the toxin-coated shards that bounced back at me.

I made a mental note to myself to reevaluate my understanding of normal cover and concealment. Projectile firearms have a nasty habit of disabusing people of the notion that concealment is actually cover. Most pistol bullets will go through car doors and can easily kill. Unfortunately, the glass splinters didn't penetrate very well and weren't heavy enough to break glass. Their effective range wasn't too great either. After about a hundred feet or so, they lost much of their velocity and accuracy.

The next thing I knew, Liz had reached past me and shot his window out with her pistol. I fired again with my splinter gun and this time the driver's number was up. The van drifted away into the other lane, rebounded off the center railing and flopped onto its side.

I slapped on the brakes and skidded to a halt about three hundred feet down the road. I was out and running back. Fortunately, there wasn't too much traffic on the road as yet; it was before rush hour. The traffic in our lanes was stopped on the other side of the wreck, since it was blocking the middle two lanes.

The Pugs must have been stunned, because they didn't come out until I was almost there. It was like shooting fish in a barrel. One would look out and I'd shoot him. Unfortunately they were taking their own sweet time about looking around. Once the first one was killed it took quite a while for the second one to decide to take his chance.

After I'd shot two of them, I remembered that I was carrying a grenade.. Throwing the grenade through the side window of the tipped-over van blew a number of holes in the metal side and roof. There was no more sound from within, so I dashed back to our car without taking the time to check.

Liz said, "That grenade must have given them a headache, but it looks like any advantage we might have had from being unknown has disappeared."

I took a deep breath, "Thanks for shooting out that window. I didn't realize these splinter shooters wouldn't break the glass." I paused, and then added, "Yeah, it seems as if they now have a line on us. We'll have to move faster."

I took the first exit, then worked my way through a maze of connecting streets until we could get back on the parkway. There was almost no traffic since the wreck had blocked the lane... There was no one on the road where we got on, so I took off as fast as the Mercedes could go.

Liz said, "There's a connection with another highway in about two miles and, if we take that, we can work our way into DC by another route."

That's what we did. It might seem as if the Pugs should have continued to track us, but they apparently failed to do so because we didn't have any more trouble. I couldn't figure why they weren't in better communication with each other, but it may have been that they seemed to consistently underestimate us. Meanwhile, I was recalling the van episode.

"What's the problem?" Liz asked, sympathetically. She had taken a couple of glances at me and realized that something was bothering me, something more than the general situation. She was already getting used to my responses under stress.

"I got a look at the driver," I said. "He wasn't human."

"He looked human from what I saw of him."

"He had a human face and didn't look like a Pug, but his face had slipped off by the time I got back there. It was lying on the road. It looked like some kind of skin-like synthetic mask." I looked at her, wondering if she'd get it.

"Uh oh. You mean that there are more of them like my boss? That will make it difficult to find anyone we can trust."

We discussed it for some time, but the problem of how to tell if a human was human and not a Pug seemed to have only one solution and that involved drawing blood in some manner. We didn't think that the Pugs could disguise their yellow fluid for normal human red blood. However, any humans we encountered would be sure to resent our rather simplistic test. Of course, any Pugs would also resent being tested, but in their case, we didn't care what they thought.

We drove through the main part of DC on the way to her headquarters . When we drove past the Senate, Jefferson went into full attack mode. I observed that he kept his face oriented towards the building. He must have sensed an alien somewhere. Even though there was hardly anyone in sight, he kept up his hissing and growling for several blocks.

"That settles it! I've always thought those guys were from outer space." Liz remarked with a silly grin on her face.

"Well, it does explain a lot, but if it's true, it's going to make it difficult to get this mess straightened out. I'm going to make the assumption that he is only partially correct," I added, trying to keep from laughing.

There was nothing we could do about it. It would be a little inconvenient, hunting Pugs down on the street and looking for them in the Senate building was totally out of the question. The local gendarmes would definitely not think highly of the idea.

We drove on a few blocks and got some more bad news. Her headquarters was obviously overrun. There was no help there for us. We found that out by simply driving by and watching Jefferson. Once again he went into attack mode.

I had started to really appreciate having him around. He seemed to have an unerring instinct for locating the enemy. I know that cats don't have a very good sense of smell, so I guess he was identifying the Pug infested buildings in some other way. I didn't care how he was doing it. The information was useful.

13

WEAPONS AND A MAP

As we drove, it became apparent that there were several centers of alien activity. We saw Pugs on the street in many locations. They blended in well unless they moved too rapidly. Their faces looked very human-like with the masks they were using. Even so, finding them was easy. Jefferson saw them and we watched him since he told us when he did.

As we were moving along K-Street near some row houses, Jefferson flashed into attack mode by one of them. By now, I'd had my fill of driving around. I was ready to take some action; almost any action, so we parked, not an easy thing in this crazy city of wall-to-wall cars and on-street parking. We got out of the Mercedes and then went up to the door of the row house and knocked; no answer. The place was locked, but I picked it as fast as I could and we entered carefully. We both had our splinter-guns ready to go as we came through the door and prepared to clear the building, but there was no need.

The front door opened to reveal a small room. There were no other exits except for a transporter installed on the wall a few steps away. The entire space represented only a fraction of the house and I wondered what was in the rest of the building, but there wasn't a clue in sight. I poked at the blank walls, but there were no hidden doorways. I mentally shelved the idea of going outside and trying to figure out how to get into the rest of the building to see what it contained. It could have been connected to the adjacent building or there might be another way in.

Liz picked up Jefferson and we summoned the transporter and entered. There was only one activation button inside. This seemed to me to be an unwelcome development. I couldn't conceive of a transporter without at least a couple of alternatives as to destinations. This one might take us to someplace that we really didn't want to go. Of course, that was kind of a silly thought. They all went places that no one in their right mind would want to go, especially considering the likelihood of being captured or killed at the end of the journey.

We checked the transporter's video screen for problems. All we could see was a large room full of miscellaneous objects. They were indistinct, but looked like rows of storage racks fading off into the distance. In any event, we could see no living creatures.

We looked at each other, I shrugged and then Liz pressed the button. There was the usual wave of disorientation and then the door opened and we walked into a large space. It was apparently a warehouse or storage room. It was dark, but the lights flared up automatically with our arrival and stayed lit at the low level preferred by the Pugs.

Just then Liz said, "Ow!" Jefferson was struggling and was so eager to get down that he scratched her. This was the first time that he'd actually made a mistake and used his claws on one of us. Once on the floor, he stayed very close to my feet. He acted like he was not very confident in this location, but maybe he was simply being conservative and playing it safe.

As I looked around, the first thing that caught my attention was a large map on the wall to the right of the transporter door. There was a sort of open briefing area facing the map. As I got closer, it became apparent that this was the break we'd really needed. The entire transporter system was marked out clearly. There was even a "You-are-here" pointer. For some reason, I found that hilarious and got a laugh out of it. I wondered if there was such a thing as interstellar transporters and I could envision a "You-are-here" pointer pointing at the Earth in general. It just seemed funny to me, but Liz looked at me with disbelief, shaking her head.

We realized later that the pointer moved around as the map's location changed. Something in the map was interactive and must have read some signal from the transporter system. The map itself looked like a slick type of plastic that hung on the wall by static electricity or surface adhesion. After studying it for a bit, I took hold of one edge and pulled lightly. It came right off in my hands.

It was thin enough to fold up and take with us. When I began to fold it, it seemed to fold up almost by itself. I ended up with a small packet that was about the same size as a conventional road map.

I unfolded it again and laid it on a nearby table and it grabbed right onto the table surface as we huddled over it. There were about a hundred transport stations marked in the US. They were generally located in the larger cities, except for a few that were scattered across Texas, Wyoming, Colorado and Kansas.

The interesting thing was that three of the connections led off the edge of the map. Curious, I turned it over and found a line drawing of our solar system. There were connections shown that led to our moon, one of the moons of Jupiter and one of the moons of Saturn.

I wasn't too strong on the astronomical side of things, so I wasn't sure about the moons aside from ours. Liz had a better knowledge base on matters astronomical and stated categorically that one of the transport routes led to Io, orbiting Jupiter and the other definitely led to a moon of Saturn. She wasn't sure which one it actually might be though. The only name she could come up with was Titan. We decided to do some research on it later, if we were still curious. We weren't planning on going there, since it was a good assumption that the place was full of Pugs.

We'd both been to the Jupiter location and while Liz had run into Pugs there, I hadn't. I wasn't sure what they used that location for, but she thought it was simply for equipment storage and possibly for storing more counterfeit bills.

The general atmosphere inside the warehouse was kind of creepy. It reminded me of the subway in some fashion. We'd seen the Pugs' pets before in a similar place and I half expected to be fighting them off again, but there was no sound other than echoes that bounced back and forth in an eerie manner as we spoke.

We finished and folded the map up so Liz could stick it into her pocket. Then we headed for the racks of equipment that were arranged in neat lines throughout the main part of the storage area. Along the first part of the rows, there were various human-made weapons. Deeper into the rows, we reached a point where we walked between racks of splinter guns. Everything there was portable by a single person. There were no large weapon systems, although I did see a rack with some of the flared mouth long weapons that fired energy bolts. They seemed to me to be too cumbersome, so I ignored them

The more advanced Pug weapons were towards the far wall, so without any more indecision, we both turned and headed in that direction. Jefferson sensed that we were on to something and he jumped up from where he'd been resting and followed.

Liz said, "This is some really weird kind of place. I thought at first that it was an armory, but it looks to be sort of a combination of both an armory and a museum. I don't understand why they have all of those human guns."

"Maybe those are simply for them to learn to recognize or to experiment with," I hazarded.

The closer to the far wall we got, the more interesting things became. We moved out of the human produced weapons and into areas with alien ones. There were projectile weapons that made our UMPs look primitive. I looked at Liz and said, "It's almost like we're walking into the future. I wonder what some of these do and why we haven't seen them using them so far."

She replied, "I don't know. I don't think that any of our current science could have created these, though. Perhaps some of the advanced ones aren't normally carried. Maybe they are being saved for pitched battles."

We decided that it was a mystery that would have to wait until later for a solution. Right at the moment, we simply accepted that we were incredibly lucky to have a chance to get our hands on samples of the Pugs' weapons.

On the last rack, we found a weapon that looked as if it were a toy. It was a lightweight, rifle-like thing with a telescopic sight. I guess it was built for the Pugs, but, since they have a humanoid build, it fit my grip just fine. It wasn't apparent what the thing shot or projected. I took it back to where I had a clear view of an antique Windsor chair on the other side of the room near the transporter door.

I shouldered the thing and looked through the scope. The rifle must have somehow read my eye's focus, because the scope's view automatically narrowed down until the chair was the only thing visible. I motioned Liz to get back and then gritting my teeth, I pressed the firing button. It didn't seem as if anything happened except for a slight clicking noise followed by a soft crackling sound. No recoil, no boom. I kind of flinched; I'm ashamed to admit it, but I was expecting something more violent and the crackling sound made me jump, so I didn't immediately see what happened.

"Holy crap..." Liz breathed out quietly.

I raised my head. The chair was gone. No muss, no fuss. Just gone. "Did you see anything happen?" I asked her.

She answered, "There was a sort of half-visible ripple which showed over the chair for a moment and then it just faded out like it was being erased."

I examined the weapon. There were some markings on it, but not in any language I recognized. The interesting thing was there seemed to be no way of easily reloading it. It did have a kind of catch on the bottom of the receiver, but I was too intimidated to open it. Perhaps it didn't need reloading.

"We'll take this with us," I decided with a thoughtful grin. "It would be nice to be able to erase any of a number of things."

I smiled at her and she gave me a charming smile back.

She'd turned back to the last shelf and was digging in a box. She rummaged for a bit, and then came up with something that looked very like a grenade.

Given that the shape was approximately similar at least, I made the assumption that it was intended to explode and blow things up. Liz, however, had other ideas about its function. Just another reason why I wanted to keep her around.

"Since this was located beside the eraser guns, I think it's an eraser grenade. Want to try it, too?" she asked.

I looked it over. There were several boxes of the little bombs. They weren't as large as a comparable human grenade would have been, but they still had enough heft to be easily thrown. There was a simple mechanism with a small timer and an obvious safety pin. A small knob adjusted the timer and I thought I understood exactly how to use it. The thing was actually kind of cute, but I'm a sucker for things that make loud noises and are destructive.

"Let's get back to Washington. We can take some of these with us and I'll set one on this shelf with enough delay to give us time to transport out before it goes off."

"OK." she agreed and we headed for the transporter door. I left the grenade setting on the shelf with its timer clicking over merrily. It seemed to run in another scale than our seconds and the numbers whirled by a little too rapidly for comfort, so we headed out fast!

The closer we got to the transporter door, the more nervous we got and we sped up until we were almost running when we reached the door. It opened and we darted in preceded by Jefferson. I hadn't realized that a cat could run so fast. He'd waited until we had almost reached the door and then he'd realized that we were leaving. He shot across the intervening space and arrived at the door ahead of us.

Liz pushed the activation button and we were in the row house again. I held the door open with one hand and we stood in the transporter cubical while she activated the view screen and we watched. Our timing was impeccable.

One moment the shelves were there and then the next moment, the screen went blank. No booms or flashes or anything. I shrugged and said, "Well that was a big let down. Let's get."

After a moment, she said, "I wonder if the eraser bomb destroyed the entire cavern or maybe it knocked out the pickup for the viewer?"

I shrugged again, "I'm not going back to find out, just in case the transporter was damaged and we end up as a stream of disassociated atoms going nowhere in particular."

14

Extent of the Threat

Carrying the cat, we got back in the Mercedes SUV, drove down the street a block, and then parked again.

Liz was playing with the radio and suddenly stopped it on a news station. The announcer was saying something about a possible earthquake or sinkhole. He wasn't clear which it was, but he was very excited. Apparently, a large section of farmland in Virginia had suddenly dropped out of sight and there was only a large hole there now. The local residents had heard a loud sound that they thought was a thunderclap. The military was cordoning the area off and a research team was on the way.

Liz and I looked at each other. The little grenade was actually not so little after all.

I thought about it a bit and then it hit me, "Anti-matter! The eraser gun and the grenade are anti-matter weapons."

"I'd always thought that there was supposed to be a huge explosion when matter and anti-matter came together," she ruminated. "It doesn't sound like a blast zone according to the news."

"No one's really done the experiment before, but maybe the thing works like the eraser gun and simply erases the matter. The loud noise the reporter mentioned might have just been air filling the suddenly vacated space. I wonder why the chair didn't make much of a sound besides that crackle. Maybe the gun creates anti-matter at a rate slow enough to dissolve the target rather than to cause it to instantly vaporize."

"Oh, by the way," Liz said. "I found something else while you were busy with the map."

"What was it?" I asked, looking at her, appreciatively. I seemed to be making more and more of an effort to look at Liz. It was a worthwhile view.

"Only this little book," she said. "It's not in English, but it does have pictures." She leafed through the pages slowly.

"Look at this! This must be representative of interstellar travel," she said, pointing at a page. "Why, it's a kind of directory and it shows planets connected by the transporter system!"

The opened booklet showed what was obviously a solar system with planets. The symbol for transporter on the pages was the same as on the wall map. That symbol was superimposed on each planet. There was a line linking each planet with a transporter to some of the other planets or moons in each system.

There was no linking line between solar systems. Instead, there was a picture apparently representing some kind of space ship imposed on a dotted line moving from star to star.

"I know what it means," Liz said excitedly. "The transmitters must be limited in some way and they've got to use a space ship to move from star to star. That's got to slow their expansion."

"Yeah, but who knows how long they've been at this expansion game." I grumbled. Then I added, "And, besides their space ships might be really fast."

She looked serious and commented, "They'd have to be faster than light. Anything slower wouldn't be a drop in the bucket when it came to interstellar distances. They must have FTL ships."

"Well, if they don't, they must take a really long-range view in their planning."

We looked through the book and found that each page had a different solar system diagram along with side notations that we couldn't read. By some of the planets, there also were small, but life-like drawings of what must be the inhabitants. The pictures showed Pugs and a few other creatures.

We found our system on the twenty-fourth page. We both recognized it at the same time. It was easy to tell it was ours because the drawing showed a man and a woman by the third planet out from the sun.

"This is Us," she exclaimed and then pointed, "Look here!"

The dotted space-ship line was going to one of the moons of Saturn. There was a transporter there and it was linked to one on Earth. I opened the map and the connection showed in the book was obviously to the transporter in Colorado. There was an identical squiggly symbol by both diagrams.

I tried to joke. "I guess they have a hard time spelling 'Colorado'."

Liz looked like she was trying to ignore my attempt at humor, but she nodded in agreement. Then paging through the rest of the book, she said, "There are thirty-six total solar systems in here and we're on the twenty-fourth page."

I grabbed the book out of her hand, in sudden speculation. Leafing through the first twenty-three pages, I noted that most of them showed drawings of Pugs and some other creatures. The fifteenth system had a fierce-looking creature that was reminiscent of a tiger and the line drawing was in a bright yellow. There were no Pugs showing on that page. It looked like the spaceship line went to a moon or something beside the planet, but there wasn't a transporter link from the moon to the surface.

There was another clue also; some of the solar systems were illustrated in a dull gray, while the rest were blue. The Pugs were only to be found on the blue ones. The gray ones had other forms of life, but none of our invaders.

There were some other pages in the back with diagrams, but I ignored them in my excitement.

"Look at this! Most of the first twenty-three pages show Pugs along with some other creatures that may be associated with them, but only the fifteenth and the gray ones have some other kind of life with no Pugs."

I flipped to the Earth page. Our planet wasn't gray, but it was a faded out blue compared to the ones that the Pugs seemed to favor. I wondered if that indicated their incompatibility with our atmosphere.

Continuing to turn the pages rapidly, I said, "Ours and all of the ones after us show other creatures. It looks like they are moving through the systems in this book one after another."

I continued, "The gray ones aren't compatible with them for some reason! The yellow creature? Well, we put dangerous things in the color of our blood, by a kind of convention. Their blood is yellow, so, assuming that I'm correct..."

My voice trailed off as Liz smirked at me.

"I know, I know. Assume makes an ASS out of U and ME," I sighed. "But, if I am correct, that thing on the fifteenth page is too much for them to handle. If the enemy of your enemy is your friend, we might do worse than contact those creatures."

Liz said acerbically, "We might also do better. Did you look closely at that picture? Those things might easily be worse than the Pugs. How do we know they'd work with us, and – "

"OK, OK, it was just an idea," I interrupted, "Anyway, I think we understand from this book that we're next on the list to be invaded and extinguished."

I shook my head and then asked, rather rhetorically, "You think they've been transporting our people off the planet to some moon or someplace, but what's been happening to the people when they get there?"

"You know I don't know the answer to that," she responded. "But, I'll bet that whatever is happening to them isn't good."

We looked at each other and it was obvious that we were both pretty much ready to lose hope. The situation hadn't really changed for the better. In fact, despite the mess we'd made of one of their facilities and the Pugs we'd killed, they were now actively looking for us. We, on the other hand, were only starting to suspect the extent of their occupation and capabilities.

Our enemies were far advanced past our human technology. While we might know about such things as anti-matter, matter transmission and space ships, even making a voyage back to the Moon was currently beyond our capabilities. And, there was no way we were close to creating something like the eraser gun or the bomb.

All-in-all, it seemed like human-kind was suddenly faced with an existential threat. If Liz and I didn't come up with a rabbit-out-of-a-hat trick soon, we agreed that things were going to get out of control very quickly.

The Pugs knew that there were rats running around in their system and that might force them to accelerate their plans. Plans that had some final goal that was unknown to us.

The question that was in the back of both of our minds was, "Were we up to the task?"

I didn't know the answer.

15

Monsters

Well, when you don't know what to do, taking some kind of action is usually a reasonable choice. In this case, I decided to delay while we thought the situation over. So, being slightly more brilliant than usual, I suggested, "Let's go back and check out the space in the row house behind the transporter room."

It took a couple of minutes to go around the block and park in front of the place again. We left the cat to guard the vehicle and walked across the sidewalk. We weren't thinking about the front door this time, even so, getting in turned out to be fairly easy. There were some stairs that we'd previously taken up to the front stoop. We hadn't paid much attention then, but below and to the left of the stairs was a door possibly leading to the basement. The door was partially obstructed by a beat-up trashcan, some cardboard boxes in the final stages of decay, and a rusty bicycle frame. I quietly moved these items so I could reach the door.

It was locked with a heavy padlock, but, as usual, that didn't keep me out for long. We carefully poked our heads through the opening and found ourselves in a vacant room that had the connections for a washing machine and dryer on one wall. The door to the next room was shut. There was a strong odor of mildew and something more, a rank scent.

Once again we eased the door open, but this time jumped back as we heard a stir and rustle of movement. The smell coming through the crack was pretty nasty, too. We looked at each other and Liz said, "Sounds kind of like those spider-thingies that we fought off."

"Smells like them, too," I whispered as I pushed the door open further.

The room beyond was dimly lit from the sun shining through a dirty window. The room was full of racks of cages and each cage had one of those nasty spider-like things that we'd encountered previously. Every single one of them, and I mean every one, was facing directly towards us. They were pressing up against the cage wire to get as close as possible.

"Looks like we're lucky they're caged," I observed. "There's no doubt that they'd be coming our way fast, if not."

We walked along the row between the racks of cages. The things slowly moved as they tracked us. They followed us across the inside of their cages and pressed against the other side as we walked to the stairway that was at the end of the aisle. We sneaked quietly up the stairs and approached the first floor.

As we came up the stairs and the floor above became visible, I could first see the bars of a very heavy and much larger cage. We slowed and proceeded with more caution. There was a single larger cage here holding another type of creature. This one, like the spiders, was fixated on us.

As we came into the room, it made a low moaning noise through some openings on the lower sides of its thorax. It was about the size of a bear, but it wasn't fuzzy or cuddly and not even as friendly-looking as a grizzly bear, which is about as dangerous a creature as exists on earth. It was large, perhaps weighing in at six or seven hundred pounds.

Its carapace looked like a beetle's;: hard and shiny. There were eight, multi-jointed legs holding the alien perhaps four feet above the floor. The legs were flexed at each of the several joints. The thing had sharp claws and mandibles that left no doubt that it was a predator. If it was as durable as the spiders, it would pose a real problem if we encountered it when it was out of the cage.

We sidled past in the aisle and jumped as it crashed into the side closest to us, rocking the cage wildly. It reached through the bars with both front appendages. We were just a little too far away for it to be successful and it moaned again, more loudly. This time there was a kind of harmony in the moans that created a pulsating and eerie beat frequency. Then it was silent, waiting. I could see that its eyes were fixed on us. They weren't like our eyes, but were flat, glossy pads with facets. You could tell it was focused on us. The pads first bulged out and then retracted into a concave, focusing configuration as it zeroed in on its two intended targets. As they did, I suddenly got the feeling that I should just drop to my knees and submit to it. I shook off the strange idea and glanced at Liz. She was staring fixedly at the thing and her mouth had dropped open. I shook her shoulder and she recovered with a jerk.

There was no other noise in the place as we turned up the stairs to the top floor. That floor was a combination lunchroom and wardrobe out of a nightmare. There were two dead humans wrapped in a kind of plastic. They were the lunch. There was little odor, so the plastic probably kept it in. Nevertheless, it was gruesome. Their faces were missing and portions of their bodies had been eaten. I remembered the Pug that I'd killed while he was snacking on the bookstore owner.

The wardrobe part of the room was almost as bad. There were two trays of a milky-looking solution on a table near the wall and the missing faces were laid out in them. Below the table were some boxes filled with a creamy-colored, compressed substance that looked like some sort of meat. Not knowing what it might be, I didn't touch the stuff. It could be toxic for all I knew. I was more interested in the faces at the moment. I remembered the Pug that looked like a human that I'd killed in the van and how its face had come off and ended up on the road.

"It's no wonder some of them look so human-like," Liz shuddered. "They must be using real faces somehow."

We slid back down the stairs as quietly as possible. Then I got the bright idea that I didn't want to leave that bear-sized thing to possibly follow us later, so I yanked out my splinter-shooter and popped one off at it. The splinter shattered on its hard side without penetrating.

It must have hurt, because part of the exo-skeleton started to dissolve and the thing let out a moaning screech. It jumped at me and almost tipped the cage over. I felt a kind of mental buzz that I did my best to ignore. It made me kind of shaky. I aimed carefully and sent the next splinter right down its gullet, between the clashing mandibles. This time, it had the desired effect and the creature screeched, belched and kind of dissolved into a lump with ooze coming out of the openings on the sides of its thorax.

Liz said, "I don't like those things. When you shot it, I felt terribly afraid. It was like we were doing something we had no right to do. We'd probably better use the anti-matter projector on that kind of creature if we ever encounter one when it's free to move."

I nodded in complete agreement. "It's that or possibly an anti-tank missile," I tried to joke.

When we came back into the basement, the spiders began to make a low susurration that was similar to the moaning of the larger creature, but softer. We used the splinter-shooters as we worked our way backwards along the aisle, taking care to get far enough past the creatures not to be splattered by any of the fluids that came out of them when the needle toxin hit their systems. We shot the last of them from outside the door.

I locked the door and we high-tailed it back across the sidewalk to the SUV . The vehicle was still there and Jefferson was fine, though he had amused himself by clawing the back seat thoroughly. When we got in, he acted like he didn't like the way we smelled. His tail bushed up and he looked at us with slitted eyes. He eventually calmed down as we drove off and the wind blew the bad scent away through the cracked-open windows.

16

HOTEL

Liz and I had gone nearly to the outskirts of town when I came up with our next step, "Let's find someplace to stay for the night." Sometimes I'm so brilliant that I astonish even myself, but the fact was, I couldn't come up with anything else except to delay while we thought things over.

"Yes, let's. I'm tired," she assented.

Not too tired, I hoped. I usually find women somewhat distracting, but she was the most distracting one I'd ever encountered.

We got on the interstate and headed west through Virginia. After driving for only about fifteen minutes, we pulled off and located a hotel. It wasn't anything special, but the rooms all had outside doors. I thought that might be good since we had to sneak Jefferson into the room and I didn't want any hassles about pets.

We brought our weapons and kit into the room and I drove around to locate another vehicle while Liz and Jefferson cleaned up and rested in the room. I figured it was about time to dump our white SUV. It was pretty scarred up from the road incident and that made it easy to recognize. I wasn't specifically looking for another M-Class, but I found one parked in a shopping center parking lot.

This Mercedes was black and exactly as easy to lift as the white one. I walked up to it and broke the antenna off to prevent any tracking. Then I used my electronic key spoofer and was shortly on the way back to the hotel. Before I got there, I stopped and changed the tags with those I found on a junky looking pickup. I figured the pickup owner wouldn't notice the different numbers for a long time. Considering the shape of his pickup, it looked like he didn't pay much attention to it.

My two companions were waiting when I got back. I cleaned up and then we left the cat in the room while we walked to an adjacent cafe for some supper. I had a rather greasy hamburger and Liz had some chicken strips. She wrapped a couple of them in a napkin and tucked them into her pocket.

When I looked surprised at this, she smiled and said, "I'll bet you're so involved in trying to come up with a way to set the Pugs back that you didn't even think that the third member of our team would want something to eat."

"Oh. Right! I should have thought of him first," I admitted.

We made it back to the room and Jefferson greeted us with a rather irritated meow. He cheered up tremendously when he received the chicken pieces, "Now this is more like it." You could practically see his thoughts. "Maybe those humans aren't totally hopeless after all."

He ate carefully and then licked his whiskers thoroughly. Then he nosed the bathroom door open a crack and disappeared. We heard him use the toilet with a tinkling sound followed by a flush. We looked at each other and burst out laughing. That was one smart cat!

"I'm next," I said and went into the bathroom, pushed the door to and sat down. Five minutes later, I came out.

"What's with you?" she asked. "You look like you lost your best friend."

"Liz, I've tried to come up with an idea, but the best I can get is to try to reach the transporter that they're using to come onto the Earth and then see how much damage we can do," I was pretty dejected at my lack of a viable plan.

She looked sympathetic and after a bit, I added, "It seems to me that the only link off the planet is the one we saw in the book and on the map that was in Northern Colorado. That one transporter may be the key, but I'm not sure. I guess we'll just have to go there and see."

"I don't want to depress you, but the situation is even worse than we thought," she said as she looked through the little book she'd picked up. "The first part has the list of planets that we looked at before. That part is useful in that it shows the connections off the planets to local moons or asteroids."

She continued, "There's a second part that we didn't look at. Or rather, you didn't look at it, since you were so excited about understanding the meaning of the list of planets. I've been trying to intuit the meaning of the last three pages while you were answering your call of nature."

"What did you come up with?" I asked.

"It's bad, if I'm correct. You see this picture, here? I think it is an illustration that represents setting off a massive nuclear burst over the central part of the country. It has an atomic symbol that is almost the same that we use and this must be a rocket. The pages have a symbol that I think is a key. I found the same symbol on the page with Earth."

"Let me see that," I took it from her hands. "Hmm. It looks as if they want to create some fancy fireworks. The picture shows it exploding at a very high altitude. See this line. I think that represents the edge of the atmosphere. If that's so, the missile will be – " I paused. "Oh, damn! It's an EMP burst! They're planning on disabling all of our electronics and the power grid."

"That's what I thought," she interjected. "The electromagnetic pulse will blow all electronics that are un-shielded. They must have used this technique against other civilizations before. I looked and found the same key on a couple of the other, earlier pages. That must mean that they used an EMP there also."

I knew that only last year the US House had authorized action to defend America's power grid against an EMP or solar storm, but the Senate eliminated the contingency plans. The thought of our lack of providence made me shake my head in dismay as I answered, "We've had coronal mass discharges before which caused problems with the electric grid, but the historically bad ones occurred before people were so dependent on electricity and all that it does, so they were largely non-events for society. Our cell phones will go out. We won't be able to pump gas even if our cars will still start and it's far from certain that cars won't have their electronics fried. Hell, even the food we rely on will spoil without refrigeration and we won't be able to get clean water."

"That domino effect," she added, "would cause deaths in the millions."

"Yes," I agreed. I'd read some reports that hypothesized the likely outcome and I told her about it, "The cities will have a death zone surrounding them that extends outwards about a hundred to one-hundred and fifty miles. Most people will not be able to travel farther than that on foot before they starve to death. The ones that leave first will actually be the ones that are more likely to get through. The ones that leave later won't have enough food and will find all of the resources have already been stripped. By then they will also meet extreme resistance by the few survivors in the area." She nodded in agreement.

"This is clearly not something our society ever wants to experience first hand, it could lead to millions of casualties," I added. "I've read estimates that suggest that an effective EMP attack would leave nine out of ten Americans dead. It would likely be at least as bad for the rest of the electricity-dependent parts of the world."

"What a way to neutralize all of our defenses," she was thinking out-loud. "They'd be able to move in and eat the rest of the population with hardly any resistance."

"OK. Now we really have to come up with a smart way to throw a wrench in their works. I vote for finding some reinforcements and heading to the link off the planet. That is probably the point at which we could disrupt their plans. If we could stop them from getting here, even for a while, we could try to get organized to counter their invasion. Maybe we could use the anti-matter grenades to blow up their interplanetary connection," I realized as I said it that my plan was weak, but I was completely out of ideas.

She interrupted my reverie momentarily, saying "There are already a lot of the aliens here that will have to be taken out also."

"I wonder exactly how many they have here now?"

"I don't know, but I believe a lot of them. When I was a captive, I saw a bunch of movement back and forth. It looked like Pugs coming in and humans going out somewhere," she answered as best she could.

She had a very worried look on her face and I couldn't take it. It really seemed to tear me up, emotionally.

"What are you doing?" she exclaimed as I moved over to the couch and sat down and put my arm around her.

I ignored her question and bent my head to kiss her. Her next vocalization was a sigh and she relaxed into my arms.

The cat gave a snort of disgust or perhaps derision and turned his back on us as he settled down on the armchair and pretended to go to sleep.

It was a long night, but we both felt like a million dollars the next morning. The promise of a sunny day with nice weather cheered us and it seemed like we had fewer limitations. We were also enjoying each other's company and that made everything look more positive.

We got ready to go out. Liz fed the cat and I searched in my bag and eventually pulled out a couple of burner phones that I had stored in my office desk and brought along, just in case.

They were inexpensive cell phones with pre-paid minutes. I'd purchased them in Walmart several months ago. Normally, I keep one or two at every one of my "offices" for emergency use. They have gotten so cheap that there is no reason not to have several.

I will mention that some of the cheaper ones, especially ones that are unbranded, come from factories in south-east Asia and can be loaded with spy software. Someone, a while back, tested several of these phones that they'd purchased off the Internet and found enough malware in them to make them very undesirable. They were loaded with software that would grab your credit card number and any passwords that you used and forward it to some unsavory people elsewhere on the globe.

Liz looked on with interest and commented, "Burner phones, huh? Are you sure they're secure."

"No." I explained to her, "I generally purchase a specific brand that I have a hacker test several times. He never found any malware in their internal code, so I think that I'm relatively safe using them. Nevertheless, I keep my conversations short, mostly ambiguous and never, ever mention names."

She grinned, "We were briefed on their use. My trainers indicated that burners were a curse on our law enforcement work. They wanted those types of phones to be made illegal."

I smiled in acknowledgment and reminded her that I was more interested in privacy in my activities and appreciated the phones.

Now that we know the true extent of our own government's surveillance, not to mention the snooping by hostile foreign powers, people in my line of work are very reluctant to use phones at all. I use a voice-distorter and a cheap cell phone that I discard after one call. Any snooper can still hear the content, but the disposable phone keeps them from tracking a known number linked to my name. Changing phones often keeps them from following numbers that have had "interesting" conversations.

To help keep any hostile systems from latching onto more than the meta-data of a call, I always spoke in careful generalities and didn't mention any key words that automated voice recognition systems might glom onto. I carefully limited my calls, since the meta-data can be quite damaging. It contains the approximate location of both parties, the time, and phone numbers with associated names, if any.

17

CALL FOR HELP

Over breakfast, we discussed how to get assistance. We agreed that we couldn't go to the government for help considering their possible involvement, but some of my underground contacts might be possible. We thought that they'd be less likely to be infiltrated by human-disguised Pugs. They made a habit of vetting everyone with whom they worked, just like I did, and their vetting process was so thorough that it made government standard procedures look like enrolling in kindergarten.

Anyway, the upshot of our discussion led me to call my old friend and sometime collaborator, Rudolph Belachick, on one of my burners.

Rudy was a little upset that I'd called him without using a more secure line, but he agreed to meet us in Lexington, Virginia. He wouldn't say exactly where he was located. He never does and I appreciated that act of caution. Everyone hates to have their safe house blown; especially someone who isn't a citizen and doesn't belong in the country.

Liz wanted a summary of what Rudy said, but I asked her to wait until we got in the SUV.

Before we left, I wedged the phone in the crack between the seats. That works about as well as dumping it in a trash bin. With any luck it would be found by someone who'd use the remaining minutes in personal calls, confusing any trackers.

We went back to the hotel and got the cat, the weapons, and the black Mercedes, in that order.

Jefferson seemed to be content being carried in an open duffle bag. He'd poke his head out, if he was interested enough to look at where we were going, but mostly he kept down, out-of-sight.

The trip was at least a three-hour drive, being just shy of two hundred miles. I pulled into a gas station to fill up. I paid with cash to avoid being traced. The national database collectors have made every effort to keep tabs on every credit card in the country.

Now, I know that they believe this is necessary for counter-terrorism, but it hasn't proven effective. However, it really was a good way for the Pugs to track people, assuming that they had the relevant credit card numbers. My cards were all corporate and billed to the usual variety of shell-corporations, but my system might still be traceable and that would be really inconvenient in the current circumstance.

Jefferson sat on the back of the rear seat and watched as I filled up the tank. At first, I was a little concerned that he might look suspicious, but who looks at a cat in a car anyway? You might look at a dog, especially if it were barking, but not an ordinary, orange cat. As I thought about it, it seemed like a good idea for him to watch. His vision was so sharp that it made me feel more comfortable. I knew that, in a sense, he was covering my six, as the fighter pilots put it.

Liz had gone across the street into a pawnshop. She came back with a portable GPS that she'd found. It was exactly what we needed to locate our rendezvous point. The Mercedes was nice, but the owner hadn't thought to purchase the navigation option. I'd broken off the antenna, anyway, feeling more paranoid than usual. I didn't want any possible tracking going on.

As we started our cruise down the highway, I told Liz about my conversation with Rudy, "Good news! It looks like we've finally found some reinforcements. We're going to meet an old friend of mine and he's bringing some experienced fighters with him."

"I hope they'll bring plenty of firepower," was her response.

"Don't worry," I assured her. "They're all professionals and I told him to make sure they're heavily armed, although I didn't tell him how hard targets the Pugs are."

It was about three hours later when we rolled into our rendezvous. We used the GPS to locate the specific point where we were to meet. It was in an abandoned warehouse located near the railroad tracks. There wasn't much traffic and the nearest residences were quite a distance away, so I felt that this would be an acceptable site. We were pretty far from the important parts of town, too.

I felt good about our trip. There had been no problems and, as far as I knew, we hadn't been tracked or seen. Also, we'd arrived early enough to check out the location for potential problems, like unexpected ambushes. We took some time nosing around the place and then, since Rudy and company weren't due for another three hours, we located a nearby restaurant. Leaving Jefferson in the car with the windows partially open, we went in and had a nice lunch. There was a pretty strong breeze blowing and Jefferson had plenty of fresh air. For water, Liz had poured out most of a water bottle into a bowl we'd accidentally borrowed from the cafe that morning.

Per my normal operations manual, we sat in a booth by the front window. It's always a good idea to have a position to observe anyone setting up a potential surprise. This time it proved to no exception.

The restaurant was in a run-down part of town and about halfway through our meal a couple of low-life types came scrounging up to our car. By the time I'd gotten out there, they'd made the mistake of trying to reach through the window and open the door. Both were bloody and scratched and were sporting some nasty looking bites on their fingers. The overall volume of cursing was loud as I walked up. Jefferson was making a series of yowls, daring them to try to stick their hands in the car again.

"Say! Is that your cat, buddy?" one asked, simultaneously trying to appear ingratiating, threatening and innocent. "I'm going to call the cops on you. He nearly ripped my arm off! He should be put down. He's dangerous!"

I tried to be reasonably nice, although I was laughing pretty hard at the time, "You shouldn't be reaching into other people's cars. It's not polite."

"I was just worried about the cat, Mister," he whined.

As we talked, the other guy tried to flank me, thinking that I was distracted. Some people don't seem to learn easily. I'd been watching for him to make a move out of the corner of my eye. Even if I'd not, Jefferson let out a yowl and tried to reach through the window, leaving no doubt about what he'd do to the guy, if he could only reach him. That was another reason to like that cat. He was a really good watcher. If there was some way to make him leopard-sized, he'd be about the most deadly partner you could wish for.

When the guy to my rear pulled out a knife, I dropped his friend with a low round kick to the knee and spun, bypassing his rush and knife. He must have felt somewhat stupid as I locked his arm up and removed the knife by twisting his fingers open. As the other guy was staggering to his feet, I stepped to the side and swung the man I was holding into him. They both fell down in a heap, cursing loudly as they tried to disentangle themselves.

By then Liz was in the Mercedes and had started the engine. I jumped in and we sped off through the light traffic. The fight had been so quick that not many people had even noticed. We didn't want to attract any more attention than we absolutely had to, since we needed to stay in the area to meet Rudy.

Jefferson was still brushed up with his hair standing on end. I'd pulled the cargo cover over our weapons and he sat on it as he watched through the rear window, just in case the two managed to somehow catch up with the car. We'd gone around a couple of corners when a police car came down the cross street headed towards where we'd been with siren wailing and lights flashing.

"Oh-oh!" I groaned. "Looks like someone called the cops."

"Let's park and wait for awhile," she said, pulling over as the cop car went out of sight. "I'll walk back and take a look to see what's going on. You stay here and watch Jefferson."

So I petted the cat while she headed around the corner. Jefferson enjoyed himself, purring loudly. It wasn't more than five minutes and Liz was back in the car, giggling.

"What's wrong with you?" I asked as we drove away. I didn't think that the situation merited her amusement.

"Those dopes tried to argue with the cops, cussed them out and both of them got tazed and arrested. I couldn't think of a pair of lunks who deserved it more," she broke out into another somewhat suppressed giggle.

"Well, at least they won't be hanging around messing up our meeting. The only problem is someone may have given the police our description and they may still be cruising around here."

"We'll have to park down the street and keep an eye out for your friend, then," she said as she maneuvered the car through the narrow streets back towards the warehouse. She parked and then we changed places and settled down to wait.

18

Help Arrives

Some minutes later, I was napping behind the wheel, when she elbowed me and said quietly, "Is that him?"

I looked and it was. I started the car and pulled out, timing my approach to intercept Rudolph as he crossed the street. He gave the car a flat glance and then a second, quick look as I stuck my arm out of the window and gave a low wave. I pulled up beside him.

"Man! You're lucky I didn't give the signal to have you taken out!" he said softly in his Eastern European accent.

"Got backup somewhere?" I asked conversationally, already knowing the answer.

"Since when have I not made sure I was covered in a meet?" he grinned.

"We had a little trouble here about an hour ago," I told him, "and we probably should find somewhere else to talk."

"Already heard about it on the scanner and I've located another place where we can discuss whatever it is you want to discuss." Then with a slightly puzzled expression, "What's with the cat?"

"You've got your back-up, I've got mine," I said with a smile.

This elicited a rather rude snort.

"Don't snort at what you don't understand. Underestimating him would be a mistake," I warned. Rudy shook his head in disbelief. He walked back around the corner and shortly a dark, older Buick pulled around beside us with him driving. We followed.

It was only a few minutes before we were located in a run-down and quiet bar. Rudy still hadn't brought his backup in, so I figured that we'd be warned if anyone suspicious headed into the establishment.

We had walked in and sat down near the back in a booth. At this time of day there were only two other customers sitting near the front of the place. The barmaid came over and was disgruntled to find that we wanted soft drinks. Once she'd brought them, we began to talk in earnest.

It didn't take more than about ten minutes to bring him up to speed on the important parts of what we'd been through. The main problem we had was convincing him that we weren't crazy. We solved that by showing him the splinter-shooter gun and then the map. The map was helpful in convincing him, especially the fact that the "You-Are-Here" arrow showed our approximate location.

He looked both over carefully and then sighed, "If you hadn't saved my life and we didn't have such a long history, I'd still not believe it, but this weapon is pretty convincing. I can't figure out how it actually works."

"Don't fire it off here!" I exclaimed as he moved his finger near the firing button. The button was located in the trigger position, but wasn't as comfortable. I guess the Pugs didn't have quite the same hand structure as humans, so it must have made sense to them. Personally, I preferred a trigger, but that's what I'm used to.

"Don't worry, I'm smart enough not to let off a round, errr, needle or splinter or whatever you want to call it," he said, putting it down on the table. He drew a napkin over it so it couldn't be seen accidentally if the barmaid came over to our booth.

We spent some time discussing the situation and finally decided that we'd need Rudy's "A" team of five in addition to the two of us. He had access to a rather large store of military-grade weapons and his men would bring them when they came. They had their own equipment and some communications gear that we were missing. For our part, we had the anti-matter weapons in the rear of the SUV and the two splinter-shooters, along with our normal human weapons.

We parted company after agreeing on our next meet. Rudy went out the back door of the bar, while we sat and finished our soft drinks. About fifteen minutes later, we sauntered out the front, got in the car, greeted Jefferson and headed off to find a motel.

19

RUDY

When I first met Dec, it was on a battlefield. I'm not saying exactly where, but it was in an Eastern European city. I was leading a small group of experienced fighters; some people would call them mercenaries, but unlike those people, we actually believed in what we were fighting for.

I remember Colin yelling, "Rudy, I'm going to clear that two-story building on the left side of the street. I think that may be where the rifle fire has been coming from."

I motioned to the rest of the group to provide covering fire for him as he dashed across the street. Sure enough, there were a couple of shots from the upstairs windows in return, but Colin was already under the portico and out of their direct line-of-sight.

Seeing that he was safe for the moment, I detailed Chandra and Joe to continue shooting at the windows just to give the occupants something to keep their attention. As they began to fire sporadically, I slid along behind a low, garden wall on the other side of the street and gradually approached the corner. My thought was to flank the building on the northern end and keep anyone inside from exiting.

The fighting was basic urban conflict – house-to-house and nasty. The sectarian nature of the conflict meant that neither side offered mercy to the other. I don't know why ostensibly religious people who should exhibit merciful behavior never do. They can be as vicious and bloodthirsty as a pack of wolves when it comes to fighting over a difference in belief. The international rules of war are largely meaningless in such a situation.

I moved to the end of the wall and waited for a moment. Colin had entered the front door with no shooting, but as I waited, a grenade went off in one of the upstairs rooms, so I figured he'd made it up the stairs. I took that moment to run across to the opposite corner. From there, I could see a rear alley behind the building. It looked like the most likely egress for anyone trying to exit, so I moved down the wall until I reached a sunken stairway that led to a basement door. I started down the stairwell to check out the door.

There was a shooter on the other side of the street that I'd not seen until he opened up at me. I ducked down into the stairwell, but not fast enough. A bullet bounced off the wall and hit me in the calf. It felt like a cow had kicked me in the shin and I dropped to the bottom of the stairs.

It hurt so much that I initially thought the bone was broken and to compound the problem, it must have nicked an artery, because I was bleeding badly. I wrestled around and got out a small first aid pack that I always carry and worked at getting a pressure bandage on my leg. All of the time I was doing this, some idiot somewhere was groaning loudly. As I finished tying the bandage and the blood-flow slowed, I realized that the noisy person was me.

There was a sudden burst of firing from the alleyway and then a stampede of boots on the concrete coming towards me. I tried to grab my weapon and prepare, but by the time I looked up, there were six or seven guns pointed at me. Colin had chased the opposition out of the house and they'd run right up on my hiding place!

Before they could finish me off, there was a burst of automatic fire from right behind them and they dropped. Incredulously, I managed to work my way up a couple of steps and there he stood, smoke trickling out of the muzzle of his assault weapon.

He smiled at me and said, "Hi, I'm Declan and you might be?"

He paused, looked up and raised his hands in a sort of acknowledgment that he wasn't fighting as Joe and Chandra ran up, covering him with their guns.

"I'm going under the assumption that the enemy of my enemy is my friend," he said. "I've been working around the back of this place for thirty minutes trying to figure out how to clear those guys out of there and now you've done it for me."

We've been friends ever since and, while we don't work together all of the time, there have been many jobs on which we've collaborated. I owe Dec my life and that's a debt that I don't take lightly.

That's why, when he called, I came immediately, even though I was actively working on what seemed to be a totally separate issue.

We'd been under contract with a private corporate group for some months. They had us working against some radical groups in a couple of places that I also won't mention. Most recently, we'd come into the US because they had an idea that we could provide some direction to their training initiative. Collectively, we had more experience than all of their trainers combined.

We'd come across the southern border somewhere in Texas and made our way to their headquarters in Virginia. Joe is the only American citizen of the group, but that didn't slow us down. The border security of the USA is highly compromised.

I know there are lots of Homeland Security agents, but their job is mainly to put up a good show and to intimidate the citizens. They don't do much by way of sealing the borders. So, we got across easily and then rented a car in Texas. Within a couple of days, we were in Virginia.

As soon as we got there, we were reassigned to investigate some kind of massive explosion in the western part of the state and as we were working on that, Dec called.

20

WAITING

Liz and I found that Lexington was smaller than we'd expected and only had a few likely looking places to stay. We finally settled on an inexpensive motel near Washington and Lee University. Like our previous motel, it had outside access to the rooms and we were able to sneak Jefferson in with no problem.

We'd agreed to give Rudy a day to gather the necessary equipment, so we loafed around the room and then drove around sightseeing for the majority of the next day. It was a pretty area, but the town was a little too small to make me feel safe. There's a lot more security in crowded cities than most people think. In a small town, you definitely stand out, while you can simply and easily blend into the crowd in a city. Blending in is made easier by the city dweller's studied inattentiveness to other people.

Of course, even in a city, there are those that will notice anything out of the ordinary. The biggest danger is that you'll be too distracted to notice that you're being hunted, since the hunter can also blend into the crowd.

I'd come to rely on Jefferson as a potential early-warning source. He was probably more observant than a watchdog. He seemed to be able to keep an eye on everything that might concern him and, by association, us, without looking as if he were actually looking. He would rest his head on his paws, peeping out of slightly slitted eyes from his position on the cargo cover in the back of the Mercedes. He was the perfect picture of contentment, but one that could explode into a fuzzy ball of fury, if he saw anything that alarmed him.

We both felt more at ease when we left the city and drove out into a rural area. There were enough cars passing by that we didn't stand out, but not so many that we couldn't keep track if we were followed.

The scenery was pretty with very steep and forested hills; we saw some wild turkeys in a clearing and several whitetail deer browsing at the edge of the woods next to a farmer's feedlot. Considering the pressure we were under, it was a relaxing interlude. Especially when we found a nice overlook and parked so we could cuddle in the back seat for a few minutes.

We opened the door, chancing that Jefferson was smart enough not to wander off. He slipped out and scratched a hole in some sandy soil in order to do his duty. He kept an alert lookout, wandered around the car for a few minutes and then meeped to come back in. He had a funny meow, when he wanted our attention. Instead of being a simple "meow," like most cats, he somehow put an elongated "p" on the end of it, so it sounded something like, "MeouPP!"

No one came along, but we were still a little jumpy and eventually headed back to town. By now it was mid-afternoon and we went back to our motel to freshen up. I parked across the parking lot from our room and we sat for several minutes checking out the place. Nothing showed as suspicious and my sixth sense didn't kick up, so we moved over and parked in front of the room next door to ours and went inside.

The maid had made up the place, but we hadn't left anything other than what anyone else would leave in a room. Liz had left some small toiletries she had purchased in the drug store and I'd hung up a few extra clothes I'd grabbed on the way. These were arranged on the wire hangers in the wall closet. We both guessed that we'd successfully eluded any pursuit and the Pugs must be scratching their heads, if, in fact, their brains were in that part of their anatomy and they actually did that sort of thing.

At supper, in a cafe near the motel, we had a decent country-fried steak, with biscuits and white gravy that was a little lumpy. Some cooks just can't seem to concentrate on the job for a long enough period of time to effectively stir the lumps out. Good gravy takes concentration to make correctly.

There were a few left over pieces of steak and they somehow got wrapped in a paper napkin, deposited in Liz's purse beside her splinter-shooter and taken back to the car for the cat.

The restaurant had a "No Guns!" sign in the window. Since the splinter-shooter was not exactly a gun in the sense that most humans used the word, we felt that we weren't violating the owner's misguided antipathy towards self-defense. Putting up a "No Guns!" sign is just inviting criminally minded individuals to waltz in and rob you. I said to Liz, "It's about as stupid as wearing a sign on your back that says, 'Kick Me'."

I've often wondered why people blame inanimate objects for violence. Violence is the exclusive province of living creatures and it can take all sorts of forms. Guns aren't necessary to the spirit of the act.

21

The Team

The next morning we met in the abandoned warehouse where we were going to meet originally. It was littered with the remains of some kind of packing material; cardboard and plastic with metal straps. Rudy and company were in a cleared area near some stacked-up wooden pallets that had probably held the items that had been enclosed in the cardboard boxes.

We greeted each other and Rudy made introductions. His team was five in number, including him. I already knew three of his people, but the other was new to me. My job was easier; I only had to introduce Liz, since the cat had been left snoozing in our black Mercedes.

We decided to go over the general plan first. I asked Liz to brief the others on what we were up against. There was a lot of disbelief on Rudy's side. However, our story became more believable to them when we got to the part about the anti-matter bomb and the crater in Virginia. This part of the story provoked some exclamations along with a couple of curses.

"Damn!" Colin said. "So, that's what caused that!"

Rudy interjected, looking at us, "What you don't know is that we were sent to Virginia on a call from our employer. They are intensely interested in that event. Your 'eraser bomb' as you call it, created a real stir, both on the part of NSA and the rest of Homeland and also a number of private corporations. We've been working for a private security contractor who has been using our services elsewhere. They would like to get their hands on whatever caused that crater."

He looked at the other men in his group with an apologetic smile, "I've probably said too much, but, as you know, we go back a long ways. Dec will, perhaps, come to the conclusion that he should help us with our contract, since he's the cause of the situation."

"Wait a minute, Rudy," I said, "it wasn't me that started this mess. The Pugs have been working on this for what seems to be a long time. Long enough, anyway, to have assets in place over most of the USA and also in a large number of places across the globe."

"How do you know all this?" asked Chandra, speaking for the first time.

This was a good time for me to pull out the map., I spread it over the top of the stack of pallets. We all clustered around and Liz briefed them on how to read it and what our conclusions were from our studies of the thing.

"How do you know that the transporter in Colorado is important?" asked Rudy.

"The answer to that is to be found on the back of the map and in this little book," I replied, pulling it out. "We found this after we found the map."

I flipped the map over and showed them the links off the Earth and then opened the book. I took the time to explain what we'd figured out about it. I did meet some disbelief with the idea of interstellar travel and the different occupants of the illustrated planet directory. However, they began to get involved in the story, since it was a little too elaborate to be a practical joke. When I got to the EMP attack, they definitely sat up and took notice.

"That's not funny," said Colin. "We can't let that stand. Too many people will be killed and our whole society will go down."

"That ain't good!" added Joe, with a distinctive southern accent.

Finally, it was time to discuss what we hoped to accomplish. I explained that we'd decided that the best approach was to somehow destroy the Pugs' ability to reach the Earth. They didn't seem to be using any sort of spacecraft as shuttles to bring their forces down. According to the map, the only point where they were transporting onto the Earth was in Estes Park.

Liz thought that this allowed them to more easily secure the access point, so we could anticipate it being heavily guarded. If this were so, they'd be likely to keep a close eye on all transporters and roads leading to Estes.

This speculation seemed to be justified since the map only showed one transporter route into Estes Park and that came through Loveland, a nearby town. There were two links in the system that led to Loveland. It was connected to Lander, Wyoming and Pueblo, Colorado.

Pueblo was a dead-end, having only the single connection to Loveland. Lander connected to Loveland, but was also connected to Carlsbad, New Mexico. This oddly structured bottleneck in the system seemed to allow the Pugs to more closely monitor comings and goings.

There was also a nearby connection from Dodge City that led to Denver. Dodge City was, for some odd reason, also linked to Singapore, but that was worthless for our purposes. However, Denver was just an hour's drive from Loveland, so that was a possible alternate route.

It looked to me like the aliens were not much into automation. Their development apparently hadn't made much use of computers. This was puzzling, because we couldn't envision how the transporters worked without a sizable cybernetic component.

I would have immediately placed computerized monitoring on the entire transporter system, but we'd seen no sign that they viewed the system as anything more than a series of doors that didn't need much guarding. They seemed to be very confident in their plan and so far, it was justified. They'd built a huge number of transporters, kidnapped a lot of people and messed around with our financial system without being caught.

Those made me wonder if they already had been discovered, but had somehow bought the cooperation of the people in charge of any investigations. Thinking about Liz's boss didn't really clarify the matter much. We thought he was collaborating, but we weren't absolutely sure that a Pug that had stolen his face hadn't replaced him. It would have had to speak better English than most of them, but that was a possibility.

Despite their apparent lack of monitoring the system, we wanted to be sure we got through, so we planned our approach through the transporters in two separate groups. One would go to west Texas and the other directly to Lander, Wyoming. We hoped that at least one group would get through.

The Lubbock, Texas group was Rudy's responsibility. From there, they would drive to Pueblo. As I mentioned, there was no direct jump from Pueblo to anywhere except Loveland, so driving was the only way to reach that end of the link. Once at Pueblo, they'd find the transporter and move to

Loveland. Liz noted they could drive to Dodge City and jump directly to Denver, but then they'd have to drive on from there to Loveland.

Joe scratched his head and asked, "Why don't they make things more direct?"

Liz answered, "I guess when you can go any distance instantly, any spot on the globe could be viewed as equally convenient to any other spot, so maybe they don't have to worry about keeping transporters close to each other...but I don't know, that still doesn't explain it very well."

Liz and I were going to jump to Lander. The map indicated that the in and out transporter stations there were separated by several miles, so we were going to need a vehicle once we arrived. When we reached the link to Loveland, we'd move there and wait for Rudy's group to show up.

When they arrived, we would try to sneak into Estes Park through the single transporter link and raise hell with whatever we found. We hoped to be able to disrupt the Pugs' operation and somehow shut down their ability to bring reinforcements to Earth.

As for the EMP problem, we thought that we would have to get the military involved. Liz and I didn't think the Pugs had their own missile. Given all we'd seen, they had arrived on Earth with less equipment than a human expeditionary force would think adequate. They apparently thought they could steal or confiscate enough of our weapons to take us down. It looked as if they were probably correct, especially if they could get hold of a missile capable of reaching Earth orbital altitudes. This wouldn't have to be extremely large, but that depended on the size of the warhead that they would use. On that point, I hadn't a clue, but I imagined that it would probably be smaller than any of ours. That is, if they used their own technology and didn't simply steal and use one of our own nukes.

Everyone tentatively agreed that this rather sketchy plan was about the best we could do, given the lack of time and lack of specific information from which we were suffering. Rudy said that he thought the Pugs would be forced to launch sooner rather than later because of our actions. He had some good military connections and thought that he could alert them to be on the lookout for anything suspicious happening with our store of missiles.

Our access plan relied on keeping the Pugs unaware of our approach. If we were able to keep their response unbalanced, it might mean that we could sneak into our objective before they had a chance to fully prepare a reception. By dividing into two groups, we hoped to ensure that at least one got through.

The next phase of our meeting involved various weapons and other equipment. We first tried the communicators that Rudy had brought along. I placed an earphone in my ear and turned on the small battery pack while Colin walked away with another one.

"Range of three-thousand meters and the battery will last for four hours of continuous broadcast. Turn them on standby and your body heat will slowly recharge the battery." The sound came in in stereo. I could see Colin talking and hear him while the earpiece echoed his speech in my ear.

Joe handed out survival gear, bullet-proof assault vests with first-aid packs, night vision units, and Levi provided a choice of conventional weapons with ammo. We vetoed the nine millimeters. They were too light to really stop a Pug as Liz's attempt to kill them with her Glock had demonstrated.

It was a bit of an argument, since Levi, an ex-Ranger who was apparently an excellent marksman, and Joe favored the round, especially when used in a sub-gun. Joe had a great deal of kinetic experience in urban combat settings. We won out by simply showing them our two eraser guns.

When I pulled them out of their case, there was a collective gasp and everyone gathered round wanting to handle them. I called a halt to that impulse immediately by simply pointing one at a box lying at the far end of the warehouse and pulling the trigger. The box obligingly disappeared with a crackle. Then I looked at the guys and said, "There is no safety on this thing. When you pull the trigger, something WILL be destroyed. Make sure it isn't one of us."

Well, that slowed them down a bit. After visually looking the weapons over, Levi asked if he could try one and on my assent, he picked it up, shouldered it, pointed and clicked the trigger. Unfortunately, he happened to be aiming at the wall at the end of the warehouse at the time. The gun did its stuff and a hole appeared in the wall and rapidly enlarged until he released the trigger with a exclamation. The blast had narrowly missed Chandra Singh, who exclaimed loudly, "You need to go back to basic training, you crazy, stupid Jew!"

It was pretty egregious of Levi. To give him credit, Rudy commented that he'd never seen Levi shoot anything by accident. I think that he hadn't really believed the eraser gun was a real weapon. It did have a rather toy-like appearance, since it was very light and made mostly of a plastic-like material.

"The next shot will take your head off, if you call me 'crazy or stupid' again!" Levi retorted. He didn't mind being called a Jew, since he was proud of his heritage, but he drew the line at insults to his mental acuity.

"That is an example of what I'm trying to tell you," I said, trying to distract them before things became more acrimonious. Chandra was a demolition expert and we really needed him with his head intact.

"The hole is going to attract attention, but I'm still glad you made it. I learned something by watching."

Liz interjected, "The gun continues to project the anti-matter field, or whatever it does, until the trigger is released. It looked like you could successfully wipe out targets of any size."

I finished up with, "I'm not sure of the range. It may keep going until it hits something to destroy or it may eventually attenuate due to erasing molecules in the intervening atmosphere. In any event, I also don't know how long the power supply will work, so let's reserve these for actual targets that we want to make disappear."

There was a general agreement on that point. I then reached into the bag and pulled out the four other eraser bombs that I'd managed to shove in my pockets before blowing the armory. I explained that these worked about the same, but were incredibly powerful and needed to be used with extreme caution.

"No worries, boss," Rudy responded. "We have been out to the collapsed crater and it's pretty seriously large. Did you say just one of these did that?"

"Yes and we were on the other side of a transporter portal, so we didn't have to worry about getting caught in the blast."

I couldn't think of what else to call it. I'd heard there was a fairly loud boom when it went off, but it was more of an implosion than explosion. I thought it was probably like the one made by a lightening bolt vaporizing the atmosphere and leaving a vacuum. The vacuum causes a thunderclap when the air rushes back in. That must have been the cause of the boom. In either case, it was obvious that the eraser bombs had to be reserved for use when extreme prejudice was required.

We also took a couple of minutes to demo the splinter-shooters. Unfortunately, we only had the two of them and Liz and I were keeping those. I regretted not gathering more of the weapons at the armory, but I hadn't felt we could carry any more weapons at the time. I rationalized that the chances were pretty high that we'd pick up more sooner or later. I could see through the indicator that both of ours were down to their last quarter load. In addition to several bricks of C-4 and detonators with timers, Rudy brought some other useful tools. I made a mental note that the C-4 could be handy to blow up transporter cubicles, if there was no time or space to use one of the erasers.

We finished outfitting in good spirits. Rudy seemed confident that the exotic weapons we'd liberated from the Pugs would be helpful.. We broke up into couples as we left the warehouse. We'd meet at the Steinway building in Astoria that housed the transporter in precisely thirty-six point five hours.

22

Astoria to...?

A little over a day and a half later, we were all inside the rather cramped lobby of the building on Steinway. Three of the men were facing the transporter door with weapons ready. The other two were facing the sidewall. I'd previously briefed them on the disappearing door and they were keeping alert, just in case it appeared at an inopportune time.

I wasn't very comfortable with the arrangement. The lobby was too small and bunched us together tightly, making an easy target, if one of the doors opened suddenly with an armed and ready Pug on the other side.

It had also been a real problem for us to get inside the building without attracting the attention of too many of the local shopkeepers. We'd separated our entry out over a period of about forty minutes, entering one at a time every few minutes. Liz and I had come last, carrying a bag that held Jefferson and the eraser bombs along with some other spare equipment.

The first thing that Jefferson did was jump out of the bag and sniff around each person's legs. I figured this was his idea of a quick check to see if anyone smelled in a way that might be suspicious. He gave the men a thorough inspection, one at a time. Satisfied, he settled down nonchalantly in a corner to lick his tail.

I pushed the call button and the transporter door opened immediately, we crowded in; it was a tight squeeze. Jefferson sauntered over, looked in disgust at the maze of legs on the floor and leaped into Liz's arms. The door snapped shut and the transporter did its normal disorienting thing, then the room changed to a slightly smaller configuration with iron walls.

We were pretty squeezed and I was glad when the door popped open in the hall where I'd first met Liz. I looked and nothing had changed. There was no one in sight.

We'd checked the map thoroughly in preparation. The door at the end of the hall, the one with the red light beside it, led into another hall that led to a transporter. That one linked to a location in Kentucky, which then linked to a place in St. Louis that was near a group of five transporters. According to the map, two of the transporters were linked to destinations that would put us closer to our goal.

Liz had made a special effort to study the map and noticed that one of the Pugs may have mistrusted his memory and made annotations on the thing. It was rather convenient, because the marks often showed which of the two buttons in a transporter went where.

We weren't sure of that last conclusion, however, and it was complicated by the fact that some transporters only had one connection while others had two. To top it off, the map wasn't marked consistently. Only a few of the locations had been annotated, but we were appreciative for the cues, nonetheless.

We hustled down the intervening space, checked around the corner and then got ourselves arranged for a possible firefight. Colin opened the door at the end of the hall to confirm that there were no Pugs that might surprise us. He let it close immediately.

"Just as you said," he shrugged. "It leads to Central Park."

Rudy tried the door beside the red light, but it seemed to be locked.

Liz stepped forward and showed him that it simply required a little knowledge to open. "You've got to slip two fingers into this finger-slot and spread them apart in an opening motion. Closing it is just the reverse, slide them into the slot and pull them together," she demonstrated.

In short order, we were through and standing in front of another transporter at the end of a narrow hallway. Liz reached for the call button, but before she could, the door popped open revealing two Pugs. They seemed flabbergasted at our presence and that gave me the edge I needed to shoot both of them with my splinter gun. They died in the usual messy way.

Rudy dropped down beside them and scavenged their splinter guns and a couple of extra magazines full of splinters. "These splinters really make a mess of the Pugs," he observed. "What do they do to people?"

"Nothing you'd want happening to you," I responded, grimly.

We piled into the transporter, trying to avoid touching the dissolving Pug corpses. This was a single destination unit with only one button. I pressed it and the door opened onto an unbelievable scene.

It was a huge space that was dimly lit. There were hundreds of Pugs held upright in frames that supported them by two bars under their armpits. They didn't look to be alive at first, but as I watched, the eyes of the nearest ones slowly rolled to look at us. They were in some sort of suspended animation and didn't seem able to move more than their eyes. Perhaps these were reinforcements that were being awakened after their journey through the transporter system.

Another thought occurred to me. They could have been placed into this state to conserve food. If all of them were fully awake and feeding on humans, it would be far more difficult to conceal their activity. We would have become aware of their presence faster.

As we started forward, we saw a man, definitely human, off to one side. He had long hair and a beard that looked ragged and scabby. He was wheeling a cart that was full of some gel-pack-like things.

When he saw us, he yelled, "Get out of here, you morons!"

When we didn't move, he began to push the cart in our direction, gradually accelerating to a run. Joe, who was in back of the group, grabbed a chair that had been sitting next to the transporter door and threw it under the front of the cart. This worked wonderfully well, if his intent had been to spill the contents all over the place. The cart tipped over and the gel-packs flew out in a cascade onto the floor. The man let out a howl and immediately forgot about us, dropping to his knees and trying to gather up the packs.

He was alternately moaning and then screaming, "The Chosen must be serviced!"

He scrabbled around on the floor picking up the gel packs and placing them almost reverently into the hastily righted cart. He paused to place a pack on the abdomen of a Pug that was conveniently located. It had been watching us, but had slowly moved its eyes to look at him as he scrambled around on the floor among the packs.

Once in contact with its abdomen, the pack immediately lit up with a yellow glow and began to suck in and out as if it were pumping something into the Pug. For his part, the Pug immediately perked up and began to make somewhat vague movements with his arms and feet as if he were beginning to realize that they were still there. When his eyes chanced on us, he ceased moving and became rigid with a hostile glare. His mouth moved and a few syllables spewed out at which the guy ceased his frantic activity on the floor and hurled himself at us again.

As he jumped at us, he screamed, "Help! Help! Invaders! Help!"

He paused for a moment to look around for reinforcements and then seeing no one coming, he turned to us with a snarl as if he were truly going to attack.

I'd had about enough of this, so I stepped forward and popped him on the left cheekbone. Not too hard, but he fell over on his back, kicking his feet in the air with a wail.

At that point, Rudy yelled, "Look out!" and unloaded a single shot from his splinter-shooter into the now fully conscious and angry Pug.

This had two immediate results. The Pug died horribly as the toxin took him down and the scabby man let out another, even higher-pitched scream and began to cry, "You've killed one of the Chosen! They'll make us all suffer and then they'll eat us!"

He continued in this mode until Liz tried talking to him. He became quieter, seeming to calm down, but as he did, he got a funny, surreptitious look on his face and slipped his hand into his pocket for a moment. The next moment, he chanced to look at the dead Pug and went off again with his screaming and crying. We simply couldn't convince him to shut up.

Rudy said, "I've had about enough of this!" and motioned to Joe, who stepped behind the man, placing his arm around his neck in a rear-naked choke. This stopped his moaning and after a brief spasm of kicking, he lost consciousness. Joe dropped him and stepped back.

Rudy had a sudden thought and examined the guy's pocket. After fumbling around for a few seconds, he removed some kind of remote control unit that looked very similar to a garage door opener remote.

"He may have signaled someone or something with this," he said, waving it in my face.

I looked at it and the hanging Pugs and made a quick decision. "We're going to have to use an eraser bomb on these guys. There's too many to leave behind us, especially if they can be rejuvenated!"

We dragged the bearded man down the hall and into the transporter we'd arrived through. Rudy used the now broken chair to reach around the corner and activate the Go button.

As he was doing so, the door shut on the chair and automatically bounced open. It was good to know that the system wouldn't take off an arm or leg. When he pulled the chair leg out, the door tried again. This time it shut and hopefully took the man back to the short hall we'd come through from the Astoria transporter.

That's when it hit me, I knew that guy! Only the last time I'd seen him, he was drunkenly stumbling down Steinway. I realized that he was more than just a slave to the Pugs. He was some kind of helper, a true sycophant, who was likely to regain consciousness and cause us some sort of problem.

Wanting to recapture him, I pushed the summoning button and the transporter showed up almost instantly, too quickly, in fact. The door popped open and three Pugs started shooting at us.

Fortunately, they only had conventional firearms. Why no splinter-shooters, I don't know, but they immediately hit Levi. He grunted in pain and sat down, almost squashing Jefferson.

The good thing about him dropping out of the line-of-fire was that it cleared my way for three quick splinter-shots and the Pugs all dropped. Jefferson jumped on the nearest one's head and made its last moments even more painful by clawing its right eye to ribbons.

After the Pug died, the cat stopped, sniffed at his prey in disgust and then leaped off, turned and symbolically scratched at the floor as if he was trying to cover something that didn't smell good.

Levi was groaning and holding his left shoulder and it was obvious that he was going to need medical attention. Rudy and I helped him get his jacket off and plugged the hole, but the slug had broken his collarbone on entry and exited through his shoulder blade and the broken bones were causing him a considerable amount of pain. Liz found one of the first-aid kits and we gave him a pain killer shot and then wrapped the wound.

Helping support him while we worked, Rudy said, "Levi, thanks for the help. You'll get a combat bonus for this, but I think that you should head home now!"

Joe nodded as Levi groaned again.

Rudy asked, "Can you make it, or will you need help getting out."

He answered, "Just let me up and I think I'll be OK."

We helped him to his feet, but he turned pale and looked so shaky that I though he was going to drop again. Then he took a couple of deep breaths and said, "The pain medication is working now. I think I'll be fine. Let me get out of here without running into any more of those guys." Colin volunteered, "I'll take him through and come right back."

They stepped into the still open transporter that had been busily trying to close on one of the last deceased Pugs' legs, bouncing open again as it trapped the leg against the doorjamb. Colin gave the leg a kick and the door slid shut.

Liz was inspecting the wall behind where I'd been standing when I finished off the Pugs. She looked at me with a disapproving glance and shook her head as she pointed to three bullet-holes located about head high for me. I realized that it was a good thing I'd ducked when I did. She commented, "I suppose those guys were the ones the bearded, crazy man alerted."

"Maybe," I thoughtfully replied. "Maybe not. In any event we need to get moving."

In about three minutes, Colin was back. "I took him through to Astoria. He's in a cab and heading for the ranch." He was a frustrated cowboy, even though he was actually Irish and had been no closer to a ranch than Chicago, as far as I knew.

"I saw the bearded guy across the street, but he ran as soon as I made him. I didn't think it was a good idea to chase him, so I came right back after getting Levi into the cab."

"That's OK, but we're probably going to have company shortly. We'd better figure out where the next transporter is located, blow the room with the stored Pugs and get while we still can," I said as I pulled out one of the eraser bombs.

Liz was looking at the map as we went back into the large room. "It looks as if the door we want is on the far side of these guys."

Joe was looking at the Pugs as we walked rapidly along the space between the nearest row of the stored creatures and the wall. He carelessly dragged his fingers on one's face and it nearly bit him.

"Wow!" he exclaimed. "They may be inactive, but they must still have some level of consciousness. We'd better hurry before they wake up fully on their own."

I responded, "It looks to me like they are aware, but have no energy. Those gel packs must provide enough energy to get them active. Don't poke any more of them! We've got to move, now!"

We passed at least a hundred rows of the creatures and finally came to the transporter door that Liz had found on the map. Jefferson had been weaving in and out of the rows of Pugs, but somehow still managed to arrive at the door at the precise instant we got there. When I looked at him, he was looking off the way we'd come and his hackles were up!

"Get ready!" I whispered. "We may have some company." Colin focused on covering our back and the rest of us turned with our weapons ready. Being somewhat taller than the average Pug, I could see over the tops of the rows by a little bit. It was obvious that something was coming our way quickly. It was pushing through the rows and the suspended Pugs were swinging wildly as it came.

We heard some of them fall to the floor with thumps, but whatever it was that was coming was quiet. It was still about twenty-five rows away when the transporter door beeped and opened. Liz had pushed the call button while the rest of us were trying to see what was approaching.

"Get in now!" she hissed. "There's no room to fight that thing. I think it must be one of the bear-sized things like we killed in the row house. It won't go down easily, so let's get out of here!"

She was right. The rows of Pugs were too close for us to get a clear shot. If what was coming was worse than one of the Pugs, and it certainly looked much larger, I didn't want to face it without a lot of space to shoot. We jumped into the door and Liz scooted in last, carrying Jefferson.

There were the usual two buttons and I hesitated, looking at them and wondering which one went to St. Louis, until Liz shouted, "The left one! Quick!"

Her shout was answered by a nasty sounding bass moan with a disconcerting beat frequency from a few rows of Pugs away. The thing accelerated and the remaining Pugs flew out of their hangers, landing on the floor, as it came. I pushed the button before it cleared the intervening rows.

The wave of disorientation hit and passed and the door popped open and we were in St. Louis. I knew because we could see a large window on the opposite wall with the St. Louis arch showing against a cheerful, clear sky about a mile away.

Oh. I forgot to mention that I'd left our moaning friend a little gift as I'd pushed the button. It was now dealing with the effects of the eraser bomb that I'd thrown at it. I'd set the delay for five seconds and it was now that time, so I figured that the stored Pugs wouldn't be a problem any longer.

23

St. Louis

The St. Louis transporter turned out to be in an inconvenient location because the six of us (seven, if you counted the cat) had to walk a couple of miles to reach the building that housed the junction of five transporters. I thought that it would have made more sense for the stations to be located in close proximity, but the Pugs were alien and thought in alien patterns. Humans have enough trouble understanding other human cultures, so you'd expect an unearthly alien culture to be even more incomprehensible. The only saving grace was that our unknown annotator had written the street addresses on many of the locations, otherwise we'd have spent an inordinate amount of time searching.

We descended to the street level of the building without seeing anyone and, once on ground level, we exited through a service door in the alley and filtered out onto the street. We came out in an area of town that was depressed looking. The stores were old with faded signs and not much merchandise displayed in the windows. The goods that were on display were shabby and covered with dust. The whole area gave off a tired and dispirited feel. Even the people were hostile in their looks.

I guess that we looked a little too affluent to be walking through their neighborhood. A couple of groups of young men acted as if they were thinking about giving us a try, but then backed off when they met our eyes. We weren't in the mood for any trouble right then and it showed.

We hiked for a while and ended up in the middle of a street near a restaurant. The restaurant promised the world's greatest rib eye steak, which seemed unlikely given the shabby look of the place. The map had indicated that the transporter hub was around this area someplace. As we looked around, there were several buildings that might have housed the things, but one nearby location seemed more suspicious than the others. Of course, it may have been because we saw a Pug entering the door as we turned the corner. That was a distinct sign that we were in the right place.

As we approached the building into which the Pug had disappeared, we saw a small sign over a stairway door indicating that no-fault divorces could be obtained for $99.00 upstairs. We duly opened the door and ushered ourselves into the divorce attorney's domain.

Once we reached the head of the stairs, we saw that there were several offices there. As luck would have it, we were saved the trouble of opening all of the doors because the Pug came out of the one farthest down the hall. He took about half of a step and dropped with two splinters in his brisket.

We cleared the door he came out of, but there was no need for alarm. It opened into a large room with no occupants. There were five transporter doors spaced out on the walls; two doors on each of two walls and one on the third.

We entered from the hall through the door on the fourth wall dragging the Pug's body in after us. No sense leaving a mess that would alarm any of the divorce lawyer's prospective clients. I didn't want them to think that deceased bodies were a normal part of the divorce process. That might or might not be the case, but in either event, it was unlikely that they would be as ugly as the dead Pug.

I've heard about divorces where one of the parties, usually the husband, would have probably been better off dead, rather than in the condition the judge left him. Most recently I read about a sailor, deployed on a submarine in the South Pacific, who was ordered to appear in court for a child custody hearing within three days or go to jail. The judge didn't seem to think that it mattered that the sub wasn't going to come into port for at least three months. Sometimes I worry about our society's direction, that and the fact that common sense is no longer a prerequisite for sitting on the bench, if it ever was.

As we entered the room with the transporters, there was the continuous sound of a small flat-screen TV turned on with the audio on low. It was located on the third wall beside the single transporter door.

The news was on and the announcer was finishing a story about a massive explosion under Fort Knox. It had apparently destroyed the entire gold supply that was stored there.

I had a suspicion that there hadn't been much gold there for years, based on the strenuous resistance to auditing that the government had exhibited. I figured that at least a few bureaucrats were actually breathing sighs of relief. Our eraser bomb had given them a perfect cover.

The next story was shocking to us, both in content and the speed at which it had appeared. Somehow our enemies knew about both of us and either had close ties to the government or had infiltrated the TV news system. There must have been a camera system located in or near the Astoria building, because our pictures were on the screen with a headline that identified us as unknown terrorists. The news babe was reading a script that indicated that we were the subject of an APB and were wanted by the FBI, NSA, and various other alphabet soup agencies because we were suspects in several bombings and were likely to blow other things up, if not apprehended.

Well, they got that last part correct. If we could, we were going to blow up a lot of stuff, all Pug-related, of course. Overall, the implications were not good as to the success of our self-imposed mission.

Liz had the map spread out on the floor and we hovered over it as she squatted down to point with her finger at locations. The map showed the five transporter heads in the room, and their destinations, but it didn't identify which door was which.

Our plan was to split into two groups; one for Lubbock, Texas, while the other would go to Lander, Wyoming. The remaining three transporters in the room were connected to San Francisco, our Moon, and back to Astoria.

The Astoria connection wasn't to the transporter we'd come through. It looked like it connected to the door that I had noticed appearing and disappearing on the wall. The symbol for that transporter on the map was in a different color than most of the others, and there were only a few like it. I thought this was fortunate, because a transporter that only appeared when it was in use was likely to prove an inconvenient surprise for us at some point. It was a good idea to keep close track of those units. The map indicated that they were coming in at Estes Park, or rather a location that was partway up the summit of Rocky Mountain Park. Then, from somewhere in southeast Estes Park, they were jumping to Loveland.

From that point, the transporter links gradually fanned out into the full system. We thought that might be their idea of securing the off-planet connection. It wouldn't have been easy to get off-planet or to even know that the off-planet link existed without the map.

For some reason known only to the Pugs, the transporter loop that I'd taken previously to one of the moons of Jupiter only went there and back. The loop to our own Moon was similar. I couldn't think what they wanted with these locations. Perhaps they thought they were nice places for sightseeing or romance or whatever. Anyway, the map indicated that our Moon was a dead-end and as far as we were concerned, it was of no interest.

The full network covered the globe with hubs located in many of the major cities. The Pugs had their own definition of major cities, though, because Alanya, Turkey had twenty different transporter heads converging in its downtown area. As nice as Alanya might be (and I had been there, once), it was not what would be called a major city, although the residents might argue with you about that.

Judging from the number of stations scattered across the world, it was obvious that the Pugs were either hyperactive or had been working on their invasion plan for quite a number of years. Either way, it created a huge problem for us, because we were playing catch-up in a game that we'd only just found out was being played.

I previously mentioned that the link they were using to access the Earth was in the Rocky Mountain National Park. That transporter led to one of the moons of Saturn. Liz thought it was Titan, but I wasn't sure. I'd decided to look it up on Wikipedia, the next time I had access to a computer, but for now, I tentatively decided to accept her identification at face value.

I'd been to Io, or at least that's what Liz called it. I was dubious about that also. I mean, how does one know? I had been on another planet-sized object and knew that it was orbiting a larger planet, but I couldn't tell the difference between Titan and Ganymede. It was hard enough to recognize that I was on a moon.

I pulled my mind back to the fact that I had Pugs to discourage. I didn't care where I discouraged them, as long as they remained in that state permanently.

We figured that our species' best advantage was if the Pugs were effectively banned from our solar system for as long as possible. We really wanted to get to the Titan connection and figure out how to break it. If we could break that link either on Titan or on the Estes Park side, it would slow them down. They wouldn't be able to continue to build up their forces on Earth.

If we could break the link on Titan, it would probably prove more disruptive than breaking it on the Earth. We knew that it would be better to destroy their main base on Titan. That might give us the time we needed to develop an effective response to their next attempt at invasion.

Of course, they could eventually come back. Based on the booklet we'd found, it was hard to tell how long it would take for them to do so. The good news was that it looked as if they had left one of the more troublesome planets to the local inhabitants. Liz and I were hoping that they'd end up classifying Earth as another one that was more trouble than it was worth. If we had anything to say about it they certainly would.

Our immediate problem here in St. Louis was the five unidentified transporter doors. We only wanted to use two of them; the two that went where we wanted. We couldn't read their script on the map and there were no apparent markings on any of the doors anyway.

The best we could figure was to go through each of the transporters sequentially and hope for the best. This is not a great plan if you want to remain unseen by the opposition. The chances were high that at least one of the doors would open to reveal one or more Pugs.

We'd been lucky so far, since we'd never run into an overwhelming force of the creatures. They had to think that we were some kind of super-heroes at this point. They'd been on the losing end of every encounter with us. However, our luck was bound to change for the worse, eventually.

As we were looking at each other over the map and scratching our heads figuratively, if not literally, the single transporter on the wall by itself dinged and popped open. Our old acquaintance, the bearded sycophant stuck his head out, cursed and took a shot at us with a sawed-off twelve gauge. It was lucky that he wasn't too stable. He'd apparently been drinking again and staggered as he shot.

The load of shot struck the TV right in the middle of a commercial for a sexual performance enhancement drug. This seemed to me to be an appropriate comment on the idea that two people sitting in separate bathtubs is somehow sexually enticing.

The TV flared and went dark and so did Mister Beardy Guy. His eyes crossed as at least two different splinters of toxic glass struck right between them. He flopped in the doorway. We'd eliminated one of the transporters courtesy of his abortive ambush.

I observed, "That door must lead to the Astoria building. That's where Joe left him."

Rudy said, in his acerbic fashion, "Why don't you try telling us something that's not so obvious."

In the spirit of the thing, I said, "Well, did you know that some owls aren't so smart?"

Apparently he missed my insurance commercial reference or he wasn't in the mood for trivia. He stooped over the bearded guy and pulled out a wallet.

"Says here his name is Vern Wardell, from Kansas. Wonder what led him into this mess."

"It makes no difference to either him or us. His song's ended," I answered, earning a look of puzzlement from all, but Liz. "What we really want to know now is how do we separate out the other transporters."

We kept coming back to that problem. We decided that our entire group would enter each one in a clock-wise direction. If we could, we'd identify the location and pop right back without disturbing anything or anyone. If one of the locations was Lubbock, Rudy's group would stay and Liz and the cat and I would go back and try the next transporter. If we hit Lander first, my group would stay, while they went back.

We were quite aware that splitting up wasn't a recommended strategy.

Despite that consideration, we'd still decided to approach the Estes location from more than one direction. This was the only way we could accomplish that kind of forked attack. Our rationale was based on the idea that coming from a couple of different locations would allow at least some of us to get through. We weren't sure if the routes were being watched. If they were, we hoped that they'd ease up on their surveillance, if they caught some of us coming from one direction. If they intercepted one group, perhaps they'd miss the other prong of the fork.

Based on that somewhat dubious logic, we summoned the first of the four remaining transporters and got inside. These four transporters were apparently single route ones, since there was only one activation button in each. They must have been earlier models or perhaps the Pugs felt that they were totally secure, because the video function was also missing from them. The map wasn't marked clearly and there was no way to check our destination until we arrived.

Rudy's hand hovered over the button as he looked over his shoulder to ensure that we were all ready to shoot, if need be.

"I'll keep my hand on the button to return, if we don't like what we see," he assured us.

I nodded, grimly and said, "OK. Go!" and off we went.

24

HiPPieS?

We ended up in the uni-sex restroom at the back of an incense-filled head shoppe in Haight-Ashbury in San Francisco. We exited the restroom, coming out of one of the toilet stalls and then going through the door. In so doing, we totally freaked out the owner, a beaded, hippie-type leftover from the sixties. He was so leftover that his expiration date had long run out, but there he was, still in his glorious garb with a headband tying back his long, gray hair and wearing a peace symbol on a leather thong underneath his leather vest.

We weren't too sure where we were at first. You can still find people like him in about any major city and this might have been Astoria if we'd been wrong about the bearded Vernon Wardell's origin. The hippie wasn't able to speak much, he was so frazzled over all of us coming out of his toilet, carrying guns!

"Guns!" He was apparently aghast over the very concept.

We poked our heads out of the front door to verify where we were. Sure enough, we were right at the intersection of Haight and Asbury. These two streets commemorate two early San Francisco notables, banker Henry Haight and politician Munroe Ashbury. The hippies of the sixties would have probably decided to have their Summer of Love in another location entirely if they'd been aware that the streets were named after such establishment types.

Mr. Hippie was not happy as we turned and trooped through his shop again. We passed some nice macrame hangings, headbands, leather watchbands and turned left by the psychedelic posters into the restroom.

He was able to say, "Hey, you all can't...," but then he paused, possibly thinking about what we were all going to do in his bathroom; five guys, a beautiful woman and a Tom cat.

San Francisco is a strange place full of strange people doing strange things, but it must have given him a mental paroxysm, because he started stuttering at that point, "can, can, ca, ca, ca."

It really didn't matter what he said, the fact was that we were all going to pile into his restroom anyway. As we entered, Joe turned and gave him the peace gesture. He stopped stuttering and returned it.

We got back to the St. Louis location and moved to the next transporter. We now had identified two of the five, so the odds were greater that the next would be one of our destinations. Only it wasn't. We ended up on the Moon.

Oh, sure. Everyone thinks they want to go to the Moon. I mean it was pretty cool and we felt lucky to be able to see the Earth from there, but I was kind of put out over it. It seemed like we couldn't catch a break and we were spending more time on a kind of lunatic tour than on approaching our enemies' strategic point.

We came out of the transporter door into a crater. This could have been deadly for us, but this crater had a transparent cover about halfway up the walls. The crater was deep, too. The covering glass or whatever it was looked as if it was about four hundred feet over our heads and the crater walls went on up from there for at least another five hundred feet or so.

The glass itself had some dust on the top of it that obscured our view of the Earth a little. I don't know how dust travels around on the surface of the moon, but this had obviously fallen down from above. There was no wind on the Moon that I knew of, since there was no atmosphere, but later Liz mentioned to me that the solar wind consisting of photons and other particles ejected from the sun was possibly to blame. The Pugs probably didn't bother to clean it off because the dust would go a long ways to obscure activities on the base of the crater from viewers on the Earth.

There are telescopes at various locations on Earth that are easily powerful enough to see the bottom of lunar craters. There was activity in the bottom of this one to see, but with the dust covering part of the glass, it may have broken up the view to the point that nothing was obvious to any observer. There wasn't much to see at the moment; the floor of the crater held a stack of large, solid looking crates, but no Pugs.

We looked at the view of the Earth like Kansas farmers look at the New York skyscrapers when they first wander into Times Square. Yes, we gawked. It was amazing and brought a lump to my throat. I got over it soon enough, though, because suddenly some Pugs entered the crater bringing more boxes towards the stack. They didn't have any equipment aside from their own muscles, but they were moving the big boxes easily in the light gravity.

They saw us after a few seconds and let out a perfect hissing storm of their language, ending with one of them speaking into some kind of communicator. The response was a series of hisses. That tore it! They all started running our way in their snake-like fashion and we started shooting at them. Liz screamed, "Use splinter guns, you idiots."

Joe and Colin were blasting away with their 45's and the bullets were bouncing around. She was afraid that they'd break the glass with a ricochet, but she needn't have worried. Any substance that is strong enough to withstand even a minor meteor strike should be able to take a pistol shot with no problem. Even so, they pulled out their splinter guns and went "Poof" rather than "Bang" at the Pugs. Two of the aliens went down immediately and the other three started bouncing back towards the boxes, looking for cover.

The communicator must have summoned help, because another Pug poked his head out of a door on the far side of the crater. He became an immediate problem, since he had one of the long, energy-bolt shooting tubes. He lowered it onto its mount, pointed it at us and let fly. We could see the bolt coming and we jumped to get out of the way.

We were surprised to find that our adrenaline powered jumps moved us high above the surface. The light gravity was a great help in dodging the shot.

We jointly sailed through the air and came back down about the time he let off a second shot. It went wide of our location because Rudy had managed to somehow shoot him with a splinter. How he managed it while flying through the air, I don't know. He kept firing as he jumped and landed on his shoulder pretty hard, because he was concentrating on shooting. When he landed, he let out a groan and stopped shooting, but it didn't matter by then.

There was one Pug remaining. He'd been hiding behind some of the crates, but now he was bounding for the door where the bolt shooter was positioned. We all unloaded in his general direction and he obligingly staggered and died before he reached it.

Rudy recovered rapidly, because he jumped up and leaped over to the dead Pugs in an attempt to recover some additional weapons. He found one splinter gun on the Pug that had shot the bolt at us. We yelled at him and he came running back, giving the gun to Chandra, who didn't have one.

We retreated back to the transporter door in a hurry. Jefferson was already there, as usual. I realized that he had remained by the door rather than risk his neck in what seemed to him to be an uninteresting exercise. Somehow he always seemed to know when we'd be backtracking. That foreknowledge saved him a lot of walking at times.

We were all breathing heavily when the transporter dumped us back in the room in St. Louis. The combination of looking at the Earth from the moon and being shot at was a little too exciting and I wouldn't recommend it.

The good thing was we now knew that the last two transporters would take us to our intended destinations and, although we didn't know which one went where, we really didn't care that much. Rudy, Colin, Chandra and Joe turned to us and saluted in a military manner and then went into the next transporter. Just before the door shut, Rudy re-adjusted the strap holding the eraser-gun I'd given him, grinned and said, "Tonight we dine in Lubbock!"

"See you in Loveland," I rejoined. Their door shut and we turned to the last transporter. Its door opened when Liz pressed the call button and we entered.

25

Rudy's Group

The transporter door slid shut on Colin, Chandra, Joe, and me. Joe reached out and put his hand on the activator and looked back at the rest of us. "Anyone want to place a bet on where we'll end up? My bet is that it won't be Lubbock." He grinned widely at me and added, "What do you think, Rudy?"

He was always trying to bet on things, but his gambling luck was so terrible that he never won. We had taken to doing the merciful thing by not betting with him, just so he could keep his money.

Considering Joe's luck, it didn't surprise us when we went directly to Lubbock. Since we'd eliminated the other three options, I assumed the last transporter would take Dec and company to Lander. If so, they'd probably get to Loveland before us. Lander had a direct link to Loveland, although that link was separated by a few miles from the one they'd arrive through.

We'd providentially called ahead to both places and reserved cargo vans, thinking those would be the least likely vehicles to arouse suspicion. For our part, we had a much longer drive to make, but we figured that we'd time our arrival in Loveland in order to meet up.

We came out in Lubbock in the lady's restroom in Jones AT&T Stadium at Texas Tech. This would have been fine, but we immediately ran into the custodian who gave us a hard time for being in the "girl's room" as he put it. I pulled out an FBI shield that I kept for appropriate times, flashed it at him and said that we'd received a report of a hidden camera installed in the facility.

I asked him to keep his eyes out for video cameras, because we believed that a Mexican narco-terrorist was using them to target good-looking Texas girls to kidnap and use as sex slaves. I don't know what got him the worst, the idea of video in the "girls room" or the sex slave thing. We left him, looking suspiciously at the entrance to the restroom, rubbing his chin and muttering, "Sex slaves!" in a speculative tone of voice.

It didn't take us long to find a municipal bus that went near the car rental bureau and shortly we were on the road to Loveland. We had a long drive, it's about six hundred miles which is a little over nine hours, not counting stops to refuel.

Everything went well for the first fifty miles and then we ran into trouble in the form of a Homeland Security VIPR squad. We weren't anywhere near the border, but these guys had set up a checkpoint and were halting all cars that came through. Perhaps they thought they were far enough away from Mexico that their chances of being bothered with an actual illegal immigrant were slim.

I slowed down and hung back until they'd cleared the previous car. There was no other traffic in sight in either direction. Then we approached, pulled over dutifully and I rolled down my window. Colin, who has an Irish brogue, and I with my Slavic accent were in the front. The other two guys were laying low in the back, trying not to be seen, since they were sitting on the floor amid a considerable amount of weaponry.

"Are you CITIZENS?" the officer barked in an accusatory tone of voice as he walked up to the van. When I nodded, he tried to poke his head far enough in the window to see in the rear, but I simply pushed my face almost up against his and smiled.

He recoiled and demanded, "Where are you going?"

I took my time and pulled out my FBI badge, hoping that it would work. When I showed it to him, he grabbed my hand to inspect it further. I pulled back and put my finger on my lips and made a shushing noise, implying, I hoped, that we were on a clandestine mission.

He said, "Just a minute," and walked back to consult with his superior. I think that Dec had mentioned that our pictures were on the news as wanted terrorists. The superior was a little smarter and obviously recognized us when he looked at me. This was a highly undesirable situation, but one that we'd planned on in St. Louis.

We didn't really want to shoot these guys, whether or not they were lazy or simply doing their job, they were still approximately on the side of the good guys. I gave the sign to my friends in back and they jumped out of the right-side door with our two M-4s. I dropped out of sight as they made a show of covering the four patrol members from the ends of the van.

The supervisor started to draw his service piece, but stopped when Chandra shouted, "Don't do it!" The other men had already dropped their weapons, including two rifles, which were every bit as deadly as ours.

What they needed with such weapons was beyond me. They were basically just harassing citizens, so I didn't think they needed that much firepower. I jumped out of the van and in the interest of keeping the weapons away from some child that might happen along, I took them. I've noticed that almost any action can be justified, if it's paired with the statement:, "It's for the children." I felt pleased with my confiscation.

These guys were obviously the "J-V" team and we rounded them up before another vehicle came along. They had some plastic zip ties to handcuff any miscreants they encountered, so we trussed them up like the Christmas Turkey, leaving them in their air-conditioned van. We stuck a knife in the van tires and then as a last act, we disabled their radios, hoping that would make them wait for assistance. I walked back and threw the checkpoint signs face down on the ground. No point leaving them up to stop someone who might take pity on the captives.

This all took only a few minutes. While I was throwing down the signs, Colin was looking at Google Earth on his phone and he came up with an alternate route that involved a bit more driving. I didn't like to change, but the odds were good that an APB would go out for us as soon as the patrol could figure out how to get free. If we changed our route, it might make it a little harder to track us down before we reached our destination.

We started off down the same road until we found an intersection and turned, now on our way to Kansas instead of Colorado. We'd opted to head to Dodge City which was four-hundred and thirty miles from Lubbock. We knew that there was a transporter link from there to Denver.

The only problem was we were not exactly sure where the Dodge City transporter head was, since we didn't have a copy of the map. We knew that it was somewhere in the vicinity of the Boot Hill tourist area. We'd have to search for it when we got there.

Once in Denver, we'd get a car and head north on I-25 to Loveland. Meanwhile, we were worried about being stopped. We resolved to get a different van at the first possible opportunity.

That opportunity came up quickly. We passed a cowboy walking back the way we'd come. He stuck out his thumb for a ride, but we didn't slow down. About two miles farther on, there was a king-cab pickup with a flat beside the road, we jumped out of the van and put our spare tire on it. Thankfully the vehicles were the same make and the wheel fit.

Then we were on our way again. The king-cab had a nearly full tank of gas and we figured we'd have possibly an hour before the word got out that it was stolen. Then it would probably take an hour more before the alert went out tying us to the van, assuming the border patrol had freed themselves or been discovered by then. I fully expected them to be free within a few minutes after we left, but there was a wide margin of error in that estimate..

Nothing happened for the rest of the drive. We pulled into Dodge City and parked at a bar near Boot Hill a little after mid-day. It was picturesque in a seedy sort of way. I guess that Kansans don't have much by way of excitement. If this was representative of the state, it was a boring place.

We got out and stretched and, as we did, Chandra and Colin began to laugh. "If it's anywhere, it's in there," they said, pointing at the Boot Hill Museum, "Located," as the sign said, "on the original site of the Boot Hill Cemetery."

We sauntered over with our thumbs hooked in our belts and paid the admission to go in. There were some tourists trying to find amusement for themselves, but it was difficult, unless they were really a western aficionado.

Chandra poked into one of the storage closets while Colin kept the attendant engaged in conversation. It was easier for him, because she was a good-looking young lady, although she did have a rather ugly tattoo on her neck. Colin made small talk with her about his tats. He could charm almost any woman; the man had apparently kissed the Blarney Stone in his youth and it showed.

Shortly, Chandra moseyed over to where I was looking at some faded postcards and nodded his head. We went out and loaded up all of our equipment while Colin kept talking to the girl. She was so enthralled with his accent that she kept laughing at almost everything he said. She barely gave us a glance when we came back in. Colin asked her if she cared if we went into the storage room to look around and she just laughed, thinking that it was another of his jokes.

"Oh, Colin!" she giggled, "You're so funny! No one goes in there except the boss and he only shows up after we're closed."

That was informative, so in we went. She was still giggling as we went through the door. Colin turned and waved at her and she waved back. Once inside we were through the transporter in seconds.

26

Denver to Loveland

Despite the mile-high altitude of the city, Denver was about ten degrees hotter than Boot Hill and a lot more polluted. The men and I came out in the back of a hardware store. We exited the store through the open loading dock without being seen by anyone. This was going very well. Since we'd met the border patrol, we'd had nothing but good luck and it continued.

Joe went around the corner and shortly came back driving an older Cadillac. It was somewhat rusty with the vinyl landau top starting to peel. He said that it belonged to a drunk who had just entered a bar. He'd looked in and the guy was ordering another drink. Joe didn't think he'd come out for some time.

We hit the road, got to the right highway and headed out of town, heading north, finally. It was only about sixty miles and the road was relatively clear with sporadic, light traffic, so it looked as if we were going to be there in plenty of time.

We did have one fright when a highway patrol unit came by us under lights and siren, but he was going to an accident that we passed a few miles farther on, so we kept up our steady progress. We'd all been in this kind of situation before and it was difficult not to speed. When trying to get away or avoid being stopped, speeding is not a great strategy. Joe tried the cruise control, but it didn't work, so he simply kept his eye on the speedometer and cruised along at a steady sixty miles per hour.

In an hour, we'd arrived at the outskirts of Loveland. The transporter was apparently located in some structure about a mile to the east of the city limits. We cruised downtown and then turned east on a convenient street.

When we hit the edge of town, we started looking and Joe shortly saw a likely possibility located a few hundred yards from an intersection with Larimer County Road 1.

It was a stereotypical red barn, somewhat dilapidated, with the words, "See Rock City" painted on the shingles. The nearby farmhouse did not look as if it was occupied, but we approached carefully none-the-less. It was a good idea that we did, too, because just as we pulled into the farmyard, a Pug came out of the house, took a look at our disreputable vehicle and ran back inside.

We bailed out of the car with our weapons and spread out, covering the house and the barn, just in case some came from there.

The Pug suddenly appeared at the front door carrying one of the long electro-bolt launchers. He immediately fired at the Cadillac and the shot barely missed the vehicle. I think he couldn't decide whether to aim at the car or the group of us. As it was, I was a little too close and was scorched, but was basically alright. The Pug wasn't. Both Colin and Joe shot him with splinter guns at the same time he shot at us. He was down and no longer a threat.

Joe went to the house and cleared the entrance. He took the time to grab the deceased Pug's splinter gun before he entered. He popped back out in a minute and announced that the place only had two rooms and they were empty, so we turned our attention to the barn.

We were just in time to catch a Pug who was trying to get a bead on Chandra from the open haymow door. Chandra ducked behind a tractor and the glass splinter broke on the wheel. There were three more Pugs hiding inside the front barn door, and they were also taking potshots at us, but missing. It didn't seem like they could see us very well. It was quite bright out and the sun was over our shoulders, so they had it in their eyes.

Another group of Pugs suddenly showed up near the corral at the back right corner of the barn, possibly having just come out of a transporter inside. Things were starting to look bad, but then Joe shot one and Chandra got another one and I got two and the odds were a little more even.

Nevertheless, it looked like we were in a standoff. They'd pulled back into the barn where it was dark and the sun was starting to go down behind the mountains to our west. We figured that they'd be better shots in the twilight, so we kept carefully under cover and waited for a break that would give us a chance.

27

LANDER

I felt a sense of trepidation and slight depression when Rudy and his men entered the transporter in St. Louis. Apparently, Liz also felt much the same, because she let out a deep sigh.

I turned to her and speculated, "I wonder if they went to Lubbock or Lander?" She simply shrugged her shoulders in response while she held Jefferson cradled in one arm. I was loaded down with the majority of our equipment, but, after all, I'm the man and it's my job to carry things.

We went through the transporter and came out of a door marked "Service" in the back of a gas station. We walked until we saw a motel sign that said, "Lander Dew Drop Inn." I snorted; it was so stereotypical. Liz ignored me and said, "We've got to get a car, somewhere so we can locate the Loveland transporter head. This place doesn't look like it will be so easy."

She was sometimes a bit too pessimistic. It was easy. We walked down to the Dew Drop Inn and watched as a heavy-set man wearing a cowboy hat and boots got out of a pickup. He limped with an uneven stride by an older Ford holding a slightly overweight, but still good-looking woman.

He went into one of the rooms and shut the door. The woman looked all around and slowly got out of the car, still on the lookout. She paused and bent down to inspect her reflection in the rear-view mirror. Apparently, her hair and make-up weren't exactly perfect, because she took a moment to re-arrange her bangs and refresh her lipstick. Then she straightened and looked around again. She didn't see anything to alarm her, so she rapidly went to the same room and entered without knocking.

Liz looked at me and sort of snickered, "I'll bet those two will be in there for at least an hour, unless her husband finds them."

"Well, let's make it a little more interesting for them. We'll take the guy's pickup."

It was an older model and easy to take. It helped that he'd parked it down at the far end of the strip of rooms without locking the doors. It had a loud muffler, but we eased away slowly and they never looked out. I guess things were too interesting inside the room.

We started out of town on highway 789 and we didn't have to go far before we found a group of mobile homes with a kind of Quonset hut near one end. Our map had indicated a rounded structure at the location of the transporter head and we decided that the hut might be the place. We pulled in and stopped in front of it. None of the nearby trailers looked as if they'd been occupied recently.

When we got out of the pickup, we were surrounded by some Indians. They were silent and were wearing hostile expressions. One of the men was obviously the leader.

He stepped closer to us and said, "You folks lost or something?" His friends suddenly seemed to be holding knives.

I lifted my windbreaker and pulled out my pistol. He said, "That don't scare me, Mister. I'd a lot rather face that than the strange guy that grabbed my friend's sister. I think you'd better get back in that truck and git while you can."

He slowly removed an over-sized machete from a sheath on his belt.

"So, you've met the Pugs?" I responded. "They're hard to kill."

He looked over his shoulder at his friends and they started putting the knives away. The atmosphere eased up considerably and he turned back to us and smiled, "That's a good answer, cause it means that you've killed some. We'd like to kill some more of them."

He motioned us to follow him and he went over to one of the dilapidated mobile homes. It was open and we all went inside, not perhaps friends, but not enemies either.

There were seven of them in total. They introduced themselves as members of the Shoshone tribe. The leader was named Freddie Stormbreaker. He said he preferred to be called "Stormbreaker". He didn't like his first name because i t sounded like a leftover from the white culture.

The other men laughed and one of them said, "Don't let Stormy fool you with that humble crap. He was Special Forces and he's a lot tougher than he looks."

"But not as tough as he smells," joked another.

"Aw, shut up, Charlie Short-leg!" Stormbreaker answered.

I could see that it bothered him.

"I didn't mean nothing by it, Stormy. You know I was just foolin' with you," was the answer.

Stormbreaker looked at me and explained, "Charlie, here, is Arapaho. The rest of us are Shoshone. We used to fight, but now we mostly get along, except Charlie thinks he's better than we are."

Charlie denied that, but he had a kind of half smile that showed me there was some truth in it, too. After that, things became friendlier, particularly after I mentioned my service record. That seemed to help with these guys.

We explained what we were up to and they let us know in no uncertain terms that they'd like to be in on the hunt. I was feeling kind of nervous about getting more people involved, but it sounded like each of them had maybe lost a relative to the Pugs.

I thought maybe the Pugs were feeling more confident away from the cities and as a result, they were engaging in open hunting of people. Perhaps it was for sport, perhaps for other reasons, but they'd really pissed-off these guys and they were ready to go on the warpath.

28

STORMBREAKER

The trouble on the reservation had started a few weeks before. The first thing that happened was old Lucy Black Hat went missing. According to her niece, who lived with her, she'd gone out in the evening to walk to the liquor store and hadn't come back.

It had happened before and it was usually because she'd gotten drunk and ended up sleeping it off in some bushes someplace. This time, though, it'd been a couple of days, so me and some of the boys went out to her place and tried to track her. It was mostly because her niece is sweet on William and he told me, "Stormbreaker, I really need some help tracking. You know I ain't any good at it." That, and the fact that I like him, convinced me to get the guys and go check on her..

He spent more time talking to the niece than actually looking for tracks. I'm a better tracker anyway, but it wasn't much use. Lucy had been gone too long and the wind had been pretty high, so there was hardly any sign left.

We managed to track her down the road a ways, but when the tracks petered out, William said, "Stormbreaker, why don't you and the others go on down the road a piece and see if you can pick them up again. I'm going back to her trailer, just in case Susannah might happen to remember anything else that could help."

I snorted and a couple of the others laughed out loud at this transparent excuse, but we turned and walked off down the road. William is a pretty likable young guy and we wanted to give him a chance with her.

We walked about another half mile and then I picked up Lucy's tracks again. This time, she wasn't alone. There was another footprint set that was walking behind her. In places it covered her tracks partially, so I knew it was following and from the condition of those tracks, they had been there about as long as hers.

There was one dusty stretch where the following tracks were very clear and they caused us some consternation. There was something funny about them. They looked like a man wearing some kind of shoes, but they were very narrow and the depth of the impression showed that the follower had a very strange way of rolling his feet.

About a hundred feet after that, there were some odd marks on the road and both sets of tracks ended. It looked as if they'd gone off into the weeds and we poked about off to the side of the road. There were some broken branches in the sage and the smell of crushed leaves was heavy in the air.

We walked along trying to figure out where they'd gone until we finally picked up the tracks of the stranger, but not Lucy's. His tracks were deep enough that it looked like he could have been carrying Lucy. We followed them out from the road towards a bluff and finally came across what remained of Lucy in a dry arroyo that snaked along across the flats.

There had been some coyotes there, but they hadn't touched much. Even so it looked as if something that was not a coyote had chewed on her throat and upper arms. Overall, it was a pretty bad thing to see and a couple of the guys turned pale and stepped back a ways.

Well, we finally got the police out there, but those numskulls thought that Lucy had gotten drunk and fallen into the arroyo and died and then been set on by coyotes. We didn't think too highly of that theory, but we've learned not to argue with those guys. It don't do any good and it makes them angry and they like to take that out on us.

The next thing that happened was Jessie Nine-Toes turned up missing. He'd gone out in the morning to cut some firewood and hadn't come back that night and his wife was mighty putout about it, too.

"How am I supposed to cook without any fuel?" she complained. "And, what's going to happen if it turns cold? This house ain't too warm as it is and it ain't even cold yet."

She had a reputation as a terrible complainer and we often kidded Jessie about it. A couple of the guys also made some fun of him going out to cut wood.

"Maybe he missed with his ax again."

"Yeah, and this time he done cut his whole leg off, not just his toe."

Jessie had been splitting wood a couple of years ago and drinking pretty heavily at the same time. As the bottle got low he took a swing at a log to trim off a stub branch and the ax glanced and cut his little toe right off. It didn't slow him up much. He tied a rag on it and poured some whiskey on the rag and it healed up just fine, but people still made fun of him sometimes.

I looked at the jokers with a mean look, trying to indicate that they should shut up around his wife. She was pretty worried for all of her complaining.

"Don't you worry, Mrs. Smith. We'll go take a look for him. He's probably in town at the bar or thrown in jail," I said, trying to be reassuring.

"Oh, God, no!" she exclaimed. "The last time that no-good fool got drunk in town, it cost us three hundred dollars in court costs! He'd better have cut off his leg, and you can tell him that for me." She had worked herself up into a pretty temper, so we got out of there as fast as possible, before she started in on us.

William thought that Jessie would have driven down the road a couple of miles and then turned onto a dirt road which led to a small stand of trees on the edge of the Res, so we decided to hike down that way. When we got there, we saw his tire marks and followed them into the treed area. His pickup was sitting there under the pines with the door open and an empty bottle lying by the rear wheels.

"It looks like he drove in here and started drinking, but I don't see no tracks where he walked out," I observed after walking around the area. It was kind of rocky where the pickup was parked and that made it hard to find any trace of trail.

After I looked around for several minutes, I found another one of those strange footprints. This one, like the ones by Lucy, looked as if the maker was heavily burdened.

"Here's one of those weird tracks and it may be that he carried Jessie off," I said.

The others agreed that Jessie could have been captured., He wouldn't usually put up much of a fight when he was drunk. Some people get fractious when drinking, but Jessie mostly became passive and ended up comatose.

We continued our looking, but we never did find anything else. William took the pickup back to the wife and she told him that it might be better for Jessie if he didn't show up for a few months, so that was the end of that.

The only problem in my mind was the odd footprints. I was pretty worried about those, so when William's kid sister disappeared on the way to school, I decided that enough was enough. William was out visiting Susannah, but his mother called me and I rounded up some of the other guys to go look for her.

When we found some more of those strange tracks, we worked at it until we traced them to the old Quonset hut. We were conferring on how best to proceed, assuming that the weird-footed guy was carrying a gun, when this big, white guy and a beautiful blonde showed up driving a pickup that I recognized as belonging to a local rancher named Dan Dayle.

Dayle wasn't the type to loan anything, so I figured the two had stolen the pickup. We thought they might be part of the group that took little Kimana, so we were pretty hostile at first, but it soon appeared that they knew more about what we were faced with than we did. We discussed the situation with them and the man told us he was going after the kidnapper through what he called a transporter. We were angry enough to go along, so we asked him to wait while we all went and got our deer rifles.

29

MORE HELP

As it developed, the Indians had tracked one of the Pugs here and were trying to figure out how best to get it out of the Quonset hut. I explained the transporter system and they seemed disappointed.

"You mean that he's not in there, then," said Charlie. "We were hoping to scalp him. We know for certain that he took William's kid sister. We've been following their trail for a couple of hours, but it don't look good. We found some of her clothes about a mile back along with some blood sign."

"I can understand it if you guys want to go, but it's going to be dangerous. The transporter in that building leads to Loveland, Colorado, and probably into a mess of those aliens as well."

"I ain't never been to Loveland, but I think I'd like to go and check it out," said Stormbreaker. "Why don't you all wait here for about an hour while we go get some more useful weapons."

It was more of an order than a question, so we assented.

It wasn't more than thirty minutes before they all came back. Five of them had AKs with boxes of cartridges, and Stormbreaker and Charlie both had AR-10s. I briefed them about the Pugs being hard to kill. Frankly, I didn't think the AKs would do much to a Pug. The cartridge is a good, close-range deer round, but the Pugs were a lot harder to kill than a deer. The good news was that the AR-10s shot a lot more powerful rifle round. That might just get the attention of the Pugs, especially if they were hit in a sensitive area, which would be... Oh, I don't know where. They seemed to be tough all over without any weak points.

We opened the Quonset door without any problems and found it to be empty except for a pile of a few clothes. The men looked over the pile and Charlie said, "This hat belonged to Lucy." He had a grim look in his eye that implied that whoever had taken Lucy out from under the hat was in trouble.

There was a kind of an office in the back of the hut. It was cubical in shape and partitioned off part of the rear quarter in the middle of the structure. The transporter door was on one side of the outside of this room. One of the Indians opened the door to the cubicle and looked inside.

"There's nothing in there at all," he observed. "That funny door on the outside end of this room don't go through. There's just another wall with a little space behind it."

The others looked puzzled and turned to Liz and me.

"The transporters don't go through into another room. They're like an elevator. You get in, press the button and then get out someplace else, only the someplace else might be a long ways away," I explained again in what I hoped were terms that they'd grasp.

I immediately realized that I'd underestimated them, for Charlie said, "It's just like that TV series with the matter transmitters."

The others nodded and I affirmed the speculation. "We've both been to another planet through one of these, so they can take you anywhere. The only thing is that they don't all connect and sometimes you have to take a round-about path to get somewhere that's nearby," Liz explained.

"That's OK, lady," said Stormbreaker. "I'm fine with going through as long as I ain't going to be converted into some kind of mutant fly or something."

"No, they seem to be reliable. We haven't had any problems with growing wings or anything," I responded perhaps a little too facetiously. The Indians gave a collective snort of disbelief and looked at each other.

We finally got organized, lined up and squeezed into the transporter, weapons ready. When it opened, we were in some kind of animal stall. We could hear some shouting and there was the poofing sound of splinter guns shooting near one end of the structure. We worked our way out carefully through the outside exit to the adjacent corral to see that we had come out of a stable door near the back of a faded red barn. Looking towards the front, I could see the backside of several Pugs looking around the corner at something.

This was an opportunity that was too good to waste. I indicated to Stormy that he should get his guys to shoot the Pugs while Liz and I went around the other way to see if there were any more. We'd barely gotten halfway around the back when the Indians started shooting with a noise that reminded me of several battles in which I've been involved.

The cat jumped out of Liz's arms and dashed off somewhere into the nearby tall-grass, staying low. I thought that was just as well. He couldn't help in this situation.

We continued on around the back and peeked around the other side of the barn to see another batch of Pugs working their way towards the front of the building. Unfortunately, one of them saw us, and they started shooting in our direction. We both returned fire and then ducked back. There was a whiz of splinters flying past the corner and we waited for a moment. The Indians were still banging away on the other side of the barn, but it was quiet on our side.

The remaining Pugs were laying low and waiting their chance to shoot splinters at us. I poked my head around the edge and almost caught a splinter, so I pulled back with a curse.

Liz grumbled about me being stupid and dug in her clothes. She finally pulled out a compact from somewhere. Women seem to have the ability to have those things stored just about anywhere on their bodies.

She flattened out on the ground and opened it, holding the mirror so she could see around the corner.

One good thing about the splinter guns, from our perspective, was they had almost zero penetrating ability when it came to things like wood, so she was perfectly safe in her action. If one of the Pugs had been shooting a human rifle, the corner of the barn would have provided next to no cover at all.

She looked at me and hissed, "There's only two of them left. One's looking this way and the other one seems to think that someone is coming around the other end of the barn."

Just then, Jefferson let out a battle-screech and showed himself briefly in the tall grass out to the right of us. He was about ninety degrees out from where the Pugs were and as they turned to look at him, Liz slid forward and shot the one that was oriented towards us.

That left one. He was trying to shoot at the grass and I hoped that the cat was out of the way. The splinters might not go through wood, but they clipped right through grass blades like a lawn mower. He was intent on killing the cat, as if Jefferson was more of a danger to him than we were.

He was wrong. I took aim and planted a splinter in his arm. That abruptly stopped the cat-shooting exercise. Suddenly there was a whole chorus of rifle and splinter shots and someone around the front of the barn yelled, "All clear!"

It sounded like Rudy and it was!

30

Spiders

L iz and I, along with our new Indian friends hurried around the barn and met up with Rudy, Joe, Colin, and Chandra. They were somewhat surprised to see our new, tribal helpers and I spent a few minutes explaining the Indians' desire to come to grips with the Pugs. Rudy's guys listened and nodded at the appropriate times. It seemed like we were going to have a working group.

About the time I finished talking, Jefferson came up and sat by Liz. He was still bristled up and keeping an eye on the barn. He finally turned towards it, stood up, and let out a low yowl.

Stormbreaker said, "What's wrong with that cat? He looks pissed."

Charlie obviously hadn't noticed our cat previously and thinking that Jefferson was a stray, said, "I'll just chase him off."

His statement was met with a chorus of "No" from the guys and me and "Don't you dare!" from Liz.

He looked puzzled, but meanwhile Jefferson was making more noise and it looked like he'd sensed something in the barn. He was watching the door while standing side-wise to it with his back arched up and every hair sticking out at right angles. It made him look at least twice as big as he actually was.

"Get ready! There's more Pugs in there. Maybe they came through the transporter link," I said.

I was wrong. We had killed all of the Pugs, but the barn had a bunch of those nasty spider-things in it. A group of them came out of the door, moving towards us in a scuttling rush across the sparse grass and dirt in the barnyard.

Liz and I pulled our conventional pistols and were banging away immediately. It took Rudy's group about a half-second to follow our lead. The Indians were a little slower, but not much. Between all of us, we shot all of the things before they'd reached where we were standing.

"There's probably more in there," I said. "We'd best be really careful about going in."

"Why would we want to go in there?" asked Charlie.

"To get to the transporter," Liz replied in a tone of voice that implied that she thought she was talking to a child.

Stormbreaker added, "You want to kill some of them Pugs or not?"

Charlie responded by starting to walk towards the barn while looking over his shoulder at us, "You ain't calling me no coward, are you?"

Coward he may not have been, but foolish, he was. As he got close to the barn, another rush of spiders came out.

We started shooting them, but he was in the way and we couldn't hit them all. He turned and shot a couple, but one ran right up his front and latched onto his cheek with those nasty fangs. He let out a scream and slapped it down to the ground, but it was too late. Colin shot it. By now we were close and it was an easy shot. Charlie was thrashing his arms around in the air, he'd dropped his rifle, and he suddenly sat down and then fell over on his side. His face looked awful, cheek swollen out like a football. The swelling burst and green fluid came out and ran down his neck.

He let out another scream and thrashed around as his neck turned black and dissolved. The corruption suddenly reached his carotid and opened it up causing blood to spurt in the air in large gouts as his heart raced. The blood turned black as it arched through the air, the poison was so fast acting.

"There's nothing you can do!" Liz yelled as the Indians jumped forward to help. "Stay away from him!"

Her warning was too late as one of the men got splashed by some of Charlie's blood. It was barely a drop on his arm, but it caused his arm to immediately turn black. He stood there looking at it in shock as the skin dissolved and the bones began to show. I was sure that was the end of him, but Stormbreaker had the presence of mind to whip out his machete and slash the poor fellow's arm right off.

He let out a scream as he saw his forearm drop to the ground, but by the time it hit, only the bones and some rapidly liquefying flesh were left. Stormbreaker and one of the other men grabbed him and wrapped a belt around the bleeding stub.

"We've got to get him to the hospital," Stormy said. "Bull, you and Mad Crow take that Caddy over there and drive him into town for help. Bull, keep him from loosening the tourniquet. Crow, you drive like hell."

Rudy spoke up, pointing, "It's not very far back that way and the hospital is easy to find."

The men grabbed the moaning victim and hustled him into the car. They took off in a cloud of dust on their mercy run.

Stormbreaker looked at the remaining two Shoshone. "Still game?" he asked in about as grim a tone of voice as I've ever heard.

"Damn straight," one of them said. The other didn't say anything, he simply contented himself with picking up Charlie's AR-10 and shoving some more .308 cartridges into its nearly depleted magazine.

Stormbreaker said, "Get the other rifles and those alien guns. We're going to need them." Then he turned and started towards the barn.

"Wait!" I exclaimed. I was watching Jefferson. He was slowly approaching the barn, bristled out as much as before.

"There are still some in there," Liz said, excitedly.

We all moved forward on either side of the door to more easily avoid another rush.

"Don't shoot each other," Rudy cautioned.

"We weren't born yesterday, paleface," Stormbreaker muttered.

I peeped around the corner and saw a couple of the creatures moving near the back of the structure. There were two AK shots and the things shattered. No more appeared, so we moved carefully into the barn.

It was hard to see in there. There were some holes in the roof that let beams of light shine down into the gloom. Dust motes drifted in the shafts of light. The whole place smelled of dust, moldy hay, and dried manure. The contrast between the dim barn and the brilliant rays of light made it difficult to see.

Jefferson let out a yowl and there was a rush of scrabbling creatures from the back-right stall. We fired until there were none in that group left alive.

While we were looking at the dead creatures, Liz heard some clicking from the hay mow and shot two moving shadows that were preparing to leap off at us. We looked at each other. Except for the light breeze blowing around the corner of the door and the sound of some distant crows cussing at a hawk, all was silent.

"The transporter we came in on is in the back left stall. Spread out and look for the other one and be careful. There might be some spiders left," I ordered as I turned to look in the front stall.

Directly, Joe called, "It's over here in the feed room. It's all clear."

We gathered in front of the door and Liz pressed the call button. The door snapped open.

"We're going into Estes Park from here," I said. "Get ready, because they will be there, somewhere. We may have to shoot our way in."

"And, out!" muttered Colin in a thicker brogue than usual.

31

WICHITA

Something was wrong with the transporter system or the map. We didn't end up in Estes Park. We came out in an airplane hanger in an airport on East Central in Wichita, Kansas. The small airport was part of an aircraft manufacturing facility, but we didn't stick around to look. None of us were in the market for an airplane anyway.

We immediately tried to use the single button in the transporter to return to Loveland, but it didn't work. Nothing happened when we pushed it. We tried repeatedly but had no luck.

Liz said, "It looks like they're onto us. They must have rerouted the Loveland transporter to here and turned off the return link."

"Have you ever seen that happen before?" I asked her, hoping that she knew some way to turn it back on.

"No. I haven't and you probably know just about as much about the transporter system as I do, by now," she retorted.

This started me thinking. To this point, the Pugs hadn't used technology the way humans would. I'd have a monitoring system that kept careful track of every use of a transporter. I didn't think that they'd been doing that, because, if they had, they would have caught us easily. Perhaps they simply viewed the system as unlikely to be discovered or maybe they thought so little of us that they didn't believe we could operate it. In any event, despite the ability they'd shown in apparently hacking into our communications feeds of various types, they didn't apply simple computerized tech the way we would.

I finally quit speculating on the problem. They were alien to us after all and they apparently didn't utilize the same mental processes we did. Mentally shrugging my shoulders, I pulled out the map and we unfolded it between us. The rest of the group gathered close as we looked at the Wichita area.

"Look! There's a set of portals in a mini-warehouse off Hillside Avenue about a quarter mile north of the University. Let's head for them," I said.

Rudy and I sneaked out of the hanger and located a couple of unattended blue SUVs in a nearby parking lot. We had them in front of the hanger in short order. Both of them had three rows of seats, but we were still a little crowded with our group and the weapons. Rudy's group stayed together with most of the kit and the remaining Indians rode with Liz and me.

Jefferson had a bit of an objection to the extra people. He seemed to think that his usual rear window lookout space was being infringed upon by the three. After pacing around while crawling over everyone in the process, he finally settled down on Liz's lap.

We went west on Central until we hit Hillside and then turned north. The traffic was light and the stoplights seemed to be all green as we approached, so it only took about fifteen minutes before we were parked in the back of the warehouse. There was a muddy parking lot there. It had been graveled at one time, but the gravel had sunk into the earth, leaving only the mud from a recent rain. We got out and stretched momentarily before unloading our stuff.

The warehouse building was one of those strip-type structures that are seen in poorer commercial or light industrial areas. It was a metal building with a flat, sloped, metal roof and it had five bays that opened in the direction of the street. The parking lot entrance was on the west side of the building and the bay doors opened on the east side facing a narrow asphalt drive that provided access to them. It didn't look prosperous or busy, most likely because the Pugs were using it.

Jefferson immediately went over towards the warehouse building and showed his usual signs of having detected Pugs. He slunk around with his hair bushed out making low growling noises as if he were looking for something to fight. He finally slid between the side of the building and some tall weeds, and stayed there, half-hidden.

We rushed to get our weapons out and divided into two groups. One group headed around the building's north end and the other the south one.

Just as we got to the front corner, the warehouse doors opened and about fifty Pugs came out.

We were immediately in a heated battle with splinters going everywhere. We shot around the corners at the Pugs. They retreated inside the doors and fired back steadily. This wasn't getting anywhere and seemed likely to result in a standoff until they were able to summon more help.

In the midst of the confusion, a policeman came wheeling up, stopped his car on the street and jumped out with his pistol in hand. He seemed confused about what was going on and pointed the gun in our general direction. He could see us hovering around the south corner of the building and he decided that we were the troublemakers. The Pugs shot him just after he yelled, "Drop your weapons on the ground!"

He slowly turned towards the open bay doors holding the Pugs and then simply toppled over. There were two cars driving by at the time, but they sped up, not wanting to be involved. I hoped that they'd keep that impulse in their mind and not immediately phone for more police. We didn't need the complications, having our hands full at the moment.

We hadn't realized that there was a regular entrance door facing the street at the south end of the complex. We'd been shooting right past it, but one of the Pugs got a bright idea and opened it just in time to put a splinter into one of our Shoshone friends as he leaned out to shoot.

He was the brother of the other Shoshone, who despite Stormbreaker's hasty order to stop, immediately jumped around the corner and rushed the door. He got inside and shot the Pug that had gotten his brother and maybe a couple more, but almost immediately after going through the door, he staggered out backwards and fell dead.

Stormbreaker looked as if he was about to rush them also, but I grabbed him and said, "Wait! I've got an idea."

We hadn't used the eraser guns to this point, because they seemed to be a little too destructive, but this was a dangerous situation. I thought I might be able to blow through the back into the building and surprise the Pugs. I didn't want to damage any of the transporters inside, but something really needed to be done quickly.

I raced back to the SUV and grabbed one of the anti-matter rifles that had been left in the back. We'd been carrying the two weapons, dutifully, but we hadn't had an opportunity to use them. As I said, they seemed to be a little too destructive and too hard to limit their effect to use in a limited firefight.

I spun around and triggered it off at the back of the building near the south end with gratifying results. Most of the Pugs had clustered at that end of the building, preparing to rush us and the disintegration of the back wall caught them by surprise. When the wall crackled and then faded from view, it left the group of Pugs looking towards the front door of the warehouse.

I swept the gun over the tight group and the Pugs also disappeared with a crackling sound. I was aiming a little high and that somehow managed to leave their lower halves hanging around, but that wasn't the dangerous end, so I didn't mind. The disconnected legs flopped and twitched a bit, but the Pugs and their guns were no longer a threat.

There were still some combat noises coming from the north end of the building as I carefully checked inside the bay holding the Pugs' legs. There were some internal partitions between each warehouse bay and I burned through the next one to the north. There was nothing in there but some motorcycles and parts. I picked my way through the motorcycles and then disintegrated a door-sized hole through the wall.

The next bay held a paint booth and a couple of Pugs, but they disappeared with a sweep of the gun. Unfortunately, that sweep also opened part of the wall into the last bay. That alerted the few that were left in the final room.

They'd been clustered near the door and had missed being erased, so they started shooting at me, recognizing that I posed an immediate threat. Since I hadn't seen any transporters in the rest of the building, I thought it was safe to assume that they were in the room with the remaining Pugs. Not wanting to damage the transporter, I used the splinter gun while ducking behind various obstructions. We poofed back and forth for a bit with no result.

Suddenly, Rudy and his guys appeared around the corner of the open bay door and there was a burst of splinters that finished off the Pugs.

I yelled for Liz and Stormy to come up and they came running through the shell of the building behind me, along with Jefferson. When we entered the final bay of the warehouse, there was a single portal there. I thought for sure there were supposed to be more. Perhaps I'd dissolved them coming through the building.

I panted, "We can't wait around. I'm not sure where it goes, but let's just take it and get out of here."

We all piled in and ended up in a hotel's conference center in San Diego.

32

Split up in San Diego

As Liz and Stormbreaker were coming through the cleared-out office of the warehouse complex, she'd somehow had the time to take a look at a desk. There were some papers there and one of them had a hand-sketched map of part of the transporter network.

It was actually a cheap road map of the United States with some inked lines on it. It looked like the Pugs were very like us in some ways. One of them didn't trust his memory and had made some notes that showed how the network had been reconfigured.

When we came out of the transporter from Wichita, we were standing in a narrow room in our new location, wondering where we were. The room looked like a hotel conference room. I'd been in many of these and this one was nice, with large chandeliers hanging from the ornate ceiling. The movable walls had been configured to make this space about fifty by one hundred feet. We looked around suspiciously, but the place was quiet and empty. It was dimly lighted in the fashion that the Pugs preferred. There were a couple of doors marked 'Exit' on the far wall. There were also two other transporters, one on each side of the transporter we'd come through.

We could faintly hear some kind of meeting going on in one of the other rooms, but this one was currently vacant. It's a good thing it was, because I'm fairly certain that our appearance, loaded with weapons, would have completely disrupted any get-rich-quick conference speaker, no matter how polished his presentation.

We were all relieved when Liz pulled out the marked-up road map. With a little study we were able to see that the link to Loveland had been rerouted and Wichita now only led to San Diego. The other two Wichita transporters hadn't survived my use of the eraser gun, so whether or not they'd been rerouted was a moot point. However, it looked as if one of them would have returned us to Loveland while the other had been linked to somewhere in the general vicinity of Eldora, close to Boulder. Blast it all!

It was bad luck and we agreed that the eraser gun was a mixed blessing. It got rid of things quickly and irrevocably, but the bad part was that it was too indiscriminate. Unless you were very lucky, you'd end up destroying your target including everything around it.

Looking at the modified map led us to conclude that we were in a hotel near the Embarcadero in San Diego. We didn't know which one, until Joe came up with a piece of hotel stationary that was left in a wastebasket. It didn't really matter, though, because we weren't planning on staying overnight. Nice though the place might be, we wanted to leave immediately.

We realized that the Pugs must now be alerted to our presence, since they'd felt the need to reroute the system to stop us. Because we didn't have any way to shut off the transporters I was worried that they might send a group after us. As a result, I felt an overwhelming urge to get us out of the hotel as rapidly as possible.

The road map had some notations on it in squiggles, but of course we couldn't make anything out of them, so that was no help. We were reduced to carefully studying the diagrams that were drawn on it. The key was obvious, once we started paying attention.

The door we'd come through was in the middle of a line of three transporter doors and looking at the map, we were able to see the line linking it directly back to Wichita. The hand-drawn line from our exit door led to one of three small boxes in Wichita that I presumed were in the warehouse. There were three San Diego boxes marked on the map and they obviously represented the transporters directly in front of us in the conference room.

When we traced the links to the other two San Diego boxes we found that one linked to Carlsbad, New Mexico, but the other one linked directly to Estes Park. Now we were getting somewhere!

The Pugs still needed that Estes connection, since it led to the only transporter link that went off-planet to Titan. From what we'd been able to understand from the maps and booklet, Titan was their only entry point to our solar system. Rather than shutting down transporters that led to Estes, they'd simply used a little misdirection to mess up our plans by changing the links.

Judging from the speed at which they'd re-routed the links, they were able to make on-the-fly changes to the network. This concerned us, because, if that were true, they could easily change all of the routes and render our maps useless. We decided we'd better move quickly into our attack, before they decided to take that step.

Liz said, "If it were me, I'd wait until I was sure that my enemies were approaching through the network before I changed it. If you go and make changes needlessly, you're simply going to cause a huge disruption to your own forces and I don't think they can notify all of their people quickly. They seem to be largely self-directed and only work in loose coordination."

We faced the three transporter doors and compared them to the drawing. It looked like the Estes one was on the left, while the Carlsbad one was on the far right.

In order to better study the maps, we'd converged on a small table that was located about twenty feet from the wall with the transporter doors and at the far end of the room from the normal entrance door. This meant that the Estes transporter link was the farthest away from where we were standing. That turned out to be a problem.

Just as we'd finished our map studies and had folded the maps in preparation to move out, the center transporter dinged and then opened to reveal a full load of Pugs.

I didn't think that the Pugs in Wichita had enough time to call for help, but they might have or it might have been the first Pug we'd seen in Loveland. He had retreated into the house by the barn and while he was getting the bolt shooter, he might have signaled for back up. Since there were only two ways out of the barn location, Lander and Wichita, the Pug back-up team might have divided in half. Either way, the ones facing us had transferred through from Wichita surprisingly fast, considering the necessity of driving to the warehouse location. They came out of the door angry and wanting revenge on whoever had killed their fellows.

It got nasty really fast. We didn't have any cover or other place to hide and they were ready to shoot. Thinking rapidly, Colin and Stormbreaker tipped the table over and we all crouched behind it as a perfect hail of splinters broke against the front.

The space behind the table was too tight and I suddenly noticed that Chandra's leg was dangerously near the edge. As I reached for him to pull him closer, he was hit in the calf. He stiffened and gagged. I knew that he was dead right then even though he was still moving.

I felt bad about it, but there was nothing I could do. He was jerking around from the toxin and gasping his last. I rolled over, put my feet on his chest and shoved him out into plain view of the Pugs in a last-ditch attempt to distract them.

The Pugs seemed to sometimes lack the judgment that makes humans so dangerous. Rather than continuing to shoot at us, they immediately focused on his spasms and shot him repeatedly. Splinters struck all over his head, face and shoulders, making him practically dissolve into a puddle of blood and gore.

While they were amusing themselves and feeling good about shooting one of us, I slid over to the other end of the table, crawling over the prone men and Liz, who was trying her hardest to hold onto the enraged and squalling cat.

When I reached the other end, I rolled out into plain view and fired the eraser gun simultaneously. The Pugs vanished with a crackle as did the surface of the wall behind them. It looked like I'd grazed the middle transporter framework, but the door was still there and it could become active any moment. I thought about wiping it off the wall, but I was afraid that I'd hit some necessary part of the electronics of the other portals. They were that close together.

"Let's get the Hell out of here," I shouted and everyone ran for the Estes link. I lagged behind to grab Jefferson from Liz and that slowed us up enough for the rest of the guys to get ahead.

When I grabbed for the cat, he wriggled and slipped out of my grasp. He ran directly towards the wall adjacent to the Carlsbad transporter with Liz and I chasing him, while the other men ran towards the Estes door.

I caught up with Jefferson near the Carlsbad door. I was trying to get hold of him and as I did, another group of Pugs came out of the still operational Wichita link. This must have been the other half of their response team, that had found nothing in Lander or it might have been reinforcements from somewhere in Wichita. Regardless of their origin, the rotten luck was that they had come through in time to cut us off.

Liz and I had absolutely no cover, so we were forced to jump into the Carlsbad transporter. She had slapped the call button when the center transporter became active for the second time. The Carlsbad door opened just in time for us to miss being riddled with splinters. As it was, some of the projectiles broke on the door framework as the door closed.

I held Jefferson and Liz grabbed my arm as the walls wavered and then when the wavering stopped, the door popped open and we were facing a dark cavern. I expected the Pugs to be right on our heels and we moved quickly to the right of the door. When it slid shut, the cavern was pitch black.

33

Rudy--The Stanley Hotel

The rest of the team and I watched Dec and Liz hop in the door nearest to them. Luckily most of the Pugs were looking their way as they came out of the middle door. This gave us a chance to shoot five of them immediately. The splinter-guns were too deadly to take chances with and we were happy for the opportunity to shoot them in the back before they could return the fire. That left two more and they weren't so anxious to die. They jumped back into the still open middle door. Colin yelled, "Rudy, hit the button. Let's get out of here!"

By chance, I was standing right beside the transporter door and I did as he'd said and pushed the Estes Park call button. This time the blasted thing seemed to take forever to come. I guess it was quick, but time seems to slow down when people are shooting at you.

Meanwhile, one of the two surviving Pugs tried to stick his head out low, about a foot from the floor to shoot at us, but Joe got him before he could shoot. That left one and he suddenly got the idea that he'd be a lot healthier if he simply went back to Wichita. The door shut and he was gone.

Joe observed, "That means trouble will be following us shortly. He'll call for help."

The Estes Park transporter interrupted us as it dinged and opened. There were two more of the dratted creatures standing there. Colin had his gun already pointed that way, just in case this happened and he killed them instantly.

This was getting a little too interesting. None of my crew minded a good firefight, but the addition of the deadly splinters made it seem even more serious than high velocity lead. With a normal human weapon, a man has a chance of being shot and living through it. With these things, not so much.

We were unhappy about Chandra. He'd been part of our team for years. It seemed a little cruel of Dec to push him out to be shot, but I realized that he was dying and couldn't be helped. Even so, Colin was cursing Dec under his breath. I told him that Dec wasn't to blame. Chandra had gotten careless, but I could see that he'd probably still take it up with Dec the next time they met.

I made a mental note to keep a precautionary eye on that situation. Colin was like a lot of Irish. He made a great friend and an even worse enemy. He would never stop fighting until he had won or was dead. I didn't want him and Dec to come to blows, if they did, I'd probably have to pick up the pieces and I might be missing at least one friend.

We piled into the Estes transporter and in a moment, we'd gone through, but we weren't quite ready for where we came out. We were prepared for a fight, but we came out of a closet marked "Janitor" on the second floor of the Stanley Hotel.

There was no one in sight. The dimly lit corridor was very quiet, with dust motes floating in the air. The row of closed doors along the hall made my hair stand on end. Pugs could come out of any of them at any time.

I glanced across the corridor and saw room 237. I half expected a Pug to suddenly chop through the door with an ax and wildly shout, "Here's Johnny!" After a moment, I got control of my mind and realized that I was fantasizing about a movie and not actual Pugs.

I could hear some noise that sounded like talking from the back courtyard, but it seemed hushed. The sound was floating in through a partially open window in the stairwell. It sounded a little like human speech. I wondered how people would be able to survive around a place that was most likely full of Pugs, but I shelved that mystery for later. Perhaps they were collaborators or maybe captives.

We checked both directions then went around the nearby corner and headed down the ornate stairs that led to the main floor. As we got to the lobby, the first thing we saw was an antique Stanley Steamer sitting in one corner. The second thing we noticed was that the three staff members, two behind the front desk and a bellman were all Pugs. True, they were concealed with realistic human faces, but we responded quickly when they pointed guns at us.

We were totally amped up on adrenaline and they didn't have a chance.

I'd noticed that as fast as the Pugs were, their reaction time was still a little slower than that of an aroused human. Given an equal start at drawing and shooting, a trained human operator would walk away nine times out of ten. It was only when they surprised us or outnumbered us that they had the advantage with guns.

We were getting ready to congratulate ourselves for having finished those guys off when another Pug jumped down the stairs and landed on my back. He didn't have any weapon, so he attacked with fists and teeth.

The creature hit me like a ton of bricks. They weren't as heavy as us, but he'd leaped down the entire staircase in one jump and had a lot of momentum. They weren't quite as fast as us, but they were definitely stronger. They didn't look it, since their musculature was smooth, giving them a sleek look, but this one was a real handful.

I'm not as good as Dec in hand-to-hand. We rolled across the floor with the Pug trying to keep me between him and the rest of my crew who were trying to aim their guns in his direction. We were moving too rapidly for them to have a sure shot. Joe said later that we reminded him of a whirlwind with teeth and fists flying out of it.

I kept pounding on the Pug's face, but it wasn't doing any good, even when I got in two, really hard, elbow strikes. The creature was incredibly tough.

As we rolled under a grand piano, I somehow got hold of his upper lip without being bitten. He had no compunction about using his teeth either. He'd been trying to bite me in the neck the whole time. Dec says he's seen them eating people, so I guessed that he thought I might be a very difficult lunch.

I yanked on his lip and his face split away from his skull. It seemed like an actual human face, but there was a synthetic layer under it that sealed off his true skin from the atmosphere. This synthetic layer tore as I pulled and he let out a shriek. He continued to fight, but now it seemed like he was fighting to escape rather than to kill me. I got into a full mount position and started raining down elbows on his head. The face tore fully off with the third really hard strike I made.

His skin was bubbling from contact with our air. It looked horrible and I jumped up and backed away as he thrashed back and forth. The skin of his face dissolved and melted through the underlying supporting structure. His skull didn't look like bone; instead it looked somewhat like brown cartilage or a heavy, leather-like material. He suddenly quit moving and I saw that he was dead.

"Wow! That guy was tough," I gasped. Colin replied, "Remind me never to get in fight with you. You play dirty!"

Stormbreaker had been mostly silent, since we lost the last of his friends, but he came over and put his hand on my shoulder and said, "You can fight on my side any day, paleface!"

As I recovered, I said, "The next thing we have to do is to locate the transporter head that leads off the planet. It's likely to be heavily guarded. I don't know why there aren't more Pugs in this place, but – "

I was interrupted by Joe, who'd been looking out the front door, "We'd better move now, there looks like about a hundred of them coming up the front steps!"

34

CARLSBAD

Liz and I came out in a dark cave. The place echoed weirdly when we spoke and even more so when Jefferson let out a meow. We immediately reduced our volume to whispers in case there was something lurking in the darkness that might hear us.

We couldn't see anything and it really freaked us out for a moment. Then I remembered that I still had one of the high-intensity lasers in a belt clip. I pulled it and adjusted it to its broadest beam, shining it around to examine our surroundings.

There was no doubt that we were in a cave. There were stalagmites rising from the floor with corresponding stalactites pointing down from overhead. There was a large curtain-like formation in the distance and when I looked down, there were bat skeletons lying around on the floor. I could hear water dripping in the near distance and the air was a cool sixty degrees or so with high humidity.

This was a part of the cave where people didn't normally come. There were no pathways for tourists, but after looking around for a little, we did find some strips of yellow plastic tied around stalagmites, obviously put there as markers.

We set off following from marker to marker and soon crossed the room. It was a little over one-hundred feet in width, so it didn't take long, even though the floor was uneven and the footing was slippery. As we approached the far wall of the room, a dark hole came into view in the wall. The markers led directly to that hole.

I whispered to Liz, "Here, hold Jefferson. I'm going ahead to check that opening. It may be the way out."

She took the cat, who'd been very quiet. I started towards the hole, when Liz quietly said, "Watch yourself! Jefferson is bristling up."

I looked back and saw that she'd put him down and his hair was standing up on his back and his tail looked like a bottle brush.

"Get your gun out and put him down! We're in for more spiders unless I'm misreading him." I followed up on my instructions by pulling my splinter-shooter and readying it. I still had my .45, but I was low on ammunition and it was so confined in the cave that I was fearful of letting it off. The explosion would have probably deafened both of us.

Liz pulled her splinter gun and started to unsling the eraser gun which she'd been carrying since we entered the cavern. I motioned her to stay there and observed that Jefferson was crouched at her feet, trying to look fierce while attempting fruitlessly to keep his feet dry in the moist environment.

Listening carefully for the spiders' clicking and rustling noise, I approached the opening. There wasn't a sound.

I kept close watch for moving shadows and walked closer. As I reached the dark opening, a huge shape lurched out, scrabbling in my direction while emitting a moaning, multi-toned shriek with a disconcerting beat frequency.

Liz screamed in response and at the same time Jefferson let out a screech and darted off into the darkness.

I had my splinter gun up and was poofing away, but the creature didn't seem to be very vulnerable as some of my shots skidded off its hard carapace. We'd seen one of these things in DC and it had proven to be hard to kill there, confined in a cage as it was. This one was jumping around violently due to the splinter-gun's toxin, but it still came towards me with evil intent. All of its movement made a killing shot right down the mouth even harder.

I backed up and dodged behind a massive stalagmite as it reached me. That was nearly a fatal mistake. It reached around both sides of the stone formation with its front appendages dripping some noxious fluid from the claw tips. I reasoned that if it were related to the spiders, the fluid would be deadly and I rapidly backed around a nearby, second stone column that was nearly as large as the first.

The thing gave up its effort to reach me and came around the first stalagmite, but it hung up as it tried to go between the two. It moaned again so loudly that I felt almost paralyzed by fright. Then it rapidly moved around the second column. As it came, I could see that my splinters had eaten holes in its carapace, but that wasn't slowing it down.

It made a lunge at me and I jumped back. As I landed, my foot went in a hole beside the first column and I ended up flat on my back on the rocky floor. It moaned in a lower tone and moved towards me more slowly as if convinced that I couldn't get away. As it neared me, I could see its dull eye pits focused on my chest and it raised its front legs for a killing strike.

At that juncture, Jefferson leaped out of nowhere and landed on my leg. It didn't help that he had all of his claws out at the time, but the creature actually backed up slightly as the cat screeched his battle cry. It moaned again, louder and raised its front legs, flexing the claws back and forth. What would have happened next was mercifully forestalled by a crackling noise as the entire rear of the creature's body dissolved.

Liz had finally gotten the eraser gun unslung and into play.

Jefferson leaped off of my leg and disappeared again as the front of the thing collapsed. It made a couple of twitches with its remaining legs and then all was still, except for the cat who was still making a throaty growling from the darkness somewhere nearby.

I shakily climbed to my feet and made a wide path around the remains of the creature.

"Keep that weapon out and ready, in case there are more of those things in here," I managed to stammer out.

Liz let out a kind of shaky laugh and said, "Now you really owe me one." Her voice wasn't very steady either.

"You can collect any time," I responded.

"I thought for a moment that I wouldn't be able to," she breathed. "Don't take risks like that again!"

"Don't be mad at me! I didn't know the thing was going to jump out like that!" I responded.

"Well, don't do it again, anyway!"

You simply can't get the last word in with most women and she was one of them. I shook my head in agreement and turned to get the light.

My laser was lying on the floor, still illuminating a large part of the cavern with its bright light. I retrieved it and we circumnavigated the creature's corpse again and approached the dark opening. As we reached the opening, Liz cried, "Jefferson!"

We couldn't hear him any longer and no matter how much we called, he wouldn't come. We spent a long while trying to find him, but it was no use. He'd disappeared.

We had spent more time than I thought we had, being afraid that some more Pugs would follow us through. After nearly thirty minutes we finally gave up.

I tried to reassure her, but didn't have much luck, "He can find us anytime. Cats can see in the dark and he's probably waiting until he feels secure. I'm sure he knows where we are."

"Oh, Dec! He's our kitty and he's... This is a horrible place! I hate caves!"

She was distraught, but we had to move on, we felt like the future of the world depended on us. In my mind, I realized that if we were the world's only hope, it had a pretty slim hope of salvation.

We both felt miserable. Losing Jefferson was, in some mysterious way, a real blow, but we couldn't wait any longer.

After one last look around the room, we entered the dark opening.

35

Eggs!

The next room in the cave was much smaller. We could easily see across it and it appeared to be only about the size of an average living room. It was filled with formations, though, and that made for quite a number of pockets and hiding spaces that we couldn't immediately verify were empty.

We moved slowly to the approximate center of the room. It was difficult since the floor here was not as sandy as in the larger room. It was wet and floored with limestone deposits that were slippery and covered with some kind of slime.

As we stood there, I thought I heard something. It wasn't more of the moaning that our late antagonist made, but sounded like someone talking at a distance. I briefly turned off the laser and, as our eyes adapted to the darkness, we turned around slowly.

The combination of the silence and the heavy, velvet darkness was frightening. Humans are visual beings and an environment with no discernible light is unsettling. Add silence to the darkness and it immediately becomes far worse. We could hear drips of water coming down from the ceiling in the distance, but the faint patter made the sense of unease greater.

Despite our disorientation, the tactic actually worked well. At a certain point in our rotation, we were able to see a very dim glow that came from behind a thin curtain of limestone. I switched our light back on and we started to move in that direction. The glow was so faint that we'd never have been able to sense it with the light on.

We were unable to take a direct path and had to detour around some rough areas that would have proven harder to climb over than circumnavigate. As we clambered over the slippery stone and around the stalagmites, we came to a sand-filled depression in the floor that housed what appeared to be a nest of eggs. They were brown and about the size and shape of a football. I looked at Liz and she had her knuckles held to her mouth in horror.

"It looks like that thing that attacked us was a mother," I observed. "It must have come in here to lay these eggs."

"It's not that," she gasped. "It's what might hatch out of them that is freaking me out!"

I turned back and looked closer. The shells were not brittle and hard like bird eggs but more leathery, like reptile eggs. I tentatively poked one with the toe of my boot and saw the creature inside move slightly in response.

Liz gasped again, "We've got to smash these. We can't have more of those monsters hatching out in here."

I reached to the back of my belt and removed the knife that I carry there. It's handy for fighting and I keep it razor sharp. Carefully, I sliced at the egg and the casing cut with some difficulty. As it opened, we could see movement and then a pair of insect-like arms came out, followed in short order by the rest of the creature. It was weak and unable to move easily, which was fortunate.

Liz said, "Why, it's one of the spider-things! They must be the immature form of the bear-sized things. These are going to grow huge and – " She paused for a moment in shock, then exclaimed, "Oh crap! Think of all of the spiders we've seen!"

"Crap is right!" I answered. "We're going to be up to our eyeballs in those things before long. Judging from what we've seen of them, the bear-sized creatures might be the Pugs' answer to how to get rid of all humans. They're really difficult to kill and one of them would make hash out of any number of conventionally armed men."

"The Pugs might be waiting for a huge crop of the big creatures to develop and then they'll release them on the populace as shock troops." Liz was speculating, but it was probably a pretty good speculation. I really hoped that she wasn't correct.

"We can't do anything about that right now, but we can squish these little bastards!" I said as I gritted my teeth and smashed the spider with a handy stone. It was starting to exhibit more strength and didn't look like it was going to hang around forever waiting while we discussed its life cycle.

Some of the rest of the eggs were moving slightly and suddenly a pair of legs erupted from one. It looked like they were going to hatch right at that moment. I thought about shooting them with the splinters, but realized that we should preserve our ammunition, so we both searched frantically for loose rocks. There were several broken limestone formations around the hole; perhaps a result of the mother creature's movements. We rapidly picked up stones and bashed the life out of the eggs.

As we crushed the brown eggs, some of them released a nasty odor. It grew worse the more we smashed. Quite a few of them were obviously rotten and had no hope of hatching, but several of the leathery things burst open and the immature spiders started staggering towards us, clicking their mandibles. Working as fast as we could, we crushed them all.

We verified that all of the eggs were broken and then started working our way towards the formation where we'd seen the glow. As we moved across the floor, we were horrified to see three more eggs that had rolled around an intervening formation. Two of them had obviously hatched and the spiders were not in view. The other was making determined motions as if it were on the verge of breaking out.

Having no convenient rock, I simply stomped on the unhatched egg. It broke and the creature inside was crushed. I didn't want to think about what I might have on the bottom of my foot, so I scuffed it back and forth against the dry sand.

Liz grabbed my arm and said, "Look, there's no time for that. Those other eggs hatched long enough ago for the spiders to be able to move away. They're probably strong enough to fight now and we know they can move rapidly. We can't stay here, one of them might be stalking us as we speak."

"You're right! Let's get going," I agreed.

We rounded the limestone curtain formation and saw that it covered an opening. I ducked down and there were a couple of ropes secured to the limestone with steel pitons. The ropes led downward into a hole and, on closer inspection, turned out to be a rope ladder.

"Someone's been up here and this is the way out," I told Liz.

We slid into the hole, arranged ourselves on the ladder and started down, Liz leading. After we had descended a few yards, the passage opened up and we could see that we were dropping down into a huge cavern.

This was the more frequented part of the cave, because we could see fixed lights off in the distance and a group of tourists moving down a path towards our position. We climbed down as fast as was safe, reaching the bottom of the ladder long before the tourist group got near. They'd stopped to listen to the guide discuss the cave's features.

"Liz, let's not make a fuss with these people. It won't help and the ranger would probably want to detain us. Let's just stay out of sight and then follow them from a distance," I said.

We moved behind another curtain formation and waited. It didn't take too long before they stopped right in front of us. We listened as the guide said, "We're below the most recent discovery in the cave. We're in the Big Room right now. In 1985, balloons were used to attach a rope to a formation above and the rooms that compose what are called The Spirit-World were discovered. Most recently, in 2013, an explorer found a large room in that hidden section that he dubbed "Halloween Hall," since it was found in October. It's about a hundred feet in diameter." He paused and then said, "Now please follow me."

We trailed along for a bit, until we could see the Underground Lunch Room at the head of the Left Hand Tunnel that connected to the Big Room. There were elevators there and we waited in the shadows until the tour group had moved on. There were other people about and additional tour groups, so we watched for the largest break we could see and then dashed over to the elevators.

I really didn't want to have to discuss our weapons with any nosy park rangers, so we tried our best to keep them shielded from view. There were a few other self-guided groups about and we figured that we weren't too out-of-place, at least until someone got a really close look at us.

In short order, we were up in the above ground Visitor Center and happy to be there. We slipped outside in a crush of visitors. The only persons who questioned us were two small girls who saw the eraser gun on Liz's shoulder.

The girls looked remarkably similar and I figured they were sisters, but they seemed to have two different sets of parents. The situation resolved itself when the father of one of the girls asked the other girl's mother, "Hey, Sis, where are we supposed to meet the guide?"

Lagging behind their parents, the two girls goggled at Liz and the long gun. The younger of the two asked Liz, "Is that some kind of gun, Lady?"

Liz smiled and said, "Yes, but it's to stun bats for easy capture. We're scientists and we are studying the bat population of the cave."

This explanation seemed to be perfect, because the girl's father grabbed her arm and admonished both of them, "Now Hazel, you and Rowan better not bother the scientists. They're really busy with scientific stuff."

They walked off and it was just in time, since Liz had to use the rest room. She looped around and went into the facility. In a little longer than I thought it should take, she came out with a grin.

"There's a transporter head in there!" she exclaimed. She'd found it inside a large, janitor closet at the back of the main rest room. "There are two here according to the map, but we'd have to keep searching to find the second one. It looks like it might be some distance away, see here!"

She used the map and pointed out the location in the bathroom. The transporter had one connection to someplace in the Yucatan, but the other one went to Loveland. When we inspected the second Carlsbad transporter location on the map, I observed that both of the connecting lines led to locations that didn't seem useful. One went to India and the other to Spain. I didn't try to puzzle out where exactly. We didn't really need to know.

"Come on, let's go. I think that the restroom might be empty now," she said.

"Well, I'll just have to act like a woman," I grinned.

"No chance of that! You wouldn't fool anyone," she assured me. "But, don't worry, I've thought of everything. I'll chase all of the women out and we'll put the 'Closed for Cleaning' sign that I found in the closet at the entrance door."

I took her hand and said, "You continue to amaze me. I'm ..." A sudden realization hit my mind. I hadn't really understood it before, being, like many men, somewhat out-of-touch with my feelings. I paused, gulped and said, "I... Look, I'm not used to saying things like this, but I think I – "

She stepped closer and pressed her freshly washed finger against my lips, "I know. I love you too. Now let's go. We can talk this over when we get somewhere safe."

I was shocked; so that's what I was feeling! I loved her! It had just sort-of sneaked up on me. I'd known that she was very dear to me and that I was ready to do anything to protect her, but I hadn't actually put a word to it. The worst part was I also didn't know when we'd have time to talk about it, since it looked like the whole world wasn't safe.

We turned towards the rest room just as a group of women entered. I sighed, resigning myself to waiting.

36

Jefferson

T he battle-scarred warrior, for that was how he viewed himself, moved silently into a small pocket in the rocks. It was dark, but his eyes were very sensitive and he was able to make out most of the details of his environment. He was still angry. The big moaning thing had intended to kill his people.

He'd been independent most of his life and had resisted getting too close to any humans, but something about the big man was attractive to him. The very first time he saw them in the subway tunnel, the tone of the big man's voice made him feel that he'd met another warrior. He immediately wanted to be part of their pride.

They'd fed him, carried him with them and he'd rubbed the scent glands in his cheeks on them until they were his exclusively. They even knew what to call him. He readily accepted the name 'Jefferson' as his, realizing that it was their word for 'stealthy-battle-scarred-warrior'. As far as he was concerned, the two of them belonged to him and he was ready to fight to protect them.

Right now, he could hear some quiet, clicking sounds in the rocks over to the right. The noise didn't puzzle him. It was one of the spiders. He had survived enough encounters with them in the subway and later to know their ways and he realized that it was stalking the two humans as they made their way into the other, smaller room.

He was well aware that the two wanted him to come, but he knew that, if he did, he'd lose the opportunity to surprise the stalking spider. They called him for a long time and moved around looking for him, but fortunately, they didn't come close enough to the spider to give it the chance to ambush either of them.

The spiders would rush if there were a large group of them and they would attack directly if they were cornered or desperate, but they were reluctant to attack boldly if the odds were against them. He didn't think about it in exactly that way, of course. His mental processes were more elementary than that. He simply categorized the spiders as cowards.

He heard Dec and Liz stop and crush the eggs in the smaller room and, although he didn't know what they were killing, he recognized the sound of violence and was satisfied when he heard the crunch of one of the spider's hard parts. He knew he could depend on them to fight and fight well.

The stealthy spider was moving closer to the entrance to the nest room and he needed to do something about that situation. He silently moved out of the pocket and around the formation that concealed him. Padding swiftly with a sensation of anger rising in anticipation of the coming attack, he moved closer to the spider.

It didn't sense him. He knew the things were good at seeing motion, but they seemed to be unable to hear well and were totally unable to smell. He kept out of its sight until he was able to slip around in front of it by running up a slanted rock.

The rock overhung the path to the entrance of the next room. The spider thing was approaching more rapidly, now that the humans were out of sight. The Warrior crouched lower as his intended prey approached.

His attention was momentarily distracted as his keen ears made out the sound of a second hiding spider. It was in the room in front of him and was currently cowering from the humans as they destroyed the eggs.

He realized that his attack would have to be silent, so he could stalk the second spider without it knowing he was there. He refocused on the approaching creature and, as it reached the optimum spot, he silently elevated into the air, propelled by his strong, hind legs. Turning in the air as he descended, he landed exactly on the spider's back, the only spot that it couldn't easily reach with its venomous fangs.

The spider made a dismayed clicking and hissing sound at being flattened to the stone floor, but the sound was not loud. Most of the air had been knocked out of it by the impact.

The Warrior clung madly to the ridged edges of the spider's slippery carapace. The edges around its back were the only solid purchase point for the cat's claws. The creature was gnashing its jaws, but unable to bite its attacker.

With perfectly timed slashes, the Warrior clawed out both of the spider's eye sockets. This had worked well in the past and it had the expected effect. Just like Declan had found with the Pugs, the optic processes were directly attached to the brain in some highly sensitive fashion. The Pugs would die if too strong a light was shined into their eyes and the spiders were similarly sensitive.

The destruction of its eye sockets sent the creature into a shuddering form of paralysis and the Warrior then lurched to one side, rolling off its back and simultaneously turning it over to expose its underside.

There was a surface nerve plexus there that the cat carefully bit, spitting out the bad taste immediately after the bite. Severing the plexus caused the spider to flex all of its legs in repeated spasms that gradually slowed. It was still alive, as evidenced by the repeated opening and closing of its jaws, but it was now unable to right itself and walk. The Warrior knew that it would soon cease all movement and die.

Congratulating himself on another successful battle, he sidled into the next room just as his humans disappeared behind a curtain of rock and descended out of the room. The odor of the crushed eggs was overwhelming and the rank odor momentarily distracted him.

The second one must have somehow sensed the death of the first spider. It came at him in the gloom as he sneezed to clear his nose of the broken egg odor. He responded by leaping straight into the air over its back to avoid the rush.

The spider halted as the cat came down on the rocks to its right side. It swiftly turned and approached more slowly, its jaws clashing.

The Warrior knew that he must avoid the business end of the thing at all costs. He bounded into the air again, bounced off a convenient rock and leaped over a fallen stalactite disappearing from view.

Once out of sight, he ran swiftly around to the rear of the puzzled spider and simply charged out from behind a formation, leaping onto its back before it could turn. From that point, the fight went as before. The Warrior had learned the technique well and the second spider was reduced to a quivering, soon-to-be-corpse in short order.

If he'd been able to speak and someone had asked him, he would have characterized the spider as much easier to defeat than another Tom, especially if the affections of a lady cat were at issue. The stinky things weren't much fun to bite, but he knew he had to do a workman-like job to dispatch them and so that's what he did. He didn't waste time quibbling about it either. His basic philosophy was: See something that needs fighting, start fighting right now and do whatever it takes to win.

The cat didn't wait around for it to die. He trotted past the destroyed eggs, sneezing again in disgust. Once at the side of the room, he was easily able to see the glow coming up from the lights below. He found the rope ladder and could smell the scent of his humans on it.

Being mostly a city cat, he had climbed buildings and fences, but had not previously encountered anything like the ladder. However, he was nothing if not adaptable, so he dug his claws in and backed down one of the supporting ropes. It was a long climb for him, but he accomplished it in good order.

Once down, he started to look for his pride members. That was a bit of a problem, because they were out of sight and, in fact, already going into one of the elevators. As he was standing by the path, a group of tourists came along and two little girls, lagging somewhat behind the main group spied him.

He was always ready to respond to children. These girls smelled and sounded as if they were simpatico, so he allowed them to make over him and he didn't struggle when one of them picked him up. This got him a nice ride as they hurried to catch up with the group.

Once the girls reached the group, their parents admonished them to keep up and then exclaimed over the cat.

"It was as if they'd never seen a Warrior," he thought.

The discussion attracted the attention of the guide who walked back and was quite upset about finding a cat taking his tour. He grabbed at the Warrior who let him know with both claws and teeth that his attentions were not appreciated.

The guide's attempt to grab the cat raised an immediate outcry from both of the girls, "Leave our kitty alone!" Their objection was merged with rather vile cursing as the guide's second attempt to grab was met with a serious bite on the thumb.

The girls couldn't hold Jefferson while he was attempting to fight. He easily slipped to the floor and then dashed off down the path at a high rate of speed, while the parents of the two girls tried to assist the guide in stopping the bleeding.

He came to a large room that smelled of food. There he saw some people eating and some others coming out of an elevator. The elevator seemed somewhat familiar. Although it obviously wasn't one of the transporters, he sensed that it would take him to a different location. Waiting his chance, he slipped into the box as the doors closed on a load of tourists exiting the cave.

He was so close to the floor and quiet that no one noticed him as he silently wove through their legs and stopped at the sidewall in a pocket clear of feet. He sat down, curling his tail tightly around him on the wall side to prevent it being inadvertently stepped on. The elevator moved up slowly, eventually reaching the surface and he exited casually along with the rest of the tourists.

He walked towards the exit of the building and outside. The light momentarily dazzled him, but as his eyes adapted, he saw both of his people going into what turned out to be a bathroom.

With a glad "Meowp," he dashed over and nearly tripped both of them as he rubbed on their legs in an ecstasy of greeting. It was obvious that the happiness was mutual, much to his satisfaction.

37

Cichen Itza

We were overjoyed to see Jefferson at our feet. We had no idea where he'd been or what he'd been doing, but the fact that he'd somehow managed to get out of the cave and find us seemed like a miracle. After a brief, but intense greeting, I picked him up, while Liz went into the restroom and set out the "Closed for Cleaning" signs. She shooed out the two women who were lagging behind their group and eventually waved at me to come in.

We entered the janitor's closet to find that it was considerably larger than I would have thought. There was a desk in there with some papers on it, in addition to the expected cleaning supplies. The transporter door was at the rear of the room and we hustled towards it.

As I walked by the desk I happened to look down and saw Pug squiggles mixed with human writing on some of the papers. That was curious enough that I stopped to look more carefully. It was a good thing that I did.

"Here, take the cat, please," I told Liz as I picked the papers up.

She took him and walked on back to the transporter door, "Hurry up! We don't have all day," she commented over her shoulder.

Why these papers were left there in plain view, I didn't know, but they contained some additional information that seemed to go with what we'd previously discovered about the EMP plan. These papers had enough incriminating information to hang a number of well-known political appointees.

I scanned over them and it became apparent that the Pugs had bought several highly placed politicians who were now aiding and abetting the enemy. I sorted out the papers that seemed to be related and shoved them in my pocket with the map.

"Hey! What are you doing in here?" The speaker was a man dressed as a Park Ranger. He looked scruffy. He was either trying to grow a beard or hadn't shaved in a couple of days and the look didn't make him any more attractive. Liz was summoning the transporter and I was distracted by the papers on the desk when he burst in. I turned towards him to see that he had a nine-millimeter service pistol pointed directly at my middle. I raised my hands slowly.

"Look. We're with the FBI," I thought I'd try to bluff my way through this.

"I don't care," he snapped. "You've found stuff you shouldn't know about and the Masters are going to have to decide what to do with you."

Another one! I really was developing a lot of antipathy for collaborators.

As I was mentally preparing to take action, Liz dropped Jefferson, who yowled. The Ranger looked at the cat in surprise and failed to react as Liz drew and shot in one smooth motion. The splinter struck his gun hand and acted instantly, causing him to drop the gun as he started the spasming phase that preceded the toxin-caused death.

I dropped my hands and said, "Let's get out of here, there might be more coming!"

We jumped into the open transporter. Jefferson, evidently deciding that he didn't want to be left behind again, dashed between our feet to the rear of the transporter box. Liz hit one of the buttons and we went elsewhere.

As usual for our luck, when there were two choices, indistinctly labeled on the map, and we had to make a quick choice, we ended up somewhere that we didn't intend.

"Oh, crap! Not another cave!" was the first thing that Liz said.

"No, it's some kind of man-made structure. See the joints in the walls," I pointed.

"Yeah, there's some light coming in over there, too," she responded.

"But, where are we?" I pulled out the map, dropping the recently purloined papers on the floor in the process. Liz helped me pick them up and I stuffed them inside my shirt to keep them out of the way. We both looked at the map with the help of my laser in flashlight mode.

"We had a choice at Carlsbad to go to Estes Park – Damn! We blew it again! Let me see, or to – " I paused.

"To the Yucatan! We're in Mexico!" she interrupted. Then she added, helpfully, "I pressed the left button at the Visitor's Center. Let's mark that on the map, so we'll remember that the right button goes to Estes."

That was a great idea and she started to mark the map accordingly, but before she got that done, I turned and took her in my arms and kissed her.

"What was that for? Not that I'm complaining," she murmured while snuggling closer.

"I thought I'd better take the opportunity while we're in a more peaceful location and also it's because you're a clever girl! I hadn't thought of marking the map," I told her.

We held onto one another for a few seconds longer, and then she sighed and said, "It looks like we're in some kind of ruins."

I picked up the map from where it had dropped on the floor.

"Looks like we're about ninety miles from Merida," I said after I'd had a minute to study it. I concluded, "I'll bet that we must be in the Mayan ruins at Chichen Itza."

38

JUAN

I was correct, for once. When we'd stumbled our way out of the structure, I could see the main pyramid, El Castillo, a few hundred yards over to one side. Looking back on the building we'd exited, I realized it was the Caracol or Tower of the Snail. It was an unusual structure since it was spiral in shape rather than the more standard, pyramidal form.

I knew that Chichen Itza is a large pre-Columbian city built by the Maya people of the Post Classic period. The archaeological site is located in the municipality of Tinum, in the Mexican state of Yucatán. I'd been there previously, in another life, almost. It was when I was a kid and my parents took me to Cozumel on a dive trip.

We'd taken a couple of days to visit the site. I remember being impressed by all of the skulls carved on the stonewalls. The guide had said they represented people killed in battle. It had made me think that the Mayans were pretty bloodthirsty. I also remembered how hot and humid it was. That hadn't changed. The jungle was still there and I could hear the screech of parrots and the sounds of other birds in the trees surrounding us.

Liz and I stood in the hot shade, occasionally batting at the insects that were attracted to us. The humidity was so high, it was like we were under water. That was compounded by the temperature, which was easily over one hundred degrees Fahrenheit. Liz tried to look like a tourist while I unfolded the map.

A brief study convinced us that the only way out was through the transporter we'd come in on. One of the two buttons returned us to the Carlsbad location, but the other went to a location in Nebraska. We wanted the Carlsbad location, obviously. Nebraska didn't seem to have any advantage.

We knew that from Carlsbad we had arrived in Chichen Itza rather than Estes Park. Just to make sure of our understanding, we crosschecked the original map with the hand-drawn one and both agreed. The other link from Carlsbad definitely went to Estes Park. Once again we'd been unlucky and ended up at a destination that was forcing us to backtrack.

Liz observed, "You know it would be really convenient if we could read their script. That way we wouldn't have to keep guessing about destinations."

"Well, let me know if you find a Rosetta Stone," I retorted. "There's just no way... No, wait! Look at the Estes connections – they do have the same final squiggle marked beside each of them. I'm willing to bet that could be the clue."

I hastily looked at the Wichita location and the Loveland location on the original map. The squiggle was on both, although it wasn't really necessary because the destination could be also seen from the connecting line. I guess the mapmaker felt that he was being complete when he double marked each transmitter link. It was irritating; if we'd been able to read the whole message by each box, it might have said more than just the destination, but we couldn't read it and speculating wasn't worthwhile.

"Come on, let's go back inside and check the buttons to see if they have the same mark," she was eager to get going.

I remembered that some, but not all of the buttons that I'd seen were marked. It wasn't like the Pugs had any sense of standardization. Sometimes their lack of systematic organization made no sense, however it did seem to give us an advantage. If we worked on the problem logically, we might keep ahead of them. I didn't know if they operated more or less randomly, had a penchant for allowing chance to intervene in their affairs, or used some form of alien logic that only made sense to them. It was a continual puzzle that bothered me. How could they be so dominant across numerous solar systems without systematic thinking?

We had been gathering up and resettling our kit while I thought. Jefferson was sitting at Liz's feet. He'd shown no interest in exploring or running off. It was as if he knew we'd be leaving quickly and wanted to be sure to stick close to us.

I turned to Liz and helped her arrange the eraser gun strap across her shoulder. It was a little inconvenient to carry, since the shape was not quite what humans would have designed. I finished and said, "OK. We're ready."

She was looking around at the ruins in the distance with apparent interest and replied, "This place looks amazing! I'd like to come back someday and take my time to see it all."

A voice came from behind us, "That's what many people do, Senorita."

We turned to see an impeccably dressed man standing there. He was shorter than me, but he had a brilliant smile that carried a considerable amount of presence.

"You realize that you're in an area where tourists aren't supposed to go? The archaeologists are studying this part right now and don't want any disturbance," he explained.

"Well, we, ah... That is...," I fumbled for a suitable and convincing explanation.

"We're trailing some evil creatures and we must go back into the building," Liz interjected. She'd obviously decided that the direct approach was best. I put the map away, so my hands would be free if I needed to move rapidly.

"Ah!" he exclaimed. "I, too, have an interest similar to yours. Both my fiancee and my sister are archaeologists and both have disappeared. They've been missing for nearly a week now. I'm not supposed to be here either, but I've narrowed my search to this part of the ruins."

We relaxed and explained a little bit about the Pugs. As we talked I could see his expression become grim. He frowned, "You will, therefore, please, allow me to accompany you. I must rescue them or assure myself they are beyond succor."

"This has been very dangerous so far. They've been doing their best to kill us," I warned him.

"I have nothing to live for now that my fiancee is missing," he assured me.

"Do you have any combat skills? Have you been in the military?" I wanted to know if he would be an asset.

"I am a black belt in Brazilian Judo and, while I'm not ex-military, I can shoot well. Regardless of my qualifications, you must either take me or kill me, because I will not accept you leaving me here." He was resolute and it showed in his face.

The discussion continued for a little longer. He agreed to follow orders from either of us and we divided up the load in order to lighten the weight that Liz was carrying. I gave him my .45 and told him that we'd get him a splinter gun at the first possible opportunity.

We were finally ready and entered the ruin. Only then did we get down to the basic social amenities.

"I'm Liz and this is Dec," my beautiful companion performed introductions as we walked through the columns. "This is our cat and advance-warning, alien detector. His name is Jefferson."

"I am charmed to meet you all. My name is..." he paused, thinking. "But, let me shorten it to just the two names that would be more common in your culture. I'm Juan Cruz. My ancestors are both Mayan and Spanish and both parts are calling out for vengeance upon those who have taken my dear ones. You see, I'd first thought that their disappearance was related to the drugs."

"Drugs? You mean cocaine?" I asked.

"Si, cocaine. The cartels have been bringing a lot of shipments in here and from this point no one knows where it goes. My fiancee told me that she had been threatened not to say anything and to leave the deliverymen alone. Whenever they came, she would busy herself with paperwork and stay away from this tower. Now..." He paused, since we had arrived at the transporter.

Juan seemed puzzled. "I've never seen this here before." He shook his head, "Is this where the cocaine could have gone?"

"They may have only just installed the transporter, but some of the things seem to have the ability to come and go or perhaps simply camouflage themselves," I explained as we entered through the portal.

Juan looked down and then stiffened to attention as he noticed a small bit of plastic in the corner. He bent and picked it up to show me that it had a distinctive mark. "This is the mark that the drug-lord places on all of his packages."

I looked at Liz and she nodded her head, "This looks like a link to the drugs that have been coming into New York. The quantity and quality is enough to destabilize the market and law enforcement is being pushed to the max to try and counter the flow. It's not something I was directly involved in, though."

"Just another thing we have to thank our alien friends for," I said, fondling the handle of my splinter gun.

Liz had been examining the two buttons and turned to me with a disappointed look. "The stupid Pugs! Neither of these two buttons is marked at all."

"We'll just have to guess again," I sighed. "If we end up in Carlsbad in the rest room, we've got a problem with a dead body and someone may have found it by now. The good news is, we'll recognize the janitor closet and we can push the second button and go directly to Estes."

She interrupted me with distress in her voice, "I don't remember which I hit to bring us here. What if those two aren't marked also?"

"No, wait! You labeled that one on the map," I remembered.

"No I didn't," she cried. "You grabbed me right then and I forgot to actually write it down."

I took a deep breath and let it out slowly. "Alright, let's see. If we end up in the rest room closet, we hit a button and we'll either come back here or go to Estes. If we come back here, we go back to Carlsbad and hit the other button. If we don't end up in the closet, we'll most likely be somewhere in Nebraska and then we can come back here and try the other button. Does that sum it up?"

She nodded. Juan simply looked at each of us in turn with his eyes wide. I guess that it was a bit much for him to suddenly try to come up to speed. His confusion wasn't helped by the fact that neither of us were good teachers, being about as confused by the transporter system as he was, despite our traveling experience.

"Wait," she said. "Now that there are three of us, let's prepare a little better."

I agreed and traded Juan my splinter-gun for the Sig, holstered it and then took the anti-matter weapon from Liz's shoulder. I positioned myself between them, as Liz briefed Juan on how to activate the splinter-gun, cautioning him on how deadly the splinters were.

"OK. Now, which one are you going to push?" I asked her.

She hovered her finger over the two and waved it back and forth, then more or less randomly pushed the left button. The door slid shut and the disorientation came and passed quickly. Juan looked definitely pale.

"Is it always the case that you feel dizzy when these things operate?" he asked.

I nodded and then the destination door popped open. We weren't in the janitor closet in Carlsbad.

39

Prison Camp

The door had opened in the back of a different-sized room. Our preparatory steps were rewarded because we were facing a squad of Pugs. They hadn't been expecting the transporter and weren't oriented in our direction, but they were turning rapidly and most of them already had their weapons out.

Liz shot first, followed, after a brief hesitation, by Juan. After three quick shots, all into the same Pug, his gun was empty. I took a second longer. I had to assure myself that whatever was behind my target wasn't something that was so vital that we couldn't afford to disintegrate it.

Some of the Pugs were down when I erased the rest, but if I hadn't fired when I did, they would have gotten us for sure. It's really nice to have an overwhelming weapon that is quiet and leaves no mess. It makes for less cleanup afterward.

On a serious note, I wondered why the Pugs didn't use the eraser-gun on us. I thought it was most likely to be due to the over-kill problem. They didn't want to randomly destroy everything surrounding and behind their target. I also suspected that they were complacent about human fighting capabilities and didn't think that it was needed, since they'd been unopposed to date. In addition, their splinter guns were totally lethal when used in close-quarters fighting. The only defense was to duck behind something the splinters couldn't penetrate.

There were a couple of dead Pugs that Liz had shot on the other side of the room. Their splinter-guns were still on their belts and I salvaged both weapons. Liz's gun was also nearly empty and I gave one to her. Juan was watching me closely as I did and I held one out to him.

"Waste not, want not," I said. "You can't get these things down at the local gun store, so we've got to pick them up when we can."

"I understand." He took it and shoved it into his belt.

We stepped over what was left of the corpses, Jefferson giving them a wide berth, and paused by the door exiting the room. Liz held her finger over her lips in a gesture to be quiet. There were people in the next room based on the sporadic, low conversation we could hear coming through the door. It sounded like several groups of people engaging in quiet conversations. We couldn't make out individual speakers with any accuracy, though. I looked at Liz and said, "Could be a lot of people in there."

She frowned and replied, "Might make it hard to see the Pugs, if there are any in there. Be careful. Shoot first if you're unsure. We can always apologize to the survivors later."

I carefully cracked the door inward while Liz stood ready with her splinter gun. The first view through the crack showed groups of people standing around in a large room and talking quietly. There were some sitting in groups on the floor also. As I looked to the side there was the distinct outline of a Pug's face about five feet to the right of the door.

If there was one there, there was probably another one on the other side, I reasoned. It was a good thing the splinter-guns were so quiet. They allowed us to have more chances at stealth than if we'd been limited to explosive weapons.

I turned to Liz and pointed towards the enemy standing to the right. She nodded and positioned herself to my right with her gun ready. Readying for action, I handed the eraser-gun I'd been carrying to Juan. He slung it over his shoulder and I gave him a thumbs-up in approbation. I drew my splinter gun and took a deep breath, then opened the door fully.

Liz leaned out and shot the Pug to the right. As she did, I spun to the left with my right hand pointing the gun around the left side of the doorjamb. There was a second Pug standing guard over the door. He had been watching the mob of people and only caught my movement out of the side of his eye. I plugged him as he started to respond to the motion.

There was a murmur in the crowd as people turned towards us. The nearest were five Marines wearing utilities. A sergeant looked meaningfully at me and waved his hand both directions, signaling that there were more

Pugs. He gave a quick order to the other four and they merged backward into the crowd making an effort to get people not to give us away by looking at us. After a brief pause, the nearby conversation started again, but more loudly this time.

The room was huge. Judging from the aircraft-sized door directly across the space from us, we were in a hanger designed to hold large jets. There must have been two hundred people there. They were bunched in the middle, away from the walls. I thought this was strange, but then I realized that it must be to give the Pugs some clear space around the edges of the group. Fortunately, there was enough noise and confusion to disguise our presence momentarily.

The sergeant walked a little closer, moving sideways and not looking directly at us. When he was about fifteen feet away, he stopped and said, "There are six others in here. They're spread evenly around the room. Two on each of the other three sides. They move back and forth every so often, so they can keep an eye on all corners of the room. Move out here with me and you'll blend in with the crowd. We aren't allowed to get too close to that door."

I looked him over carefully. He was about my height and gave the impression of calm competence and also complete honesty. I liked what I saw. He appeared tough and intelligent.

We casually moved out and blended in with the people nearest us, deflecting questions as we walked. Everyone wanted to know if they were being rescued and we simply nodded and told them to act as if things hadn't changed. The sergeant walked along with me.

"We're going to have to kill the rest of them before they give an alarm," I said. "Let's get the splinter guns from the two we killed and we can arm you and one other man."

"We've got to be careful that we aren't seen," he spoke softly.

"You get the one to the right and I'll pick up the left one," I told him.

I sauntered over along the front of the crowd of people until I was in front of the Pug I'd shot. He was lying in a heap about twenty feet to the left of the door and his splinter-gun was still on his belt. The people nearest were looking at him and I could see a couple were trying to get up the courage to go for his gun, but it looked like they were so fearful that they really couldn't make the decision.

I had no such problems and I ducked down and shortly had the creature's weapon. I worked my way back to the sergeant, telling the people that I passed, "Just act normally until we kill the others."

To give them credit, they did their best, but a guard on the left wall got curious and I suddenly saw him walking our way. The people along the left wall made an attempt to move closer to the center of the room as the Pug went by them. It was easy to follow his progress, since I could see the motion of people's heads as they moved away from him.

A sudden inspiration hit me and I dropped quickly to the floor close to the door we'd entered from. I tried to act dead as if I'd gotten a little too close and the guard had shot me. My ruse worked well. When the Pug reached a point where he could see along the back wall, he saw both me and his two comrades lying on the floor and he took several quick steps in our direction in order to see better. He neglected to alert his compatriot as he did and it was a big mistake.

He had raised his gun to cover the standing people and they shoved back from the door. As he scanned them suspiciously, I shot him and he dropped. This time one of the other Marines grabbed his weapon. I motioned the man to come over and we conferred as a group.

"Can we work our way through the crowd until we can shoot the rest of them without their being aware anything is going on?" I asked the sergeant.

"We've got to avoid some of the people near the middle of the room. They're with the Secretary of State and they'd be likely to try to alert the Pugs," he cautioned.

"What! The Secretary of State? What's she doing here?" I asked in surprise.

Her name was one of those on the incriminating papers I'd picked up from the desk in Carlsbad. If nothing else, I had a serious conversation to have with the woman. The idea that the Pugs had grabbed her led me to believe that they were nearly ready to roll out their invasion plans in full force. They wouldn't have taken someone so easily missed otherwise.

"She's been a real problem since they dumped her in here with us," he commented. "A lot of us have been here for several days. Some as long as a couple of weeks. My men and I were captured when we escorted a couple of trucks that were loaded with ordinance to a fire base near Kandahar. They brought us in here through that thing in the back room. The Secretary has only been here a couple of days. She's already convinced the aliens to start selecting the military personnel for the nightly round-up."

I paused at that, and then refocused on practical matters, "OK. You'll have to fill me in on the whole situation later. Liz, you move through the crowd near the edge until you can take out the other Pug on the left side. Sergeant, you and your man see about getting the two on the right and Juan, you and I will slip around to try and get the ones on the far wall by the hanger door."

It wasn't a great plan, but it did account for all of the Pugs. The sergeant nodded and said, "We'll do it."

He looked at his gun and asked, "Any briefing on these things?"

I explained that there was no safety, except keeping your finger off the trigger. I needlessly emphasized that they were deadly. He assured me that he'd seen a number of people shot and already knew that.

Juan looked nervous, but said, "I'm ready. This will be my revenge on these despicable creatures."

He and I started to move. Liz had already gone off, moving in a meandering fashion towards the left wall as she threaded through the captives. Juan and I followed after her moving rapidly enough to catch up.

"Let us get ahead of you and I'll try to catch his attention when we've gone past. When he looks at me, you shoot him," I instructed.

She simply nodded in response.

We gradually worked our way through the edge of the crowd until we were near the single Pug who was looking down the wall to see if his companion would show up soon. As we passed him, he fixed his eyes on the two of us and hissed something sibilant while raising his gun. He didn't get the chance to shoot before Liz stepped out of the crowd behind us. She moved away from the people in order to get a clear shot and he started to swing his aim towards her. The arc of his gun's movement suddenly stopped as he dropped. The three of us had shot him simultaneously.

At that moment, I heard loud hissing from across the room. The Marines had eliminated one of the guards stationed there, but the other had seen him fall. The Pug had cleverly dashed into the crowd and people were starting to try and get away from his vicinity. He was apparently shooting randomly and it was going to be a mess. Literally everyone hit would die.

Juan and I ran full speed to the large door and cleared the edge of the crowd just as the two Pugs there were reaching the far, right-hand corner where they could aid the one that was calling for help. They were fast, but they couldn't out-run the splinters.

We shot both of them in the back before they knew we were there. As they dropped, I realized that the crowd was a little quieter. I didn't hear any more hissing. The Marines had killed the last Pug, leaving us in control of the hanger.

40

OPPUT

We continued on down the wall past the hanger door. There was a person door to the left of the main hanger entrance that the other two Pugs had been guarding. As we approached, a group of people detached themselves from the bulk of the crowd and reached the door slightly before us. They made as if to go out, but I jumped in front of them and told them to back off. One of them was the Secretary of State and she looked greatly offended at my order.

She huffed and snapped, "Get out of our way! We've got to alert the Chosen Ones. You're all going to die for killing these guards."

The four men with her were her personal security and the Pugs hadn't disarmed them. Three of them had pulled their pistols and were aiming at me. I slowly raised my hands.

"Take that gun away from him!" she ordered.

One of her guards started forward, but a hand reached out of the crowd and grabbed his pistol. It was a well-trained hand, too. The owner was one of the other Marines and he knew exactly how to disarm an opponent. The other two guards started to jump forward, but one collapsed as a Marine stepped out of the crowd behind him and expertly struck him in the side of the neck with a knife-hand blow. The other went down as the sergeant and his other man piled on his back.

The fourth security guard was distancing himself from the Secretary with his hands raised. I motioned him over to where I was. As he started forward, I instructed the three Marines to take the Secretary back to the rear wall and hold her near the door to the transporter room.

"Don't let her get in any trouble," the sergeant ordered.

She cursed and struggled a bit with the three men, but was quickly out-of-breath. She quit fighting, although if looks could kill, I'd have been dead three-times over. When she started to say something else to me, I raised my palm and told her, "Stuff it!"

That got another huff and caused her to struggle a bit more, but the Marines hustled her over to the rear wall.

Liz came up holding Jefferson. He'd been staying out of the way, but now was relaxing comfortably in her arms. I looked around, but couldn't see Juan anywhere.

We gathered in a clear space near the small door to the left of the main hanger door. What developed then amounted to an intelligence briefing from the sergeant paired with a similar report from the Secretary's security man who turned out to have been a Navy Seal prior to his work in the secret service.

The sergeant started it off as he described being captured by a large group of Pugs who had been dressed like Afghans. He and his men had been delivering ordinance to a fire base and had simply been overwhelmed by the Pugs. After two of their compatriots had been killed with splinters, they realized the futility of fighting and gave up.

The Pugs had taken them to a village that housed a transporter. After a couple of transfers between transporters, including one where they had to walk around a building at night and into an unoccupied restroom, they arrived in some ruins that I thought must have been the Caracol.

They waited there for a couple of other groups to arrive and then the Pugs transferred them in two large groups back through the same transporter they'd come through, only this time they ended up in this aircraft hanger.

I figured that they'd come into Carlsbad using the second transporter near the Carlsbad Visitors Center. That was the one we hadn't had the opportunity to locate. I guessed that the Pugs had held them near the Caracol and finally brought them from Chichen Itza through to here. This duplicated our final couple of transfers and seemed to make sense.

The Pugs had provided MREs and the people had been using a couple of restrooms that were located on the third side of the hanger, the only wall I hadn't visited. Since many of the crowd had been here for days, they were beginning to suffer. There was no place to sit and most were unable to sleep comfortably on the concrete floor. The Pugs didn't seem to care, though. Their primary role was to keep the humans bunched in the middle of the space. Anyone who got too close to the walls was shot immediately. The corpses were hauled out, so the air didn't smell much worse than a locker room in a football stadium after a championship game with five overtimes.

For a fact, it was pretty rank, but we got used to it quickly.

The sergeant couldn't quite figure out how the Pugs were able to transport from one location to another, but he had accepted the fact that they were aliens with unknown technology.

As for where we were, the building was a hanger at Offut Air Force Base just outside Omaha, Nebraska. The hanger was one of two that were involved in some secret project. He thought that the ordinary human personnel were not allowed near the two hangers and hadn't encountered the Pugs. Those few that had, ended up inside the hanger. That's how he knew where we were. One of the captured airmen had told him.

When I asked where that man was, he explained that the Pugs would herd a group of humans through the small door that we were standing near and into a covered deuce and a half truck each night at about ten PM. The people had never come back, so he was unsure where they were going, but it couldn't be far, because the truck had lately been coming back in ten minutes to take on another load of people.

The Pugs had been bringing in more people from all over the globe right along, so the number of people in the room hadn't varied much from day to day. The ones that went out were usually replaced by several groups ushered in through the transporter that we'd arrived through. The Secretary of State and her guards had been shoved through the door only a couple of days before.

She'd been speaking to the Pugs. They seemed to know who she was and allowed her to approach them when they came in to select people to take out. She'd apparently told them to remove the military members first and that hadn't made her popular with the sergeant.

He finished by telling us that there were a few women in the group and they had been carefully shielded at the center of the hanger by most of the men. There were also quite a large number of civilians from a number of different countries. I could see several different nationalities standing in smaller groups as I scanned the room.

I reasoned that the Pugs had so many transporter heads scattered all over because they were using some of them as access points to gather human captives. They didn't want to pull in hundreds of people from one location at once. That would be a little too obvious, so spreading their hunting around was a better approach. Considering that nearly a hundred thousand people go missing in the USA annually, it was obvious that the Pugs' strategy wouldn't prematurely alert the human authorities as to the large volume of people they'd been capturing.

Everyone was watching us covertly as if they expected us to pull a rabbit out of our hat. It made me feel bad, because, so far, I didn't have much of a clue as to what to do. Even a mini-lop rabbit with a switchblade and an evil disposition couldn't help in this situation.

The secret service guard wanted to speak next and his story was about as enlightening. He'd been a long-term member of the Secretary's security detail and he was very unhappy about it. He started by mentioning that she had an extreme amount of disdain for her security and held a particular animus towards military members. That explained her volunteering the military men to the Pugs.

He told us that she'd been approached by a delegation from Russia a few weeks back. The people she met were, as he recalled it, obviously Pugs. He didn't quite know what to make of their human disguise at first and thought they were simply odd humans. Now that he knew, he was livid. He hadn't been a party to her planning with the Pugs, but she'd dropped plenty of hints in a grandiose and smug way. She'd implied that she would soon have a more important position and they'd better watch themselves or she'd take some unspecified actions that they wouldn't like.

Since she was always talking more or less in that vein, he didn't think too much of it, but right before they were brought here, she had the Pugs drag one of her assistants out of a meeting for cautioning her about negative political ramifications of her proposed actions. The man had never come back.

According to her security guard, she'd gotten crosswise with the Pugs over a discussion about some kind of missile launch. He'd been present and had heard some of the discussion, but it had been rather vague and he was unsure what was being planned. He did know that the launch was to be from a Russian site in the Urals, but he wasn't sure of either the target or what kind of payload the missile was supposed to carry.

The choice of target was where the rift had occurred. The Secretary had kept insisting that they should target Beijing after the Pugs had indicated that it would be somewhere in America. The ex-seal wasn't sure where.

The argument had increased in volume and the Pugs had finally given up and solved the problem by pulling their guns. The secret service guards had started to pull theirs in return, but like the Marines, they had given up after the Pugs had shot one of them. As he said, there was no point protecting a woman whom they all despised when it was a sure bet they'd be killed.

The ex-seal concluded by saying that he was ready to rebel due to her turning the Pugs on the military personnel. His anger over her had already convinced him to resign, but that was the last straw. Our killing the Pugs was the most positive thing he'd seen recently. He especially liked my suggestion that she "Stuff it!"

The sergeant pointed out that in about an hour it would be time for the Pugs to come and get a load of people and we'd better be prepared for that. Usually a small group of five came in to select the people to leave. They then ushered the humans out of the door, where they apparently got into a truck.

Just at that juncture, Juan came up, his face radiating joy and smiles. Two nice-looking, dark haired women were close behind him. I realized that he'd found his fiancee and sister.

"Well, my friend, it looks like your quest is fulfilled," I congratulated him.

"I'm so happy! They were there in the center of the room. They have been here for the whole week they have been missing and the chivalrous men have kept them safe for me!"

He would have continued, but the presence of the two women made me think. I turned to the sergeant and said, "We'd better begin moving people out of here as rapidly as we can. It's likely to become even more dangerous shortly."

41

TREACHERY

The Pug that had moved out into the group of humans had killed eighteen people before he'd been taken down. If the transfer detail consisted of at least five Pugs, it could be a massacre. I didn't like the odds of having a group of Pugs shooting randomly into the hanger. It could easily end up with most of the captives dead.

We went back to the transporter closet, ignoring the vituperative Secretary and opened the door. The closet could accommodate about twenty people and I calculated the transporter could hold about half that.

I summoned it and the door opened. I suddenly realized that we'd been lucky not to be flanked by Pugs coming in through the door behind us and I asked the sergeant to have two of his men guard the door with splinter-guns. That left one to keep an eye on the Secretary, but the secret service guard said he'd be pleased to watch her. He walked out with a glint in his eye and I knew that he would enjoy holding her captive.

Liz and I looked inside the door and saw that this was one of the older transporters with only one button. We'd been so busy shooting Pugs when we had come through the first time, that we hadn't noticed. I pulled out the map and verified that it showed only the one connection to Chichen Itza. The ruins must be a pretty busy place with all of the traffic in captured humans. I asked the sergeant about that and he said that everyone he'd talked to had been brought in at night, so I figured the Pugs were still worried about detection, since they waited until the tourists were gone before transferring prisoners. This might not be the case any longer, though. The capture of a politically prominent individual, such as the Secretary of

State, would seem to indicate that they were ready to come out into the open.

"Juan, if we start sending people through to El Caracol, can you direct them to safety?" I asked.

"Si." He thought about it. "I think I can organize them as if they were groups of tourists. If they can wait, my brother owns a bus concession and we can set up transportation to Merida. From there – ," he sighed and shrugged. "Well, they are illegals and Mexico is aiding such people to go to the southern border of the USA. Perhaps we can smuggle them into the USA."

I laughed aloud at the audacity of the concept while Liz looked at me with a half-smile. Smuggling refugees from an alien attack across the US border as illegal aliens was absurd enough that it tickled me. The sergeant just snickered at the thought.

I asked the sergeant to instruct people to press the activation button when they'd packed the transporter full and we got started transferring the crowd by sending Juan and his ladies through. They were accompanied by several of the nearest people in the hanger along with the fifth Marine, who'd just then worked his way through the crowd to where we were standing. He was going to act as a messenger, coming back to let us know if it was OK to keep sending more people.

Juan would wait for the escapees to begin coming through while his fiancee would go and contact his brother for buses. His sister said that she knew of a more remote area where she could lead the crowd so that they would be safe until the buses arrived for them. That seemed to take care of that end of things, but I cautioned Juan to keep his splinter-gun ready, because there was always the possibility of running into Pugs transiting the system. He agreed to be ready and off they went.

Directly the transporter dinged again and the Marine poked his head out and said, "It's all clear. Start sending more through."

We started the group moving and the only problem we had, besides the Secretary of State cursing at us, was that people tended to bunch up anxiously. They all wanted out as fast as possible, but I couldn't blame them for that.

I don't know how we managed, but we got everyone through the system before the hour was up. The people moved rapidly and packed into the transporter as tightly as they could. We found that if they squeezed, the thing would hold fifteen people, so that accelerated the transfer and the hanger emptied rapidly. When it was empty, except for the last group of captives, the five Marines, the secret service man and his charge, and Liz and I, we still had fifteen minutes before the Pug transfer team was due.

I mentally allocated that time, giving myself five minutes to interrogate the Secretary. That left about ten minutes to get in position to ambush the Pugs' human-herding detail.

42

BLIND AMBITION

I hoped that I could get all the information that I needed from the Secretary in just a few minutes. That was partly because I didn't like her and didn't want to speak to her longer than necessary. As I walked towards her, I could see from her face that she knew I was going to be a serious problem.

"Madam Secretary, I don't have time to fool around with you. I need answers and I need them now!" I snapped as I came close.

She recoiled and then snapped back, "I demand to be released. I'm the Secretary of – "

She didn't get any farther, I slapped her, jarring her teeth together. Normally, I'm the last person to resort to violence – yeah, I know – from my story, you wouldn't believe me, but she had a way about her that really annoyed me. She shut up and held her hand on her cheek.

I hadn't hit her that hard and I knew that she was posing while she thought about how best to handle the situation.

"I've got evidence that you're a traitor. You have conspired with an alien race to destroy our communications and electronic infrastructure so they can invade safely," as I spoke, I removed the incriminating notes from my pocket and held them up so she could see that there was really something to my charges.

"I don't know what – " she got out.

I interrupted her, "These are plans to detonate a high-altitude nuclear EMP burst over the United States. Your name is written here as one of the conspirators. That is treason and it carries the death penalty. The problem is that we don't have enough time to take you to court, so I'm going to make you this offer. Either you tell me what you know – in full," I amended, "Or, I'm simply going to shoot you with this alien weapon."

I displayed my splinter-gun and pointed it right at her stomach. She flinched and started to stutter. For sure, she knew what the gun was capable of.

"W – Wh – What happens if I tell you what you want to know? Do I have your assurance that you'll get me out of here and let me live?" she asked.

She obviously believed me. I was using my dead-serious face and it apparently was convincing. She was shaking now and holding one hand out to me in a pleading manner.

"I can do that. I guarantee I'll get you out of here and I won't kill you, nor will anyone in my command," I answered.

Liz interrupted, "Wait a minute, Dec! I'm minded to start by cutting off her fingers and then kill her."

She gave every sign of meaning what she said. Her face was red with anger. To top it off, she had pulled my knife out of my back waistband and was waving it around making vicious cutting motions.

"Don't let that bitch get me!" the Secretary moaned.

"That 'bitch' as you call her is the woman I intend to marry!" I snapped back.

Liz stopped waving the knife and looked at me as her face lighted up and said, "Really? This isn't the time or place, Dec. I'd kind of imagined that it would be on a beautiful tropical beach, but I don't care. The answer is, 'Yes!'"

She was looking at me in a way that I'd only dreamed of. I knew that there would be no backing out of this backhanded and clumsy proposal, if we lived through the situation. Thinking it over, I decided that I didn't care. I grinned and said, "My timing has never been very good."

I turned back to the Secretary, whose mouth was hanging open in amazement. I guess she'd never seen true love in action before. I nodded at her and said, "I meant what I said. I can only give you three more minutes to convince me that you've earned your life. Now, talk!"

This is what she told us: Some people had approached her about three months ago. She initially thought they were from the Russian Embassy, since their credentials checked out. They had set up a meeting for her with a private business group that turned out to be accompanied by some of the aliens.

I told her, "We call them 'Pugs'. That's what they call themselves."

She responded by telling me that they told her they were to be known to humans as 'The Chosen Ones' and they had conquered numerous planets in the past. They convinced her that their technology was superior to ours and told her that Earth was to be theirs next. She was told that she would have a position ruling humans after the conquest. They'd need someone to control the remains of the human race and they had selected her.

At this, I mentally thought, "Yeah, and I've got a bridge in Brooklyn for sale," but I didn't interrupt her.

Their plan was to destroy part of our communications ability with an EMP burst. She had been trying to 'save' the United States by arguing that the explosion should be over Beijing, but they preferred to take out the most dominant military power first. They said that the rest of the world would give up after that.

She had actually been trying to preserve her power base in the USA; even so it was sort of in her favor. I asked, "When and where is the missile being launched and where will they set off the explosion?"

Her answer wasn't very favorable. She told us that the launch was set for zero-six-hundred Eastern Standard Time, tomorrow morning. The missile, which was coming out of the Urals in eastern Russia, would reach its approximate detonation point about forty-five minutes after launch. That gave us barely a little over eight hours to prepare. We were interrupted then by the sergeant, who cautioned us that the Pugs would be coming within a few minutes.

As he warned us, I glanced around the nearly vacant hanger just in time to see the last of the captives exiting through the closet door on the other side.

That left only the few of us to worry about. I turned to the rest of the group and told them what I'd been thinking of as a course of action.

"The Pugs have taken a large number of people out of here in the past several days. We know that they aren't taking them very far, because they come back for a second load within minutes. I believe that we should see if we can rescue those people also. To do that, we'll need to kill the squad that comes through the door and then see if we can force or fool any one left outside into taking us to wherever they've been carrying the missing people. Since, we haven't been able to convince any of the aliens to do anything – they just fight until they're dead – I'm hoping that we can fool one of them into driving the truck."

I paused and looked at the group, then continued, "Here's what we'll do. The Pugs will be startled that the people are gone from the hanger. Most of us will lie on the floor as if we've been killed along with the eighteen dead that the Pugs killed, but two of us will be against the wall beside the door. When the aliens come in, the farthest person away on the floor will make a noise and I'm hoping that they will step forward to investigate without looking too closely to the sides. The large steel girder that supports the hanger door will provide shelter for one of our two shooters. The other shooter will have to be over there in the corner where the beams that support the roof come together."

The secret service man asked, "What about the Secretary?"

My answer was, "The Secretary will cooperate or she'll be shot. She'll be lying on the floor closest to the door. If she moves, they'll be likely to shoot her first and if they don't, I'm sure Liz will."

Liz nodded with a glare at the woman.

"Now get to your places. Sergeant, you and I will be the shooters. The rest of you get down on the floor. Scatter out! Now!"

It wasn't any too soon. Everyone had barely reached their places, when we heard a large truck pulling up outside. The door rattled, signaling that it was show time.

43

PΛYBΛCK

The door flew open with a bang and a Pug walked through. He was talking over his shoulder to the one behind him. They stepped in far enough for the next two to come through and then looked around in surprise.

There was something about their response that gave me hope for our chances in the coming conflict. They didn't adapt as rapidly as we would have in the same situation. They looked wildly back and forth as if they couldn't believe that everyone was gone.

The other two came in speaking in their hissing speech. The first two began to aim their guns at the people lying on the floor when the last of the five came through the door. He was somewhat quicker on the uptake and hissed an order for the second two to cover the sides of the hanger in a belated attempt to clear the place.

Just as they turned, Jefferson stepped out of the shadows on the far side of the hanger and yowled. The Pugs refocused on him, crouching and aiming at him. I didn't know if they thought he was responsible for the missing crowd, but it was obvious that they were going to shoot him. They were taking their time aiming because he was such a small target and moving.

The door started to swing shut on its automatic closer when the sergeant and I opened up with our splinter-guns. All five Pugs went down. I ran forward and the sergeant stepped out and gave me a high-five. It was silly, but I guess he was pretty glad to get some revenge on the creatures.

We scavenged their splinter-guns and passed them out to the unarmed members of our team as they came forward. I gathered the group at the door and carefully opened it to peep outside.

I could see the rear of the canvas-covered truck with the cargo gate open, but there were no other Pugs in sight. My spirits fell. It looked like we'd killed the only ones that were there, leaving us without any clue as to where to go.

I opened the door slowly to clear the space. Seeing no one, I stepped out to the rear of the truck, passing through the exhaust of the idling engine as I did. I leaned out to look around the driver's side of the canvas and was able to see a Pug's head in the rear-view mirror. He was looking across the way at another hanger and didn't see me.

I quietly got everyone on board, pulled the gate closed and then hammered on the rear of the cab. The driver, thinking all was normal, shifted the idling vehicle into gear and we rolled off.

We didn't go far. He drove us a hundred yards to the next hanger and backed up to the person-door. I was able to see that the hanger had a bright red sign that said, "Top Secret – No Admittance!"

The truck stopped and this time the driver opened his door, got down and came around to the rear of the truck. We weren't quite what he expected to see and he tried to run away, but not fast enough. One of the Marines jumped out and shot three rounds, bringing him down about forty feet away from the truck.

"Now, everyone out, and we'll see if we can save the rest of the captives," I optimistically said.

The sergeant stepped up to the person-door and opened it. I could hear his gasp as he looked through and I ran up to look over his shoulder. It was a horrific sight. The first thing we could see was that the floor of the hanger looked like the floor of a slaughterhouse. There were parts of bodies and skeletal sections scattered all over. The second thing we encountered was the awful smell of death and putrefaction that rolled out the opened door.

I had barely started recovering from the shock, when a wave of spiders came out of the darkness in the rear of the hanger, moving towards us. They were not like the ones I'd previously seen. These were bloated and swollen and many had grown so much that it looked like their spindly legs wouldn't support them. The big ones had vastly larger bodies in proportion to their legs and some of them were almost as large as the bear-sized creature that was so hard to kill.

It was obvious that, just as we'd suspected from seeing the eggs, the spiders were the immature form of the bear-sized thing. Thinking about it, I realized that the damned Pugs had been feeding the spiders in order to grow the bear-sized things. As if my thinking about them had summoned them into existence, the throbbing, moaning noise of an adult came from the shadows and then there was a scrabbling rush as a full dozen of the adults ran at the door. I slammed it shut.

In my excitement, I somehow conflated the Pugs with bears and inadvertently created a more usable name for the large creatures. I turned to the others in alarm and yelled, "Pug-bears!"

Liz shouted, "Take cover!" and followed her own advice by crawling under the truck so that she could shoot while protected by the chassis.

There was a scraping sound, then a loud bang as claws penetrated the door. At the same time, I felt a mental wave of fear that seemed to be projected through the door. Without thinking, I unslung the eraser-gun from my shoulder where I'd been carrying it after retrieving it from Juan. I stepped back and triggered it at the door.

As I swept it back and forth, the front of the hanger gaped open and I was able to direct the weapon at the collection of nasties inside. They responded by trying to rush out at us and this grouped them so that I was able to dissolve them back into their primal energy state.

Unfortunately, I missed several of the smaller spiders and they swarmed over two of the Marines before we could get them. The sergeant was cursing and shooting the blamed things with his splinter-gun, but not having much effect, so I turned to the side after clearing the oncoming horde and wiped out the spiders and the dead Marines' bodies at the same time. I felt bad about dissolving the Marines, but they were dead and there was no time to be picky. I immediately turned back to the opening and blasted a few latecomers.

The last thing to come out was one of the adult Pug-bears. It wasn't moving as fast, since it was missing two legs on one side. I waited until it was fully out in the open and then pointed the anti-matter weapon at it. As I did, a strange thought passed through my mind. "Perhaps I shouldn't kill it; it deserved to live."

The Secretary of State had been standing to one side, wringing her hands and moaning in distress as we dissolved the creatures. I shrugged off the odd impulse to let the last one live and as I prepared to finish it off, she darted in front of it with her arms spread wide in order to protect it.

"You've killed the Masters!" she screamed. "That will be met with total annihilation of all humans."

I was puzzled, but Liz was quicker, "What do you mean, 'the Masters'?"

The Secretary gasped, "The humanoid aliens are the Chosen Ones! They were chosen by the Masters for their ability to work with technology."

As she started to speak again, there was a wave of mental anger as the 'Master' behind her brought its remaining front leg up and stabbed downwards into her back with its venom-dripping claw. She gasped and then practically melted in on herself.

I'd seen enough and the eraser-gun put a period on that act, leaving nothing of the Secretary or the last of this group of so-called 'Masters'.

44

Backup Plan

We looked back to the other hanger. It wasn't that far and I wondered why the Pugs had used the truck rather than simply making people walk from one hanger to another. Maybe it was to ensure that they kept together and possibly to keep other humans from realizing what was going on.

We turned and walked back to the first hanger, taking only a few minutes to cross the intervening space. The lights of an automobile came around the corner of our destination as we reached the person-door and it rapidly pulled towards us.

We got ready to shoot, should the occupants prove to be Pugs, but an Air Force captain climbed out and immediately said, "Hey, where the heck is everybody?"

It turned out that he was a pilot and had been on leave to visit his ailing mother in the western part of Nebraska. He'd been gone for two weeks and had just returned. The base was completely deserted and he had been startled by the lack of security as he drove through the gates. It wasn't immediately apparent as to what had happened, so he drove around for a while and ended by discovering our little group. As we re-entered the hanger, we filled him in on the situation.

I had left Jefferson behind in the hanger. As we stood there, the cat came up and rubbed around my legs to show me that he didn't hold it against me. He thought that everything was fine now that we'd come back. I could tell, because he sat and purred as we told the captain what we knew.

It turned out that he was a good person to meet. He had been assigned to the airborne laser-testing project for over a year. This project had been in the news and had been largely discredited, but that was simply for disinformation. They'd continued on with the research and the Mark VII version was now ready for field use. It was currently undergoing testing over the Atlantic. The basic idea behind the weapon was to mount a super-powered laser in a Boeing aircraft and use it to shoot down missiles. However, that was all I knew.

The captain was kind enough to brief us on the system, "The Boeing YAL-1 Airborne Laser weapons system is a megawatt-class chemical oxygen-iodine laser mounted inside a modified Boeing 747-400F. It was primarily designed as a missile defense system to destroy tactical ballistic missiles in boost phase."

"The YAL-1 was first test-fired in flight, at an airborne target in 2007 using a low-power laser, and then a high-energy laser was used to intercept a test target in January of 2010. The following month, the system successfully destroyed two test missiles and this was viewed with considerable alarm by various opposing nations. For this reason, funding for the program was cut in 2010 and the program was ostensibly canceled in December 2011. The funding cut and subsequent mothballing of the project was intended to get the system out of the public eye until it was readied for actual use in the field. The testing of the final modifications to the system is now nearly complete," he concluded.

To me, it sounded like this was exactly what we wanted, provided that it could be deployed and that it could hit an orbital target with enough power to burn out the electronics.

The captain thought he could contact his commanding officer and fill him in on the situation. The test unit, itself, was located at Patrick AFB on the east coast of Florida and the test group had been flying it out over the Atlantic to a relatively unfrequented location in the Sargasso Sea for low altitude tests on drone targets.

While the primary use of the weapons system was to burn out missile electronics as they launched and boosted through the atmosphere, there were also an optional plan to use it on a target in low Earth orbit. He thought that there was a chance they could hit the EMP warhead hard enough to prevent it from going off.

It was going to be a real problem getting ready to shoot down the missile, but he immediately made a call on his cell to his commanding officer. He finished and turned to us, "My colonel thinks I'm half-crazy, but he agreed to launch the plane early for a mission that he was going to fly tomorrow at eight in the morning. He'll wait until there is a confirmation of a launch in Russia, but if there is one at 0600, he'll go ahead and get it in the air early."

That gave us a little hope. The pilot agreed to stay in touch with us, but he wanted to try and get back to his mother's place. He knew exactly what an EMP would do and thought he had about enough time to get there if he left immediately.

I took some solace in the fact that his commander had been alerted and there was a chance that the warhead would be taken down. We'd successfully rescued all of the people we could and we didn't see what else we could do. It looked like our best course of action was to go back through the transporter and try to reach Estes Park. I still had the feeling that we could seriously disrupt the Pugs' plans if we could only find the transporter head that led to Titan, besides I was concerned about Rudy.

We turned into the now vacant hanger. It was empty, except for a bad odor and some pieces of clothing that the crowd had left behind.

As we walked across the echoing space to the transporter room, I considered the events that had led us to this point. We'd seen many spiders in numerous locations and the newly christened Pug-bears in the room with the hanging Pugs, in the cage in DC, in Carlsbad and here. It was now obvious that the spiders and Pug-bears were one and the same. That had dire implications, because a large force of Pug-bears would be nearly impossible to combat with small arms.

Then it hit me. Somehow in the heat of action, I had only focused on the immediate necessities. I had heard the Secretary's explanation of the relationship between the Pugs and the Pug-bears, but only now did it really reach my conscious level of processing.

The Pug-bears were the dominant race! The Pugs were only servants or helpers. I couldn't see how that could possibly be. To this point the spiders and Pug-bears had not exhibited anything other than a savage willingness to attack. They'd shown no understanding of weapons and no signs of intelligence.

I finally came up with a tentative theory that had to do with the way they grew up. Their reproductive strategy led to the immature creatures scattering out and fending for themselves. Perhaps they didn't develop the capacity for intelligence until they reached their adult size.

That explained the spiders, but I was still left wondering if, when, and how the Pug-bears became intelligent. The one in DC had seemed totally animal-like, unless the moans that it made were an attempt to communicate. So had the one in Carlsbad, but then we were unknowingly threatening its eggs..

The ones that I'd just erased could have been recent adults and not smart enough to know to run from an eraser-gun. Then I remembered that the one that killed the Secretary had a more developed head section. As I recalled, its head was larger than the others. In proportion to their bodies, their heads had appeared all mandibles with fangs and the space behind and above their eyes was flattened. The last one had a much larger - I guess you could call it - brain case.

It seemed like their brains only developed after they became fully grown. That thought led me to realize that life on a planet with the monsters would be difficult. They were pure, vicious, bundles of predatory instinct as they grew and might only acquire a tempering level of intelligence when they became adult. I thought that would mean that they would have no family instincts. Perhaps only the most robust of them survived to adulthood. It would also mean that, once they spread over the Earth, our species' days were strictly numbered.

As we reached the back wall, I came up with another unanswered question. If the Pug-bears had chosen the Pugs, how did they communicate? I had to leave that line of inquiry for later. The rest of the group was already in the transporter and I hurriedly entered, turning to face the front as I did.

Liz freed one hand from carrying Jefferson and pushed the button. She'd become, by default, sort of our official button-pusher. The transporter did its thing, but it didn't bother any of us. We'd all been there and done that numerous times.

We came out in El Caracol as expected. There was no one around, so we simply let the door open and then shut. As soon as it shut, Liz hit the Carlsbad-connection button and we transited instantaneously through space to that location.

This time, the door opened to reveal the backsides of two Pugs wearing New Mexico State Police uniforms. They were in their human guise, but we all recognized them now. They were bent over inspecting the remains of the Ranger that we'd dealt with on our earlier pass through. His body was still where it had fallen, so they must have just found his remains. Police officer uniforms or not, our splinter-guns poofed and they dropped beside the Ranger's corpse.

"It looks like they've infiltrated a lot of our law enforcement organizations," commented the sergeant.

"Yeah!" I responded. "Tell me, have you seen any of them in military uniform?"

"No, but that doesn't mean they haven't somehow inserted themselves into the military also," he answered.

"We can sort it out later! Right now we've got to get to Estes," Liz snapped. She was plainly worked-up.

"Alright! Everyone, listen, we may be walking into a hot-bed of the creatures where we're going. Make sure your guns are ready. Also, please make sure of your shots as we exit the door. It's tight and we don't want any friendly-fire casualties," I told the group.

"Ready to go?" Liz asked, her hand hovering over the right-hand button.

That was another reason why I loved her. She had a great memory. Until she reached for the button on the right-hand side, I'd forgotten that the left one would take us back to the Yucatan. She was great with details like that, at least when I didn't distract her.

45

Estes Park

The Estes Park transporter link led to a door on the second floor of what turned out to be the Stanley Hotel. We verified that the dimly lit hall was empty, but the closed doors gave us a rather uneasy feeling. There could be a lot of Pugs in there, just waiting to pop out.

I turned a nearby corner and found the stairwell. I led our group quietly down the carpeted stairs. There was a window at the landing, but we ignored it, trotting down the steps as rapidly as possible.

The scene at the bottom of the stairs was enough to clue me that Rudy had been there before us. There were dead Pugs all over the place and the furnishings looked like a series of grenades had been used. It was a mess and the owners of the hotel were doubtless going to be angry. No, wait. The owners were most likely dead, killed by Pugs.

Combat-like sounds were coming from the rear of the hotel. As I listened, it became obvious that there was a fight going on there. I could hear faint "Poof" sounds from a number of splinter-guns shooting in ragged volleys. There was also a lot of hissing that sounded like enraged Pugs.

Keeping my head down, I sneaked over to a convenient window and looked out. It was past dusk, but I could see that there were a lot of Pugs in the well-lit, garden-like courtyard outside. They had their backs to us and were keeping low behind whatever cover they could find. Just then Rudy's face popped into my field of vision. He was high up, looking down over some rocks near a waterfall that descended into the rear courtyard of the hotel. The rock wall was about a hundred feet from the back porch of the main building and about twenty feet higher. As I watched, I could see that

Rudy was aiming at something. He sighted and shot, and one of the Pugs below dropped its gun and started thrashing about.

That was enough for us. We slipped quietly to the rear door and prepared to flank them. As we moved around the free-floating stairway, the sergeant put his hand on my arm and pointed up, indicating that he'd go to the landing halfway up and shoot out of the window. I nodded, and he and the other remaining Marine slipped back around to the front of the free-floating staircase. In a few seconds, I heard them running up the stairs.

The rest of us arranged ourselves on both sides of the door in such a way that we could shoot out at almost any angle. I ducked down and unfolded the attached doorstop, then shoved the door hard. The stop dragged behind, wedging the door open..

None of the Pugs had seen anything, but I caught a quick wave from one of the men on top of the rocks by the waterfall. They had seen us and that relieved me a lot. If given the choice I'd rather have a whole roomful of Pugs shooting at me than any one of Rudy's group.

We picked out as many targets as we could and then let fly all at once. The Pugs were thrown into total disarray. They first didn't know where the additional fire was coming from and then they apparently thought that Rudy's group had gotten behind them, because they all turned towards the hotel.

We had to duck back as a hailstorm of needles flew past us to shatter on the underside of the stairs. This, however, was perfect for Rudy, because his group popped up and fired rapidly at the Pugs' exposed backs until some of the enemy turned to shoot back and his guys dropped out of sight.

The Pugs had set up in a spot with a couple of low stonewalls, some heavy planters, and some tables. It was well lighted and there was no difficulty picking out our targets. The walls offered them no protection from shots fired from the hotel side. They could hide from us behind the planters, but that exposed them to Rudy's group. A few of the Pugs had thrown tables on edge between them and Rudy and they tipped more over when we started shooting and hid between them. That was the best cover they had.

This was kind of like a shooting gallery, and I was almost enjoying myself. With the exception of the chance of being killed, it was entertaining. There were still over fifty Pugs between us and the rest of our force. I unslung the eraser-gun and swept it across as much of their line as I could see from my position.

The remaining Pugs jumped up and started to run up the stairs beside the waterfall. They knew the eraser-gun would wipe them out if they stayed in sight. I followed them up the stairs with a long burst of anti-matter and got most of them. Rudy's group shot the remaining few as they crested the top.

I'd over-timed that last burst. The waterfall was now running into a deep hole where the base of the stairs used to be. It looked like we'd be climbing over the stacked rocks to get up to Rudy's location.

He stood up at the crest of the hill and waved at us to come up. He shouted down, "There may be a bunch more of them coming along, so get up here now."

Behind us, I could hear the two Marines running down the stairs. We exited the door and headed for the rocks, stepping over dead Pugs and watching carefully for living ones as we went.

We had made it partway across the open garden when I heard someone shout an obscenity inside the hotel. The shout was followed by the "Poof" sounds from a couple of splinter guns. Right after that, the sergeant came running through the door at a full sprint, but he was alone.

"One came out of a room and shot James!" He was cursing as he ran.

"Did you get him?" I yelled.

"Yeah! Damn his eyes! I should have been more careful!"

You could see that he was really torn up about James. He'd already lost two other members of his squad. The only other survivor of the group was the Marine that went with Juan. I hoped he was OK.

We ran the rest of the way across the garden area and scrambled up the sloping rock wall to where we were greeted by Rudy.

"Man, I've never been so glad to see someone in my life!" he exclaimed. "We weren't making any progress against those Pugs, and I was about to try and run for it when I saw you looking out of the door."

My first question was in the nature of criticism of his strategy, "Why the Hell didn't you use your eraser-gun?"

He looked embarrassed, "I broke it."

He shrugged his shoulders and explained, "A Pug jumped on me and in the scuffle, I landed on the thing and it broke. I could have used it when the recently deceased – " Here he waved his hand at the dead Pugs scattered out down-below, " – first chased us through the hotel. I tried and the only thing it would do was spark a little around the receiver area. I thought it might explode, so I ditched it under the seat of that antique car in the lobby."

"That's a Stanley Steamer for your information," I responded.

Liz came up carrying the cat, as usual. She seemed concerned about the time and was trying to get a glimpse of Rudy's watch. When she saw what time it was, she drew a deep breath, composing herself before speaking.

"We only have about eight hours before the EMP detonation. I think we'd better see if we can get to the off-planet transporter link and cause some kind of problem while it's still dark. If we wait, it might be too late to do anything."

46

PITCHED BATTLE

Liz had thoughtfully taken a local area map from a display in the lobby, as we came through. I don't know how she manages to think of those things, but it was a convenient thing to have. We studied it along with the Pugs' transporter maps. Using the information from both of those, we thought we'd located the key transporter. It appeared to be partway up the summit of Rocky Mountain National Park. Specifically, it seemed to be located about halfway up Old Fall River road.

We folded the maps and gathered up as many splinter guns as we could from the deceased Pugs. We still had the single remaining anti-matter gun and two of the hand-grenade-sized, anti-matter bombs.

We divided into two groups. Rudy, Colin, Joe, and Stormbreaker in one and the sergeant, the ex-Secretary's Navy Seal guard, Liz, and I were in the other. I commented that our group might be the stronger because we had Jefferson, but Liz told me that I was just being silly. I know I have an odd sense of humor, but it still seemed kind of funny to me.

The whole battle had taken long enough and been loud enough for some kind of official response to show up, but I hadn't heard any sirens coming down the road. We had made so much noise, despite the lack of actual gunfire, that I was sure that someone, somewhere, would have called the police. I was bothered by the fact that no one had shown up to investigate. The hotel must have been empty of humans and I was beginning to suspect the city was also.

We walked to the nearby parking lot and found that we had a great selection of automobiles with tags from all over the country. Pairing that with the lack of response from the hotel, gave me the impression that the

Pugs had killed everyone in the area. It kind of gave a new slant to the horror movie that had been filmed there years ago.

It wasn't long before we'd stolen two cars. Both started easily and we piled in and headed around the hotel, down the long, curving drive and off the grounds. We had a momentary fright as we rounded a clump of trees when a small herd of elk came trotting across the drive, directly in front of us.

I wasn't prepared for the animals and I jammed on the brakes hard. Jefferson was caught by surprise and came flying forward between the seats. He might have been injured, except that he lashed out and snagged my shirt collar with his claws as he flew by. He swung around under my arm and landed with his pointy little feet right in my groin. It took me a moment to regain control of the car. Getting hit in the crotch by twenty pounds of cat is not a happy experience!

After I regained my breath and Jefferson regained his composure, we continued on to Business 34. It shortly turned into West Elkhorn Avenue and led us to a tourist-oriented area with lots of small shops and restaurants. The place was deserted and we slowly drove through town heading west.

Liz turned to me and said, "It just seems like it should be harder."

Still sore from the cat bouncing off my sensitive parts, I answered, "That's easy for you to say!"

The guys in the back laughed and Liz shook her head, but at least she looked sympathetic.

About a block farther on, she was proven right. We'd reached the intersection with Rock Ridge and were moving through it, when something heavy crashed onto the top of the car. The vehicle swayed violently from side to side and I nearly ran off the road. A wave of fear washed over me as I swerved back onto the asphalt.

We were left with no doubt as to what had hit us; clawed legs appeared on both sides of the car and scrabbled at the windows. The sergeant hastily rolled his window up and accidentally trapped a claw. The Pug-bear moaned loudly and yanked its leg, pulling its claw out of the crack and shattering the window.

While that was going on, I glanced in the rear-view mirror to see that three of the fully adult creatures had blocked Rudy's car. While I was looking back, another one ran right out in front of us and we bounced into the air as the front of the car went over the top of its hard carapace.

This was bad and getting worse, because there were about twenty more of the things coming down the street in front of us as fast as they could move. There were more coming up Rock Ridge also and a few were coming out of broken storefronts on the other side of the street. We'd been ambushed very effectively. The things seemed to arouse an extreme fear response in everyone. We were all panting and shaky as they approached.

Everyone was shooting out their cracked windows with their splinter-guns, but those weapons had little effect on the Pug-bears. The toxin seemed to make them shaky, but it wouldn't stop them rapidly enough to help our cause. I struggled out of the seat belt and grabbed for the eraser-gun that was lying muzzle-down between my right leg and the center console of the vehicle. It was difficult to move the longer weapon around in the narrow confines, but I somehow managed.

The sergeant was madly trying to dodge a couple of clawed legs that had come in the window reaching for him, while he shot two more creatures that were headed our way from the nearby sidewalk. I rolled around on the center console, ignoring the shift lever poking me in the right kidney. I shot as soon as the gun was covering what I thought was most likely the center of the alien on the car roof.

That worked; the claws quit waving around and the thing slid off the rear of our vehicle. I then set up and discovered a novel way of exiting an automobile. I swung the gun forward and shot off the entire front. That cleared my view so that I could get the Pug-bears coming our way. I took a little too long, though. The ones that were farthest down the road saw what was happening and tried to scatter.

As soon as I'd gotten all of them, I realized that the ones coming up from the south side of the intersection were almost upon us. So, I turned that way and burned through the driver's door. I wiped out that group and then used the gun to carefully enlarge the hole a bit.

I stepped out of the car and carefully picked off the ones that were blocking Rudy's group. While I was doing this, the Navy guy yelled for me to watch my back. Heeding his warning, I spun just as another one came out of a building on the north side of the street and jumped onto the car roof. I was so close that the weapon disintegrated a hole through its body. The Pug-bear's massive weight collapsed the front of the now unsupported roof before the others could get out. As I spun around, I had a momentary glimpse of Jefferson, his tail bushed out, running towards the cover of a building on the south side of the street.

Despite the front of the car being collapsed, Liz wiggled her way out through the vacant space where I'd inadvertently dissolved the majority of the engine. The other two were able to slide out of the broken rear window.

Now that his roadblock had been removed, Rudy pulled up to our position.

"Try that pick-up over there!" He pointed at a late-model 4x4 sitting at the curb.

I ran over to it and smashed the window. When I got in, I found a spare key hidden over the sun visor. The truck started right up and the two men jumped in the rear while Liz got in the front. I started to pull out, but stopped as Jefferson came flying through the passenger window with a yowl. Liz somehow caught him as if they'd been training for a circus. He wasn't going to let us get out of his sight and that was good. We'd become very attached to him and we now saw him as an indispensable partner in our enterprise. His ability to react to unseen aliens was a great early-warning system.

We took off like the gates of Hell had opened behind us and, indeed, it was true. The whole street behind was filled with Pug-bears following as fast as they were able. I judged that they could move at about twenty miles per hour, so we could easily out-run them. The problem would come if they had enough endurance to follow us to our destination.

The ex-Seal reached around to Liz's window and yelled for her to hand him the eraser-gun. She did, but not without some trepidation, as it was the only weapon we had that was even semi-effective against the things. He carefully shot brief bursts at the following crowd and they soon got the idea they weren't welcome on our trip.

They faded out to the sides into some trees and nearby buildings. He stopped shooting as they disappeared. When he did, I mentally made a note that we needed to all have a discussion on how best to use that gun. He could have continued to shoot, destroying any intervening barriers until he reached the Pug-bears. Being used to human weapon limitations, it didn't occur to him, so several of the things got away.

We built up speed and careened out of town on West Elkhorn Avenue, lurching around the "Y" where it became Fall River Road. We were on our way into the park.

47

Old Fall River Road

We passed through the park gates with no trouble and then began the long climb up to the point where the old road intersected the new one. Old Fall River Road was gravel and was much steeper than the modern asphalt highway. I, for one, wasn't looking forward to it. Even though it was nearly summer, there was a lot of snow lying around in drifts and banks, especially where the trees or cliffs sheltered it.

Twice we saw what might have been Pug-bears crossing the road ahead of us, but nothing ever attacked. The shapes could have been anything, but I thought that the aliens were roaming the whole area. Searching for what? I didn't know. Food, perhaps? That seemed most likely, but if they liked people sandwiches, their best bet was to be in a city.

After what seemed like an amazingly long time that was filled with tense driving around steep mountain curves, we passed Sheep Lakes. The turn-off to Old Fall River Road was just before we reached the point where Fall River crosses the highway.

The gate was shut, and a sign warning us that the road was closed due to snow put a damper on our hopes of driving right up to the transporter head. The part of the road that I could see in the headlights looked clear of snow. Making the decision to go ahead was easy, since we didn't have any choice about the matter.

I stuck my head out of the window and asked the sergeant to use the eraser-gun on the gate. He stood up in the truck bed, complaining that he was nearly frozen. "This is a miserable location! I'm freezing and the two of us back here won't have to worry about Pug-bears much longer! We're going to freeze solid before we go too much farther."

Liz, rather unsympathetically told him to, "Man-up! Just shoot the gate!"

Once he got to his feet, he leaned on the top of the cab to slow down his shivering and the Seal handed him the gun. He used it to effectively clear the gate from in front of us. We proceeded slowly after that, moving along the rough gravel road that clearly hadn't been maintained since last year. We drove past an area of alluvial debris and then crossed Fall River.

Our pick-up had a much easier time of it than Rudy's sedan. I could see his lights bouncing wildly as he tried to find a path between the water-washed stones and potholes. Even with the higher suspension, we still had a rough ride and I worried about the guys in the bed. They were getting tossed around a lot. I stopped and asked them to hand the eraser-gun back inside. I was worried about it getting banged on the bed walls and breaking. We needed it too much to risk any damage.

After a while, we came to a turn-off going left, but Liz waved me on. Several minutes later we came to our first real switchback. It was quite steep and we zigzagged across the face of the mountain as we ascended. Directly after that we went by a waterfall. She said it was called Chasm Falls on the map. I couldn't see much because it was dark and I was concentrating on the road, but it seemed like it might offer a nice view, if the circumstances hadn't been so dire.

We went more or less straight for a time and then came to a series of three steep switchbacks. After we'd crested the third, Liz motioned for me to slow down. She had been looking out of the window in the dark, trying to make out the skyline to the north. She finally gave up.

"We'll have to stop here and turn off the lights for me to see anything. It should be around here to the north of the road, up the slope, but I couldn't find any distinctive markings on the map other than a kind of ridge."

I stopped and shut the truck off. The guys in back dismounted and were shortly joined by Rudy's group. Liz and I got out. It took me a moment to get my hands unclenched from the steering wheel. Taking that road in the dark with the potential for alien attacks gave a new meaning to 'white-knuckle' driving.

After about a minute in the dark, our eyes had adapted. It was clear with no moon, the stars shining brightly in the sky jumped out at us. We could see what seemed to be millions of stars. It was dark, but we finally made out a jagged ridge-back silhouetted against the night sky high above us.

Liz pointed at it and said, "I think that's where the transporter head must be."

"I hope so," Rudy grumbled. "It would be a shame to climb all that way and find nothing."

"Look, we don't have any choice. We've got to find this thing," I interjected.

Stormbreaker had been searching for the best way to start. He now motioned us to follow him over some rocks and up a steep climb. After the group cleared the tough terrain, the climb was smoother and less steep as we approached some stunted trees.

Stormbreaker led us along an open area where an avalanche had cleared a path through the small evergreens. We were moving uphill by a clump of trees when he suddenly paused and held up his hand. It was visible against the sky above us and we all halted.

"I heard something," he whispered.

Just then we all heard it. It was the sound of a heavy body crunching through the dried branches on the other side of the small clump. I swiveled, tracking the sound with the eraser-gun. The creature came around the edge of the trees on the downhill side. As soon as it sensed us, it let out one of the Pug-bears' distinctive moans.

I made sure that no one was in the way and then triggered the gun and swept it back and forth. The trees crackled and toppled, and a lot of rocks gave way, rolling downhill as the thing shrieked. Its sound was cut off suddenly as the beam struck it.

I lifted the gun, pointing the muzzle upwards. Suddenly Stormbreaker grabbed my arm and wrenched me around to face the other side of the avalanche path. He didn't need to tell me to shoot. I'd already felt the mental sensation of fear that the things created. There was another Pug-bear rapidly approaching and it was keeping quiet. I got that one too.

Uphill from us was a third Pug-bear. It had remained still and looked like a medium sized boulder as it crouched there in the starlight. I caught it with my peripheral vision as it started to rise and come at us. Snapping a shot off in the poor light, I dissolved the legs on one side of the beast.

Whipping its other legs and shrieking, it rolled down upon us. I tried another shot, but it was too close. I jumped out of the way and yelled, "Watch out!"

It rolled out of control down the slope, clattering past the others without getting close to anyone. I didn't think that it would be able to climb back up the slope after us with only the legs on one side, so we left it alone. We turned back towards our goal and continued upwards for several yards until we were stopped by a most unwelcome accident.

When I had hit the creature's legs, the beam had severed them, but not dissolved the entire length of the legs. One of the claw tips had been cut off and it landed on a large rock that the ex-seal happened to lean on as he passed. The claw barely nicked his palm, nothing more, but his arm immediately went limp. He staggered and let out a groan, then dropped to a sitting position.

We clustered around to see what had happened. Rudy had a small light that he shielded with his coat and we looked at the wound. The man was breathing hard and starting to shiver. We tried putting a belt around his arm and tightening it, but it was no use. In a few minutes, he gasped loudly, convulsed and then died.

"Damn! Those things are simply too deadly!" the sergeant exclaimed.

"We can't let them penetrate our skin with anything. That was one of the rear claws and I would have sworn the poison was only in the front ones," I added.

"More importantly, we can't lose anyone else. We're too few as it is and we don't know what we face up ahead," Liz said.

"That's right. We've got to get through. There isn't any choice," Rudy concluded.

We regrouped and started off again. We were nearing the ridgeback and the trees had thinned out. What few were left were small and stunted and hardly tall enough to provide cover for a Pug-bear. The moon had barely peeked over the ridge during the last few minutes of our climb and the breeze was blowing down the hill directly into our faces. It brought a stench of decay with it, reminiscent of the odor from the slaughterhouse hanger.

Stormbreaker sniffed and said, "We're getting close. That odor ain't comin' from nothing we want to see. It has got to be a human corpse. I've smelled enough of them to know."

We reached the bottom of the ridgeback formation and I could see a transporter door inset into the stone. Sure enough, lying beside the door was a dead human, or what remained of him. He'd been dismembered and partially eaten. The blood and gore was all around and the smell wasn't good.

Stormbreaker thought that we'd interrupted the supper of the Pug-bears we'd killed. "They must have been guards for this door," he speculated.

We faced the door and pushed the call button. I was ready with the eraser-gun just in case.

48

Breaking In

The transporter door opened without a sound. Some of the things made a small dinging noise; this one didn't. Maybe the bell was broken or they had some other reason that made sense to their thought patterns.

The transporter was empty. We looked in and saw a single activation button and no video screen. The unit was an earlier model, which made sense. It was probably the first one installed on the Earth.

None of us were anxious for the next phase of this operation. We had to make sure we knew where this door went and doing that had a high probability of getting us killed.

"Look. You all wait here and I'll go through and take a look around, then I'll come right back," I said.

Before I could step in, the sergeant jumped into the compartment and struck the button. The door slid shut and he was gone.

We stood there looking at each other in surprise. The breeze blew coldly down from the crest of the ridge and the moon provided an eerie pale light that illuminated the rocks around us. It was truly a desolate place. The desolation was enhanced by the sudden sound of moaning from down-slope somewhere. There was another Pug-bear coming our way.

We could hear the stones clatter and fall as it scrabbled up the slope. The blasted thing was playing it cagey though. It was making use of every available bit of cover as it passed the trees. Finally, though it got close enough that I thought I could make out the moonlight glinting off of some shiny places on its carapace. Aiming just below the shine, I fired a brief bolt and struck it dead center.

The legs scrabbled a bit, but the entire middle of the thing had dissolved.

Liz breathed, "Will they never stop coming?"

As I lifted the eraser-gun to the ready position, I happened to notice something new about it. There was a tiny flashing yellow light on the left side of the weapon.

"Uh-oh!" I exclaimed. "I think that might mean that it's about out of power."

"Not good! We really need it now!" Liz answered.

Then it became obvious why Rudy's group was so solid. Jointly, they were very resourceful and Joe proved it. He stepped forward with something in his hand.

He explained that he'd looked at the other eraser-gun after Rudy broke it and noticed that there was one part that was detachable. He'd taken that part off before Rudy had left the gun in the Stanley Steamer.

I'd seen that there was a kind of clip-like device on the right of the receiver area of the weapon, but I hadn't dared mess with it. Since it hadn't blown Joe up, I felt a little more confident. It took about thirty seconds to figure out how to pull the thing off my gun and replace it with the one from Rudy's. When we did, the flashing light went out. I gave a sigh of relief and said, "It looks like we've got a recharge."

"We'll see shortly," said Rudy, just as the transporter door popped open again.

The sergeant was there, wild-eyed; "There's a small room and another transporter on the other end of it. I don't know where the small room is. I went through the second transporter and it came out in a large, glass-enclosed dome on some other planet. I could see what looked like other domes in the distance. There were a lot of aliens there! They saw me, but I ducked back through before they could do anything."

"They'll be coming soon, then!" I observed. "The good news is that it sounds like you reached the link on Titan. We'll have to go through to it and then blow the dome. Maybe that will slow the bastards down!"

The transporter door behind him started to close and we rushed to enter the compartment, before it did. It struck Colin's arm and popped open again. We all piled in and turned to get our guns aimed at the door. Liz activated the button; we went through the disorientation and then the door opened to a small, rectangular shaped room.

There was another transporter door on the far wall, but between it and us was trouble!

There was a squad of Pugs waiting for our door to open with their guns aimed right at our faces. Before they could think to shoot, I triggered the eraser-gun.

The Pugs didn't have a chance. Nothing could withstand the anti-matter. They disappeared with a crackling sound. I released the trigger and heard a gagging noise. Spinning towards the sound, I was horrified to see that Colin was on his knees with a splinter in his throat. His head was turning to mush as I watched. He gasped once and fell forward on his face.

One of the Pugs had managed to get off a shot before disintegrating. The splinter had passed above the anti-matter beam and hit Colin square in the neck. It was a hard blow to the rest of us.

Rudy turned away with his face screwed tightly, shaking his head violently in denial, while Liz simply stood there holding the cat with a very pale, taut expression.

We were too few and some of the best of us were dying too easily. In the back of my mind, I doubted that we'd get through this.

"They probably think we won't make it through this room, so let's go on and make them pay!" Rudy had recovered enough to want revenge, even though there were tears sliding down his cheeks. He and Colin had been especially close. They went back farther than the rest of the team and I knew that Rudy would be hard put to deal with the loss.

We walked forward to the transporter door on the far side of the room. There we found a serious problem. Once again, the eraser gun had proven to be a mixed blessing. I'd burned up the call button and a portion of the workings of the transporter.

I could see some kind of mechanism, but it was incomprehensible to me. I mean, I know a little about electronics, but electronics composed of gel bands connecting lumps of something that looked like silly putty? No, sorry. I couldn't make any sense out of it.

I was figuratively scratching my head as I inspected the problem. There was no button left. There was a hole in the panel where parts had been exposed to the anti-matter beam for too long. I could see little sparkles of what appeared to be electricity, but might have been some other kind of force, leaking from the edges of the partially disintegrated putty lumps. Altogether, it was a huge mess.

I turned to the others with dismay on my face, "I think we're screwed. We can't get the door open and I may have killed the whole unit. I don't know what we can do now."

Rudy said something unmentionable about the Pugs' mothers. It was kind of nonsensical, because we didn't even know if they had mothers. He continued cursing their entire family tree back to the primordial mud from which they might have arisen.

Joe, however, had a useful suggestion.

"Now, let's don't go jumping to conclusions. The door may be jammed from our side, but it may be that you only burned the call unit out. If we wait, I'll bet that the Pugs on the other side will get curious and come through. They will either think we haven't arrived and no messenger has been sent back or they will think that we arrived and killed the squad."

"Which, of course, is what happened," I added, taking up the thought. "It's a good idea. I think you're right. They can't wait too long before they send someone through to check out the situation. They'll be expecting the worst, so we need to be ready as fast as possible."

I looked around the chamber. It was empty except for some remnants of the Pugs I'd erased. The bare metal walls were the only things there. All of a sudden I had another brilliant flash of mental acuity. I guess that old phrase, 'necessity is the mother of invention' is correct. We needed some shielding from the Pugs' splinters and there was nothing in the room, but the metal walls.

"The metal walls!" I exclaimed. The others looked at me in surprise.

I took the eraser-gun and disintegrated a hole in the metal. There was a brief hiss of equalizing atmosphere and then nothing. Using my laser torch,

I could see that there was rock behind the metal. This encouraged me and using the anti-matter gun, I made four long, swift passes and cut a large, irregular square of metal out of the wall. It fell to the floor with a crash, revealing a basalt wall behind.

We levered the metal plate up; it was unusually heavy and required all of us to lift it onto one edge. Then we worked it around so that it blocked the chamber about half way from the end.

I'd started cutting in the middle of the wall and we were able to brace one of the metal plate's irregular ends against the rock. The plate was thus partially supported by leaning against the edge of the initial cut in the metal wall. It wasn't resting there very securely and had to be kind of balanced by someone holding it on the opposite corner, but it did offer a good shield that we could duck behind.

We arranged ourselves behind the barrier and settled down to wait for the Pugs to show up.

49

Breaking Out?

An hour later, we were beginning to doubt that our plan would work. It seemed like they had no curiosity. Nothing was happening. We speculated that the door was completely broken or that they had a view screen on the other side and could see us. We were also getting tired of holding the metal plate in place, even though we alternated periodically.

The sergeant said, "Look, if they can see us, they'd open the door right away and pitch a grenade through. That would take care of us with no problem."

We thought about it and realized that he was probably correct. They couldn't use one of the anti-matter bombs, because it would amount to massive overkill, but it was unimaginable that they didn't have other, less powerful explosive devices. So, we were still left waiting.

"I hope the Air Force pilot gets some action with his commanding officer and they manage to get the airborne laser into play. The country couldn't take an EMP burst," Joe looked agitated.

He continued, "There's been no decent leadership in Washington for years. Just look at the mess the Feds have made of weather-caused disasters. They can't do anything but spend money on useless actions. I think those hundreds of mobile homes that FEMA ordered for that hurricane are still rotting away in some field somewhere."

Joe didn't have a good impression of our government. Actually he was so independent that he despised all government, claiming that there had to be a better way for humans to live together. I considered his position for a moment. From the mess our leaders had made of the world, it appeared that he was mostly justified.

The room was getting hotter and more humid with our breathing and that was compounded by the amount of heat radiating from the rocks that I'd exposed. I felt them and they were warm to the touch.

"I think we must be a fair distance underground here. The rocks are warm," I said.

Rudy responded, "You might be right, or we might be just under the surface and the sun might be heating up the rocks."

"Wait. It was night when we came in here. What time is it now?" Liz asked.

Rudy looked at his watch, "We've been in here an hour and twenty seven minutes. They're probably not coming through."

We were all sweating and the air was getting positively moist from our breath. Things didn't seem as clear-cut as I remembered. I was feeling mentally foggy, when I suddenly realized that we were suffering from lack of oxygen.

"One of us has to go back through the transporter to the mountain-side and then come back in. That way we can transport a load of fresh air into this sweat box," I said.

"I'll go," said the sergeant.

He stepped back to the transporter to Estes Park and pushed the button. The door popped open releasing a Pug-bear right on top of him. He didn't have a chance. It ripped his head right off his shoulders and his blood splattered all over the room. A terrible wave of fear passed over us as he died and I felt the urge to simply lie down in front of the creature.

The alien thing was fully adult and terrifically strong. It threw his body directly at me, knocking me down and taking the metal wall with me as I fell backwards. The eraser-gun skidded over to the side of the room. The shock cleared my mind of the fear and left me able to act. I scrambled and rolled, desperately stretching to reach it.

Liz, Rudy, and Joe were firing away with their splinter guns at the thing as it slipped about in the blood from our friend, its claws digging for traction.

That slip gave them the chance they needed to shoot a second round of splinters. One of the shots happened to go right down the alien's gullet as it opened its fangs. The effect was the same as when I shot the one in the cage in the row house. The creature practically exploded internally. Fluid gushed out of the spiracles on its carapace and it collapsed into a twitching hulk on the floor.

I shakily regained my feet while Liz tried to calm the hysterical cat. I recovered the eraser-gun and handed it to her. She took it in one hand as she distractedly stroked Jefferson who was yowling as he stood against the wall.

Together, Rudy, Joe, Stormbreaker and I laboriously replaced the piece of metal and reconstructed our ambush. The only good that came of the sergeant's death was we now had a transporter full of fresh air that had been released into our cubical.

We settled down to wait again. After awhile, I decided that I'd better let in another load of fresh air. This time, I opened the rear transporter door myself with the eraser-gun pointing at the ready.

Nothing came through, but some fresh Rocky Mountain air, naturally air-conditioned by Mother Nature. It was downright frosty and Rudy said, "Global warming is a crock! I'm cold."

Stormbreaker replied, "Those people who think that humans can change the global climate, probably also think that the Earth shakes when they let a fart!"

We all laughed at the idea and, encouraged, he continued in a more sober vein.

"The Great Spirit makes all things work in cycles. We understand some of them, like the peak in rabbit population every seven years. It's always followed by a die-off and the eighth year you can't hardly find a rabbit anywhere," he paused and looked at us seriously. "If I thought like those people do, I'd be placing the rabbit on the endangered species list and forbidding hunting. It's a good thing the rabbits don't think that way. They get to humping other rabbits, like they do, and the population builds up again so that the foxes and coyotes and hawks and owls have good years and build up their population. Everything is interrelated with cycles."

He looked at the still closed transporter door, then started again, "I'll bet that there is some kind of relationship between us and the Pugs, if we only understood..."

As he spoke, the damaged door opened and we started shooting for all we were worth. The transporter was full of Pugs.

50

The Jump Off Point

Their splinter-guns were firing from the moment the transporter opened, but the splinters either went high or broke on our shielding metal plate. The very number of the splinters they were throwing at us suppressed our return fire. None of us wanted to risk being shot. Since the splinter-guns had a magazine that a cowboy in an old black and white movie would have envied, the volume of fire coming at us didn't slow.

I got an idea from Liz's earlier use of her compact and pulled out my only remaining phone. The cover glass on it was reflective enough for me to use as a mirror so I poked the end of it out near the floor around the end of the metal plate.

It worked. I could see Pugs well enough to poke my splinter-gun around the edge and fire a burst into their legs. That slowed the volume of their fire down considerably.

The next time I pushed the phone out, it drew a hail of splinters and I dropped it as the things broke near my fingers. None actually cut me, but pieces bounced off my hand. I desperately hoped that the poison wouldn't migrate through my un-cut skin as I drew back and inspected my hand. I wasn't cut and there wasn't any yellow fluid, so I re-focused on the battle.

Thinking fast, I shoved the end of my splinter-gun out and it too, drew their fire. As they were trying to shoot it, Rudy and Joe stuck their heads over the far end of the plate where it leaned against the wall.

Stormbreaker was doing his best to prop the end up over my head and couldn't shoot, but the two of them managed to kill the last three Pugs. One of the aliens fell, blocking the transporter door open. Its body kept the transporter inactive and prohibited the aliens from possibly sending reinforcements through.

I got up and helped Stormbreaker push the plate back to where we could lean it against the wall. We might still need it, I thought, and it was too heavy to pick up easily.

Clustered around the open transporter door were seven Pug bodies. They were pretty gross from the poison's action, but we carefully moved them into the transporter and stacked them up so we could squat behind the pile. This would give us a modicum of cover when we came through to the destination. I got the eraser-gun ready and pointed over the Pug bodies at the door opening and everyone except Liz squatted down behind the pile and prepared to go.

Liz was trying to pick up the cat, but Jefferson absolutely balked at this point. He wouldn't let her get close, dodging from one side of the room to the other while staying as near the first transporter door as possible. Even dodging about as he was, he was careful to avoid the random splashes of poisoned-glass pieces on the floor. When she finally picked him up, he refused to come in the second transporter, wriggling out of her arms to the floor and yowling. I guess he thought that the dead Pugs smelled too bad or maybe he thought we weren't going to make it. In either event, I couldn't see how he could survive, if we left him locked in that room.

I jumped up and grabbed him before he had time to react, than ran to the other door at the far end of the room, dodging around the Pug-bear's carcass as I did. I pushed the first transporter's call button and was rewarded by another burst of fresh air when the door opened.

As it popped open, I tossed the cat into the back of the transporter box, simultaneously reaching around to push the activation button. The door nearly slid shut on my arm, but I got it out in time. I figured Jefferson would have a better chance on the mountainside than with us. I only hoped that there weren't any aliens close enough to grab him as he came out.

As I turned back, I could see that Liz was upset by my throwing him out, but she took a deep breath and said, "He'll be able to avoid any danger out there. He's smart and knows to stay away from Pugs."

Stormbreaker had to ruin that happy thought, "I hope he knows to stay away from coyotes, too. They'll take a cat quicker than anything."

I didn't know if Jefferson even knew that such a thing as a coyote existed, but the elevation at the Fall River transporter head was high and there was probably little around to attract coyotes. I hoped they'd also stay away from the area because of the Pug-bears. I tried to make myself feel more confident for him.

Digging in my belt pouch, I pulled out one of the anti-matter bombs. Hefting it in my hand, I looked again at the timer dial. I remembered how I'd set the others and decided to set this one to explode with only enough time for us to transport away, assuming that we were alive to do so.

As I examined the bomb, Stormbreaker asked, "What's that thing? It ain't a bomb is it? It's too small to be much good."

"It's plenty good. It'll make more of a mess than any conventional bomb," I assured him.

We didn't know what was on the other side of this final transporter. The sergeant had said that it led off the planet to some domes, but where that was, we could only assume. If it was the Titan location, we hoped that shooting off the bomb would seriously disrupt the aliens' plans. However, there was no guarantee and I was having second thoughts about the idea. It seemed like one bomb wouldn't be enough for the whole moon. I thought briefly about using the second one also, but I figured it had better be kept as a reserve.

We got in position and readied our weapons and Liz pressed the button.

51

Somewhere Else

We came out in a dome, just like the sergeant had said we would, but, to our great relief, there were no aliens of any kind in sight. This was unexpected but welcome. We carefully exited the transporter, watching for any opposition to show up. It was set flush against the front of a square building on one side of the dome. There were a number of such structures around the perimeter of the place. They were cube-like in the front with the sidewalls curving down from the roof, joining smoothly against the dome wall. All of the structures had doors in the middle of their front and all of the doors were closed.

The dome, itself, was at least two hundred yards in diameter and made out of some transparent material that looked like glass. I reckoned that it was something far stronger. It would just about have to be. There's always a higher chance of being struck by falling space debris when the atmosphere is thin. Earth's atmosphere is thick enough to burn up much of the fast-moving, smaller stuff before it causes a problem on the ground. The only things we have to worry about are the rocks large enough to crash through our roof on up to the ones big enough to cause global disaster, but they are fortunately rare.

The pressure inside the structure was about Earth normal, but the air had a funny smell. It left us short of breath, too. Either the oxygen level was low or maybe the CO_2 balance was off. That squared with the Pugs' nasty reaction to Earth's air. We could breathe theirs with difficulty; they needed some kind of thin suit with, I presumed, a built-in respirator to protect them from ours.

The center of the dome gave us all pause. It was a lush garden filled with alien plants. The growing things were far more alien than the Pugs and their colors were shocking to us, used as we were to green as the predominant plant color. There were numerous varieties of plants mixed in a wild exuberance of growth. They ranged from a light, sky-blue to almost ultra-violet in color and stood up to thirty or forty feet in height.

As we wonderingly approached the garden, several of the plant-like organisms slowly moved to orient towards us. One particularly large tree analogue had numerous tubular, flower-like structures that hung down from its multitude of branches. It slowly lifted them as we approached. The flowers gradually moved until they all pointed directly at us.

The things looked too much like projectile weapons for my comfort and I motioned for everyone to stop and back-up. As we departed, the farther tubes drooped to their original position, but those on our side of the tree kept pointing at us. There was a piece of a broken, plastic crate that had been conveniently left on the floor of the dome and Joe picked it up. He tossed it towards the tree and the 'flowers' convincingly demonstrated that they were deadly.

As the plastic flew towards the tree, seeming to almost float in the lighter gravity, the closest flowers launched reddish, harpoon-like things from their tubular centers. The harpoons were attached to the flowers by a white, thin fiber. The things were able to shoot with accuracy and almost all of them bounced off the piece, knocking it to the ground.

The flowers retrieved their weapons by somehow sucking the fiber back and in a few seconds they were ready for action again. One of the last shooters had missed the target as it dropped and the harpoon had embedded itself in the dome's floor. The flower strained to pull it back and the filament tightened until the entire branch was bent. It finally gave up and relaxed.

It was enough of a lesson for us. No doubt there were other organisms in that alien garden that were as dangerous. We weren't interested in taking any chances, so we sheared off to check out the other cube-structures.

We had no difficulty opening the doors of each; they were simply set up to be pulled open with a cable-like loop. That handle would work for both the Pugs, who had more or less human-like hands and for the Pug-bears' claws.

The first cube was full of packages of compressed wafers. We didn't even try to guess their purpose, although Stormbreaker said the material looked like pemmican. Perhaps it was some sort of food supply. If it was for the aliens, it probably was meat. That's all I'd seen them eat. Of course, there weren't any suitable vegetables on Earth, if the central garden was any indication.

The second cube was packed with padded cases that proved to be full of eggs. The outsides of the cases were marked in the Pugs cursive script and also in English. The labels were destination cities, many corresponding to the transporter heads we'd previously located.

The fact that they were co-marked in English was a nasty reminder that some of our fellows were quite ready to sell out our race. I browsed around a little bit, hoping to find some kind of a list of collaborators. I knew this was probably a vain hope, but it would have made it much easier to locate the people who'd been co-opted to help the Pugs. However, it turned out to be a fruitless effort.

Liz wanted to blow the eggs with one of the anti-matter bombs, but I wasn't ready to give up on our search. It was proving informative and information was what we were short of. I'd been playing catch-up ever since I stumbled into the transporter system and I was sick of it, so I vetoed her idea.

"What I want to know," said Rudy, "is why they are making the effort to transport the eggs. Are these eggs dormant in some way? And, why not simply send Pug-bears through and let them lay eggs in each location?"

"Maybe they don't reproduce very quickly," I said, but I knew that couldn't be correct. The damned things had taken over at least fifteen planets based on the booklet we'd found. I thought they had to be very fecund. I desperately felt the need for more information.

We walked on to the next cube building. The door of this one was locked. We tried pulling on the loop, but it didn't move. Tiring of this, I used the eraser-gun on the door to cut an irregular shaped opening through the wall, dissolving the entire door in the process. We carefully entered the cube.

When my eyes had adapted to the dimly lit room, my hair practically stood on end. The place was packed with what appeared to be nuclear warheads. They looked like bombs and even had conventional human atom symbols on them. If I'd held the anti-matter beam on a little too long, the things might have gone off or released some nuclear material that could have proven deadly to us.

The implications of this stockpile were grim. There were enough weapons here to decimate the Earth. If the aliens could simply drop these things from orbit or even somehow launch them from Titan, humans would have no effective defense. The presence of the things also implied some form of spacecraft. They'd have to get them into position to drop on us somehow. I briefly wondered if there was a spaceship around somewhere, but I decided that I'd better focus on screwing up their plans.

We snooped around and examined the bombs. They might have had some form of proximity detonator on them, but we couldn't recognize it.

At the rear of the room, I found another type of bomb. These were also nuclear, but they didn't look aerodynamic. They had timers and were meant to be placed near their targets. The timers were exactly like the ones on the eraser-grenades, so I knew how to set them.

"Let's check the next cubes and then set these things to go off," I said.

"OK. If you're sure we have the time to explore farther," Rudy replied. His tone of voice indicated that he was doubtful about the idea of additional exploration.

"I don't know how the aliens even get in here. The sergeant told us the place was full of them, so there might be a transporter in one of the other cubes or even a tunnel to the other domes," I gestured vaguely at the transparent wall.

The clear dome now provided a view of Saturn, framed by jagged mountains and partially obscured by a light, patchy fog of some kind of vapor. The planet had risen while we were looking at the bombs. There was a slight mist of falling methane snow, but the view, while stunning, didn't give me a warm and fuzzy feeling.. Instead, it looked cold and totally inhospitable to humans.

I glanced at the other domes. There were several in sight and I thought I could see a large mass of creatures moving across the floor of the closest one. I decided that this was undoubtedly their main base.

The next cubical only contained some ragged human clothes. It looked like there had been some captives here, but they weren't there now and the only clue was the clothes, w appeared to have been torn off their bodies. We presumed the worst had happened to them.

We looked at each other sadly and went on. It was too late for those people. I felt a wave of anger wash through me. I had to make the aliens pay for their attempted invasion.

52

The Ancient One

The last cube was almost all the way around the dome near the transporter door through which we'd entered. I walked up and casually pulled the loop handle. As the door swung open, I felt like my body was exposed to a vibrating shock that made me become numb. I could stand, but wasn't able to voluntarily move. A shadow moved in the rear of the dark cube and a horrific visage appeared out of the darkness. It was a huge Pug-bear.

This one must have been much older than the ones we'd disposed of earlier. Its body was almost twice the size of the largest I'd previously seen and its carapace gave the impression of being old. It was actually ragged around the edges where it had chipped and been broken by use. The huge creature's mental projection was far stronger than that of the younger ones I'd previously encountered.

The thing moved closer to the door and I could see that its braincase was likewise enlarged. As I watched it approach, in my horror, I tried my best to move my gun hand, but nothing happened. I was panicking. I wondered briefly why one of the others didn't shoot the thing. Then I suddenly felt a combination sensation that was like nothing I'd ever felt before. It was a kind of mental pressure, combined with a rapidly increasing headache in my temples.

As I wondered where the others were and why they weren't shooting, the pressure became unbearable. It mounted in my skull to a crescendo and then something seemed to rip with an agonizing, tearing feeling. The alien had torn through my mental defenses and ripped its way into my conscious mind.

In spite of the pain, I understood that this was how they communicated and it was obvious the old alien was far more adept at sending than I was at blocking. I was completely unable to defend myself from the thoughts and emotions it inserted into my mind. It was a helpless, outrageous feeling, almost as if it were raping me. I ached from my loss of control. It was terrifying being at the thing's mercy, but beneath my terror, I was coldly and utterly angry at the violation of my core being.

I suddenly felt a sense of inquisitiveness coming from it. It wasn't angry or revengeful. It was simply wondering why we were attempting to resist their invasion.

"How did we expect to stand against them, The Masters?"

The thought seemed to slide into my mind edgewise. The communication came slowly at first, as if I had to interpret patterns of emotions into concepts that I could understand. As the thought formed, the creature's self-identification also came into my consciousness. He referred to himself as, "The Ancient One."

His intrusion became more forceful. Suddenly, I unexpectedly found myself sobbing aloud. Tears welled out of my eyes as the thing manipulated my emotions.

"The Masters were wonderful. They were kind and loved humans. Why had we ever thought we were good enough to kill them? We were guilty of cruelty on an genocidal scale."

I was completely under the control of the thing. It must have previously experimented with other humans, since it had no trouble pushing all of my emotional buttons. I was practically salivating in my urge to help The Masters. The only thing was, I didn't really want to help them: far from it. There was another wave of emotion and I suddenly felt totally unworthy of existence.

"How dared our species deign to monopolize that wonderful planet? We absolutely didn't deserve it. I should kill the other unworthy ones behind me and then help them with their invasion. With my expert help, they would be guaranteed success and I'd have a cherished and honored place after the take-over. They'd see that I had everything I desired, all of the food, all of the luxury, all of the women..."

That last promise suddenly shocked my mind. I didn't want All of the women. I only wanted one and I'd just been instructed to kill her. I was horrified that I'd actually accepted that thought as my own for a moment without any question. The shock split my mind into two parts.

It was a state that was somewhat familiar to me from some of my past experience. At one point in my long and admittedly spotty career, I had spent a considerable amount of time meditating as part of a series of advanced healing classes I'd taken and I knew that those surface thoughts weren't really me.

In each human's mind, there are divisions of consciousness. The first is exclusively involved with our passing thoughts. That is the one that we normally think of as ourselves.

The thoughts that come and go through our minds aren't really exclusively ours. We think they are us, but we actually may be receiving them from someone else or they may be floating around in the quantum plenum waiting for us to become conscious of them.

There is, however, another aspect of our minds that is not part of the surface thoughts. I call it the 'Observer' and it stays separate from them. I'd learned to allow myself to passively watch the thoughts that come through my mind while I meditated. I'd discovered that they have no effect on the 'Observer' part of me. It can look at a thought and say, "That's an interesting one. I wonder where it came from?" and then let the thought go without becoming entangled by it.

This entanglement is what traps the majority of people into responding emotionally before they even think things out. They're so sure that their surface thoughts are all that there is of them, they respond instantly to any emotion that comes through their mind. I was aware of the 'Observer' watching the emotionally laden thoughts that the alien created.

It was this part of my mind that was resisting the Ancient One's control. The alien was pushing its own thoughts into my mind in a masterful way and those thoughts were so calculated as to activate my emotions powerfully. I didn't like the forced intrusion, but I couldn't cause it to cease. I found that I could avoid it by retreating into my 'Observer' state.

The old Pug-bear continued to work its controlling influence into my surface mind and as it did, the 'Observer' part of me became aware of a hidden channel. The Ancient One was obviously unaware of that flow. I was somehow receiving information about the Pug-bears and Pugs that I realized should never be released to an enemy.

Below the controlling, emotionally laden thoughts it was deliberately forcing on me was a connection to the Ancient One's entire knowledge. It may have been accidental, but information flowed out of its mind into mine on some deep level in a continuous stream. I suddenly felt as if I knew things about the aliens that I couldn't possibly know. Things that gave me a far better understanding of their invasion and strengths and weaknesses.

Retreating into the 'Observer' had given me a self-induced respite from the emotional control and I had been building up more and more resistance to the manipulation. The 'Observer' part of my mind was not angry, since it didn't feel emotion, but I, the me on an existential level, was more than ready to do something about the intrusion.

As I prepared myself mentally, the information flow from the old alien increased on its bi-level intrusion. On the surface, the Pug-bear was attempting to gain control of me, but, on the lower level, it was unintentionally dumping all of its entire store of knowledge into my sub-conscious mind. I didn't have a firm grip on the flow. It wasn't as if I was reading the information on a conscious level; instead, it was as if I just had discovered that I had memories of it that I hadn't known I had.

At that point, something even stranger happened. It must have been due to the ripping open of my individual sense of consciousness paired with the infiltration of the massive amount of extra knowledge. I suddenly was able to reach a mental depth that I'd never experienced before.

I found myself actually standing behind the 'Observer' section of my mind. Now, I found myself in an emotionless, colorless, neutral space that had no connection to thoughts, as we normally understand them. This part of me was the 'I,' the 'me,' my 'core existence'. It was untouched by the surface thoughts and the Ancient One's emotional manipulation was far away and unimportant.

From this vantage point, I was simultaneously conscious of all that was going on around me and also able to sense lines of energy flowing in what I understood was the universe. They were passing around and through my body and connecting me to the moon, the stars, the sun, Liz, my friends and everything else in existence. The connection was direct and immediate. Distance didn't seem to make any difference; something could be far or near and I could still see a direct link of force. There was a skein of these connections between my energy field and that of the Ancient One.

I reached out and tapped into these lines of force in some indescribable way. I could feel energy flowing through me, arising from my pelvic region and ascending in two rainbow, sparkling columns on each side of my back. There was a momentary pause and then the columns joined, continued up my neck and then shot out of the top of my head, connecting me to an incredible feeling of strength. The net effect was a thrilling flow of energy along my spine, paired with the sense that I could accomplish anything.

I'd heard of Kundalini energy before, but I'd never felt anything like this and I'm not sure that was exactly what I was experiencing. I did realize that the flow of force was irrevocably changing my mental structure. The change wasn't limited to my thoughts only; my ability to use my senses seemed to also have been impacted. I could somehow mentally enhance my perceptual ability. I guess a better description might be that I was developing some form of psychic ability. I didn't know how it would affect me or if it would even last, but I knew with a dead certainty that it was there and that I was different as a result.

The flow strengthened in seconds. I let the feeling build until it reached the point where I didn't think I could hold any more power. Then I used my knowledge of the Pug-bear's mental structure. The understanding suddenly welled up from the new information in my subconscious and I knew with a total certainty what to do.

I carefully formed and then sent a brilliant, white-hot and high energy thought at the Pug-bear. It was an imperative; simple, piercing, and highly focused:

"Die!Die!Die!Die!Die!Die!Die!Die!Die!Die!Die!Die!Die!Die!"

The Pug-bear reared back in shock!

"This had never happened before! The worthless human had broken its mental control and had launched an attack directly through its mental defenses. It must fight, it must – "

It began quivering and foam appeared around its mandibles and, as it did, I suddenly felt the paralysis that it had imposed on me disappear. At the same time, there was an additional rush of information that flowed from its mind to mine as it struggled to regain control.

I looked shakily down and realized that I'd dropped the eraser gun, which I'd been holding in my right hand. Fortunately, my left hand instinctively moved in the muscle pattern engraved through years of practice. I yanked the splinter-gun from my belt holster and shot a single splinter down the creature's opened gullet.

The Ancient One let out an incredible, moaning shriek and the telltale green fluid ran from its spiracles. The splinter mortally injured it. The creature's body was beginning to succumb to the poison. It fell over on one side and its legs moved slowly.

The mental control it had been exerting on me was destroyed. I could sense that it was dead or dying as I made an effort to return to my normal reality. As I came out of my mental depths, the information I'd received from it seemed to recede into mist. I still had the sensation that I knew a lot about them, but it wasn't so easily accessible, now

I was trying to regain my equilibrium when Liz suddenly grabbed my arm and shook me. "What happened? I was frozen! I was paralyzed and I couldn't move and then you did something and I could move again and – and then you killed the thing!" She was screaming directly into my face. She moved to grab both of my arms, still trying to shake me.

I was so stunned at the outcome that I couldn't immediately answer. All I could do was to put a hand on her shoulder and weakly nod. The sense of energy flow receded rapidly back down my spine with part of it moving out around my ribs. My head felt like it was about three times its normal size and the sense of knowledge about the aliens had now simply faded out.

The others were recovering as if from some huge emotional binge. They were rubbing their eyes and staggering around as if they were inebriated. They moved towards me and Stormbreaker pointed at the dying Pug-bear as it slowly moved one leg in a reflexive action.

"It's a good thing you're a powerful Shaman, paleface," he said.

I'd noticed that he used 'paleface' in moments of approbation. He was giving me a compliment. I took it in the spirit in which it was offered.

I had recovered enough to joke back with him, "That's OK, Redskin! I'm here to help any time you need me."

He laughed and said, "You better not use that term around any politically correct devotees. I don't care, cause it describes me perfectly, but some busybody might think it's meant as an insult."

It was apparent that they had somehow sensed the mental exchange on some sub-conscious level, but not been able to follow it. The Ancient-One had been holding us all in its control, but had been communicating only with me.

Now recovered to the point where I could think more or less rationally, I turned to the others and said, "Let's set those bombs and get out of here. I could feel the old Pug-bear mentally summoning help while he had me captive."

We dashed to the cube where the bombs were stored and I carefully adjusted the ones with timers to go off in what I judged would be about fifteen minutes. They were at the back of the room and hidden from easy view by the non-timed bombs, so I thought that the Pugs probably wouldn't find that they were set until too late.

It took me a couple of minutes to set them all, so I tried to stagger the settings in order to get the timing correct. I was hoping that they'd all go off at the same time. If not, the first explosion might simply destroy the other bombs before they fired. I didn't have a great deal of confidence in my timing expertise, but I hoped that it would work.

The only problem was that the cubical door was dissolved, so I decided to remove that indicator by camouflage. As I stepped out of the cube, I turned with the eraser gun and dissolved all of the other cube doors that were in sight. That made them all look similar and kept the bomb storage room from standing out.

We cut and ran for the transporter cube. As we reached the point where I could see the other two cubes around the central jungle, I burned out their doors. We then dashed into the transporter as soon as it opened, jumping over the stacked Pug bodies as we entered. With a button push, we left Titan and returned to Earth.

As we came out of the transporter door into the small room, I mentally sent a message to my compatriots to "Run!" I had intended to yell it out-loud, but somehow it came out mentally instead.

No one seemed to notice that it was not audible. They'd been looking around at the room, but now they scampered to the other end rapidly, bypassing the stinking carcass of the Master we'd previously killed. I started after them, but then stopped and turned back to drag one of the stacked-up Pug bodies partly out of the transporter to block the door from closing.

The others were yelling at me to hurry as I turned back to them.

"That might keep them from getting through so quickly," I panted as I arrived at their end of the room.

Liz hit the call button and the door swung open. We bailed in and, just before she hit the button, I set the timer and threw one of my last two eraser-grenades into the room. It was adjusted to go off rapidly, so I slammed my hand down on the transporter activation button, brushing hers aside and we were out of there!

53

The Park

The mountain wind was still from the north and had picked up so that it felt a lot colder. There was a trace of frost forming on the rocks as we came out of the Fall River transporter head and the stars appeared even brighter than before. I shivered and looked around for Jefferson, but there was no sign of him near the door.

Rudy, Joe, and Stormbreaker started down towards the car, walking cautiously in the moonlight and stopping to listen for Pug-bear sounds every few steps. Liz started after them and then realized that I had turned up the slope and halted to see what I was doing.

As I stepped upwards into the chill wind, I realized that whatever had happened during my encounter with the old Pug-bear had made a permanent difference to my perceptual ability. I was now aware of my surroundings in a way that I'd never experienced. It was kind of like having super-sensitive hearing and sight, but I realized that my eyes didn't need to be open to see! My feeling of more acute senses was paired with a mental receptivity to thoughts and patterns of energy.

I stood still and looked up at the stars. They suddenly seemed brighter and looked as if they were coming down on me for a moment. I felt dizzy and my head felt strange, but then everything straightened out. It was like plunging into a cold pool of water. It was a shock, but then I got used to it.

My perception opened and spread out. I was aware of little nuances in the wind; of the pattern of light and shadows that the moon made and of... Something pulled at the edge of my mind. Something that was familiar and was up the hill from my location.

I focused my attention, sensing a feeling of desolation and loneliness along with a distinctive impression of total self-confidence. That could only be coming from Jefferson. Following the energy flow in some way that I couldn't describe, I walked up the hill about a hundred yards as Liz watched.

I used my newfound ability to send thoughts and summoned him, putting a sort of signature flourish on my thought as I did. I could sense that he viewed me in a particular way and that flourish that I created contained some of the elements he associated with me. My mental signature had equal parts of strength, large size, fighting ability and kindness. As I sent it, I realized that I had created a personal identity pattern that would be helpful in sending messages to humans as well as to our feline partner.

I heard a querulous "Meowp?" carried on the wind from behind a boulder farther up slope, then a quick rush as he ran full speed down to me. I had to shift gears and come back to my normal sense pattern in order to catch him, as he jumped at me from about ten feet away.

Don't let anyone tell you that cats are light. You try and catch twenty pounds of furry lightening coming at around thirty miles per hour. It wasn't easy and I had a hard time keeping my footing on the slope. It was worth the effort, though. I could hear him starting to purr even before he hit my arms.

Now reunited with our cat (I'd say 'kitty' affectionately, but that would be too demeaning to our furry warrior), we started down after the others. As we walked, I extended my senses, seeking for any aliens. The area seemed clear and we hurried to catch up.

Stormbreaker cautioned us that we'd better slow down and watch for ambushes, but I told him not to worry about it. That necessitated a discussion that took several minutes. The main problem was due to my being unable to find satisfactory words to describe my suddenly increased abilities. I couldn't seem to make them understand that something had happened to my senses.

There was considerable resistance on their part and I got the impression that the idea offended Stormbreaker. He felt that one of the strengths that he brought to our group was his ability to track and to encompass the natural environment to the point where no animal could surprise him. He was upset because I was now telling him, I could sense the presence of other creatures better than he could.

We discussed it for awhile, but I finally told them to watch my lips and then held them very still as I mentally broadcast to them, "Enhanced perception isn't all I can do."

This caused Joe, who hadn't been paying much attention to jump. Rudy tapped on the side of his head in a puzzled manner, while Stormbreaker only muttered something about, "Damned, weird white-men."

I was going to send them a second thought, but the transporter suddenly exploded. There was a flash and a loud 'boom' as the thing went off. We spun around and saw a large part of the ridgeback structure fall into its component pieces. There was a rattle as debris fell around us. A rumble followed as many of the larger pieces came rolling down in our direction.

We scrambled up the side of the shallow valley we'd been following on our trek downward and huddled behind a large boulder. The rock slide rattled past us, staying mostly in the gully. There were a number of loud cracks as good-sized rocks hit the other side of our shelter. Some of the debris flew over the top and Rudy yelled out an imprecation as he was struck.

The landslide faded out, still moving downhill, and we took a deep breath of relief.

"What made that thing blow?" Rudy asked, rubbing his head where a goose-egg was forming.

"I'm not totally sure," I answered, "but I have an idea. Remember, we've never noticed any time lag as we went through the transporters. It's as if the trip has been instantaneous, no matter whether we were going next door or to the alien base."

I paused as I realized that I somehow knew far more about the transporters than I'd realized. The subconscious knowledge I'd received from the 'Ancient-One' seemed to bubble up when I needed it. Now that I'd had some time to start to assimilate the knowledge, I suddenly realized that the 'Ancient-One' had not really understood it. The information had been lifted from some other creature's mind that the 'Ancient-One' had dominated. Perhaps that was why it leaked it to me on a secondary channel; it didn't recognize the value of what I was assimilating.

The thought made me stutter a little, but then I continued, "Th-The only thing that can move that rapidly are so called 'torsion waves' that are movements in the quantum plenum. These waves can travel about a billion times faster than light and are responsible for things like quantum entanglement."

I took a deep breath, "If I understand correctly, the transporters are linked on a quantum level. We didn't travel through space when we went through them; we de-materialized somehow into an energy field. Then we were transmitted far faster than light in torsion waveform. We re-materialized into our bodies as we exited from the linked destination portal."

"That's why most of the transporters only have one or two connections. It's too difficult for them to build ones that can be 'tuned' to numerous destinations. They simply use quantum entanglement to link the structures of two of the transporter heads together. They've only recently gotten far enough along to be able to place two such linked heads in the same mechanism, each activated by its own button." Liz was shaking my arm, trying to interrupt the flow of subconscious information that I was spewing. "How do you know all of that?" she demanded.

"Yeah. Where did that come from? You've never acted like a theoretical physicist before," Rudy added.

I thought about it for a moment, "I received a lot more information from the Pug-bear than it thought I was receiving. There was kind of an undercurrent of... I don't know how to describe it."

I shook my head in frustration and then went on, "I think the alien somehow imparted a lot more knowledge than it intended. In its surprise, when I was able to resist its control and then struck back, it shoved even more information into my mind. It was totally shocked that I could send a mental strike through its control. I remember feeling like I understood everything clearly for a moment as I attacked. I think I'm going to begin to remember things from that connection that I couldn't otherwise know."

"But, what caused the transporter to explode?" Rudy hadn't forgotten the point of my original monologue.

"I was getting to that when I was interrupted," I looked at Liz with a smile. "The transporters are linked instantaneously and the central controlling unit was the one on Titan. When it blew up, this one lost the controlling influence of the other and it blew up also. They're inherently unstable without that central control. The control linkage passes through the entire network. Why – ," I stopped as it hit me.

"None of their transporters are working now!" Liz filled in. She'd been following me closely and understood the critical point.

"They're without their main advantage. The aliens on Earth are isolated and they can't transport," I concluded.

"I hope that's right," Stormbreaker said. He was unwilling to believe we could be that lucky.

The others looked somewhat skeptical, but even so, the ramifications of what I'd told them stopped the discussion and we started to move on towards the vehicles while they were thinking about what it might mean. Despite being able to move more easily due to my enhanced senses, it still took us some time to get back down to the road. We climbed up on the gravel and huddled to discuss our next step.

"I believe that we may have stopped the invasion for at least a few years," I started to explain, but Liz interrupted me with a question.

"How long has it been since the bombs should have gone off?" she asked.

"Well, the short answer is that they went off when the transporter blew up, but I think I see what you're trying to get at," I looked at her and she nodded, encouragingly. "Let's see. I set the timers for about fifteen minutes and it probably took us a couple of minutes to get back through the two transporters. Then I had to retrieve Jefferson and that took maybe five minutes. We caught up to the guys and that took us another few minutes. We had that argument where I had to convince everyone that we were safe –
"

Stormbreaker interjected, "Yeah. Then there was that 'boom' and we had to dodge falling rocks. We might be safe in your dreams – maybe. I'm not feeling happy until I see the last of those things dead."

"I agree completely," I responded. "But, what I was saying is that the discussion took about another ten minutes, so we've taken almost an hour to get here in total."

"That's what I thought," said Liz. "Look up there to the west," she pointed. "That's Saturn right there."

We could all see the shining planet hovering in the ecliptic.

"I think that it takes about seventy minutes or so for light to travel from there to Earth," she explained. "If I'm right – "

There was a flash of light that was momentarily brighter than the planet. It sparkled a little, but wasn't terribly bright overall. Even multiple atomic bombs aren't powerful enough to make much of a flash from almost eight hundred million miles.

"That flash was from an explosion that happened about seventy minutes ago based on light speed. It must have been from the bombs. If you're correct, and you seemed to be making some sense for a change, then all of the transporters all over the world blew up when it went off," Liz summarized.

"That will certainly get everyone's attention. A lot of those things are hidden in heavily populated areas and there's likely to be a lot of damage and casualties," I responded.

We climbed in the truck and car and headed back down Old Fall River road towards Estes Park.

54

A Flash in the Sky

We drove carefully, watching the road ahead, but nothing happened until we reached the turn-off that we'd passed on the way up. It was quite dark, down in the trees, but suddenly the whole eastern sky lit up. At the same time, both vehicles died.

The Air Force hadn't been ready in time and the EMP warhead had gone off. It looked like it had exploded somewhere over Kansas. That was near enough to the geographical center of the USA for the pulse to kill electronics all over the country.

"Oh, crap, crap, crap!" I shouted, banging my hand on the suddenly heavy steering wheel.

"They must have accelerated the launch! The transporters exploding must have caused them to hurry up!" Liz yelled.

"I know. That's exactly what they did. Now, what'll happen?" I was practically ready to bite ten-penny nails in half, I was so angry.

"A lot of... a very big lot of people will die," Liz sobbed.

"That's right. The cities will be death traps for everyone. They'll be out of water immediately and out of food in two or three days. Then they'll have to try and walk to safety, only there won't be any safety," I breathed deeply, trying to think.

"The Masters might have won after all," Liz said quietly.

"They're probably attacking all over the globe right now and we're stuck here," I groaned.

The pickup's engine had stopped and the power steering had failed, but we were still coasting down hill slowly. I shoved the transmission in neutral and the vehicle continued to roll. It was dark and that made it hard to see, but my newfound ability allowed me to sense the road.

Realizing that Rudy would be having more trouble seeing than we were, I pushed on the leaden-feeling brake pedal. The truck gradually stopped, although the power-assisted brakes had failed also. When we stopped, I set the manual parking brake and we jumped out.

There wasn't a sound from behind us. I extended my perception and knew that Rudy had stopped as fast as he could when the engine failed. He couldn't see and judged that stopping, so as to not run into anything or off the road, was the best thing to do.

We walked back a couple of hundred yards and then we could see the three of them coming down the road. The moon was still up, but threatening to go behind a mountain-peak, nevertheless there was enough light to walk by.

When they came up to us, I explained that I could get us down, but they'd have to ride in the truck bed as we coasted.

"At least it's a ride," commented Joe. He hated to walk anywhere, if he could ride instead.

We got in and they climbed into the pickup's bed. I released the parking brake. The vehicle started to roll and then hit a stone and that stopped our progress. The three in the back had to climb out and push the truck over the low obstruction. Then they had to leap back in as it started to roll again.

We bounced over the alluvial area and almost came to a dead stop as we approached the main road, but the truck retained enough momentum to roll slowly up on the asphalt. From there, it was all-downhill, literally. There were times when I was afraid that we'd get going too fast for my reduced steering ability. The wheel wasn't very responsive with no power steering. Only by using all of my strength stomping on the brake while turning the wheel could I keep us on the road.

In a little over thirty minutes we rolled back into town. As we did, I passed the eraser-gun out the window to Joe and he handed it to Rudy for immediate deployment, in case the Pug-bears tried another ambush. We coasted for another block and gradually came to a full stop as the street turned upwards. We got out, trying to be as quiet as we could and not attract any attention.

I extended my senses and I could feel Pug-bears all around us, but they seemed different, somehow. They felt less organized in my mind. They were acting as if they were simply wild animals. There wasn't the sense of centralized planning with which they'd used to coordinate their previous ambush.

I suddenly knew that the death of the Ancient One had disorganized them. They had some form of mental link that relied on a leader. He had provided their leadership and now there was a vacancy.

Suddenly, a couple of the things charged out from behind a building. They were actually fighting each other; one chasing the other and striking at it with its front claws as they ran. They reached the middle of the street in front of us before they became aware we were there. The fight stopped abruptly and they began to move quickly in our direction.

Rudy was still carrying the eraser-gun and he used it immediately. Then another one was coming our way from behind the pickup. He destroyed it also. As he did, the little yellow light began flashing, signaling the incipient demise of the power pack.

"Let's try to sneak out of here," I said, holding up my hand and motioning him not to shoot any more.

"I'll try to save the remaining power for an emergency," he answered.

We moved over to the front of the buildings and more or less tiptoed along in the shadows. A couple of times, I sensed aliens nearby, but they moved away.

I suddenly realized that I was responsible for their departing. I'd been wishing that they would go away and they did. I concentrated on sensing the nearest aliens. There was one coming through a broken store window about a block in front of us.

The knowledge of how to proceed came from the Ancient One's imparted wisdom. As I concentrated on the nearby alien, I felt my mind slip into a form of communion with it. It wasn't intelligent at all. In fact, it had about the same level of native comprehension as an Earth-born bear.

I formed the image of other Pug-bears feeding on something delicious and inserted the impression into its consciousness. It immediately began looking around for the location of the feast. I hurriedly amended my projection to include a location a couple of blocks away to the north. The creature spun around and re-entered the storefront. A moment later I could sense it moving rapidly across the street behind the store. It was hot on the trail of food.

I turned to my companions to tell them the good news. This time I was met with only a little incredulity; they were beginning to believe my story.

"I can keep them away from us. I just now decoyed one out of our path and, unless we run into more of them than I can handle at once, I can make sure we get out of here without fighting. They're not intelligent," I assured them.

We continued down the street until Rudy grasped my arm and pointed at a great discovery. There it sat in all its radiant glory; one of the most ugly vehicles ever produced, at least in my opinion. He was pointing at a VW Vanagon, probably a 1980 model. This one looked to be in decent shape, despite the unattractive green color of its paint.

We sprinted over and I opened the hood. Sure enough, the Volkswagen was original and it had only a minimum of electronics in it. The ignition used a mechanical distributor and it only took a few seconds, to get it started. It was full of gas, too.

Talk about a wonderful blessing. We climbed in, with Rudy driving. He headed down the street without using his headlights, idling along slowly, keeping the motor quiet, so as to not attract any Pug-bears. I kept my senses tuned for any possible attacks as we moved.

"You said the aliens weren't intelligent, before," Liz was curious. "What did you mean and how do you know?"

I thought about it for a moment and then answered, "OK. Here's what..."

I paused while a memory intruded and flowed up into my consciousness.

"It's another one of the pieces of information that I got on Titan," I thoughtfully said. "I keep being surprised by how much more I got from the old Pug-bear than I realize. Each time I think about something relating to the aliens, the knowledge simply flows into my mind. The creatures aren't intelligent at all. They depend on another organism for their mental abilities."

"How is that even possible?" Rudy was astonished.

"You noticed that there is a difference in the cranium size between the young adults and the older ones?" I asked.

"Yes. The older ones have bigger heads," he answered.

"Well, that is the key. They have symbionts that infect them and those organisms end up in their skulls. The presence of the symbiotic creature causes their craniums to grow and it somehow attaches to their nervous system. The symbiont endows them with intelligence. There's no direct correlation with any earthly organism for this."

"Where do the symbionts come from?" asked Liz. She was watching me intently.

"I... No, wait a minute. Yes. The Pug-bears eat those wafers we saw. They are meat of a sort," I looked at Stormbreaker. He'd been correct in his speculation.

"The wafers are created of compressed and dried symbiont eggs. They hatch in the Pug-bears digestive tract and infect it. The infection rate is very low. Only one out of a hundred thousand of the eggs successfully attaches to the Pug-bear's central nervous system. The others are destroyed by its immune system or don't hatch. The infection doesn't happen until the Pug-bear is fully adult. The spiders and the larger, immature Pug-bears can't be infected. The only ones that have intelligence are the adults. The young ones are only fierce animals. They're still deadly, though," I cautioned as an afterthought.

"That must mean that they don't have very many intelligent adults on Earth, because we've seen a lot of immature ones, but none that were as big as the one on Titan," Rudy said.

"That's right. Oh, and there's one other important thing that limits them. The symbionts aren't transportable. I mean that they don't live when the

Pug-bear goes through a transporter," I held up my hand to forestall their comments.

"Wait a minute, I know what you're going to say, we had some of the adults travel through transporters to attack us," I looked at them before continuing. "They will go through, knowing that they'll be animals when they come out if the reason is strong enough to make it worthwhile. They can always eat more wafers and regain their intelligence although it would take awhile. It's kind of like the common story of the werewolf. It's a human, but loses its human rationality when it changes to a fierce animal. When it changes back, it regains its intelligence. These things do the same, but it takes them months to regain their smarts."

Liz commented, "They must not take personal identity as seriously as we do."

I answered, "I think that's correct. Anyway, that's why they were storing spider eggs on Titan. They can send their eggs through with no ill effects. They haven't been infected yet."

"The symbiont eggs can't be transported, though. Not even in the wafer form. When they go through a transporter, it somehow kills or inactivates them. That means those wafers have to travel through normal space. Unless they have used a space ship to transport wafers to Earth, we're unlikely to see any new, intelligent Pug-bears here," I gasped. The words had rolled out of me without any pause and I had to stop and breathe.

"They might have brought some wafers here and those will be a priority for humans to destroy. Of course, we'll want to be rid of the eggs and immature Pug-bears, too," I continued spewing out words at a rapid rate. I felt like I needed to speak rapidly, in case I somehow forgot or lost the connection to the information. "The other thing is, we'll need to get rid of the Pugs. They're a subsidiary race that the Pug-bears have basically enslaved. I don't know if they're naturally as antagonistic to humans as they've been, but they can't really live in our atmosphere. That might mean they will be a self-limiting problem."

I continued, "One other possibility exists. The Pugs may revert to a more peaceful type of creature without the Pug-bears' mental influence. They've been enslaved for so long, they have a sort of Stockholm syndrome. They identify with their Masters and, right now, they exist to further the Masters' goals. Without the transporters and with no or few intelligent Masters on Earth, the Pugs might actually fall apart. They'll have no ambitions for themselves other than to return to a planet where they can exist comfortably."

I didn't know how much of this was accurate, but it flowed into my head as if I'd known it since birth.

Liz's eyes were shining as she said, "That means we'll be free of the aliens in time." Her expression turned glum as she added, "But, we're still going to lose a huge amount of our population to the damage caused by the EMP."

"That's true. The other thing I think is that our little group can't help on a large scale. We can kill the aliens we personally encounter, but we can't do much about the potential refugee crisis. People are still going to starve," I sighed.

"People will reap the fruits of their lack of preparation," Rudy added. "We've known about Earth's natural disasters and possible astronomical catastrophes for many years. If people choose not to be prepared, if expensive basketball sneakers are more important to them than survival food, then they've got only themselves to blame."

Stormbreaker slowly said, "That's right. My people know how to live off the land. If there are a lot fewer city people, it will be easier to rebuild. The culture of this country is based on debt and buying crap that no one in their right mind needs. We could easily get by without that nonsense."

"Well. We can only hope that our society will recover, but I hope it develops in a different direction. The current, consumer-based culture has about exploited itself out of its ecological niche," I contributed to his point.

"I've often thought that we need a different way of living together. Large bureaucracies haven't proven to be the most efficient things for humans. Individually, we're all naturally directed to seek freedom. As a group, we tend to sacrifice that freedom for a set of rules that get more complex year by year until they strangle any thought of individual initiative," Liz philosophized.

I didn't know that she'd thought about that aspect of our society, but I approved. I was glad my wife-to-be was intellectually aligned with my basic position. I said, "People are going to die and we can do nothing about it. We can't even warn anyone because all communications are likely to have been killed by the EMP. The best we can do is to protect ourselves and try to survive. There will come a day in the future when we'll have the chance to rebuild. It might not be in our lifetimes..."

I paused and then concluded, "It might be up to our children to rebuild the world." Taking a deep breath, I reached out and grasped Liz's hand. She looked at me and smiled as she squeezed my fingers.

"All of that is fine," said Rudy. "But, I've still got a duty that I've got to try and fulfill. Colin had a sister who lives in Miami. He made me promise that, if anything happened to him, I'd take care of her. I've got to live up to that promise."

"Oh! That will be almost impossible to do," I said, without thinking.

"I know," he answered, "but, I've got to try. I know it will be crazy-hard to get there, but maybe if you'll let me have this V-dub I can make it."

"You'll have to keep out of the cities as much as possible," I responded. "You can take the Vanagon. I only hope that it will get you through. Take the last eraser-grenade and the eraser-gun too. I know there isn't much charge, but it might be useful in an emergency."

"I'm with you, Rudy," said Joe. "I've been with you through thick and thin and, anyway, it's too cold around here in the winter. I think I'd prefer Florida if I have to become a homesteader. I hear those Florida girls are pretty hot."

He concluded with a kind of smirk that caused Stormbreaker to laugh.

"Look, you guys don't know me well, but I've about had it with the life I've been living. The only thing to do around the Res is to drink. Man, I've been batting zero in the women department there, too. Maybe the Florida girls would like me. Anyway, I'm willing to try. Can I go with you?" he ended on a quizzical note.

"We'd be honored to have you with us," Rudy said formally.

So, that was set. The only thing that remained was for Liz and I to generate a plan of our own.

55

Splitting Up

We drove the VW out of Estes on North St. Vrain Avenue. When we reached the edge of the city, it became Highway 36. I fended off possible Pug-bear encounters mentally as we drove and the drive was almost peaceful. After the majority of an hour on 36, we pulled into a town called Lyons that is roughly midway between Boulder and Estes Park. Rudy intended to turn off 36 there and continue on Highway 66 heading east. It was a smaller highway and less likely to be quickly overwhelmed with refugees. We thought it would probably stay clear for several days.

Rudy wasn't going to head into the Denver area. It was going to be a death zone there in a couple of days. It was probably already suffering from mass looting. The power would be off and the unprepared populace would be trying to get as much food and water as fast as they could.

We reckoned that the only people who would be moving around right now were ones who had access to antique vehicles and maybe some military units. Even the military would find that it had trouble, since the temptation for members to desert and attempt to reach their families would lead to poor morale. It's pretty difficult to stay focused on unrelated tasks when you know in your heart that your children are in danger.

Rudy figured that traveling through the relatively underpopulated areas of Kansas and Oklahoma would be the best route to start, but I was pretty pessimistic when I considered his probability of reaching Miami. It made me sad to think of them leaving on what I viewed as a wild goose chase. I practically begged him not to go, pointing out that our chances of survival were much higher if we stuck together.

He listened to me carefully and told me that he agreed with what I said, but he then threw it back in my face by pointing out that our loyalty to each other was the key factor. He had promised Colin that he'd take care of his sister and he had to try to fulfill that promise. If he didn't try, he said, then what good was loyalty or his word on something?

I was still unhappy about it, but I couldn't think of any argument that would influence him. His mind was made up and I realized that I had to respect his decision, even though it was a terrible idea. In all likelihood, he wouldn't get more than the few hundred miles he'd be able to drive in the next twenty-four hours. After that, people would start to get desperate and would be looking to hijack anyone coming down the road.

Of course, they'd find that they had a real task hijacking those three. They were experienced fighters and not likely to go down easily, but still, anyone can be shot by a sniper. There's no good defense against that first shot.

That's when I got another idea. It was paired with me sighting another antique vehicle. This time it was a partly restored '48 Chevy pickup. I only hoped that it had the original electrical system in it.

"Pull over by that truck," I pointed.

Rudy did so without question.

"Liz and I are going to take it, provided the owner doesn't pitch too much of a fit," I said.

Stealing the truck didn't feel quite right, since it represented a considerable resource in this emergency. I'd done worse, though, and we needed it for what I had in mind. There was no way I was going to risk my woman on a hair-brained attempt for Miami. We were in Colorado and I figured we'd find some place to hole up in the mountains until the country got through at least the first phases of the die-off that was inevitably coming.

I paused and thought for a moment. I was still worried about the poor chances of the guys on their trip to Miami. I wondered if there wasn't something I could do to help them. After considering what the Ancient One had done to me, I realized that at least some of the knowledge of how to establish mental contact with another human was available in my memory. I might be able to give others at least a portion of my gift and that would definitely improve their chances.

"Look. My mind is different because of the Pug-bear forcing his communications on me. We've seen that I have the ability to fend off attacks. If I could somehow transfer even a bit of my ability to you guys, you'd be a lot safer," I started.

"That would be nice, paleface, but don't think I'm going to kiss you or anything. I don't get intimate with other men," Stormbreaker was only half joking.

"OK. Let me try with Liz, first," I responded.

She looked into my eyes in perfect trust and took my hand, smiling.

We sat there in the VW and I looked into her eyes. At first it was distracting, I found her extremely easy to look at and my heart rate started to increase. It didn't help to see her mouth open a little as she looked at me. For a moment, the urge for physical contact overwhelmed me and I had to tell myself to calm down. This was not the time or place for that.

I took a deep breath and then something clicked. I found my mind merging with hers. There was no sensation of pressure or force involved. It was far different from the struggle and pain I'd had when the Ancient One ripped my defenses down. Instead, it was as if I were sliding a key into a well-lubricated lock.

As I felt our minds reach total synchronicity, I did something I don't know how to describe clearly. It was kind of like reaching through a window and arranging a puzzle into the form that it was supposed to be. I understood that there was a part of her mind that was disorganized. It seemed like it was isolated around the concept of individuality. I knew that discrete, individual minds were the way we normally saw ourselves, but on another level, we weren't individuals. Deep underneath, we are all connected. As John Donne said, "No man is an island."

Donne's words were true. Once linked fully, I found a way to reshape the blockage in her mind. This resulted in our suddenly becoming closer than had previously seemed possible. I could communicate with her and she with me, but on a level far deeper than merely speaking. Her thoughts were mine and mine were hers. We were, in a sense, the same person.

It was an exhilarating sensation. We were the same, but we were also different. I was aware of her as a woman and, simultaneously, I was aware of her awareness of me as a man. It was extremely intimate and would have been embarrassing, save for the fact that we were deeply in love.

Yes, I could sense that in her also. She really loved me completely and without reservation. I understood that she could also feel my love for her to the same degree.

I moved my concentration to her..., to a part of her mind that I have no name for, but which controlled her ability to extend her perceptions. It, too, was blocked. I adjusted it.

It's difficult to describe this mental action. Our normal language has no words for such things. In a way, it's like trying to describe colors to someone who is blind. The only language that works is to describe the wavelengths of light that each color reflects and absorbs. The blind person may end up with a quantitative understanding, but they still won't have an experiential knowledge of the subject. I can talk about mental contact, but the words really aren't adequate.

We gazed into each others' eyes for perhaps longer than was necessary. Rudy finally coughed under his breath and we quickly separated and looked around in a little embarrassment. We were conscious that there was still a link between our minds. I thought that we would always know that the other was there and I had no doubt that the connection would persist no matter how far apart we were.

I sighed and turned to Rudy, "It's intense and emotional. For us it was almost like having a sexual experience, it was so intimate."

I could see him flinch. He's decidedly heterosexual and the idea of getting that close to me didn't appeal to him much. He took a couple of deep breaths and looked out the window, thinking. I could see that he was considering the advantages and trying to overcome his resistance.

"Wait a minute," he finally said. "Can we keep it at a buddies-in-war level?"

"That's very emotionally close, too," I responded.

"Yes, but that's exactly what we are. I think I'm willing to do it, if there aren't sexual overtones to confuse the issue," he said.

"No. Even with Liz, it wasn't that way. We were aware of our attraction for each other, but it was on an idealistic level. There wasn't really sex," I dissembled, trying to convince him.

"OK," he said, "do your worst."

I took a deep breath and looked into his eyes. It was definitely more difficult. I'd thought that I could connect with him the same way I had with Liz, but it was sort of like trying to hold the north poles of two magnets together. The connection kept squirting off and away from the pressure. Just when I thought that I had everything ready for contact, the incipient link would break and I'd have to start over again.

There was a lot more resistance than before, but engaging in communion with Liz had taught me how to go through the process. I had to force through some barriers to reach his mind. He resisted. It was difficult, but far easier than what I'd experienced at the mercy of the Pug-bear. There came a point where we connected. We were both relieved that it was on a deeply masculine level.

Soldiers in combat can develop a deep feeling of fraternal love for their fellows. It's something that often lasts for the rest of their lives. When one of their close friends is killed, they'll grieve nearly as strongly as if they've lost their spouse or children. Humans are amazing in the level of emotional bonds they can forge. The only tragedy is that many of us have lost the ability to empathize with others to any meaningful degree.

Rudy and I finally clicked together and I adjusted his mind in the same way I'd adjusted Liz's. When we parted, there was still the sensation of a link between us, though not as strong as between my intended and me.

I turned and looked at Joe and Stormbreaker, but both of them looked away. It was obvious that the thought was too overwhelming for them. I understood. It had been difficult for me to deal with connecting to Rudy and I was much closer to him than to the other two.

"Maybe some other time," Joe said. "I don't think I'm going to be able to handle what happened between you guys."

Rudy answered with more confidence than his limited mental experience really allowed, "That's alright. You and I have been together longer than Dec's been around. I think I can maybe work with you later."

Joe let out a sigh of relief and nodded his head.

Stormbreaker looked out the window for a moment and then said, "I might get to that point, but right now, I'm going to stay happy, just being what I am. I can track and hunt fine without that mental stuff and... Well, I'll think it over and maybe someday I'll be OK with the idea."

I breathed a sigh of relief. I hadn't realized it, but the mental contacts had left me exhausted. I was sweating and felt like I needed to sleep. Only there wasn't time for that.

I looked at the old Chevy pickup and checked the street and houses. There didn't seem to be anyone around. I extended my mind and didn't find anyone. It was almost like Estes Park, where the Pug-bears had eliminated all of the humans.

I finally sensed a Pug-bear's feral thought patterns, but it was a long ways off. I didn't have to look at Liz to know that she had gathered Jefferson into her arms. Together we got out of the van and approached the pickup.

I first looked under the hood and saw that the motor was original in all respects. I hoped that it would run. It did look as if it had been maintained in good condition.

The truck was a little harder to get into, since I'd never practiced on such an old vehicle, but we managed to open the door without breaking anything. The ignition, on the other hand, was easy. I ducked under the dash and shorted the wires together and it fired right up.

I rechecked the area for the mental emanations of humans and the only people I could sense were my friends. The pickup's owner was definitely gone, so I didn't regret taking the vehicle.

I put it into reverse and backed out.

56

ACROSS THE MOUNTAINS

We waved at Rudy as he turned towards Highway 66. After he'd gone, I finished backing the truck out and we headed out of town back to Estes Park.

"What do you have in mind?" Liz asked, although she already mostly knew.

Mental rapport was new to us and it still felt like we should be talking to communicate.

"I think we should go over the top of Rocky Mountain Park and into the North Park area. Perhaps we'll find somewhere to hole-up near Grand Lake," I told her.

I'd been thinking about it and it seemed to me that living in the mountains would be about as secure as we could get. The altitude and terrain would provide a natural barrier against refugees and the gangs that were sure to form. They'd surely take an easier direction where the climate was better and walking was easier.

I knew that we'd have some years before we had to worry about the aliens returning. We'd destroyed the link to Earth and they could only install another one by bringing the equipment on a spacecraft. If they were limited in their travel velocity to something similar to our rockets, it would be a long time before they'd show up again. It took our Cassini probe about seven years to reach Saturn.

I hoped that we wouldn't have to worry about them for at least five years. In so doing, I was optimistically assuming that the ones already on Earth wouldn't survive.

We drove up the road towards Estes Park as the new day broke. The old pickup was willing, but it wasn't very fast. The seats had been redone, however, so it was fairly comfortable. Jefferson made good use of the center of the bench seat and gave us an example of exactly how to relax. If only humans could get into as many totally relaxing postures as cats, there would be no need for psychiatrists.

When we got back into Estes Park, there were a few leftover Pug-bears prowling around, but I was able to fend them off with my mind, luring them to another location with visions of food. Their appearances gave Liz a chance to shadow me mentally and learn how I did it.

It was a good thing she was a fast learner. As we reached the middle of town, we were faced with a whole group of the things and I found that there was a limit to my ability. The large group proved to be more than I could deal with all at once.

I could feel Liz split from my consciousness as I tried to decoy the aliens away from our path. In a second, I could sense that the rest of them were moving off and I glanced at her. She was deep in concentration with her eyes closed as she successfully diverted the ones I hadn't been able to influence. I'd reached the point of being able to more or less carry on physically while I did my mental gymnastics, but she still needed to shut her eyes to concentrate.

As we reached the edge of town, a lone Pug came out of a house and looked at us. He didn't have any weapons and he didn't seem aggressive. Without the Masters influence, he simply seemed forlorn and lost. I reached out and lightly touched his mind. It was bleak: "The Masters have terminated the gates for some reason and have reverted to their primitive state. My life will be over soon. My reserve breathing system is nearly ready to fail and I'll die with no glory on this miserable planet with its nasty air."

I could read a fatalistic attitude in his mind and it was echoed in his posture. I reasoned that, if he were representative of their species, none of the Pugs were likely to be much of a problem for humanity in a week or so.

We drove on out of Estes and started up the mountain road. The old pickup made a valiant effort to climb the steep grade, but I had to keep it mostly in first or second gear as we drove slowly around the turns, winding our way gradually up above timberline. It was a clear day and this time, we enjoyed the drive up to the top of the park. The views were superb.

The wind was chill and there was a lot of snow covering the ground. As the sun gradually warmed things up, the snow melted, creating rivulets that drained down the rocks with a cheery, tinkling sound. Looking over the beautiful scenery, the events of the past few days seemed like a bad dream.

It's funny how the human mind works. There might be tragedy everywhere, but if the sun is shining and you can only see beautiful things, you can forget about the problems of the world.

After a while, we crested the top of the pass and drove on past the park buildings and rest area. The place appeared to be deserted and we saw no one as we started our winding descent into the North Park region.

57

Grand Lake

The downhill trip wasn't any easier on the pickup than going up. In order to avoid getting the brakes too hot, I kept the vehicle in second gear and coasted against the motor to keep us from rolling too fast. I'd driven in the mountains before and knew enough to be a little careful. Get your brakes too hot and you won't stop when you most need to.

We had to go around some steep switchbacks and a couple of times I shifted down to first gear. Jefferson slept most of the way, taking the time to fully relax while everything was safe. He didn't seem worried by my driving, a fact that I found somewhat heartwarming.

Liz glanced down at the snoozing cat and commented, "I wish we could find time to get some rest like that. I feel like I've been on full alert for so long, my nerves are just about fried."

I responded, "Maybe when we reach Grand Lake, we can find a nice place to rest for a while. I don't expect there to be many of the aliens there. This road doesn't really lead to any place that has a large population and I'm hoping that they've left this area mostly alone."

We finally reached the western gate of the park as we approached Grand Lake. There were a couple of rangers manning the toll station and they both came out into the road and flagged us down. I rolled down my window as we came to a halt.

"What's going on over there?" asked the older man. "There hasn't been any traffic come through for the past couple of days. Our cars wouldn't start this morning and we're wondering if we should try to walk back to town."

"Yeah. No one has come to relieve us and our shift ended at eight, the power's off and the phones don't work!" complained the woman.

I considered what to tell them and carefully answered, "It's probably best if you both assume that your employment has ended. There's been a nuclear explosion causing an electro-magnetic pulse over Kansas and I'm pretty sure that all electrical and electronic systems across the entire country have been destroyed. Cars mostly won't run, unless they are an antique with a mechanical distributor. There's no one else coming across the pass at this time and probably won't be anyone for weeks at the minimum."

The man reacted well to the news, shaking his head and trying to rapidly adjust, but the woman responded differently, "Damn and double-damn it! I'm tired, I want breakfast and I need to get some sleep. Wait a minute, did you say that our jobs are over?"

"I think that the government, if it still exists, will have other priorities than keeping national parks open," I responded.

The male ranger was thinking ahead and had realized that the situation in Denver would be bad. He rubbed his chin thoughtfully and said, "There may be a flood of refugees coming over the pass."

"Look. There's nothing we can do about it here and now. If you two don't mind riding in the bed, I'll give you a lift into Grand Lake," I suggested.

They wanted to lock everything up, so we waited while they locked doors and their unusable cars. Then we got moving again. It wasn't too far to town. They could have easily walked, but we've become a nation of people who largely won't even consider walking if there's a vehicle available.

We continued down Trail Ridge road and then turned on West Portal Avenue into Grand Lake. I asked the rangers where they'd like to be dropped off and they indicated that they wanted to go downtown. That squared with our intent, so we turned onto Grand Avenue and arrived at the center of town just in time to help the townspeople with a Pug-bear.

We pulled up beside a small park-like area that was complete with a gazebo. It was located slightly past the intersection of Garfield Street with Grand, placing it diagonally across the intersection from a large building with a sign that read "Village Center."

The street was wide and there weren't many cars parked along it in the diagonal parking spaces. As we pulled into one of the parking slots a couple of cowboys with thirty-thirty's jumped out of the front of the building and one yelled at us, "Get out of here, you fools!"

Right after he shouted at us, his friend took a couple of shots across the street and we jerked around to look at his target. It was a Pug-bear that was charging wildly back and forth in the park. As the man shot, it spun around in a circle, obviously trying to localize the source of the shots. It stopped and focused on him, then started towards our location.

It didn't get more than about four or five yards when someone down the street, hiding in a mini-golf course, let off a heavy rifle that made the thirty-thirty sound like a pop-gun. The Pug-bear made a moan that was almost a squeal and turned that way. I could feel its mental emanation of frustration and anger. It made no progress towards that shooter either. It was immediately shot in the rump area by another cowboy who was balancing somewhat precariously on the steep roof of a log building located a few yards behind the gazebo.

The alien turned a little more slowly and started back that way. I could see that the combined rifle shots were having an effect on it. There was fluid foaming out of its spiracles and it was gradually slowing down.

Not wanting to let the cowboys have all of the fun and thinking that this might be a good chance for us to show our value to the community, I reached out mentally and sent a challenge into the Pug-bear's mind. It turned towards me and started back in my direction.

I jumped out of the pickup and yelled, "Cease fire!"

I had to repeat it a couple of times to get the shooters to lower their rifles, but they paused to see what I was going to do.

I thought that I could use my newfound mental ability to confuse the thing, but it proved resistant to my suggestions. I shortly realized that it was so stressed, that luring it away with images of food wouldn't work.

The Pug-bear was starting across the road by now. As it approached, I could see that it had the flattened skull of a feral Pug-bear and didn't have the symbiont, so there was no intelligence there for me to influence. My only connection to it was on a bestial level.

I pulled out my splinter-gun and simultaneously sent another aggressive challenge to it. In response it opened its mandibles and moaned as it crossed the road towards me. It wasn't moving too well. I could see that two of its rear legs had been shot off and there were some large holes visible in its carapace.

As it opened its mandibles, I fired one shot down its throat. It expired, as had all of the others that had been made to eat one of the poisonous splinters. Its legs quivered as it tried to keep on coming, then it staggered and collapsed right in the middle of the street. It wasn't one of the biggest Pug-bears I'd seen, but it was impressive enough.

The cowboy who'd been shooting from the Town Center came over with his friend and the one who'd yelled at us said, "That's amazing! We've been having to shoot those damned things twenty or thirty times to kill them and you knock it off with just a little puff gun!"

"What the Hell is that gun and what's it shoot?" demanded the other.

Liz got out of the truck, holding the cat as the two rangers climbed out of the bed. The rangers had been cowering down, barely peeking over the edge of the tailgate as the action progressed. All three of them came up onto the sidewalk where we were standing.

"It's a splinter-gun and it shoots poison glass needles," she explained as she walked up. "It was made by the aliens and "" "

"Wait!" interrupted both of the rangers and one of the cowboys at the same time. "What aliens?"

"Well, that one to start with," I indicated the dead creature and they turned to stare incredulously at the carcass. They obviously hadn't made the mental leap required to associate the creature with another planet.

"Hey! Don't touch its claws or teeth!" Liz was shouting at a couple of adolescents who were squatting down and reaching out to do precisely that. "They're deadly poison and you won't live for more than a few minutes if you touch that stuff."

They acted like they didn't believe her, but one of the cowboys reinforced it by saying, "One of them bastards got Phil yesterday. Stuck its claw in his leg and he died right away. Haven't you kids heard about it?"

"We heard that he'd been killed by a bear or somethun', Matt," one of the two answered.

"It wasn't a bear, it was one of these things!" he pointed.

"Look, Mister," Matt's friend reached out his hand to shake mine. "I think you'd better come inside and meet the Mayor and the Sheriff. We need to figure out some way to kill these things and we need to know what's goin' on in the world. Stuff quit working around here last night and hardly anybody's got a car that will run."

"None of the lights come on and the cell phones don't work either," added the man that had been shooting from the mini-golf course. He'd just come walking up the sidewalk and joined our group.

I could see that he was carrying a Browning rifle that looked like some kind of thirty caliber. "What's the caliber of your gun, friend?" I asked.

"It's only a 30-06. I was kind of hoping that it would do more damage to that thing than it did. People have been shooting them with various smaller guns and it doesn't seem to damage them much. Pretty hard to get through that thick shell, I reckon," he answered.

"We might have to move up to something like a .338 or maybe a .300 Win-Mag for some better penetration. We'd better get some heavy, solid bullets to shoot at them, too. Hollow points won't penetrate," I replied. "We'll eventually have to kill the things without our alien weapons. We're running low on splinters and I don't think the local sporting goods store carries any."

I waved my splinter-gun in the air and they stared at it. Without thinking, I asked, "Haven't you ever seen one of these before?

Then, looking at their faces, I realized that they hadn't. It was kind of embarrassing. I'd been using the things so much that they'd come to seem as comfortable and familiar to me as my Sig. I had forgotten how amazing the weapon had seemed when I first picked it up.

58

A Place to Rest

While we were talking, both the Sheriff and the Mayor came out of the building. Neither was armed and they'd been keeping out of sight until the alien was finished. It turned out that both of them had been in the back with the store owner, taking a quick nip from a bottle that he had back there, too, but it didn't seem to have had any negative influence on their behavior.

They wanted to know about us and the rangers both chimed in with, "We found them coming down out of the park and they brought us into town."

I started to give my story, but the Mayor held up his hand and stopped me. He thought that maybe he'd better get most of the citizens together over in the park and I could tell everyone at once what was going on.

"Mayor, Liz, and I are exhausted. We've been on the go, fighting these things for days straight and there's nothing that I can say to your people that will make any difference right now. Please, just let us find a room somewhere and get some rest." I was practically begging him not to force us to go through what would surely turn into a long and drawn-out meeting.

Liz reinforced my plea by tiredly nodding her head and adding, "We've been working solid to try and stop their invasion. It looks like we've finally got them stopped for the moment and we need a break."

"I see that you need rest. Y'all look like ya' been dragged through a knot-hole. We can get you a room, but at least tell us here what's happening. We need to make some kind of plans," he was begging in his turn.

I stood there on the sidewalk and briefly summarized the situation, as I now understood it. It didn't take long because I was concise and didn't pull my punches.

"Here's what's happened," I started. "The Earth has been invaded by aliens. They have been working behind the scenes to destabilize our society and disable our ability to strike back at them. They've exploded at least one nuclear warhead over Kansas, maybe others. The electro-magnetic pulse has done more to hurt us than anything else. There's likely to be immense population loss from starvation and lack of water and disease in the next two weeks, mostly in the cities. We'll have to plan on how we're going to survive."

The Sheriff commented, "We're going to need information more than anything, but, if what you say is correct, we've got a little time and I expect that you-all could use the rest. It looks like you're plumb tuckered out."

I said, "We are. Let us get some rest and meanwhile you can think over what I've told you. When we've slept some, I'll be happy to explain at length in a large meeting. Maybe as a first step, you could start to list resources and people who have survival skills. We're going to need a complete inventory of every thing that could be an advantage."

The woman ranger seemed suspicious despite our driving her to town. She said, "Wait a minute! You're a stranger. Why should we trust what you say? Why shouldn't we send you off?"

The Sheriff, the Mayor and the others disagreed. Their general consensus was that Liz and I were too valuable to run off and the dead Pug-bear was evidence that we were correct. They all felt that we'd add a lot to the survival chances of the town. I think that they also were feeling like they had been hit with a huge problem with which they weren't prepared to deal and they hoped that I'd be able to provide more guidance and leadership.

The Mayor waved at an older couple who had just come out of the building behind us. They came up and he asked them if they knew of any condos in their building that were vacant.

"Mayor, nearly the entire place is vacant. Most of the summer people went back to Denver when the announcement came about the Secretary of State being missing. The news said that there might be some kind of national emergency like a terrorist attack or something. The ones we spoke to said that they weren't going to try and wait out a national emergency in this small town. Most of them simply wanted to get back to their own homes," he said as his wife nodded in affirmation.

The couple was from Florida. They hadn't seen any sense in trying to fight their way onto an airplane when everyone else was trying for emergency flights. They readily agreed to take us over to their place and see if we could get into one of the vacant units for some rest. It wasn't far and they gave us directions, saying they'd walk back as long as no more of those dangerous alien things showed up.

That was a good point and I'd been so concerned with resting that I'd ignored my discovered ability to sense the Pug-bears. I took a deep breath and closed my eyes. It was hard to do, standing there in the sunlight surrounded by other people, but I was able to mentally verify that there weren't any of them in the immediate vicinity.

"I think we're clear of them for a while. You should be fine to walk back," I said as I opened my eyes.

We got in the truck and drove over to the building they'd described. They showed up about five minutes later and we were soon inside a nicely furnished vacation condo. While Liz and I cleaned up, Jefferson explored the place, helped by a can of tuna that had been left in the pantry. In short order, we were snugged in bed, feeling more secure than we'd felt in days. Sleep was marvelous.

59

Getting Organized

L iz and I finally woke up on our own and it was almost dusk. We'd slept
through the entire day without waking. I stretched and realized that
Liz was curled up against my side with her back to me. My stretching was
complicated by the heavy weight that was holding the covers down between
my legs, trapping them in a moderately uncomfortable position. I reached
down to see what it was and felt a warm bundle of fur. My touch
immediately elicited a burst of purring.

Jefferson stood up, stretched as only a cat can, and then walked up my
body, carefully selecting the most sensitive spots to step on as he came. I
tried not to flinch too much. His bed manners definitely needed fine-tuning,
but I realized that sleeping with humans was probably a new thing for him.
He'd always given the impression that he was an independent, street cat.

I suddenly had the idea that I should try and contact his mind. It was
more difficult than contacting Liz and also harder than touching the Pug-
bears' minds. I thought that the aliens were easy due to the way I'd been
endowed with my abilities. The 'Ancient One' had inadvertently given me a
deep insight into their mental structure, making it easy to locate them in the
energy field.

Our cat, however, had a tightly wrapped, compact mental field. I'd sensed
it before on the mountainside, but never tried for a deeper contact. This
time I reached for a level on which I could feel some of his thoughts. They
were lightening-quick flickers without much depth to them, but I got a
distinct sense that he approved of us and liked the comfortable bed.

I got the impression that he somehow could sense my contact. He turned
and stared fixedly into my eyes and then walked up my chest and touched

noses with me. I held my breath in astonishment as he gave me the ultimate cat sign of approval. He sort of kneaded my chest with his front feet and licked my nose. It was only a tiny flick of his tongue, but it was the most intimate sign of affection that he could give to a human. I read it in his mind as a warm glow of happiness that he was here with us now.

The amazing moment was ruined by his hind feet. They were, unfortunately, poking directly and uncomfortably into my solar plexus. I moved him gently off my chest and to my side where I could stroke his back. He lay down and begin a soft, steady purr.

The activity woke Liz up and she stretched and murmured a little as I rubbed my right hand up and down her back. Shortly, she rolled over and looked into my eyes. We kissed and then she happened to look over my head at the clock on the nightstand.

"Oh, my! We've slept through the whole day! We'd better get ready for the Mayor's meeting," she exclaimed.

I was more than ready to relax longer, like maybe until tomorrow, but I sighed and moved the cat so that I could swing my legs out of bed. I started to throw off the covers, but she giggled in a way that I'd not previously heard and grabbed me around the waist, pulling me back towards her.

"Maybe the Mayor won't mind waiting a few minutes longer," she whispered.

After a while, I found that she had her own purr. It was one that I wanted to hear repeatedly in the future.

We got out of bed, cleaned up and got dressed. Jefferson watched from his perch on a chair and did his own wash-up routine, licking his paws and rubbing them on his face. When we were ready, we left the condo and knocked on our Florida friends' door.

Mike stuck his head out after a little pause and invited us in. We stood just inside the door as he and his wife, Nancy, got ready and then we all left the building and walked downtown to the meeting that the Mayor had scheduled for eight PM.

When we got to the Town Center building, there were a lot of people standing around talking. The Sheriff came over to us, saying that there were too many people to meet inside, so we'd have to speak to the group out on the sidewalk.

The Mayor came up, saw us, shook my hand and then turned to the noisy crowd. He placed his index fingers into his mouth and let out a piercing whistle, which was loud enough to make my ears hurt. It forced Liz to take a firmer grip on Jefferson. .

The folks quit talking and turned towards us and the Mayor proceeded to start the meeting. He spoke for quite a while and I'll summarize rather than trying to quote him verbatim, since he was rather long-winded.

He told them that he had new information that was important. Carefully avoiding any mention of atom bombs or aliens, he said that it looked like they were on their own and would need to get organized to have the best chance of survival in the months to come. He said that he knew that the townspeople had a lot of skills and there were resources that they could draw upon to help everyone get along.

He spent quite a bit of time on the concept of community teamwork and how everyone would have to share food resources and not hog food for themselves. He'd calculated things out and he thought that they could get plenty of meat, since the local elk herd was plentiful and there were a lot of lake trout in the lake that could be easily caught. Chickens were most valuable, not for eating, but for eggs. He allowed as how they'd have to let the chicken flocks that were owned by a few of the residents grow until they were numerous enough so that some birds could be slaughtered.

Some of the people were getting restive and fidgety. Finally, one older lady that looked like she didn't take any guff from anyone interrupted him, "OK, Harvey, that's just about enough organizing out of you. What we want to know is what's happened with our power and the phones and TV. I'm missing my favorite program right now! I was given to understand that you had someone who could tell us what's going on."

"Now, Martha Perkins," he said, "It's just like you to interrupt me when I'm just getting started, but – " Here he held up his hand in a stopping motion as she was about to interrupt again. Then he continued, "This young man here has come over the pass from Estes Park and he seems to have a complete grip on what's been happening. In the interest of getting the information out as fast as possible, I'd like to introduce..."

He glanced at me and paused again, realizing that he didn't know my name. I stepped forward and began to speak.

"My name is Declan Dunham. I'm going to tell you what I know about what's happened. It's going to be difficult for you to believe, but the proof lies in the fact that nothing that uses digital electronics or the power system will work."

"Take it on faith that I'm not making anything up and hold your questions until later. I'll try and answer them when I'm done," I took a breath and mentally tried to organize my thoughts. I hadn't really planned on what I was going to say and the presence of so many people made me a little nervous, but then I realized that I only had to tell them what they needed to know.

"The Earth has been invaded by aliens," I started. This statement was met by a collective gasp and some quiet comments that didn't sound as if they were convinced.

"Elizabeth and I have been fighting the things for several days. There are three types of aliens. The one that was killed in the street this morning right in front of where I'm standing was a member of the race that is responsible for the invasion."

"There's that kind of alien; we've taken to calling them 'Pug-bears' because they are somewhat bear-like in size, but the difference is pretty extreme. They're hard to kill; their hard shell protects them from lighter caliber firearms, so it takes quite a few shots to slow them down. They also have a very deadly poison on all of their claws and in their bite. I don't know what other parts of them are poison, but it's best to kill the things and leave them alone after they're dead. I've seen a man die from simply getting a small scratch from a dead one's claw."

"The second type of alien is humanoid in shape and when they disguise themselves, they can actually pass as humans as long as you don't look too closely. They don't move like we do. Their movements give you the feel of a snake in some fashion and their native speech is largely hissing sounds. They're very tough and pistol shots won't kill them, even if you shoot them in the head. I don't know about high-power rifles. We call this kind, 'Pugs'."

"The third type of alien isn't something you'll see directly. They're a kind of parasite that grows in the Pug-bear's head. It may be the species that is truly responsible for the invasion, because it somehow gives the Pug-bears intelligence. Without the parasite, they're no more intelligent, although more dangerous, than a grizzly bear. I've been calling the stupid ones 'Feral Pug-bears'."

"As part of their invasion, the Pugs set up a matter transporter network that connected places all over the Earth. These transporters worked just about like the ones you've probably seen in science fiction movies. They were using them to move cocaine and counterfeit money around in an attempt to soften up our defenses, prior to openly invading. They have an unknown number of human collaborators and the Secretary of State was one."

I had to wait, because that disclosure created an outraged murmur in the crowd.

"We believe the Pugs and Pug-bears eat humans. We know that they have been capturing a lot of people from all over and taking them to one of the moons of Saturn. We also know that the people haven't come back."

I had to wait again while the sound died out.

"That's not the worst of the story. The Pug-bears lay eggs and these hatch into foot-long, spider-like creatures that are poisonous. We've seen them feeding on corpses. Any left alive will eventually grow into Feral Pug-bears. If they have access to the parasite's eggs, they can become infected and become intelligent. The intelligent ones have the ability to mentally dominate the Pugs and any humans they encounter."

I surveyed the crowd. They were spell-bound, but unconvinced.

"I know this is a lot to swallow at once, but there is some good news in the story. We managed to blow up their base on Titan, the moon of Saturn I mentioned. Its destruction caused their entire matter transmitter network to blow up and they can no longer travel on our planet without our knowledge. The loss of the transmitter network will keep them from bringing any more reinforcements to Earth. The parasite eggs have to be manually carried to Earth anyway. They can't go through the transporters. There may be a store of them here or there may not. I think that they had only gotten around to transporting a small amount to Earth before we blew up their main supply on Titan. If there aren't any here, it should mean that the spiders that escape us and grow to Feral Pug-bears won't become intelligent. They have to be fed the eggs anyway. They don't automatically seek them out, so we may be OK, even if there are some already here."

"The other good thing is that the Pugs, the humanoid aliens, can't breathe our atmosphere without some kind of respirator. They will most likely die in the next few days when their supplies run out. They will shortly cease to be a problem for us. Since, they're responsible for feeding the eggs to the Feral Pug-bears, there should be fewer and fewer intelligent ones. Our main problem is that the Feral Pug-bears and spiders will have to be killed individually. If we don't get them all, they may continue to breed. They're dangerous enough that they could gradually dominate Earth, even without the parasite's intelligence."

"Now, here's the worst news. The invasion plan included destruction of our ability to fight back. They planned to set off an atomic burst causing an electro-magnetic pulse that would destroy our electronics and paralyze our society. The aliens were successful in launching a missile from Russia and the bomb went off this morning. They may have shot other bombs over other countries as well, I don't know."

I looked around at the crowd. Now they were paying close attention to my words. They had seen the direct result of the EMP burst and knew that I was telling the truth.

"This EMP burst is going to cause the deaths of probably half of the people on the globe and maybe more."

They gasped and began to talk to each other.

I shouted over the chatter, "Our society was not prepared for a disaster like this and the cities are going to suffer the worst. Right now, cities are running out of water and they'll mostly be out of food in two or three days. There won't be any trucks or trains of supplies coming. Most of the vehicles are inoperable due to the EMP burst. Older vehicles with a mechanical distributor will probably still run, though."

"As the people in the cities begin to starve, many of them will try to walk out. They won't get more than about a hundred miles. The countryside will be scavenged clean; there will be no food so they won't get far. There will be some of the city folk who form gangs and prey on the others, stealing their supplies. We're located far enough here from any major cities that I don't think many refugees will make it this far. However, given time for the gangs to sort themselves out, some of them may show up and we may have to fight in order to keep our supplies and freedom."

"We'll need to do the following things: First, we have to take steps to make sure we have food and water enough for everyone that lives here. We'll need to make our food supply sustainable by gardening, fishing, hunting, whatever, because there aren't going to be any more trucks of supplies coming over the mountains. I've asked the Mayor to come up with a list of people and resources that we have."

"Second, we need to organize a defensive force against any of the aliens that show up – they're disorganized and most will be feral, but they are still very dangerous. We'll need the heaviest guns we've got to take them out and we can't afford to waste ammunition, because there won't be anymore unless we make it ourselves."

"Third, the defensive force must be on the alert for refugees. Hard though it is to think about, if we let a lot of refugees in, they can easily overtax our ability to support ourselves. If they have skills to offer that outweigh their need for our resources, we might consider letting them stay, but otherwise..." I paused to let that sink in. The audience was watching me with wide eyes as they realized what the practical aspects of turning people away would mean.

"The fourth thing we have to worry about is gangs. These will probably become more organized after a month or so. Some people are naturally oriented towards using force on others and they will form gangs to stay alive by robbing or attacking anyone who has food. They will be a threat that we'll have to fight off with our utmost ability."

"I'm going to ask the Mayor and Sheriff to figure out how we can block the roads to keep refugees and gangs out of our area. I believe that we'll have our hands full feeding ourselves. Medical supplies will also be scarce, so you'll want to avoid accidents and try to stay healthy. There may not be much we can do for you if you're injured or get an infection. Basically, we've just gone back in time to the seventeen hundreds."

I stopped and looked around, then asked, "Any questions?"

There wasn't a single one. They were too busy processing everything I'd said to think of anything to ask.

The Mayor stepped up and began to get them organized.

60

Epilogue: Mountain Life

Liz thought that I should have quit telling the story when we crested the pass in Rocky Mountain National Park and headed down to Grand Lake, but I thought that you'd want to know what happened afterward. I've got a little more to tell, some of it good and some of it bad.

Here's what happened after the meeting:

The EMP burst didn't cause quite as much damage as it might have, but it was still a showstopper for our civilization. A few years before, the trucking industry had released a report that detailed the effects of a trucking stoppage and this was about the same. The EMP disabled almost all of our more modern vehicles, leaving only the older ones still running. There were a few modern ones that had been somehow shielded in metal buildings and such, but mostly they were all kaput.

The Mayor and Sheriff proved competent and got everyone organized pretty well and although it has been touch and go, we managed to survive through the first winter without losing too many people.

We sent a party into the park and they blew up the road near Poudre Lake, so that it would be more difficult to reach us from that direction. On the south side of town, we made connection with people in Granby and they followed our lead and prepared. They now serve as a buffer for us and they've been the ones that were forced to decide to either turn away or absorb the few refugees that made it over the mountains. They used an old bulldozer to cut the roads into their town for more security.

There have been a few people who showed up, wanting refuge. Most of them were survival types who were prepared to take care of themselves and some of them have proven to be true resources for the community.

There has been little crime. The repercussions are so severe that no one is tempted to misbehave. There was a small group of refugees who sneaked into town and killed a man and his children in order to steal their supplies. We caught them and, in due course, after a speedy trial, they were hung. We took to posting warning signs outside town about it and it seems to have worked.

Water is plentiful, needing only to be sterilized due to the presence of giardia. No one wants to suffer weeks of debilitating diarrhea and fever, so we're pretty careful about what we drink. Food has been a little more difficult, but we're surviving on elk, mule deer and lake fish. There are chicken eggs, but they're pretty scarce, so we usually have them only on special occasions. There are now enough gardens and greenhouses in town to keep us stocked up on vegetables. Wheat and bread is one thing we miss, but it never was really too healthy for most people, anyway. Some of the locals owned some cattle and goats, so we've had a source of milk and cheese. One of the townspeople even had a breeding colony of tilapia and he now makes his living selling those firm-bodied fish. The crazy things have to be kept warm, but they're so productive that everyone can eat them whenever they want.

It didn't take long for us to realize that the radio in the Chevy pickup was a piece of original equipment. I pulled it out and several of us worked at rewiring it. The insulation of the original wires had deteriorated because of age and most of the contact points were corroded. Fortunately, the tubes were still OK and so it wasn't too long before we had a working AM radio.

We had to drive up the mountain a few miles to receive anything, but there were still a few AM stations broadcasting at first. We learned from them that there was a lot of damage when the transporter network blew and a lot more when the EMP went off. Planes crashed out of the skies and millions died in the first few minutes from accidents and natural causes. We estimated there were close to a million heart patients with pacemakers that stopped instantly due to the EMP. It was bad.

To top it off, although some of the Pugs simply gave up, many of them came out of hiding and attacked, knowing that they were going to die and wanting to do as much damage as possible. They killed many, many people before what was left of the military and private citizens with weapons managed to put an end to their threat. The last groups of them died when their respirators failed.

The other problem we faced was the spiders and Feral Pug-bears. We haven't seen any of the intelligent Pug-bears, thankfully, but the feral ones have proven to be difficult. They showed up in town sporadically for months and were responsible for some deaths.

The most notable sighting of one was when a grizzly came running up Grand Avenue closely followed by a huge Pug-bear. The grizzly turned at bay right in front of the mini-golf course and the two came together with a crash. It didn't take the Pug-bear more than a minute to have the grizzly by the throat and kill it. We shot the Pug-bear shortly thereafter, so it didn't get to enjoy its kill.

There haven't been any Pug-bears around for some months now, so we hope that most of them are dead by now.

We haven't heard anything on the radio for a couple of years at this point. We still check the radio frequencies every so often. Someone else, somewhere will have survived and we hope that they'll be able get civilization back together where they are. We're doing our best where we are.

It seems like the country has broken up into small enclaves. Most of the surviving people are dependent, as are we, on their local community and they haven't been traveling much, as yet.

Mike and Nancy, the people from Florida have taken over the local school. They're working hard to ensure that the kids get a useful education and know their history and science.

I should backtrack for a moment. Right after the meeting, Liz and I located the city judge and got married. It was a great decision. Liz is very happy with me and vice versa.

We located a spot of land, out of town, on North Supply creek. It has a good view and it offers a lot of privacy. We got help from some of our friends and raised a cabin and Liz and I have a nice garden, a couple of horses and a cow that I traded for. We also have a little boy, Michael. We named him in part for remembrance of Colin and also in part for our Florida friend, Mike. He just turned four last month.

Both Liz and I have continued to develop our ESP ability. It's no longer sporting when I go elk hunting. I can always locate them by their mental aura. We're also working with Michael to train him. We're making the training up as we go, but he's starting to exhibit some ability. I'm hoping that it will be similar to raising a child in a bilingual family. With any luck, he'll pick up our mental skills and blend them seamlessly into his life.

There are some limitations, though. I've tried to impart my ability to many of the local people in the same way I gave it to Liz and Rudy. Only about one in twenty of the townspeople seem to get even a smattering of it. Perhaps humans must be emotionally close in order for the mental link to be strong enough to transmit the ability.

My knowledge of the aliens, the information that I'd received from the 'Ancient One,' has gradually organized itself in my mind and I can now recall much of it at will. There are gaps in what I learned, unfortunately. The 'Ancient One' didn't seem to have an understanding of what it had learned from the original source and a lot of the information is incomplete. It's a source of frustration for me.

Jefferson has quietly set up a small kingdom around our cabin. He's older, but still in fighting trim. He has a coterie of local females who drop by at times when they're in the family-making mood. He's had a few short spats with some of the local Toms, but they all learned to stay out of his territory. In short, he's adapted and is happy. We're glad that he took up with us. He's been a real advantage to our team.

There are a lot of new kittens around town that have his distinctive, orange coloring. Everyone hereabouts knows him and his reputation as an alien fighter and detector. I think all of his kittens have been adopted as a result. Families with children seem to especially like them, which is fortunate, because there are a lot of children that have been born in the last three or four years.

We talk about what humanity had, sometimes, and we hope for the future. That's all anyone can do, ultimately. Without hope and plans, humans have no meaning in their life. We're not ready to let the race disappear, so we all are working hard to rebuild.

61

Reprise

I've got to add this update about a recent happening before I finish telling this story.

My memories from the 'Ancient One' tell me that the aliens came to our solar system from a red dwarf in the direction of what seems to be the Orion area of the sky. They have a form of space travel that is close to light speed, but it still takes them many years to travel to our solar system. I was relieved when I remembered that fact. We'd previously thought that they must have FTL travel. At sub-light speeds, I didn't think we'll have to worry about another invasion for a long time.

On the negative side, I remembered that there was a reserve base that we hadn't known about. It was on Oberon, the second-largest moon of Uranus. There was a transporter link from there to Titan, but I believe that it's probably broken. It should have gone down when the main network blew.

The Titan location was the main installation. I know that the distance to Saturn is about eight hundred million miles and the distance to Uranus averages a little more than 1.6 billion miles. That planet has an eccentric orbit and it is much farther away than that during parts of its long year.

Based on those facts, I'd been assuming that Michael would be nearly grown by the time the aliens could use a conventional spacecraft to return to Earth. We believed that we would have ample time to rebuild before we faced another threat from them. I sometimes worried that I could be wrong about my assumptions and that bothered me considerably.

Last night, Liz and I were standing in the yard watching the summer stars wheel overhead. It was a romantic night, despite the lack of the moon. The wind was from the south and the air, while cool, wasn't too cold. The fragrance of spruce and pine was all around us and I had my arm around her. Michael was in bed and we were clinging to each other, thinking adult thoughts.

We'd stopped talking and she had turned to face me. I placed my arms around her and we kissed. When we paused, she looked over my shoulder and took a deep breath. I was breathing rather heavily also, but I suddenly realized that she was gasping in surprise and not at our kiss. I turned rapidly, ready for anything and she stepped up by my side.

As we stood there, the western sky lit up as a bright falling star shot by. It appeared to have flames trailing behind it as it moved steeply downward. It passed our location heading eastward over the mountains leaving a trail of sparks in the air. I could hear a low rumble from the disturbed air.

The thing disappeared over the eastern mountain peaks and I judged that it probably hit just over the pass near Estes Park. The sight keyed my 'Ancient One' memories and I recalled that they'd sent an automated spacecraft carrying a transporter link to Earth when they'd first begun their invasion.

I somehow have the feeling that we aren't done with them yet. This time, though, they won't take us by surprise.

THE END

"How could a readiness for war in time of peace be safely prohibited, unless we could prohibit, in like manner, the preparations and establishments of every hostile nation?" – James Madison

A Possible Timeline for Events After an EMP

The first few hours:

1. All communications will be disrupted: no radio, no TV, no Internet, no phones.

2. The electrical grid will be down everywhere: no A/C, no heat.

3. Municipal water systems will begin to run out of water.

4. People will immediately panic and loot grocery stores. The shelves will be emptied within a few hours.

5. Hospitals will run out of basic supplies.

6. Service stations will begin to run out of fuel.

7. US mail and other package delivery will cease.

8. Travel will be restricted to walking, bicycles, or animal-assisted means.

Within a day:

1. Food shortages will develop and those who haven't food will begin to starve.

2. Food shortages will escalate, especially in the face of hoarding and consumer panic.

3. Supplies of essentials at major retailers will disappear.

4. Cash will become mostly worthless.

5. Service stations will completely run out of fuel.

6. Garbage will start piling up in urban and suburban areas.

7. Container ships will sit idle in ports and rail transport will be at a standstill.

8. Law enforcement will fail as officers return home to try and keep their families alive.

9. Looting will become violent, causing many injuries and further overloading the medical system.

Within a week:

1. Hospitals will shut down due to lack of supplies.

2. Water will be safe for drinking only after boiling. As a result, gastrointestinal illnesses will increase, further taxing an already weakened health care system.

3. Civil unrest will predominate in the cities and national government will be impotent due to lack of communication and inability to travel.

4. Surviving authorities will be reduced to relying on local supplies and local force in an effort to maintain order.

5. Violent criminal gangs will take over large areas.

6. Death rates will skyrocket.

7. Disease, including plagues will start to appear.

8. All trade will be mediated by barter.

Within a Month:

1. The first month will be the period of the highest die-off. It has been estimated that 9 out of 10 people will die during that time. Those who are unable to get food and water will try and walk out of the cities. They won't make it more than about a hundred miles before starving or dying from thirst.

2. The regions surrounding areas of high population density will be stripped of all resources during this time. Refugees will be met by increasing hostility and force by local residents who are out of supplies and struggling to maintain their own lives. Loners may survive for a while, but will probably eventually succumb to organized gangs or war parties.

3. Smaller towns may be areas where people can survive, provided that the citizens cooperate. There will be a danger of small groups changing into repressively ruled tribes, especially if those in power hold all of the weapons.

4. Geographically or geologically isolated rural areas where the population has a reservoir of survival talent, including farmers, mechanics, and medical professionals will be most likely to offer sanctuary for civilization. Climate factors will be important in

determining the population carrying capacity of these areas. The availability of fish and game will be important.

5. In short, man will be reduced to a 17th-century lifestyle, but most won't have the knowledge base or survival skills of a 17th-century human. Survival in such a case is highly correlated with how fast one can adapt and learn.

About the Author

Eric S. Martell set out to become a scientist when he was five. He has a PhD. in experimental psychology. When personal computers came along (way back in prehistory), he became adept with them and spent years in software design, working on projects that ranged from early childhood learning software to military training. He has been trained in various types of energy healing, is an expert in real estate investing and sales, and holds a black belt in Tae-Kwon-Do. He is also a pilot, scuba diver, guitar player, outdoorsman and is addicted to both science and science fiction.

Eric's science fiction books offer both believable science and compelling characters set against realistic action. They are carefully researched, and while his fictional science sometimes strains against the bounds of current knowledge, it is always plausible. His stories cover alien invasion in an apocalyptic setting, political structure, space travel, advanced weapons, quantum physics, hunting, war, romance, time travel, and alien worlds.

He's been published in a series of anthologies and has published many full-length science fiction novels. His writing goal is to provide his readers with stories they cannot put down, and he takes readers' suggestions seriously.

Notices about new books, free short stories, opinion posts, and preview pages for many of his books can be found on his author blog at **EricMartellAuthor.com**

A Request

I make every effort to ensure your reading experience is enjoyable. This involves multiple editing steps, interior book layout, design, and using a professional cover artist/designer. Even so, it is becoming more difficult to find readers. If you liked this book, please leave a review and tell your friends.

Reviews may be left on the platform of your choice or emailed directly to me through my blog.

Thank you,
Eric Martell
Venice, 2021

Also by Eric S. Martell

The Time Equation Series

Heart of Fire Time of Ice

Paradox: On the Sharp Edge of the Blade

All the Moments in Forever

Time Enough to Live

All Things in Time

The Belter Series

The Pirates of the Asteroids*

The Belter Revolution

Cyber-Magic Series

CyberWitch*

Nano-Magic

The Gaia Ascendant Trilogy

The Time of The Cat

Second Wave

Confederation

Other Books

Dustfall*

Asterats and Other Stories

*Florida Authors and Publishers President's Award Winner

www.ingramcontent.com/pod-product-compliance
Lightning Source LLC
Chambersburg PA
CBHW061012120726
47910CB00006B/1901